Silent Battleground

A Novel

by

D. M. Ulmer

Silent Battleground

First Edition
Copyright © 2008 by D. M. Ulmer
All rights reserved.

No portion of this book may be reproduced or transmitted in any form or by any means, electronic or mechanical, including photocopying, recordings or information storage and retrieval systems without the expressed written permission of the author and/or publisher.

ISBN-13: 978-09791642-2-4

Cover Design & Layout
Nancy Fish

Map Chorography
Ed Bradley

This is a fictional story: Use or mention of historical events, places, names of anyone or any similarity of the story line to actual persons, places or events is purely coincidental.

Published by Patriot Media, Inc.
Publishing America's Patriots
P.O. Box 5414
Niceville, FL 32578
United States of America
www.patriotmediainc.com

Printed September 2008
by Trent's Prints & Publishing
Chumuckla, Florida
United States of America

Reviews

'Captain Ulmer parlays his knowledge and experience gained from command of a US Navy Diesel-Electric submarine and earlier service as a Department Head on one of the first nuclear-powered Polaris ballistic missile submarines to craft a fascinating alternative history in the early part of the last decade of the 20th century … unusual in this "techno-thriller" genre, **Silent Battleground** absolutely reeks of both technical and tactical credibility … readers will find a delightful blend of elements from **On the Beach, Incredible Victory, Thirteen Days** and **Hunt for Red October**. Submariners will approve, non-submariners will learn, but all will enjoy **Silent Battleground**.'

James H. Patton, CAPT USN (Ret)
Technical Advisor, film **Hunt for Red October**

'**Silent Battleground** is a powerful, compelling novel. Author, D. M. Ulmer, a Navy veteran of 32 years, moves the reader through tense events with skill and expertise using his professional savvy to lace the plot with intrigue and speculation that makes the book a page-turner. Ulmer's rare talent exposes torn loyalty and self-discovery the characters endure. They serve with duty, fear, and vengeance but the human element of love and family challenges them. I found myself believing fiction to be fact.'

JR Reynolds, Author of **Sustenance of Courage** and **Woman of Courage**.

'Don Ulmer's **Silent Battleground** leaves me breathless at the end of every chapter. Don brings us, realistically, into the shipboard world. His wardroom scenes are so realistic that I found myself there. Don shows us a scenario that very nearly happened. In doing so, he not only gives us a view of professional Navy officers, but opens a rare glimpse into the war-fighters' personal lives–on both sides of a conflict we hope never happens.'

Dave Bartholomew, CAPT USN (Ret)

Acknowledgements

Las Plumas, a literary critique group that meets weekly in the King County, Washington Library System provided valuable counsel with this effort. I wish to thank Doris Littlefield, for her tireless manuscript review, editorial efforts and support, Dave Bartholomew, Dagmar Braun-Jones, Barbara Brown, June Goehler, Barbara Boyle, Margie Hussey, Wayne Littlefield, Liz McCord, Sue Meyers, Gina Simpson, Jan and Scott Stahr, and Kathie Arcide.

Dedication

This book is dedicated to Jack Liptrap, submariner, father, husband and shipmate and to submariners on both sides who sailed with Jack during the Cold War.

Glossary

1MC	General announcing system with speakers in every compartment.
21MC	Tactical communication system interconnecting the Attack Center, wardroom, captain's quarters, sonar shack, torpedo room, radio shack and maneuvering.
688 class	Identifying term for US submarines bears the hull number of the initial submarine of a new configuration.
ACC	Attack Control Console, located in the Attack Center, a digital display that enables operator to interact with tactical data to ascertain target bearing, range, course and speed.
ADCAP	Advanced capability MK48 torpedo, both ASW and anti-ship that can be controlled over a wire after it is launched.
Akula	Soviet nuclear powered attack submarine.
ASW	Anti-submarine warfare.
Attack Center	Watch station of the Conning Officer. Here ship's course, speed, tactical maneuvers and operating depth are initiated and controlled.
Baffles	A twenty-degree wide blind spot astern of a submarine obscured by the ship's hull and radiated noise from the propulsion system.
Clear the Baffles	Turning the ship twenty degrees to the right or left to expose the previously masked area to the ship's sonar.
COB	Chief of the Boat.
Crew's Mess	Compartment where enlisted men take their meals. Serves also as a lecture and recreation area for the crew.
Forms of address (regardless of military rank)	Commanding Officer — Captain by all Executive Officer — Mister by crew XO or Exec by officers All other officers — Mister by crew First names to each other Enlisted men — Surname

Gun-Decking	A Navy term for entering a job as completed into a record without performing the actual work.
Maneuvering room	Compartment where the ship's reactor and propulsions systems are controlled.
Radio Shack	Secure compartment where the ship's radio, message encryption and electronic counter measure equipment is located.
Sealance	A long range ASW missile capable of submerged launch and able to deliver a light weight torpedo over long distances.
Sonar Shack	Compartment that houses the ship's sonar equipment consoles, acoustically insulated to provide a quiet environment for operators.
Sound powered phone	A system of phones throughout the ship for general compartment-to-compartment communications. Functions independently of ships electrical power.
SSN	Submersible ship, nuclear powered.
Tango	Soviet diesel-electric powered attack submarine.
TSAM	Tomahawk Ship Attack Missile, long range, configured for submerged launch with its own radar homing system.
TLAM	Tomahawk Land Attack Missile, finds its target by matching the actual earth contour via radar altimeter with stored information over tracks to the target.
Wardroom	Compartment where officers take their meals. Serves also as a conference and recreation area for the ship's officers.
WCC	Weapons Control Console, located in the Attack Center, interfaces with ACC and transmits weapon settings to the Torpedo Room.

Prologue

Lucius Aemilius Paulus Macedonicus

'In every circle, and truly, at every table, there are people who lead armies into Macedonia; who know where the camp ought to be placed; what posts ought to be occupied by troops; when and through what pass that territory should be entered; where magazines should be formed; how provisions should be conveyed by land and sea; and when it is proper to engage the enemy, when to lie quiet and they not only determine what is best to be done, but if any thing is done in any other manner than what they have pointed out, they arraign the consul, as if he were on trial before them. These are great impediments to those who have the management of affairs; for every one cannot encounter injurious reports with the same constancy and firmness of mind as Fabius did, who chose to let his own ability be questioned through the folly of the people, rather than to mismanage the public business with a high reputation. I am not one of those who think that commanders ought at no time to receive advice; on the contrary, I should deem that man more proud than wise, who regulated every proceeding by the standard of his own single judgment. What then is my opinion? That commanders should be counseled, chiefly, by persons of known talent; by those who have made the art of war their particular study, and whose knowledge is derived from experience; from those who are present at the scene of action, who see the country, who see the enemy; who see the advantage that occasions offer, and who, like people embarked in the same ship, are sharers of the danger. If, therefore, any one thinks himself qualified to give advice respecting the war which I am to conduct, which may prove advantageous to the public, let him not refuse his assistance to the state, but let him come with me into Macedonia. He shall be furnished with a ship, a horse, a tent; even his traveling charges shall be defrayed. But if he thinks this too much trouble, and prefers the repose of a city life to the toils of war, let him not, on land, assume the office of a pilot. The city, in itself, furnishes abundance of topics for conversation; let it confine its passion for talking within its own precincts, and rest assured that we shall pay no attention to any councils but such as shall be framed within our camp.'

Livy, "History of Rome", book 44, chapter 22—Livy, trans. Alfred C. Schlesinger, vol. 13, p. 161 (1951).

Foreword

In 1917, the Russian Bolshevik Revolution started what finally became the Union of Soviet Socialist Republics (USSR) better known as the Soviet Union. From the beginning and all through the 20th century, the Soviets stood at political odds with the United States and early on began creating unrest and economic chaos in small capitalistic societies of the world promoting their one-party rule. Then in 1943 during World War II, Franklin D. Roosevelt President of the United States, along with Prime Minister of England Sir Winston Churchill became allies with dictator Joseph Stalin of the USSR to fight and defeat a common enemy, Adolf Hitler of Nazi Germany.

After the war, the Soviets continued building their massive army and naval forces to spread their communist beliefs throughout the free world. Tensions between the former allies built up over the next thirty years through conflicts and proxy wars with surrogate adversaries such as in the Korean War, the Viet Nam War, the Beirut bombing, Grenada, Haiti and many lesser skirmishes. Economic confrontations in the form of sports boycotts and trade embargos erupted during this time all the while a military arms race continued in full force by both sides.

We always prepare to fight the last war, is an over-used cliché that remains ever valid. During the mid-nineteen eighties, the U.S. Navy continued to use the tactic of vast naval forces gathered around aircraft carriers, the same tactics used successfully by the allied naval forces in sweeps through the Southwest Pacific against the Japanese in World War II. If war with the Soviets ever came about, the strategy was to deploy twelve U.S. Navy Carrier Battle Groups over both the Pacific and Atlantic Oceans. These Battle Groups would push Soviet naval forces into their home waters, opening the sea lines of communication, thereby protecting the movement of men and essential war materials.

A flaw in this strategy is the failure to account for improvements in submarine warfare over those subdued by the U.S. and the allies during the Second World War. Nazi submarines patrolling the North Atlantic could submerge for only short periods and spent the greatest part of their time on the surface in transition to assigned areas, therefore they were vulnerable to search and attack by aircraft.

The advent of nuclear power drastically changed submarine tactical operations. Nuclear powered submarines are able to remain submerged indefinitely, and unlike their diesel predecessors, perform best while submerged. Soviet submarines would soon out-dive and outrun any anti-submarine warfare (ASW) weapon in the U.S. Navy inventory and were not vulnerable to the current search and locating equipment.

The United States pioneered the development and deployment of nuclear submarines, and by 1972 produced the 688 Los Angeles class attack submarines that epitomized the state of the art in underwater warfare. However, ensuring nuclear safety for this complex technical advance began to dilute the long-standing submariner importance on tactical excellence. Officer personnel selected to man the new ships began to be chosen on the basis of academic standards rather than the traditional method of evaluating operational performance.

In the meantime, the Soviet military chiefs became aware of the American progress with nuclear powered submarines via information obtained from John Anthony Walker, a U.S. citizen working as a spy for the Soviets. From this information, the Soviets realized they must reduce submarine radiated noise levels or risk annihilation of their undersea fleet. Then through the illegal sales of propeller milling technology by the Japanese firm Toshiba and the Norwegian firm Kongsberg, the Soviets made great strides perfecting their *Akula* class submarine design and began building their new underwater armada.

All during those troubled years after World War II, the Americans and the Soviets agreed in principle to resolve their differences using diplomacy to bring about peace. As charter members of the United Nations, they met often to do so, but failure after failure made things worse. During the Kennedy presidency in 1962, the two adversaries came the closest to all out war with what is now known as the Cuban Missile Crisis. The situation took a long time to de-escalate because even though the Soviets conceded to arming Cuba with missiles, they continued to push their ideology elsewhere for world domination.

Two years after being elected as the President of the United States Andrew J. Dempsey ended diplomatic relations with the Soviet Premier saying he would only return to the negotiating table after the Soviets made serious gestures toward peace. He did so without the expressed approval of the United States Congress.

Silent Battleground opens at this juncture in history.

USS *Denver* Combat Patrol Route

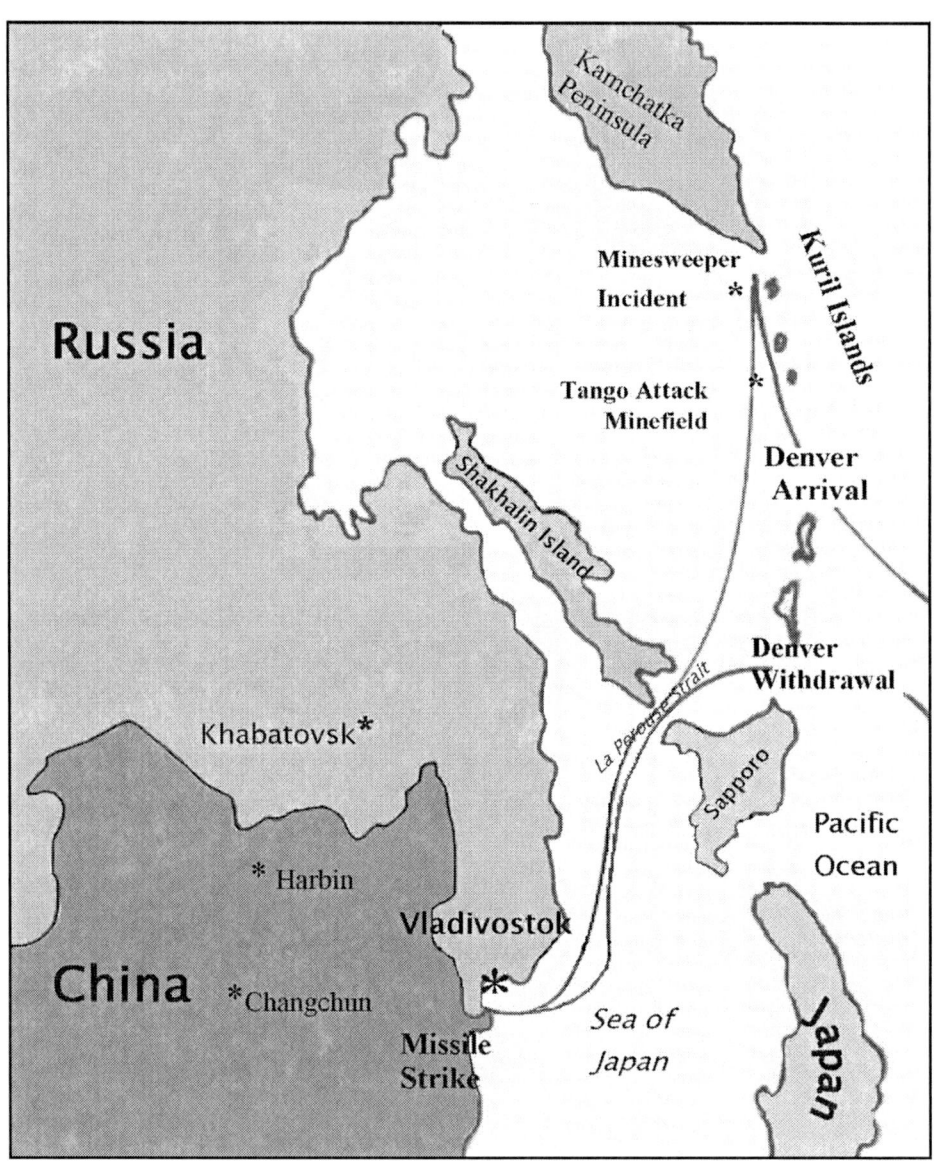

Chorography *by* Ed Bradley

Operation Macedonia Overlay Map

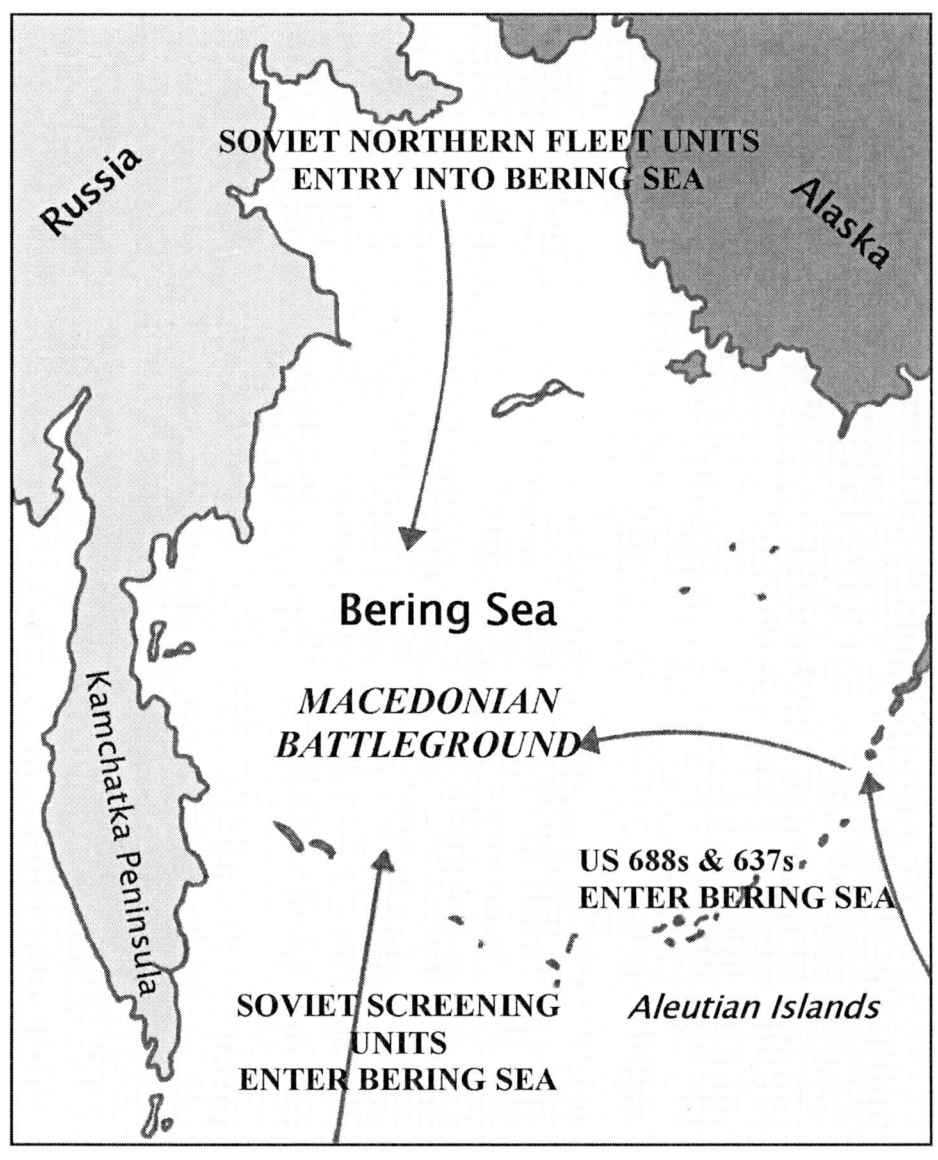

Chorography *by* Ed Bradley

Silent Battleground

Chapter 1

Neither ship nor man is intended to be comfortable during a United States Navy shipyard overhaul. The vessels are dry-docked where they are deprived of the seaborne grace and agility as intended by their designers. They rest on huge keel blocks with sides ripped open and vital organs exposed for repair and maintenance.

Man, too, is equally out of his element here. The environment is noisy, dangerous and unforgiving of careless acts. In wintertime, no amount of clothing provides adequate protection from the incessant, penetrating cold. Little has changed in the industry since the first Continental Navy, so named before it became the United States Navy, laid up wooden ships for overhaul in the shipyards in New England.

During one blustery winter day, the USS *Denver*, a SSN 688 class nuclear attack submarine, rested in dry dock basin Number Five in the Puget Sound Naval Shipyard in Bremerton, Washington. Several openings in the ship's bottom, designed for the rapid influx of seawater, allowed workmen access points of entry to do repairs on the hull. As evening descended, the huge, sleek black hull glistened in a cold rain that began falling in the early afternoon. Reflections from the welders' torches made sharp points of light over *Denver*'s entire length.

Beneath the hull, two civilian yard workers, an older inspector and his young assistant, warmed their hands around mugs of black coffee drawn from a thermos.

The younger man spoke. "If I've been in any colder places, Darby, I sure as hell can't remember where."

"Well, at least half the job's behind us," replied Darby Cameron, a veteran inspector of submarine ordnance systems, having worked at the yard ten years before his assistant was born.

After completing inspection of the starboard side torpedo launcher ejection pump and reinstalling the inspection plates Cameron said, "We'll take a little break here. Not much warmer than outside, but it keeps us out of the drizzle."

"Sounds good to me," the youngster replied. "Rain's made a mess of this damn sandblast grit," referring to the spent material blasted with a high-pressure air hose to remove the loose paint and accumulated rust on *Denver*'s under-hull.

The young man looked up at the long narrow concrete stairway leading to the dry dock's upper rim and continued, "I got mud in my shoes and climbing outta here is gonna blister my feet some, not to mention it's gonna be treacherous underfoot on the way out."

"Shift's nearly over," Darby said. "We better get started if we expect to get the port side done."

Darby shared his assistant's lack of enthusiasm for climbing back into the near frigid bowels of *Denver*'s hull. This required a difficult entry through the main ballast tank flood ports at the keel line and then through a maze of stiffeners and dividers just to reach the inspection plates.

The young helper asked, "Will the fasteners be as tough to get off as the other side?"

"Afraid so," Darby replied. "They're always exposed to seawater so that's what happens to 'em."

"We won't be able to talk in there, Darby. Riggers in the other tank are making too much noise with their knuckle busters," the young man said, referring to the pneumatic chippers used to remove paint and rust. "Damn, that noise is nerve-wracking. Why don't we just *gun deck* this one? We've seen a hundred of these shafts and never found a sign of wear yet."

Gun decking is a Navy term for entering a job as completed into a record without performing the actual work and Darby knew it was the wrong thing to do. He paused for a moment, thinking about a double shot of bourbon and the warmth in Helmsman's Tavern nearby.

The desire for a drink and a place to get warm persuaded Darby's better judgment so he said, "Okay, let's go."

Both men gathered up their tool bags and left, Darby in anticipation of breaking his body chill with a nice stiff drink while the younger man hoped the new secretary from the shipyard commander's office would drop by Helmsman's on her way home.

Months later as spring and winter battled back and forth for control over the Pacific Northwest, the nuclear submarine USS *Denver* plowed westward through huge swells from the north Pacific while in the Strait of Juan de Fuca approach to Puget Sound. Reaching the ocean, the crew began conducting sea trials to validate the work performed during her overhaul at Bremerton. As usual, far too many tests were jammed into an overly ambitious work schedule, leaving no slack time to correct inevitable problems.

Success-oriented people, despite their repeated experience to the contrary, scheduled no time for emergencies or other inherent problems while conducting a sea trial. Time needed to deal with emergencies or to correct other problems came at the expense of off duty time for both the crew and the civilian yard workers embarked for the trials. The yard workers rode in submarines during trial cruises to assist with repairs as needed, thus providing a psychological insurance against shoddy workmanship.

If a disaster occurred causing the loss of life, the civilians would be on the casualty list, as in April 1963 when the nuclear submarine USS *Thresher* sank during deep-sea trials in the North Atlantic. Seventeen civilians lost their lives along with all Naval personnel aboard, 16 officers and 96 enlisted men.

Preliminary tests for hull leaks and proper operation of retractable masts, antennae and periscopes on the USS *Denver* were conducted in shallow water. In the unlikely event of a major problem, personnel aboard had a better chance of being rescued. So far on this sea trial some minor problems had occurred, but none with the potential to extend *Denver's* stay at Bremerton.

Aboard a submarine, the conning officer coordinates all trials from the submarine's Attack Center. This assignment went to Lieutenant Brent Maddock because he had the longest tenure among *Denver's* junior officers. He also got the job because he stood well above his peers in command presence. Navy lean, Brent had bright blue eyes, stood five-eleven with a medium build at one hundred seventy pounds.

At the termination of a shallow dive, Brent reported over the 21MC tactical intercom. "Wardroom, Conn. Pass to the captain, shallow dive completed, en route the deep dive area, ahead standard on course two-seven-five at two hundred feet."

Captain Hal Bostwick answered, "Captain, aye, Conn. Everything go okay?"

"Perfect, Captain."

"Very well, Brent, let me know when you have an ETA worked out," said Captain Bostwick, referring to the estimated time of arrival.

"Aye, sir," said Brent. Next, on the 21MC again, he called the engineering officer of the watch in control of the ship's propulsion. "Maneuvering, Conn. All shallow depth tests completed satisfactorily. We're moving out for the big one."

"Maneuvering, aye," the EOOW responded.

Brent ordered the helmsman, "Right full rudder. Come to new course two-seven-five, belay the headings."

"Right full rudder to two-seven-five, belay the headings. Aye, Mr. Maddock."

To the planesman, Brent announced, "Make your depth two-zero-zero feet, no more than five degrees down bubble."

An oil filled clear circular tube with a bubble inside indicated the longitudinal angle of the submarine's hull.

"Two-zero-zero, no more than five down. Aye, sir."

"Ahead standard," Brent ordered.

He enjoyed having 3,640 tons of the world's most advanced undersea technology obey him. *Denver's* heading fell off to the right and she pitched downward in response to Brent's directions. He barely heard the chum, chum, chum as the huge propeller bit into the seawater and increased *Denver's* velocity through the ocean depths.

Denver quickly restored herself internally to cruise status. The odor of clean hydraulic oil now masked the stench of burned metal created by many arc-welding jobs completed during the overhaul on land. The rattle-bang of the yard left far behind, background sounds consisted only of muffled conversations among the crew and yard workers going about testing *Denver's* seaworthiness to the constant hum of rotating machinery.

Submariners survive through their knowledge of sounds made by their ship. Quick detection of any abnormalities, a flat bearing, lack of lubrication, or unexplained changes in a rotation rate often prevented extensive repairs and on occasion, disaster itself.

Quartermaster Second Class Jacques Henri, a handsome young black man, carefully wrote Brent's flurry of instructions into the log, an official record of each event that took place aboard *Denver*. The log began at *Denver's* commissioning ceremony and would continue until her retirement, scheduled some twenty-five years in the future.

Henri believed the sole difference between him and the officers he served was three hundred years of injustice inflicted by whites that mistakenly considered themselves superior. Henri made this point through excellent performance and spurned what he considered liberal bleeding heart programs to correct past indiscretions.

His uniforms always appeared impeccable and while the others capitalized on the informality of sea trials and dressed for comfort, Jacques maintained his dungarees in accordance with regulations and fresh from the laundry. Well-shined shoes rounded out his meticulous appearance.

Henri made it his business to know the details of the Attack Center watch better than any of the ship's officers. He felt it beneath his dignity to do just better than an average officer; he had to excel. As the quartermaster gang's leading petty officer, he made the Attack Center quartermaster-of-the-watch assignments. By his own choice, he put himself on watch with Lieutenant Maddock, who he regarded to be the sharpest officer on board and a worthy challenge.

With a deep basso tone Henri announced, "Personnel not on watch in the Attack Center clear the area," a presumptuous order for him to initiate because the prerogative of command belonged to the conning officer.

Brent took it in stride and let it slip, perhaps because of the relaxed atmosphere aboard during sea trials. Brent, unlike the other conning officers, admired Henri. The others resented being upstaged by the young outspoken enlisted man, especially in the presence of Captain Bostwick, however, Brent's self-confidence permitted him to see the value of being backed up by a competent subordinate.

The helmsman reported, "Steady, two-seven-five."

Denver headed for the next sea trial in the best possible hands.

Until now, deep dive results exceeded all that could be hoped for and a rigorous test program maintained its schedule. The few minor discrepancies encountered would not delay the final departure from the yard and there would be ample time for farewell visits to Helmsman's Tavern prior to leaving for San Diego.

The crew felt exhausted when *Denver* prepared for her final deep dive event, firing seawater slugs at maximum depth to test the torpedo tubes with full launch pressure. Captain Bostwick anticipated a routine test and left Lieutenant Daniel Patrick in charge.

Denver proceeded to maximum depth, maintaining coolant pumps in *slow* for greater reliability and lower noise levels. For precise depth control, Patrick ordered speed above eight knots then ordered watch standers stationed at hydraulic controls for major hull openings to cope with possible flooding casualties.

Lessons learned from the loss of *Thresher* remained fresh.

Initiating the torpedo tube test firings at maximum depth, Brent ordered, "Starboard bank first, Dan."

Brent stood behind the Attack Control Console and the ACC Operator as tubes one and three operated successfully. "Port bank now. Tube two ready."

"Fire two!" ordered Dan.

WHOOSH.

"Tube two away." *What the hell was that? Was that a slightly different sound during the eject pulse?* "Hold it, Dan ... I'm going forward to check with the torpedo room watch."

Dan asked, "Why for chrissakes? These shots are going off like a Swiss watch and you want to hold us up?"

Brent replied, "Just a hunch. Let me check with the room watch to see if he noticed anything."

Annoyed, Dan said, "Damn it, Brent. You call the old man and report this. Otherwise, pop off four and let's get the hell out of here."

Brent hesitated.

A rift had grown between Captain Bostwick and Brent because his combat readiness interests appeared to conflict with the captain's agenda. Captain Bostwick bucked hard for promotion to admiral and had reached a critical point in his career. He did not regard tactical excellence a significant stepping-stone and he expected *Denver* officers to support his personal program, hence Brent frequently stood at odds with him. It would not be a good time for Brent to cry wolf and although he knew it would be wrong, he caved in to Dan's request.

Brent ordered, "Torpedo room; make ready a water slug in tube four."

After the firing key, the normal shudder followed throughout the submarine as the twenty-five foot long, twenty-one inch diameter launcher expelled its contents of green water into the sea.

Dan admonished his friend. "See. I told you. Nothing to worry about."

An instant later came the sound most dreaded by submariners ... a deafening roar along with a screaming voice sounding an alarm over the 2lMC. "Flooding in the torpedo room!"

The shout erupted from the middle level operations compartment.

Dan yelled out, "Ahead full! Twenty degrees up bubble! Torpedo room, commence compartment pressurization."

At *Denver's* maximum depth, the order had minimal effect on the flooding rate. Brent hurried toward the torpedo room as *Denver* began to pitch down by the bow. He seemed oblivious to the terrified men lining his tortuous route.

Next, Dan ordered emergency blow of all main ballast and shifted engines to *back full* when the hull transitioned from an up to a down angle.

Brent had accurately diagnosed the casualty and knew that only stopping the leak would save the ship. The port torpedo tube ejection pump shaft had broken, leaving a three-and-a-half inch opening directly to sea and the entering column of water blasted into the ship as though fired from a cannon. Only securing the barn-door valve to seal off the inrushing seawater could stop it.

Petty Officer Gary Hansen had already initiated the operation at a rear hydraulic control valve inside the compartment.

Normally, this involved resetting an anti-refire valve (ARV) when the ram returned to battery. But, the ram-shaft lay broken on the torpedo room deck and could not be repositioned.

Brent would have to reset the ARV manually, a near impossible task because of its close proximity to the roaring stream. With time running out, he struggled forward, passing terrified crewmen and yard workers along the way.

He reached the torpedo room and ordered, "Hansen! Hold the control valve shut. I'll reset the ARV by hand."

Brent's lungs and eyes filled with the acrid mist created by the bombarding saltwater and he couldn't see. The shrill noise threatened to burst his eardrums and the force from the incoming water stream could easily shear off an arm or leg.

Thoughts raced through Brent's mind. *Concentrate, gotta try to remember where the valve is ... find it and reset it. Feels like the bow's down a few more degrees. Gotta watch out for the heavy stuff breaking loose, but I can't worry about that now.*

Concentrate...concentrate...three points down, fourth and long with less than a minute to play against Army. Here comes the ball. Why in hell did he have to lob it so damn high? Stretch out and give the converging linebackers a better shot. Concentrate...gotta concentrate. Beyond the first down marker, just grab the ball and hang on to it. Nothing else matters. I've got it ... squeeze it. Crunch, gold and black helmets cave in exposed rib cage.

CRASH.

The barn door valve slammed shut and the inrushing water abruptly stopped. An eerie silence fell over the compartment. Hansen's white-knuckled hands continued to hold the control valve in the shut position, his face ashen. As Brent looked at him, he felt a sudden surge of admiration for the man's courage.

With *Denver* down further by the bow, Brent had to climb back to the 2lMC station before he could activate the intercom. "Conn, secure the blow and vent the after group. It's increasing the down angle. Somebody start thinking up there!"

The emergency blow subsided. *Denver* maintained its sickening pitch angle for a moment and then began to slowly turn upward.

Captain Bostwick's stern voice boomed back over the 2lMC, "Torpedo room ... report your condition."

Recalling his last reprimand, Brent muttered, "Oh crap, more trouble with the old man is all I need right now."

He made his way back to the Attack Center through the crew members lining the way with many of them in various states of near shock. For most of the men, the close brush with a death experience showed in their faces. Some stood frozen in silence or sobbed. Others provided what comfort they could while the veterans just went about their duties.

Dan Patrick got the hull angle under control and used speed to drive *Denver* toward the surface.

At the Attack Center, Captain Bostwick cautioned, "Not too fast, Dan. Let's not pop out like a cork. Slow your rate of ascent. We're okay now. Flooding problem resolved."

Captain Bostwick saw Brent in his peripheral vision, and without facing him demanded, "What happened up there, Brent?"

"The port eject pump ram failed, Captain. It broke during the launch stroke. The momentum caused it to knock over the air piston and leave a three-and-a-half inch hole to sea. We reset the ARV manually so the barn door could be closed from the remote position. Hansen did a hell of a job for us, sir. Scared to death but he hung in there."

"Was the shaft inspected?"

The captain knew the program schedule and had argued against inspecting the shaft before the overhaul, hoping to prune the Navy yard workload and to placate the bean counters at Commander Submarine Force, Pacific Fleet, COMSUBPAC. Concerns grew over rising costs of overhaul programs and Captain Bostwick's priorities reflected those set at COMSUBPAC.

Weapons systems inspections did not rate a high priority among the scheduled overhaul programs, but strong arguments presented by Brent and the Squadron Three weapons officer, Lieutenant Commander Karl 'Dutch' Meyer, restored the inspections to the work package.

Brent said, "It was, sir."

Bostwick asked, "Did you witness the inspection?"

The captain knew full well he set the priorities in hindsight and delivered a cheap shot.

Brent's huge work assignments exceeded his limited resources, so he distributed them by priority. Earlier, Brent verbally advised the executive officer, Lieutenant Commander Jack Olsen the eject pump inspection did not require a ship's force oversight and now wished he had put this in writing.

Brent made no excuse. "No, sir, I did not witness the inspection."

"Very well. I want to review the paperwork when we hit port. First order of business … understand?"

"Understand, sir," Brent said then left the Attack Center and turned in to his bunk for a much-needed rest.

Sea trails and the near disaster had sapped his energy, yet he couldn't set aside the events of the day and fall asleep. He thought of Beatrice Zane and the last time he had seen her. It was the best of all their evenings. Thoughts of her relieved his tension and he finally slept as *Denver* sped toward Puget Sound.

In another part of the ship, Darby Cameron, though dog tired, lay awake in the chief petty officers' quarters. He'd been selected to ride *Denver* for trials and overheard the captain's intention to investigate the casualty. Darby felt a terrible fear when the submarine headed for the bottom and now he feared he would pay a price twice more for his maintenance omission, dismissal from Civil Service and the forfeiture of all his benefits accrued for over thirty-two years of working at the shipyard.

Inspecting the fasteners on the eject pump would show they had not been removed recently and reveal he gun-decked the initial inspection report.

He thought, *The days ahead are truly gonna be grim ones.*

Chapter 2

Captain Eric Danis, Commander of Submarine Squadron Three based at San Diego, sat in a huge chair behind a large mahogany desk at the Puget Sound Naval Shipyard Headquarters. His temporary office supplied with expensive furnishings made him uncomfortable, not being accustomed to such plush accommodations.

He bore the title commodore, a verbal courtesy extended to officers who command a squadron of warships, regardless of their actual rank. The COMSUBRON 3 assignment had earned him the nickname Squad Dog, a jumping off spot for promotion to admiral, flag-rank, as it is known in the Navy. His prospects were good at the time of his posting, but two years without selection, a lightning strike in Navy jargon, brought him close to mandatory retirement.

A tall slender man with premature gray hair, he had matching eyes that could bore right through a person, yet also show compassion.

Captain Hal Bostwick sat opposite Commodore Danis. Officers in the rank of commander normally command submarines, but Bostwick had manipulated the system well and gained the higher rank of captain through an early selection process.

Their meeting ran the usual agenda of congenialities incident to departure from a successful overhaul, but now they needed to address the near disaster. Responsibility had to be fixed. Despite the premium for limited space within a submarine, an unwritten rule: *There's room onboard for everything but a mistake.* Mistakes and their perpetrators were culled out.

Captain Bostwick's voice tones and body language signaled a change to a more serious note. "Commodore, I'm afraid *Denver* must shoulder a good share of responsibility for the casualty," electing to use the term *Denver* in lieu of the pronoun *I* used by commanding officers when blame is a factor. COs are responsible for all that happens aboard their ships whether triumph or failure and the skipper gets both barbs and cheers.

Bostwick continued, "I scheduled the eject pump to be inspected, but our weapons officer failed to ensure this was carried out. Frankly, Lieutenant Maddock is not measuring up. I realize the responsibility is ultimately mine, but this officer fails in setting priorities."

Commodore Danis expressed concern, "Oh? ... I'm surprised to hear that. He's got a solid reputation in previous assignments. A maverick of sorts, but us old guys need prodding now and then. Keeps us from our favorite ruts."

Believing he had no ruts, Bostwick pounced on the opening. "A maverick is a wild cow, Commodore, but it is still a cow; and they all end up at McDonald's. Lieutenant Maddock's points of view, and believe me, sir, I've heard them all, are not suitable alternatives for the proper performance of duty."

Commodore Danis countered, "I'm told he was instrumental in securing the casualty during trials."

Bostwick's frustration rose. "There are slackers on every ship that resort to rationalization for not doing their jobs. Maddock's alleged rescue of *Denver* is over embellished by some of these. I personally coerced his performance of what was a simple task. His panic, and delay, turned routine procedure into a near casualty."

Danis tried to catch Bostwick's eyes, but they avoided him. The commodore took great pains to be acquainted with each officer in his squadron, therefore, he knew of Bostwick's ambition and it irritated him, in particular his tendency to seek and establish a rapport with his boss's boss. Bostwick often implied SUBRON 3 policies thwarted his efforts to comply with SUBPAC directions.

Shifting in his chair, Bostwick looked at Danis and said, "Sir, I'm recommending Maddock for reassignment outside the submarine force. You'll have the correspondence today."

Contemplating Bostwick's words for a moment, Danis stared him down. "I appreciate your position, Captain," using Bostwick's rank instead of his first name signaled the commodore's displeasure, "but I will return any such recommendation disapproved."

Danis's statement angered Captain Bostwick, but he maintained his composure and said nothing.

Danis continued, "Hal, I have grave news. You must understand what I'm about to tell you is not be discussed outside this room."

Bostwick nodded.

"We believe the Soviets are up to something. Since the old guard reemerged and overthrew the Glasnost crowd, there's been a lot of unrest. Our Intelligence people believe the new Premier needs a major war against NATO to consolidate power. The Soviets won't like the emergent balance of power if things keep going the way they are."

Bostwick did not subscribe to this view, but made no move to challenge it. Danis's pleasure with *Denver's* overhaul success would be reported up the line and the ambitious CO had no wish to temper that.

"Pardon my saying so, Commodore, but we've been there before, starting with the Cuban missile crisis. Glasnost isn't dead. Our efforts must center on restoring it. I don't see a problem. Just like always, they'll back down."

"I hope you're right, Hal, but I think not. We've lost contact with all their submarines. It's like they know how we track them and have flipped off the switch. And we believe they're more combat ready than we are."

"May I ask, sir, what this has to do with Maddock?"

"Two things. First, he can't be replaced in the near term. If I approve your recommendation, that makes him a *short timer,* bad for both his morale and the crew's. Second, he's a good tactician because he didn't over invest himself with the high-priced tea kettle," the commodore said, referring to the nuclear reactor. "Mind you, we must know what we're doing there, but other areas need attention. If this Soviet thing continues, we'll need all the Brent Maddocks we can get. He's a rare breed that understands the sole purpose of everything aft of the torpedo room is to get our bullets within attack range."

Bostwick remained silent, but disagreed. He knew submarine CO's careers were destroyed on the spot if they ran afoul of reactor problems. All the other sins were forgivable.

"I understand, sir, but I'm firm on this recommendation. As *Denver's* CO, I must send this to SUBPAC, hopefully with your concurrence, but with whatever endorsement you choose."

Danis thought, *You brassy son of a bitch. You think I'm a lame duck and can wing anything past me you want.* Danis spoke with a soft but firm tone. "Captain Bostwick, the shorter one's tenure becomes, the less concern for opinions by higher authority. By much reckoning, not least of all yours, my tenure grows short. Let me assure you, my position will stand in this matter. If not reinforced by COMSUBPAC, then by others well positioned to do so. Those I refer to hold my service reputation in high esteem and are long of memory. Do I make myself clear?"

He showed the *Denver* skipper there's more than one route for an end run. The well positioned others mentioned had a lot of affect over Bostwick's promotional chances.

Bostwick knew he'd lost the round. "Perfectly, Commodore. I'll withdraw the recommendation. And now, if you please, sir, details on this Soviet thing."

Dave Zane opened the refrigerator and drew a glass of wine from his ready box of Franzia. He spotted two bottles of Mount Ste Michele Chardonnay.

"What time is Brent coming, Bea?" Dave asked, addressing his daughter Beatrice by her pet name.

"About six. For dinner ... okay, Dad?"

"Not gonna ask how I know?"

"Nope."

Dave liked Brent Maddock and saw much of himself in the young officer. He hoped something would come of his relationship with Bea.

Settling into his recliner, he balanced his glass of wine on the arm. Several logs crackled in the family room fireplace as he fired up the TV with his remote. A news anchor flickered into view: top item, growing Soviet displeasure over the Iraq-Iran situation.

The TV narrator said, "It seems the Iranians are about to resolve the current war in their favor," then digressed to conjecture on the meaning of this, irritating Dave.

Damn newsies believe a good voice and camera presence qualifies 'em to interpret what's not interpretable. Why the hell don't they stick to the facts instead of their half-assed theories? Maybe a body could then figure out what's happening.

The camera zoomed in on the anchor's stern look. "Earlier today, President Andrew J. Dempsey warned that any foreign military forces placed into the Iraq-Iran conflict would surely result in the gravest of consequences."

Dempsey's words are tough, Dave thought, *but he's gotta know backing an opponent into a corner leaves him one option. Fight.*

Thirteen years earlier, Dave retired from the Navy at the rank of captain, Submariner Engineering Duty Only (EDO), and now made his home on Bainbridge Island, not far from Bremerton Naval Shipyard, the site of his final posting before retiring. As a civilian, he took up a profitable second career in domestic real estate sales then lost his wife Dale after a four-year bout with cancer.

Bea set out on her own after college then moved home to recover from a disastrous relationship. Alarmed at Dave's deterioration over the loss of his wife, Bea stayed on with him. She adored her father, a rigid standard by which she measured all her suitors.

Dave's submarine career began at Submarine Base, New London, Connecticut in the summer of 1957 where he attended the Officers' Submarine School. He sired Bea in *fertile flats,* nickname for married student officers' quarters. A train roared through the base each day at 5:30 a.m., a full hour before anyone had to get up. Awake with an hour to kill, young couples did what came naturally and a high birthrate resulted with Bea numbered among that bumper crop.

Veterans of World War II ran the submarine Navy when Dave entered the service. Consequences of the Navy being caught off guard at Pearl Harbor remained fresh in their minds thus operational readiness held top priority. Performance at sea in simulated combat operations made or broke careers.

The year 1957, eleven years after Winston Churchill's Iron Curtain speech, found the Cold War at full tilt; the Kremlin conceded the U.S. Navy had an insurmountable lead in surface combatants. It planned to counter by using the same leverage demonstrated by the United States during WW II. Fifty-five percent of combined Japanese merchantmen and warships went to the bottom, compliments of U.S. submarines that comprised only 1.6 percent of the Navy's wartime complement.

The Soviets launched a vigorous submarine building program and by the early eighties force levels rose to five hundred, while their U.S. counterpart fielded only a hundred submarines.

U.S. submarine mission priority shifted to anti-submarine warfare in the absence of a significant surface threat requiring a new set of tactics and weapons. One big problem: how to attack a submerged submarine with no way of determining its range? The answer: new techniques for passive ranging, Target Motion Analysis (TMA) developed by forward thinking submariners. This gained them a permanent measure of fame, for emergent techniques bore the names of their inventors, Clearwater plot, Lynch plot and Ekelund range, to name a few. The number of practice torpedoes fired and ratio of constructed hits measured a commanding officer's success.

Dave felt proud to be part of that.

The advent of nuclear power shifted the Navy's emphasis to reactor safety and demoted mission to a distant second. Dave feared this shift might prove painful in event of war. Now, worried by what emerged on the international scene, he believed this fear might be close to fulfillment.

Lieutenant Brent Maddock held similar beliefs, hence always a welcome guest for Dave to vent upon.

Brent's vintage Porsche hydroplaned through a heavy spring rain along State Route 3 from Bremerton. He turned off and crossed the bridge to Poulsbo, a tiny fishing and resort village located at the head of Liberty Bay off Puget Sound. This lengthened his drive, but he had a liking for the town and drove through it whenever the opportunity presented itself.

He'd met Bea Zane in Poulsbo under unlikely circumstances four months earlier. One night, Woody Parnell, *Denver*'s new Ensign, Dan Patrick and Brent enjoyed a hard earned night on the town. Dog-tired from the overhaul's hectic pace, the three arrived at the same local restaurant where Dave Zane, Bea and longtime friend Commodore Eric Danis shared a table for dinner.

At evening's end, the young officers' fatigued conditions, coupled with having over-imbibed caused them to be boisterous and appeared in no condition to drive. The commodore became extremely annoyed, particularly as they wore uniforms. With a tone of anger in his voice, he told Dave and Bea that he would leave and personally drive them back to Bremerton.

Dave Zane wished to prolong an infrequent visit with his old friend and volunteered Bea to do the job. Bea agreed and after the foursome departed, Danis commented on the deteriorating conduct of new junior officers. Dave smiled and reminded his friend of a young Lieutenant Junior Grade back in sixty-five who had to be lowered into his submarine on the end of a mooring line. This errant officer had too much party at Cot House Tavern near the fleet landing of the Polaris Base in Holy Loch, Scotland. Both men sat silent for a moment and then shared a good laugh.

Commodore Danis said, "Tell me, Dave, is time really flying by this fast?"

They retired to the comfortable warmth of a huge hearth for a brandy and outrageous tales of their own junior officer days.

Brent's Porsche crunched onto the circular gravel driveway of the Zane's modest dwelling. It sat upon a quarter acre, screened from the road and the neighbors by stands of Douglas fir and cedars. The house, built on a partial bank, had two sides of the basement open to ground level to accommodate access to the garage and a sliding glass door connecting the family room with an expanse of lawn. Dave disliked puttering about the yard but did nurture a variety of shrubs and flowers planted by his wife.

Bea wished to intercept Brent before he rang the doorbell and alerted her father to his arrival. She wanted a few minutes alone with Brent before Dave found an excuse to capture him for yet another marathon conversation but reached the door too late.

Ding-dong, the bell sounded.

Dave called, "Who's that?"

"The iceman, Daddy."

Brent held Bea for a long kiss then slid a hand to her buttock as he pressed her close. "Hi, Den Mother." He used the nickname coined by Woody Parnell the night of their drive to Bremerton Bachelor Officers Quarters (BOQ).

Bea wore blue jeans and a red cotton shirt open at the neck. She perceived herself unattractive as a child, though now she accepted that time had ripened her like a rare wine. An abundance of chestnut hair tumbled to her shoulders. She smiled back at Brent through brown eyes set in a slightly oval face. Bea's firm full figure brought the top of her head to Brent's chin.

She bombarded him with questions. "Hi, yourself. How can you be so casual? What happened out there? The story is all over the yard and it scared the hell out of me, Brent. Good thing it ended before any of us heard or I'd have been worried sick."

Brent used a nonchalant monotone, "Must've been a slow day at the yard if that's all you talked about. Taxpayers won't like that."

"They say you're the hero. Tell me about it."

"There's nothing to tell."

"Okay, I know how to get it from you later."

"Promises, promises. How will you do that? Spare none of the torrid details."

"Wait and see," she teased.

Dave arrived to claim Brent; his excuse, a vino refill. "Hello, Brent. What a nice surprise. Can you stay for dinner?"

"Dad!"

Opening the refrigerator, Dave asked, "Glass of wine, Brent?"

"Thought you'd never ask."

"Good. Maybe Bea will let me crack this good stuff seeing you're here now. All I ever get is that fifty cents a gallon stuff from a box."

Patting her father's generous stomach Bea said to Brent, "Your heart just has to bleed for this poor, neglected fellow. He looks so starved."

Brent grinned and said, "Don't see how you make it, Dave."

Uncorking a bottle of chardonnay Dave poured two glasses.

Bea asked, "What about the cook?"

Dave winked at Brent and gave him a grin. "Drinkin' and cookin's bad as drinkin' and drivin'. Don't want to spoil our dinner."

"Pour me a glass, turkey, unless you plan to drive to McDonald's for dinner."

Dave poured his daughter a glass of chardonnay. "Should give ya the stuff you make me drink."

Bea embraced her father, kissed him and said, "Yeah, sure," then surrendered Brent gracefully. "You two get out of my kitchen if you expect dinner anytime before midnight."

The men retreated to the family room.

Dave turned off the television, silencing a local concern over what should be done about excessive wild geese populations that no longer migrate because tourists feed them.

Being sarcastic Dave said, "I'll sleep a lot better when they get that goose thing straightened out."

Walls of cedar backed a recycled clay brick fireplace that blended well with the Pacific Northwest décor of the room. A glass sliding door provided a view onto a lush lawn that had already begun to green under the early spring rain.

At sixty-three, Dave considered himself overdue for grandchildren to spoil and hoped Bea and Brent might remedy that.

Dave sipped the golden chardonnay. "Ah ... that's good stuff. Not as good as a stiff belt of gin, mind you, but a stomach as old as mine, well, ya gotta compromise. Sit down, Brent, and tell me what's doing in these new fangled submarines. Bea says you had some wild sea trials."

"You could say that."

"Want to talk about it?"

"There's not a lot to tell." Brent reviewed the casualty and went on, "It's happened on other ships but always on the surface. Just our bad luck to be at test depth."

Dave understood the circumstances and nerves of steel needed to perform Brent's rescue feat. He sensed Brent didn't want to discuss it further.

"It's really a lousy design, driven by the need to push torpedoes against the higher sea pressures of deeper diving submarines. Other things should have been factors, but they weren't."

"Other things?"

"War fighting capability. We had ten launchers in the ships that won World War II and only four in that 688 of yours. You got two eject pumps. If one goes down, and you just found out it can, you're left with only two launchers. Result ... we got the fastest, quietest boats in the world, but they're tactically bankrupt."

"You've witnessed a lot of change, Dave."

With an edge on his voice Dave asked, "For the better?" Then went on in softer tones, "I can get heavy on this subject, especially after a couple of vinos. Be thankful it's not after a couple of gins. We're not warriors now, we're scientists and professors. Academia has replaced initiative. Not too good, in my humble view."

"Humble, Dave? You?"

Bea entered the room. "The choir still preaches to the choir, I see. Here's the only topic more important than you two saving the submarine Navy. Dinner is served, gentlemen."

They moved to the dining room and sat down to Bea's succulent rack of lamb that could hold its own in any four star restaurant. Brent enjoyed the change of venue. With Bea around, more pleasurable topics held greater appeal.

Brent primed Dave's memories of earlier happy times, many which included his wife. At the conclusion of each monologue, Dave's face brightened, and he would turn to Bea, no doubt to capture traces of his wife's countenance so apparent in her daughter.

Next came cognacs by the fire and a few more tales before Dave excused himself for the evening.

With Dave out of earshot, Brent said, "What a guy. I can't think of your dad in any other way than he is now."

Bea gave a curious look, "Meaning?" Her tone signaled need for a good explanation.

Brent caught the signal and groped for words. "You know, old, wise."

Staring Brent down, Bea asked, "Old?"

He squirmed. *When will I learn to think before speaking to this woman?*

She went on, "You mean it's hard to visualize Dad as a young guy like yourself?"

Brent leapt on her words like a drowning man upon a sandy beach. "Exactly," he replied.

Bea said, "Let me show you." She took a photo album from the mahogany bookshelf above the fireplace and began to page through. "Here." She produced a black and white snapshot of twenty-six year old Lieutenant Junior Grade Dave Zane, Navy binoculars hanging about his neck, standing on the bridge of a World War II fleet type submarine. "There's one fine looking officer. Too bad you didn't look that good as a JG."

"Touché."

They paged through the album and shared occasional oohs, aahs and laughs, mostly over childhood photos of Bea. They came upon a five by eight folder fronted with a formal photo of Bea's mother, beneath which read *Celebrating the Life of Dale Beatrice Walker-Zane, July 22, 1930 to August 12, 1984.*

"What a beautiful lady."

Bea, pleased by his remark, rewarded him with a smile. "Really want to know Dad? Read this."

> *Remembering my Beloved Wife, Dale*
>
> *A summer hike through the Olympic National Park at Sol Duc Hot Springs brought me upon a rare orchid that would beautify the rest of my life. It came about while doing an unwise thing - leaving the trail to explore side canyons. Good fortune for me that I elected the 'unwise' path. Though searching for the elusive cephalanthera austinae orchid, I found instead my own Olympic Blossom, Dale, whose beauty exceeds that of every flower in the forest. A soft cry, "Help," floated through the balmy afternoon air, and I found a young lady lying on the ground in great pain. "I think my ankle's broken." She raised her eyes to me apologetically. A quick look proved her right. Words came to mind, you shouldn't hike alone! But then that would be the pot calling the kettle black. Depleting my first aid kit supplies, and with help from two small tree branches, I fashioned a splint, then gathered Dale into my arms for the six mile trek back to the trailhead. Such a dilemma! Speaking depleted my breath and strength, but how could I impress her without doing that? And from the first instant, impressing her became more important than anything in my life. I must have done well. The trail we walked together that blessed day extended through thirty-two beautiful and precious years. My Olympic Blossom, Dale, wife, mother*

and enduring companion of my life. I shall never walk alone, Sweetheart.

Brent exclaimed, "Wow!"

"My uncle, Mom's oldest brother read this for Dad at the funeral. Then a woman in the choir sang *You'll Never Walk Alone*, Mom's favorite song."

Taking her hand Brent asked, "Hard for you to talk about it?"

"No, Brent. The pain's gone now. Only the happy memories are left."

They looked through some remaining photos and Bea returned the album to its place on the shelf.

She rejected Brent's suggestion they drive to the Bangor 'O' club for a nightcap and check the action. He had the key to Jack Olsen's room at the Bachelor Officers' Quarters, vacant and available because the executive officer's wife's visit to Bremerton had been delayed.

"It's a waste of time to drive over there. Dad won't come down unless I call him. You don't plan to make me do that, do you?"

Brent answered with a smile, "Not if you can control yourself."

"Male chauvinist."

Later, firelight illuminated the highlights in Bea's hair as they lay nude with a small blanket and dwindling fire for warmth. They slept in each other's arms until the flames burned low and a chill awakened them.

Bea pleaded, "Don't leave. Not just yet."

They gathered the blanket over them and lingered another hour, holding each other in the afterglow of their lovemaking.

Chapter 3

Lieutenant Commander Jack Olsen, *Denver's* executive officer, barked, "Crew…a-ten-SHUN."

Shuffling feet echoed throughout the warehouse-turned-drill-field as a hundred crewmen came to a semblance of the traditional military position. Submarine crews are plumbers, electricians, technicians and mechanics and do not parade often and it showed.

Lieutenant Commander Olsen gave his impression of a salute when greeting Squadron Commander Commodore Danis, a sincere gesture if not military. An arm slithered up his right side; the hand bent ninety degrees at the wrist. It reminded him of a rising periscope.

At the same time he rendered the weird looking salute, Lieutenant Commander Olsen said, "Good morning, Commodore. *Denver* officers and crew ready for your inspection, sir."

The commodore returned the salute, hand swung in a precise and graceful arc, back ramrod straight, yet relaxed and comfortable. His crisp military bearing showed him to be a product of earlier times.

"Good morning, Jack," the commodore said, and then to Captain Bostwick, "If you would lead the way, Captain."

The inspection party moved single file through the waiting ranks, first Captain Bostwick, followed by Commodore Danis, Lieutenant Commander Jack Olsen, and Senior Chief Quartermaster Richard Cunningham, *Denver*'s Chief of the Boat. The COB, the executive officer's strong right arm, enforced directives to the crew and also assisted the first lieutenant in organizing the crew members for grunt work and keeping *Denver* shipshape. Chief of the boat ratings exist only in submarines, the position inaugurated prior to World War II and awarded to the ablest chief petty officer aboard.

Captain Bostwick introduced each officer in order of rank and upon reaching Brent said, "You know Lieutenant Maddock, Commodore.

He's been with us the longest. And if I may say so, did valuable service with his quick action during our problem on sea trials."

Brent contained his surprise at the captain's comment.

It pleased Commodore Danis that Bostwick had gotten the message and he said, "Oh? I must hear all about this, Brent. But for now, congratulations."

Ensign Woody Parnell's cherubic face looked stern from beneath the brilliant gold chinstrap on his cap. A single gold stripe, equally brilliant, circled each sleeve cuff.

The commodore said, "You're a fine looking officer, Ensign Parnell," then winked. "Don't let these crusty old submariners change that."

The officers followed with polite laughter.

Next, the commodore inspected the crew. He made random stops by a number of men and spoke to each one. Some he questioned, "Where is your home? Many of our best submariners came from the plains states. Did your family come to Bremerton for the overhaul? Bet it'll be good to get back to San Diego."

All standards for senior officers interacting with enlisted, however, the commodore's personal interaction made each recipient feel special.

With the inspection of ranks completed, the inspection party filed to a podium in the center of the warehouse as Lieutenant Commander Jack Olsen ordered, "Pa-rade REST!"

Again, shuffling feet moved to the comfortable military position.

The commodore read letters of commendation to crewmembers who made special contributions to the overhaul's success. Next, he passed out chevrons and advance rating certificates for new promotions among the crew.

Brent managed an unmilitary wink at Gary Hansen who made Fire Control Technician, First Class.

Commodore Danis addressed *Denver's* crew. "Officers and men of *Denver*. You've a right to be proud of the overhaul … your overhaul. You brought a tired ship to Bremerton and rejuvenated her. She leaves here with elevated fighting power and a top notch fighting spirit based on what I see of her crew.

"Combat readiness is paramount, I mince no words. Overtones in the news are valid and of great concern. You must depart the Strait of Juan de Fuca ready and with your guard up.

"Officers who served in World War II guided me through my early career, their agenda and emphasis experience driven. But they are gone now and lessons of the war are diminished by time. Submariners have not heard a shot fired in anger for many years and so we must avoid the complacency that grows from this.

"Our 688 class submarines have no peers in the navies of the world and will serve us well in the event of war. They run faster, quieter and deeper than our prospective adversaries. But the bitter lessons of war often show opening poker hands are seldom the ones played at the end.

"Nuclear propulsion has revolutionized submarine warfare, but its demands for attention have diluted the resources needed for other tasks. Combat readiness suffers accordingly. While I do not suggest we back off from safe reactor operation, I ask you all to dig deep and find the means to maintain a high level of combat effectiveness. In a word, be ready to fight."

Brent thought, *Ready to fight? Sounds damn serious.*

Denver's crew caught the emphasis. Commodore Danis's words departed from the normal rah-rah, go get 'em pabulum usually served up on these occasions.

Was this a war warning?

His audience stirred at the commodore's ominous words so he paused a moment to let this settle in. Then continued with, "You cannot rest upon success of your efforts in the yard, however hard you've worked. Monday, you get under way for two weeks refresher training and return to San Diego, though I would not make book on the latter. This time must be used well to ready you for combat.

"I've ordered *Denver* to depart Bremerton with a full weapons load and provisions for an extended patrol. Your sister ships are doing likewise throughout the Pacific. Be mindful that *Denver* exists only because of her need in time of war. This is the sole justification for all Navy warships. We must be worthy of the trust that accompanies a huge national investment to this extent. I am confident the officers and men of *Denver* will discharge this trust with skill and honor.

"Thank you and congratulations on a job well done."

Applause, led by Captain Bostwick, interrupted the shocked silence of *Denver's* crew.

Lieutenant Commander Olsen ordered, "At-ten-SHUN," and the commodore and Captain Bostwick departed.

After being dismissed from formation, troops reassembled in small groups, wanting to get the straight scoop.

Gary Hansen asked, "What the hell's going on, Mr. Maddock?"

Several others gathered to hear Brent's response, a testimony to their confidence in the young officer.

Brent knew this, thus chose his words carefully. "You heard what the man said. This isn't Monday Night Football. Second guesses are not worth much. We've got a job to do, but what else is new? We don't break with our tradition of doing it right.

"Hansen, our work is cut out for us if we're to be ready by Monday. A full load-out will be a first. Look at it this way. Same as all the other ones, except more bullets. So let's get out of these sailor suits and into working gear. And Hansen," he called to his leading petty officer who started to walk away, "congratulations on the new stripe. This means I can expect more and better things, okay?"

Grinning at his division officer in response, Hansen continued to walk off.

Quartermaster Henri, ever the self-starter, said, "Not sure where I'll find them, Mr. Maddock, but we don't leave here without every Pacific chart printed in the last ten years."

Brent grinned, "Don't forget the Atlantic, Henri. We can get there under the Pole, ya know."

Henri provided a rare glimpse into his sense of humor with a wide grin spread over his face. "You're tough, Mr. Maddock. Real tough."

A short time later aboard *Denver*, Lieutenant Commander Jack Olsen reported to the captain's stateroom in response to a summons by Captain Bostwick.

"Jack," the captain warned, "this is a protected conversation. Understand?"

"Of course, Captain."

Bostwick lowered his voice and glared at his executive officer. "I believe Danis is overreacting. I hear noises from an officer who's blown his flag chances and takes reckless long shots to recover them. We've got to protect *Denver* from doing something stupid. It's eight-thirty in Pearl. SUBPAC is still at morning staff. I'll place a call in half an hour and get this thing straightened out. In the meantime, keep me informed of everything we do to tilt with Danis' windmills."

"Aye, sir, will do that, Captain."

"While I'm on the phone, I'll locate an open billet in the rustiest tub in the force for a certain half-assed lieutenant."

"Brent?"

Bostwick snarled, "Bingo!"

Jack took a breath to say something in the young officer's behalf, but sensed Bostwick detected his intention so he remained quiet.

"Anything else?"

As usual, Jack's courage deserted him. "Nothing, sir." Then he rose and walked out of the captain's stateroom.

Ensign Parnell and Brent arrived at the shipyard commander's office to give testimony before a Civil Service Board convened to investigate *Denver's* sea trial accident. The near loss of a submarine is a sensitive matter, so the Board availed itself of privacy in the shipyard commander's office complex.

Brent had expected to be asked to describe the accident while Woody witnessed the post-event inspection and would be asked to describe the findings.

As he waited to give his statement, Ensign Parnell made good use of the time by engaging an attractive young secretary in conversation. His extra-curricular activity ended when summoned into the hearing room.

Past shipyard commanders looked down at the proceedings from gold framed oil paintings hung on dark mahogany paneled walls. The portraits dated back to September 1891 when Lieutenant Ambrose Barkley Wyckoff purchased the site and occupied the office as its first commander.

Five senior civil servants ranging in age from mid to late fifties comprised the board. They sat about a large oak conference table, their moods somber. Darby Cameron sat alone at the table's end.

The chairman swore in Woody and asked the young officer to state his name, rank and affiliation with USS *Denver*.

"Elwood F. Parnell, Ensign, United States Navy, sir, assigned to USS *Denver* as first lieutenant in the Weapons Department."

After the oath the chairman nodded to Darby then asked, "Do you know Mr. Cameron?"

Woody looked at Cameron who did not raise his eyes. "Yes, sir, I know him."

"Please understand that your testimony may have an impact on Mr. Cameron's tenure as a civil servant, therefore I ask you to consider each question and answer it to the best of your knowledge. Please do not speculate. If you have no specific knowledge relating to a question, state that you do not know."

"I'll do that, sir," Woody replied.

The committee produced a stack of inspection reports related to the alleged falsified inspection.

The next series of questions asked by the chairman pertained to the reports. "Have you read the inspection criteria?"

Woody answered, "I have sir."

"Did you observe any inconsistencies between the criteria and what you observed at the inspection?"

"I'm not experienced enough to comment on that, sir."

This characterized Woody's responses to the balance of questions on the alleged *gun decking* of the report. His damning testimony came during questions posed on the post event inspection when he stated, "The inspection plate was rusted shut and tough to open."

"In your view, is it possible the plates had been removed within the past two months as shown in these records?"

"Again, sir, I'm too inexperienced to comment, so I must say, I do not know."

The chairman admired the young officer's candor. He had almost lost his life because of Cameron's flagrant oversight but remained unwilling to make speculative testimony against him.

"You are certain of the difficulty experienced to open the port side inspection plates?"

Woody replied, "I am, sir."

Turning to Darby the Chairman asked, "Mr. Cameron, do you have any questions for Ensign Parnell?"

Cameron indicated he had none by shaking his head.

"Ensign Parnell, do you have any questions for Mr. Cameron, or statements you'd like to make?"

Woody paused a second then said, "Mr. Chairman, I was scared out of my wits when we almost sank. But Mr. Cameron would have gone down with us too so I think that should count for something, sir."

The chairman's stern expression softened. "Ensign Parnell, you've shown a great sense of justice and compassion for one so young. In the twilight of my career, I find it refreshing to see this quality among those at the beginning of theirs. You are dismissed, Ensign Parnell, and we thank you very much."

The chairman called for Brent and repeated the oath administered to Woody. The questions to Brent centered mainly on the accident and explored possible mitigating circumstances.

"Lieutenant Maddock," the chairman opened, "earlier testimony by Lieutenant Patrick alleges that following the first operation of the port eject pump, and you wished to delay the second. Is this correct?"

"That is correct, sir."

"Can you explain?"

"Actually, it's unexplainable."

"Unexplainable? Did you have a reason for requesting the delay?"

"It's ... it's a sort of sixth sense. I can't say for sure. Maybe something I heard, how the ship shuddered in response to the impulse ... an additional delay between the time we hit the firing key and bottoming of the ram or maybe a combination of all three."

"You believed this to be a problem?"

"No, sir. Not a problem but something different. The absence of anything specific prevented delaying the event and we had a tight schedule."

Members of the board had transcripts of all the pertinent records, including readings taken before and after the casualty and descriptions of the procedures followed.

Brent said, "We conducted the test in compliance with established directions and there were no cockpit errors."

The chairman replied, "We're aware of that, Lieutenant. When we interrogated *Denver*'s weapons department personnel, we found them knowledgeable and well trained. This reflects credit upon you and our findings will so state."

Brent nodded. "Thank you, sir."

Invited to make a closing statement, Brent said, "Gentlemen, I have only six years experience at sea. In that time, I've learned the ocean is unforgiving and relentless. If there is any way for it to get into a submarine, it will. Mistakes by people are a concern and corrective action must follow immediately. Deliberate omissions on the other hand are intolerable. Those found responsible forfeit their right to be part of submarine service."

Darby Cameron buried his face in his hands.

Continuing his commentary, Brent said, "Whatever your findings, Mr. Cameron has burned his bridge with submariners. We are a small lot and already know his name. I recommend that he be barred from ever working on submarines again."

Pausing for a moment as if making up his mind about something Brent went on, "There's another side to this coin, however. Six months before the overhaul, we very nearly made Mr. Cameron's mistake for him."

Darby Cameron raised his eyes.

Interested expressions accompanied the repositioning of board members' bodies around the table.

Brent knew this would put him deeper into hot water with the captain, but his sense of justice required he speak out. "The overhaul work package had the usual problems. Too much needed to be done, not enough time and never enough money. The eject pump inspections fell initially among the cuts, but reinstated in exchange for having my troops pick up other items approved earlier. The inspections, dropped a second time as salve for an engineering problem, got back into the work package as a result of arguments by Lieutenant Commander Meyer, Squadron Three weapons officer.

"In fairness to Mr. Cameron, this must be considered. Experienced submariners shared his view on the low priority attributed to eject pump inspections; however, I stand firm in my recommendation he never again be permitted to work on submarines."

Brent responded to a barrage of questions on his statements with answers that presented Captain Bostwick in an unfavorable light.

"Thank you for your testimony, Lieutenant. You are dismissed from these proceedings."

Brent recognized he had blown the whistle on his captain and understood the consequences. He abhorred being disloyal but believed his testimony essential for a fair judgment of Darby Cameron.

After deliberations, the Chairman of the Board read the findings and recommendations to Darby. "As to the charge, 'falsification of an inspection record incident to the overhaul work on USS *Denver*,' the verdict is guilty. We have reached a unanimous recommendation that you be discharged from the Civil Service, effective this date. We further recommend that rights and benefits accumulated by you shall remain in force."

The chairman added, "Testimony from *Denver* officers had a great bearing on the latter recommendation. The findings of this board will be forwarded to the shipyard commander for his final disposition."

When invited to comment, Darby Cameron shook his head. "No. I expected it would be a lot worse. I'm grateful to the *Denver* officers."

The chairman adjourned the inquiry.

Returning to the waterfront, Brent found Woody had the weapons load-out well in hand. The number five Tomahawk Land Attack Missile (TLAM), out of the dozen delivered, made its way into the vertical launcher in the *Denver's* forward deck. Chief Cunningham's presence reassured Brent despite growing confidence in his young first lieutenant. The COB had amassed enough experience to supervise the job on his own, but had an unwritten assignment to prop up any new junior officer's self-confidence. Woody believed he ran the show, but Cunningham hovered about to protect the young officer from rookie mistakes.

Navy yard weapons load-out deviated from the normal procedure of conducting this at an ammunition facility because Commodore Danis rearranged the process to expedite *Denver's* departure. Weapons, barged from the Naval Weapons Station Seal Beach, Detachment Port Hadlock, Washington in upper Puget Sound, made their way into *Denver's* vertical launchers at the Bremerton facility.

Brent dropped by the *Denver* wardroom for a short break and discovered Bea had called.

He dialed her number. "Hi, Den Mother. How's life among the clerical types of Shipyard Planning?"

She replied in a mock annoyed tone, "Administrative assistant, you macho, male egotist."

"Guilty on the two adjectives, but I'm too humble to have an ego."

"And I'm too beautiful to be stuck in a shipyard, but here we are. Now tell me. The whole place is buzzing about Commodore Danis's speech. What's going on?"

"Sorry, Bea, but one thing is not going on. Our weekend on the peninsula is history. We're like a convention of one-legged men at an ass-kicking contest."

"Oh, damn. You're kidding?"

"Wish I were. Things we need to do to get out of here on Monday have all but quadrupled."

Bea asked, "Lunch maybe?"

"It's a madhouse here, Bea. I'll see you tonight, okay?"

"Okay, give me a call when things settle down, either here or at home."

"Sorry, Babe. See ya soon," Brent said then hung up the phone and went topside to check on Woody's loading operations.

The Zane family loved retreating to the modest but cozy house on the Olympic Peninsula Pacific Coast. It was also a favorite escape for Bea and Brent. Dave Zane often joined them, but knew when to turn his daughter a blind eye.

They all planned to spend *Denver*'s final weekend at Bremerton by staying at the *Digs*, as Dave termed his favorite haunt. Though Dave had not mentioned it, he also invited Eric Danis to join them.

Day wore into night before Woody and the COB Cunningham completed the load-out, but not too late for a farewell drink at the Helmsman with Brent, Dan and Bea Zane.

At the Helmsman, loud blaring disco music made it impossible to communicate below a shout. Woody spotted the young secretary he met at the shipyard commander's office that morning. He excused himself and made his way to her across the tavern. A short time later, a commotion erupted. Another young man had staked an earlier claim on the target of Woody's interest.

Brent picked up on the dialogue as he approached the scene.

Denver's baby-faced ensign said, "She looks old enough to decide by herself whether she wants to dance."

The man snapped "What the hell? You goddamn Navy guys come in here like you own the place. Hit the road you bastard, or I'm gonna pulverize that dumb face of yours."

Woody softly cautioned, "You don't want to fight with me."

"Wrong, you yellow bastard. It's you that doesn't wanna fight with me. You got no choice, buster."

The young man made a wild swing at Woody's head.

While a midshipman at the Naval Academy, Ensign Elwood Parnell learned to fight by instinct and his automatic reactions helped him to become a four-time middleweight boxing champion. His feet skimmed skillfully, right foot back on toe, left forward, flat in line ninety degrees to his opponent. His jaw took cover behind a raised left shoulder, while the attempted blow whizzed overhead. Woody waited for the expected left to follow and avoided it with ease. He straightened, anticipating the forward movement the attacker's effort would give to his head.

Snorting like an angry bull, Woody delivered the first of two-planned solid left jabs to his opponent's face. Like lightning, snap, the sound of knuckles against skin. No need for a second blow. The man's knees folded inward and he collapsed like a tall building felled by a well-placed demolition charge.

Unknown to Woody, the young inspector, culpable, but not exposed by Darby Cameron, had received a measure of punishment at the hands of Ensign Parnell.

Bea dropped Dan, Woody and Brent off at *Denver's* pier where a mass of humanity stirred about like ants making the submarine ready for sea.

Brent shared a kiss with Bea to whistles and howls from sailors and other passersby. The unmistakable voice of Gary Hansen shouted, "Way to go, Mr. Maddock."

Bea admonished Brent, "Don't do anything stupid out there."

"Make book on it, but it's you I'm worried about. I'm a lot safer at sea if this Soviet thing blows up. You listen to what Dave says. He'll know what to do. I care a lot about you, Bea."

She took a final look at him, "I will, Brent. You come back to me. Hear?"

"Make book on that too!"

They released each other and Brent disappeared into the mayhem on the dock.

Captain Bostwick sat in his stateroom and fumed as he read the transcript of Brent's testimony. He ignored the issue that confronted young Maddock, the need to state all pertinent facts to assure the defendant got a fair hearing. The Civil Service Board report cast a shadow over Bostwick, so he would not pass it along to SUBPAC. Bostwick hoped the findings would set the stage for a career ending, adverse fitness report on young Maddock, but they did not. Brent's testimony to the Civil Service Board averted a fatal blow from the captain.

Bostwick muttered, "So the sneaky bastard wants to play games. Well I'll damn well show him he's playing in the big leagues."

Chapter 4

To the east, a red dawn brightened the ridges of Whidbey Island as *Denver* sped north through Puget Sound en route to the open sea. Brent thought, *Red sky in the morning, sailor takes warning* and anticipated seas would kick up as the day wore on. He stood the morning watch, 0400-0800 as officer of the deck on the open bridge, his favorite assignment. Here, the blackness of night yields to the morning glow.

Brent developed a theory that his sense of elation, inherited from ancestors, dated back to the dawn of civilization. Early inhabitants of earth hoped each darkness would surely end, but nonetheless felt relief at the actual occurrence.

To the west, Olympic Mountain peaks caught the first rays of the rising sun and brightening skies diminished a scattering of man-made lights on the land below. The sea bore few marks of man's presence on the planet, but on occasion, even the land view presented unspoiled perspectives. For an instant, Brent beheld Peter Puget's view of this virgin land as he arrived here over two hundred years ago.

Its beauty inspired Brent to think, *God, I love this land!*

Brent recalled an evening with Bea and dinner at a restaurant on Lake Union in Seattle. Patterned after a Pacific Northwest Indian Longhouse, it featured Native-American artifacts. Its owner dedicated much effort to perpetuate traditions of the people who lived in harmony with the land since the dawn of time. Native American photographs taken close to the turn of the century adorned the walls. These depicted early tribesmen who passed their lives here feasting upon endless natural abundance.

Another time, they visited the Hiram Chittenden canal locks, built for passage of shipping between Lake Washington and the lower level waters of Puget Sound. A fish ladder bypassed the locks and facilitated annual salmon migrations to the many headwaters that fed the lake. A ladder featured windows to view these magnificent fish, overcoming all odds while heading to the waters of their birth. There, they spawned and then swam further upstream to die so their prodigy could survive by eating fragments of the decaying carcasses that washed downstream.

He decided he would live out his declining years in these robust surroundings.

Denver left Bremerton too early for lingering good-byes to friends and family and would remain at sea two weeks conducting independent exercises during the way to their homeport in San Diego. There, an extended repair period alongside a submarine tender to clean up post-overhaul material discrepancies would afford time for the crew to re-establish home and social lives before *Denver* put to sea for her next deployment. The captain explained this to his crew on the eve of her departure, but made no mention of the war scare laid upon them by Commodore Danis.

As officer of the deck, Brent guided *Denver* over the course laid down by the navigator and carried out the ship's routine as specified in the captain's night order book. Quiet prevailed below decks as the crew, exhausted from the trying final days at the yard; lay in their bunks for a much-needed rest. Only watch standers remained up and about.

Denver reached the Strait of Juan de Fuca and turned west then submerged for the final leg of her seaward transit.

Later, a stewardsman knocked on the junior officers' stateroom door then opened it. "Mister Maddock. Wake up. The captain wants a meeting in the wardroom in fifteen minutes."

"Thank you," Brent replied. He looked at his watch ... 0930. He'd slept less than an hour. *The morning watch doesn't get a fair share of sack time, but what else is new?*

Shortly, the officers assembled and Olsen summoned the captain.

Bostwick opened with an uncharacteristic jovial voice. "Damn, it's sure good to be out of the yard."

General nods of agreement followed.

"Now we get back to the real Navy. No need to say how important it is for us to make the most of the next fourteen days. Before long, we're back in the squadron and our work's cut out if we expect to keep that red *E* hanging on the fairwater."

Bostwick referred to SUBPAC's award for engineering excellence won by *Denver* the previous year.

The captain continued, "Additionally, we can expect an ORSE (Operational Reactor Safeguard Examination) soon after our return. We must be ready." Bostwick paused and scanned each officer's face. "Zero tolerance for screw-ups, but you all know that so give the executive officer your training requirements. You know where we need attention. The exec and I will set priorities as we see them."

Looking at Olsen, who nodded his assent, the captain continued with, "The ORSE is first then we concentrate efforts to insure records are updated. With the yard workload, I know much of that is on hold, but we've got to get crackin'. We've come out of the yard in great shape. No one will know this unless it's documented."

Brent thought, *Who needs to know besides us?*

Continuing the lecture Bostwick said, "Advancement in rate is next. We led the squadron last year and now I want to lead the force. Promote 'em and retain 'em is the best re-enlistment policy I know. Does anyone have a better idea?"

Astonished that Bostwick did not address the war readiness counsel given by Commodore Danis in his speech, Brent asked, "What about combat training?"

Dan Patrick frowned. He recognized the precursor to yet another Bostwick-Maddock donnybrook. *Uh-oh! Here it comes.*

Bostwick said in a tone forced to sound steady, "There's much to be done to restore pre-overhaul readiness levels. I look to you, Brent, to take the lead. However, I expect you'll not permit these measures to interfere with projects of higher priority."

Brent replied, "Understand, Captain." *Here we go again. Another situation where just doing my job gets me deeper into hot water.* "Captain?"

"Yes?"

His voice tone caused nervous glances to be exchanged among the other officers.

"We have a full load-out of weapons for the first time since I've been aboard. Two of them are new and we don't have any experience with deploying them. If the commodore's instructions are to be followed, I need to conduct a full-court press to be combat ready. But on the other hand, Captain, if you have reason to believe there's no danger, I recommend you share it with us and the crew. The troops are worried about family and friends and a word from you would relieve them immensely."

Brent had just told the captain to either put up or shut up. The officers slumped in their seats to relieve tension.

Captain Bostwick took Brent's comment in stride. "I appreciate your point of view, Brent, and you must appreciate mine. We are not robots. I've been given the commodore's perception on the state of international affairs. The final decision on how we factor this into ship priorities remains with me. I make decisions based on how I see the situation. Do I make myself clear?"

"Very clear, Captain. I'll not interfere with your agenda, but plan to work my department round the clock till we know how to use the new bullets."

"As you wish, Lieutenant," Bostwick replied, disregarding the submarine tradition of calling a junior officer by his first name, thus signaling displeasure over Brent's tenacity to the subject.

The exchange made Jack Olsen's gut churn. Concerned over growing open hostility between Brent and the captain, he also fretted over Bostwick not having shared the results of his call to SUBPAC on Danis's war warning. Bostwick liked to gloat when higher authority confirmed his assertions and he had not done this.

"Yes, Commodore?" Lieutenant Commander Karl 'Dutch' Meyer responded to Commodore Danis's summons to the temporary office.

"Hi Dutch. Grab us a cup of mud and sit down. There's stuff we need to go over."

Dutch responded with a grin, "These okay, Commodore?"

He held a pair of china mugs pirated from a submarine enlisted mess, each filled to the rim with black and bitter coffee, the preference of both officers. The mugs, more practical than the standard wardroom china's dainty pieces, held more coffee and had handles big enough for Dutch to stuff his sausage-like fingers through.

Danis said, "Should've known you wouldn't come in here empty handed. Forgive me for not noticing."

A wooden chair protested as Dutch rested his bulk upon it. "No problem, sir. What's up?"

"I just got back from SUBGROUP 9 Headquarters at the Trident Base. Pucker factor runs pretty high up there. Keep all this stuff under your hat, Dutch. It's dynamite."

"Count on me, sir."

"The Chief of Naval Operations has passed to all operational commanders that a Soviet invasion of Iran is imminent and expected within the next seventy-two hours."

Dutch whistled softly. "Dynamite ain't the word for it. What orders are being given?"

"The general belief is conventional war between us and the Soviets, likely limited to the Middle East. If the Reds make this move, they know we'll try to kick their asses out. They must believe we can't or they wouldn't be taking the chance."

Dutch exclaimed, "We're in bomber range here like a bunch of sitting ducks!"

"I know," Danis agreed, "and we've got to get our submarines away from here. Hitch is, we can't alarm everybody. The public gets a strong enough whiff and concludes *nuclear war*. Panic will hurt us a helluva lot more than a few Soviet bombs."

Dutch addressed his boss through a puzzled look, "Move every damn warship outta here and don't make anybody suspicious? How we gonna do that?"

Danis replied, "SUBGROUP 9's already buttoning up Tridents in refit to leave today."

Dutch shook his head in disbelief. "Good for them, but they got less problems than us ... security for example. The waterfront's an exclusive Navy show. No civilians. Tridents can be out in a day with no one ashore any the wiser. We're in downtown Bremerton and can't loosen a mooring line without involving fifty civilians. People will want answers when we start moving that much hardware."

"I thought about that, Dutch. Here's what just might work."

"With all due respect, Commodore, it better be good."

"Good or bad, it's gonna be our only chance. I'll tell the shipyard commander we're conducting a surprise drill, an emergency evacuation of all SUBPAC units in overhaul. COMSUBPAC ordered this and already passed the word to affected squad dogs. Expect some skippers to bitch over having their overhauls interrupted for a drill. The bright ones will see the light and cooperate fully. It's lousy to keep so many good officers in the dark, but we got to keep the train on the tracks. So far, Admiral Parker at SUBGROUP 9, you and me are all who know the right story so keep it under your bonnet."

Dutch whistled softly. "I will, sir. When do we start?"

"Immediately."

"Okay. I'll identify the boats that are seaworthy and—"

Danis wore a serious expression as he interrupted Dutch. "All of them just like Operation Agile Player," referring to a Navy drill that got every submarine out in forty-eight hours and loaded out for a ninety-day deployment.

"At least we're not plowing new ground."

"We are, Dutch. We did only the operational boats in *Player*. We got to do the same with boats in overhaul. My gut says we'll need 'em all, and soon."

Dutch shook his head. "Some of 'em got access holes in the hull less than three feet above the waterline. They won't survive a storm on the Sound, much less at sea."

"I don't give a damn. They might not survive the Sound, but they sure as hell won't survive a Soviet air raid. Let's not forget Pearl Harbor, Dutch. No Navy ought to get caught with its head up its ass twice in the same century."

Dutch received his boss's message and got behind it. "We got ships with down propulsion systems. I'll order tugs for them."

Danis gave an admiring glance to the wily *old mustang*, Navy slang for an officer who has come up through the ranks. He knew he could count on the full weight of Dutch's beefy shoulders to be put to the wheel. Together they'd pull off the impossible.

Danis said, "I called the Bremerton SUBPAC representative and told him it's a drill ordered by his boss. Told them SUBPAC will give him more if he needs to know."

"He buy it?"

"Like a low mileage used car, but he complained about interrupting overhauls."

"No surprise. Reps are engineers, not operational types."

"Listen, Dutch. Round up a navigator, a communicator and an operations officer from three boats that can best spare them. They'll report to me for temporary staff duty. Better get a couple of yeomen too. We need to crank out a practice emergency dispersal plan."

"Aye, aye, sir. I'll do that. How about the Commander, Naval Base, Seattle? Has he been cut in?"

"Hell of a way to run a Navy. I don't know, Dutch, and I'm not saying anything without direction from SUBPAC."

"Shall we advise him of the drill, sir? If the newspapers pick up on this, they're sure to contact him. If he claims not to know, that alone might throw the fat in the fire."

Danis considered the keen mind that functioned behind Dutch's unobtrusive countenance. "Real good point. I'll tell him the damn submariners are up to another Chinese fire drill. Hopefully, he won't suspect anything."

Relieving his chair of its load Dutch left. Though ordered in soft tones, he knew this to be the most complex and important assignment of his career. He also recognized omissions of specific instructions by Danis to be a vote of confidence. Another tough task lay ahead. It made no sense to pull half repaired submarines from the yard without the right people to finish the job. He'd personally pick key individuals to survive and spare his commodore this weighty chore.

The old mustang pulled a notepad from his pocket and began a list of yard workers.

SHOP	#	NEEDED SKILL
X11	3	Shipfitters
X26	5	Welders
X38	3	Outside Machinists
X51	2	Electricians
X56	2	Pipe Fitters
X67	2	Electronics
X72	4	Riggers

Dutch would ask the shipyard commander for his best men. And he'd requisition the team that had successfully installed an auxiliary saltwater pump at the remote ballistic missile submarine base at Guam. Their recent experience conducting repair operations in the field would round out Dutch's ragtag repair crew. He'd order ships in dry dock to have plates welded over nonessential underwater openings. There'd be time for only one welding pass, violating the rules, but better than nothing. These would hold out seawater but only at shallow depths. Non-propulsive ships would be towed to shallow water in the Sound, submerged to sit on the bottom till whatever might happen blows over.

A myriad of things required attention. Provide Danis with a copy of local ferry schedules so the sortie could be completed before they started running. Passengers might notice the abrupt flurry of Naval activity and become suspicious.

Commodore Danis picked up the phone and dialed after Dutch left the room. It rang only once at the other end.

"Dave Zane speaking."

The commodore greeted his old friend, "Should've known you'd be in the cockpit. Damn, I'm looking forward to retirement."

Dave Zane kept his instruments, the phone, TV and VCR remotes within easy reach of his lazy boy recliner, hence the term cockpit.

Dave replied, "Depending whether you get two or just one term as Chief of Naval Operations, I'd say you'll be retired in eight years minimum."

"I'd retire today if you could fix me up as commodore of the local yacht club. That'd be a lot more exciting."

"We'll talk about it over the weekend, old Buddy. Why don't you ride home with Bea after work tomorrow? We'll drive to the peninsula together in my car. Don't show up in that damn Navy vehicle. The neighbors worry about their taxes when they see that thing in the driveway."

"Sorry, Dave, but I gotta beg off. Navy's gone all to hell since you left it. Us old guys are supposed to sit around and drink coffee and watch the youngsters. We're not supposed to work, but that's what they're making me do. Better get you back on active duty to straighten things out."

"You're kidding. We can put it off a day and leave Saturday."

"No, Dave, I'm afraid not this time. I'll be at sea." Danis offered no further explanation and Dave pressed for none.

"You and Bea will go ahead without me, won't you? I don't want to be a total wet blanket." Danis resisted the urge to warn Dave to leave the area.

"We'll go. Some stuff we have to take care of up there. We'll miss you, though. Next time I won't take no for an answer ... understand?"

"Understand. I'll come by and see you before I leave for Dago, and you can tell me about all the fun I missed. See ya, Dave."

"See ya, Eric. Don't get seasick out there."

After hanging up, Danis felt a great sense of relief that his friend planned to be away from Bremerton for the near term. He did not buy CNO's view that the impending war would be limited to non-nuclear weapons.

An eerie red glow bathed *Denver's* Attack Center to protect the conning officer's night vision; essential in case a periscope observation is needed. Rig for red is enforced between sunset and sunrise and gives the crew a sense of conditions in the world above the waves. Brent enjoyed the quiet time.

Miracle of miracles, he and the captain saw eye to eye on reverting to the traditional four-hour watches. The previous six-hour watches brought on fatigue, boredom and a loss of touch with ship's operations.

The captain's training schedule took five full days. Brent's day began at 0330 when called for the morning watch then came a full day of drills, followed by watch again from 1600-2000. Brent kept his word and squeezed three hours of new weapons training into each day. Land Attack Tomahawk Missiles, TLAMs, loaded in vertical outside the pressure hull, got the most attention. Operation and maintenance had to be conducted from within the ship. The Tomahawk Ship Attack Missiles, TSAMs, stowed in the torpedo room, were accessible, but limited because of being encapsulated.

Brent nursed a cup of hot coffee, not so much for enjoyment but for the wakening effect of the caffeine. At 0530, he executed sunrise and the Attack Center returned to normal lighting.

Denver cruised three hundred miles off Oregon's coast, submerging deep enough to avoid motion imparted by large swells on the surface as she made her way south toward San Diego and home.

A voice crackled over the 21MC, "Conn, Sonar. Can you come in here a second, Mr. Maddock?"

Brent called back, "On the way," and then said to Senior Chief Cunningham, "COB, you got it for a few minutes."

"Aye, sir," Cunningham replied.

Brent entered the sonar shack to find a pair of operators monitoring a maze of green lines on the sonar video displays, "What've you got?"

A sonarman replied, "Don't really know, sir. I've never heard it before. It sort of rumbles at frequencies too low to get a good bearing. They come generally from the east, though. Look, sir, there goes one now."

"Run that back on the LOFAR." Then he and two sonarmen reviewed the Low Frequency Analyzer Recorder (LOFAR) trace but could make no sense of it.

"An earthquake? Or maybe Mount St. Helens erupting again?"

The sonarman disagreed, "Don't think so, sir. I've heard a few quakes and volcanoes and they don't sound anything like this. I've got some tapes if you want me to run them, Mr. Maddock."

"That won't be necessary. Keep track and log everything. We'll want trace-recorder sheets from LOFAR annotated with times. Advise me of any changes."

An ominous feeling built in the pit of Brent's stomach.

"Aye, Mr. Maddock. Will do."

Brent went back to the Attack Center and advised Cunningham of his return then he picked up the telephone and dialed the captain's stateroom.

Bostwick's sleepy voice mumbled, "Captain."

"Conning officer, Captain. We're picking up strange sounds on sonar, sir. Low frequency, very powerful, a long way off to the east. I recommend you come up and listen, sir."

A slight pause then Bostwick said, "No, but let me know if there are any changes. Pacific Ocean can make weird noises when it wants to."

"I don't think these fit that format, Captain. Request permission to proceed to periscope depth and hoist an antenna. Maybe we can pick up some traffic on what's happening."

"Alright, Brent, I'm coming up. You and your damn war scares."

Brent bit his lip. "Hope it's nothing, Captain, but we ought to be sure."

"You're right, it's nothing."

Brent accompanied Bostwick to the sonar shack. The captain listened and again classified the sounds as natural.

He said to Brent, "As long as you got me out of bed, let's go to periscope depth. Should be pretty bright now. At least we'll get a weather observation outta this."

"Aye, sir," and then pressing the 21MC button said, "Sonar, search around, report all contacts."

The sonarman responded, "No contacts, sir. Just the rumbling."

Brent ordered the helmsman, "Ahead two-thirds," and then to Cunningham, "Chief, make your depth one-five-zero feet smartly."

He turned to the quartermaster of the watch and said, "Henri, based on the last look, give me a good heading away from the troughs." This measure minimized obscuring the periscope upper optics from wave action.

"Recommend come left to zero-seven-five," came Henri's crisp reply. This heading also assured best possible depth control near the surface.

"Level one-five-zero, sir," reported Cunningham.

"Sonar, Conn, coming left to zero-seven-five. Check the baffles,"

Denver's main sonar, the spherical array of the AN/BQQ-5 baffles, being mounted forward created a blind spot by the submarine hull. Turning the ship permitted sonarmen to detect possible contacts being masked by the baffles.

Sonar responded, "Baffles. Conn, Sonar, aye," and a minute later, "Baffles clear."

Double clicking the 21MC, Brent signaled he heard and understood the report. "Six-three feet smartly, Chief," Brent ordered.

"Six-three smartly, aye, sir."

"Very well, Chief, mark at seventy and every two thereafter."

"Seventy, and the twos, aye."

Brent ordered, "Up two for a look around."

Henri reported, "Two coming up, sir." As the periscope cleared the well, he flipped the handles to the down position, rotated the optics to low power with the right handle and elevated the optics to full high with the left.

Brent fastened his eye to the scope and at once saw florescent plankton speed by the periscope head window. He rotated the scope rapidly for visual contact with the bottom of possible undetected surface ships that might be close aboard.

Cunningham called out, "Seven-two feet, seven-zero, six-eight."

Brent shouted, "Scope clear," as the optics broke the ocean surface. "Swinging around in low power. Nothing close. Raise the BRA 34." Training the scope aft, Brent observed the large antenna break the surface and extend to full length. "Henri, tell Radio the 34 is clear. Monitor all VLF and HF band signals."

Radio responded to the order relayed by Henri, "Radio, aye. Our ears are on."

A minute slipped by and the 21MC crackled again. "No joy in Radio, Conn."

"Well, Brent, looks like no war today," the captain smirked. "I'm going below and get some—"

The 21MC prevented Bostwick from finishing his sentence.

A shrill and panicked voice cried out, "Captain to Radio on the double!"

No one ordered the captain anywhere and never on the double. As he hurried to the radio shack, he snarled, "This better be damned important."

A short while later, Bostwick returned to the Attack Center, his face ashen. "Men, we're about to change our spots from peacetime sailor to full-time warrior. We've been attacked by the Soviets. Good luck to us all. We're going to need it."

Brent wondered if the other men had detected Bostwick's lack of conviction. He was not eager to follow this captain into combat.

Chapter 5

Dave Zane and Bea loved their rustic family retreat that sat on a cliff overlooking the Pacific Ocean from Washington's magnificent Olympic Peninsula. The simple, functional, cozy structure included a kitchen and dining-family room combination with a large ocean view window. A nearby cliff looked down fifty feet onto a stretch of sandy beach strewn with large boulders deposited there during the ice age. A rugged switchback trail provided access to the beach for the stout of heart.

Dave built most of the house himself, but his wife Dale drew the line and brought in professionals for the finishing work. Fieldstone collected from the site made up a large fireplace on the family room north wall. A divan and several large chairs formed a semicircle facing the hearth. Two baths, a loft bunkroom, a master bedroom and two other bedrooms rounded out the spread.

Eric Danis had to bow out at the last minute. Dave regretted his friend canceled his visit, but he didn't let it dampen the good spirits that accompanied each of his visits to what Dale had dubbed the *Digs*.

Bea wondered if the presence of Eric Danis and her dad might put a damper on her weekend with Brent. But, she had been raised among submariners and knew of their tendency for taking life in stride, so concluded it would have been a fun time.

Dave ate far too much baked salmon, the traditional opening meal established by his late wife. After several games of cribbage with Bea, he turned in then fell into a deep and restful sleep.

Hours later, Bea stood beside her father's bed wearing one of his old bathrobes. "Dad ... Dad! Wake up! Something is very wrong."

Dave quickly woke. "What, Baby? What's the matter?"

"Come outside and look. East of the Olympics."

"East of the Olympics? What are you talking about? You can't see anything from here. The mountains are too big."

"Come outside, Dad, and have a look. Unless the sun is rising three hours early, something pretty terrible is happening."

Dave emerged from the *Digs* to see the source of Bea's concern. A red glow probed the black night with such brightness that he could detect the Olympic Mountains' ridge.

My God! The dumb bastards really did it. "Bea, go inside and turn on the radio."

Electro-magnetic pulses from detonated nuclear warheads created oscillations in the ionosphere like ripples on a pond, causing distant radio transmissions to fade in and out. Bea finally found a commercial station in western Montana at just the right distance that bounced a sky wave off the ionosphere and reflected it to the Washington coast.

The announcer spoke in quiet, serious tones, "So far, enemy strikes appear limited to just Naval bases and shipyards. On the east coast: Kittery, Maine; Groton, Connecticut; Norfolk, Virginia; Charleston, South Carolina; and Kings Bay, Georgia. Targets on the west coast are the Trident Base at Bangor and nearby Bremerton Naval Shipyard, in Washington State. In California: Mare Island Naval Shipyard, Seal Beach Naval Weapons Station, and Naval Bases in San Diego.

"Pentagon sources advise American response has been limited. Also, other unofficial sources reported a total of seventeen missiles have been launched in retaliation. There are no reports on the extent of damage from Soviet warheads, but it is apparently heavy. Main thoroughfares from the damaged areas are jammed with fleeing survivors, as are those from New York, Chicago and other population centers not yet under attack."

Father and daughter listened in stunned silence to the unthinkable. Visited by a host of emotions, Dave felt gratitude his beloved Dale had to see none of this in her lifetime and it saddened him to reflect upon the impact it would have on Bea's future.

The recent conversation with Eric Danis came to mind. His friend had urged him to make the trip, likely for good reason. Dave hoped Eric had made it to sea and survived.

Captain 1st Rank Igor Sherensky, commanding officer of the Soviet nuclear submarine *Marshall Zhukov,* reined in his exhilaration. He dare not let it affect performance of the critical task-at-hand, sinking the mighty U.S. nuclear-powered attack aircraft carrier, *Savo Island*. A three second view through *Zhukov*'s attack periscope showed the giant ship lumbering toward him at a full twenty-five knots. The periscope video camera, peri-viz, recorded information to refine target range, course and speed well beyond the precision needed for a successful attack. For two weeks, *Zhukov* trailed the aircraft carrier.

Upon receipt of a prearranged signal, she moved ahead of *Savo Island* to prepare for an attack. All over the world, Soviet submarines deployed successfully in coordinated attacks against the U.S. aircraft carrier fleet and nullified it.

Zhukov and her sisters bore the North Atlantic Treaty Organization designation, *Akula* class.

Initial Soviet land attack warheads destroyed those carriers that remained in port or in overhaul. These victories dealt a severe blow to the Americans who had bet everything on survival of their carriers. It certainly appeared there would soon be none, leaving the U.S. Navy scrambling to recover control over their vital sea lanes

Captain Sherensky could not believe his good fortune. He had reached the best possible attack position, seven miles ahead of the carrier and within twenty degrees of her monstrous bow.

The captain ordered, "Make all torpedoes ready, Comrade Baknov. We cannot miss with this setup."

Their target cooperated by running at high speed. Radiated noise from the carrier's immense propulsion system further obscured the already silent *Zhukov* and diminished counter-detection probability by Anti-Submarine-Warfare surface ships. *Savo Island*'s sole self-defense measure consisted of the near futile World War II zigzag course.

Lieutenant Vasiliy Baknov would not permit excitement of the moment to stampede him into making an error. He ordered the ET 80A torpedoes to run at a depth of twenty-five meters and set the warheads to detonate in the magnetic influence created as the steel giant passed overhead. The target's back would be broken by detonations below her keel.

The young officer rechecked his ordered settings.

Vasiliy Baknov viewed a U.S. aircraft carrier through the periscope during an earlier peacetime exercise to measure *Zhukov*'s ability to reach an effective attack position undetected. The target's vast size captivated him. He considered production costs of these behemoths drained even abundant resources of capitalist America.

Captain Sherensky announced, "Comrades, attack commences in five minutes."

The zampolit, *Zhukov's* political officer Commander Poplavich, added, "We embark the Motherland on the road to world communism."

Sherensky thought, *Leave it to our half-assed political commissar to make speeches at a time like this.* He detested Poplavich, who took up space aboard *Zhukov* and contributed nothing to her mission.

Lieutenant Baknov wondered. *Perhaps we'll become the victims.*

Peacetime surveillance against the U.S. Navy succeeded beyond their wildest hopes, but concern grew over whether American 688 class submarines were present as escorts and monitored the *Akulas* from the onset. Lieutenant Baknov feared the hunter might become the hunted.

A U.S. Advanced Capability torpedo, ADCAP, fired at point blank range would add *Zhukov* to the ocean's long list of victims now resting on the bottom. He reasoned the interdiction attack probability by an enemy submarine diminished in proportion to *Zhukov's* distance from her target. If an American submarine tracked them, the time to initiate an attack had passed.

Captain Sherensky ordered, "To depth 60 meters. We will attack on sonar bearings. The target gives no sign he knows we are here and continues to close the range. What is the time to torpedo launch?"

Lieutenant Baknov could barely contain his excitement. "A minute twenty seconds, Comrade Captain."

"Good. Then launch when the target reaches firing bearing."

The lieutenant replied with an excited voice, "Yes, Comrade Captain!" and then counted off time till torpedo launch. "Sixty seconds … thirty … ten … five, four, three, two, one … launch torpedoes!"

Zhukov shuddered in the manner of all submarines expelling weapons. Four ET 80A torpedoes surged from their launchers and began their runs toward the unsuspecting *Savo Island.*

Captain Sherensky demanded, "Time till detonation?"

The sound of an explosion interrupted Lieutenant Baknov's reply. Three more quickly followed, as all four torpedoes hit. No surprise at such a short range.

A cheer went up throughout *Zhukov* to celebrate the first kill by a Soviet submarine in fifty-two years.

"Sonar, search carefully," Sherensky ordered, fearing the possibility of attack by an escorting submarine.

"No new contacts, Comrade Captain. Only the aircraft carrier and escorting surface ships."

Neither Sherensky nor Baknov understood how the Americans could be so naive. The captain thought, *Had they really based their entire naval strategy upon the survival of fifteen aircraft carriers known to be defenseless against nuclear-powered attack submarines? Do they consider us buffoons, or do they enact this merely to throw us off guard, the real plan to follow.*

Sherensky could not resist getting a view of his triumph. "Come to twenty meters."

The diving officer replied, "To twenty meters."

The Zampolit Poplavich, concerned the alerted Americans might detect them, demanded, "Comrade Captain, is this wise?"

"Consider the importance of showing our people the photographic evidence of the enemy sea giant's death, comrade. It will prove your great value to the party."

Sherensky knew how to butter up the zampolit. Poplavich made no response, his assent assumed.

Savo Island lay dead in the water and listed fifteen degrees to starboard, down by the bow with smoke billowing from a major rupture amidships. Analysis of the peri-viz tape showed *Savo Island* a doomed ship, sinking faster than Sherensky imagined. The carrier disappeared and the periscope field showed only tiny spots in the water, heads of some hundred or so surviving crewmembers.

The elated zampolit declared, "The softheaded Americans will rush to their aid. We will stand off a safe distance, Comrade Captain, and attack the rescuers with cruise missiles."

The captain pleaded, "Attacking ships while recovering survivors counters a thousand years of tradition."

Zampolit Poplavich snapped back, "You are reminded, comrade, World Communization requires overturning tradition. Be mindful that rescued men will mend and rise again to fight the Motherland with a terrible resolve."

Slaughtering helpless men in the water will probably increase American resolve by a factor of ten, thought Sherensky. He did not share this, for arguing with the zampolit is unwise and could result in a nine-millimeter headache.

As the zampolit predicted, escorting warships approached the *Savo Island's* grave and began to pick up survivors from the oil-slicked ocean. Rescue operations continued in the mistaken belief the attackers preoccupied themselves with escape and posed no further threat.

Sherensky had little heart for it, but released a salvo of SS-N-21 anti-ship missiles at the rescue operation. The 21, NATO designation *Sampson,* mimics a U.S. Tomahawk Ship Attack Missile in capability.

A short time later, Sherensky observed columns of black smoke as the rescuers burned from missile hits.

The *Sampsons* left an infrared trail to *Zhukov,* but the defeated foe had no aircraft to mount a counterattack. The captain ordered *Zhukov* to a hundred meters and increased to maximum speed in the direction of home.

Only the zampolit, Commander Poplavich, and the vengeance bent Lieutenant Vasiliy Baknov found elation in this senseless post attack.

Captain Hal Bostwick assembled *Denver* officers in the wardroom. He read a historic document, the first operational message from a flying backup TACAMO aircraft, a system of U.S. Naval communications that would continue in the event shore facilities were destroyed. Derived from an old Navy expression, '*Take Charge and March Off.*' These TACAMO aircraft did just that.

These special C130s held runway priority over all other U.S. aircraft, including the Air Force Strategic Air Command assets. The TACAMO maneuver involved streaming a mile long antenna from the back of the aircraft during a turn maneuver to hold the antenna vertical to the earth's surface. This enhanced transmission from TACAMO C130s continually airborne over both Atlantic and Pacific Oceans.

The message addressed to all units of the U.S. Pacific Fleet from the commander read:

> *The U.S. Congress has enacted a declaration of war on the Union of Soviet Socialist Republics. All Pacific Fleet Units*

conduct immediate hostilities against any/all Soviet units and resources. Good hunting.

"Gentlemen," said Bostwick, "our work is cut out for us. I know you'll give your customary best and *Denver's* chapter in this war will be a brilliant one. I expect no departure from normal routine. This has always been a warship and will continue to perform like one. But we must get better at things we have always done well.

"Perform equipment inspections and maintenance above current requirements. Correct problems before they occur. Exercise greater diligence in all areas, particularly in conduct of the watch.

"I've directed Brent to load four ADCAPs into the launchers. I emphasize, we have no release authority for tactical nuclear weapons. After the initial exchange of strategic nukes, our government and the Soviets have mutually agreed their further use jeopardizes the causes of both nations and will be withheld. SUBROCs (*rocket propelled long-range nuclear depth charges*) will remain on the 4FZ tampering monitor system and in their lower, outboard stowage positions.

"Dan, I want you to double up on sonar watch. We could encounter Ivan at anytime and I want to be damn sure we detect him before he even suspects we're in the area. We have acoustic advantage over him and in order to prevail, we must exploit this to the fullest."

Bostwick continued, "I am concerned about crew morale. We've very little information on what's happened at home. My plan is to play it straight up and let them know what we know as soon as we know it. Don't get dragged into speculating, but if it's unavoidable always stress positive possibilities."

Brent thought, *Maybe the reality of combat has turned the Captain around. I sincerely hope so.*

Bostwick went on, "Our first assignment is to screen passage for the COB's last home, USS *Utah,* from the Strait of Juan de Fuca seaward. We've a message from SUBPAC. It reads:

USS Denver proceed to area Tango Four to arrive not later than 290300Z April 1987. Conduct patrol and sanitize area for seaward passage of USS Utah, window 290500Z - 290900Z. Effect rendezvous with Utah at point Tango Four Alfa 290530Z, method November 7 (a pre-defined search plan) and escort to western limit of Tango Alfa. Instructions for subsequent operations to follow."

Bostwick looked up from the text. "I'm sure COB will be happy to hold his old shipmates' hands while we tiptoe them through the tulips."

Somber moods among the officers prevented the expected laugh. They understood the importance of training for war; but thoughts of war and the separation from family and friends overwhelmed them. Each dealt with it in their own way.

The captain asked, "Questions?" then hearing none he said, "Very well. Dan, would you join me in the Sonar Shack, please?"

Lieutenant Vasiliy Baknov's hatred of all things American made *Zhukov's* victory over *Savo Island* much sweeter for him. This anger began early against his father, a famous ballet dancer who defected to the United States shortly after Vasiliy's birth.

Yuri Baknov toured America with the Kirov Ballet Company and while there, asked for political asylum, ultimately granted by the U.S. Government. News of this shocked his wife, Ekaterina, still recovering from Vasiliy's childbirth. She and her son subsequently paid dearly for Yuri's actions. The Soviet state, embarrassed and humiliated by Yuri's defection, took retribution against his family. It barred Ekaterina, also a dancer, from the Kirov and she never performed publicly again.

For Vasiliy, the legacy left by his father made the young man's life miserable and bitter from the onset. Being the son of a defector, his schoolmates regarded him with scorn. Security considerations nearly prevented him from entering naval service, but fortunately, Ekaterina took a state official as her lover. His influence overcame this problem.

Vasiliy divided his hatred between his father and the country giving him asylum. He resolved to inflict great harm on both, if the opportunity developed and beamed with pride over his part in the attack against *Savo Island* and her escorts. He planned someday, as captain of his own submarine, he'd direct even greater attacks to concurrently satisfy his anger and hurt the enemies of the Motherland. Vasiliy had yet to formulate a plan for revenge against his father, but the topic preoccupied him often.

Commodore Eric Danis and Commander Dutch Meyer adjusted to the shock of their new surroundings then asked, "Damn it, Dutch who in hell ever executed command-at-sea from a desert?"

COMSUBRON 3 set up their temporary headquarters at the Naval Weapons Center, China Lake, just above the Mojave Desert region of California because the initial Soviet attack destroyed all San Diego based Naval facilities. Years would pass before any of the base would be tenable. Ninety percent of the civilian population believed killed outright, leaving the balance to expire from radiation sickness in a matter of weeks.

Most of the commodore's staff comprised of replacements from what submariners could be scraped up along with a handful of naval aviators off sunken aircraft carriers. They wanted vengeance and U.S. submarine forces offered the best opportunity; so the aviators accepted their assignments with enthusiasm. They would add their *right stuff* to the mix and eventually impress the skeptical submariners.

Dutch Meyer looked around their new headquarters and thought, *A far cry from the hustle, bustle and the comfort of a submarine tender* then said, "Well, Commodore, at least we got a place to hang our hat."

"Maybe so, Dutch, but I hope you brought along a hammer and some nails just in case. Look, give me half an hour to settle in ... then I want to meet with the staff."

"Aye, sir." Dutch then set out on his most important task, find a coffee pot.

Thirty minutes later, Danis addressed his makeshift staff in a hot and stuffy workshop turned conference room. An air-conditioner sat silent. The short supply of electric power precluded such peacetime luxuries.

"Gentlemen, I'm Eric Danis. I just told Dutch Meyer this is a hell of a place from which to run a submarine squadron. But at least we have a place, which is more than other less fortunate commands can say. I'm pleased to note we have some aviators aboard. Commander Carter is the number two man in seniority and as such will perform the duties of chief staff officer. We make history, gentlemen. No naval aviator has ever held this post in a U.S. submarine squadron before. Welcome and congratulations, Commander."

Commander Carter acknowledged with a nod and smile.

Danis went on, "West coast port facilities for submarines are no longer available for reasons you all know. They've all been hit with ground bursts and left too hot for anything for at least five years. It's part of the Soviet strategy. Isolate us from our allies and finish off with a blockade. To break this, we must regain access to the sea. Our job is to replace the lost seaports.

"Ships on patrol can't stay out there indefinitely. They gotta come home to lick their wounds and get back out there to kick more Soviet ass. This won't be easy and we have no experience with such a task so ingenuity is a hot commodity. The new additions from the aviation community are famous for this and I expect they'll give us submariners a run for our money."

He made it clear he would not tolerate inter-group animosity and concluded with, "And now, I'd like to go around and hook up some faces with the names I've seen on the staff register. After that, I want Commander Carter to conduct interviews and find the best fits for staff jobs that need filling."

Brent Maddock handed a steaming cup of coffee to the conning officer, Dan Patrick. "Here, shipmate. Don't say I never gave you anything. How long ago did we enter Tango Four?"

"About an hour ... and let me tell you the pucker factor has been right up there."

"No surprise. First shooting war for all of us. How are things going?"

"I'd have to say good. Never realized we could get the ship this quiet. We're bombing along at fifteen knots without a flicker on the self noise monitor."

"Fear is a hell of an incentive. What's the search plan?"

Irritation apparent in his voice, Dan went on, "Nothing formal so far. The old man's seat-of-the-pantsing it. He wears himself out bouncing between Sonar and the chart table. And he's burning out our best ears with the double watch bit. A week at this pace and we won't be able to hear a jack hammer in the Sonar Shack."

Taking Dan by the arm, Brent guided him out of earshot of the enlisted watch standers. "Back off on the captain, Dan."

"You're a fine one to talk, Brent. You bait him every chance you get."

"No, Dan, I don't. I just do my job and sometimes it gets in the way. I don't try to prove him wrong just to make him look bad."

Dan said with a sarcastic tone, "Sometimes it just happens that way. Right?"

"That's not my point, Dan. If we survive this mission, it'll be as a team. Most important, don't let the troops suspect there's dissension. That would blow their confidence, which equates to low morale."

"Yeah, Brent. But the skipper scares the hell out of me for that very reason. I don't think he really knows what to do."

"None of us do, Dan. We've got to bring out the best each of us has to offer and throw it on the table. It'll get damn tough around here if the captain suspects we're not behind him. He won't take our advice then, even when it's sound, but I promise you, it won't always be."

"What are you suggesting, Brent?"

"We make the old man look good. He's running with the ball too hard on his own. Maybe not for what we consider the best of reasons, but we need to show he can depend on us."

Dan frowned. "Let me think on it."

"Good. And while you are, I'll work up a search plan."

Brent disappeared behind the plotting room curtains and emerged an hour later. "Here's how it looks to me, Dan. Tango Four's too big for a complete sweep before *Utah* gets here, so let's focus our efforts on her projected track. We'll do this below the layer. Ivan's no fool and he knows that's where the Tridents like to hang out. We'll search passive-narrowband at low frequencies. This is our best chance to find him. But, if he's lying still and waiting, even that will be pretty damn hard. We'll search wide at the seaward end and converge to the rendezvous point. This will give us the most coverage for the time allowed. We've got to be careful about our own radiated noise levels; and Dan, fifteen knots is too fast. I don't care what the monitors say. At this speed, we concede first detection to an *Akula* laying to, dead in the water."

Dan interrupted. "Where'n hell do you come up with all this stuff, Brent?"

Brent grinned at his friend. "I'm the weapons officer and I read all that paperwork your department sends me. Listen, we must not make that rendezvous."

"For chrissake, Brent, why not? SUBPAC told us to rendez —"

Brent broke in, "I know, but don't forget, nobody on the Soviet side has any combat experience, either. We shouldn't hook up with *Utah* for two reasons. First, if an *Akula*'s out there and he finds us, he'll know what we're up to. He'll simply follow us to the real prize, *Utah.*"

"And, the other reason?"

"What can we do for *Utah* after the rendezvous? Consider the options. If we go ahead of her, anybody waiting on the track will let us pass and shoot the big guy. If we follow, anything we do will be too late. So why not take our chances and lead Ivan to where *Utah* ain't?"

Dan shook his head. "You'll never sell this to the Old Man."

"I know I won't, Dan. You will."

"What do you mean, I will? Damn it, Brent."

"Look, Dan. I'm not asking you to do anything you don't believe is right. You agree with my approach, don't you?"

"Yes, but —"

"You know I'm a burr under the captain's saddle. He gets pissed off if I tell him what time it is. This is medicine he must take … and it can't be from me. Besides, Dan, you're the operations officer and it's your job to make these up anyway."

Dan smarted under the allegation. The two glared at each other a moment.

After a short pause, Dan said, "Okay. I'll give it my best shot, but no promises."

"No promises."

Brent left the Attack Center.

An hour later Dan explained to Brent the outcome of his meeting with the captain. "The son of a bitch is dangerous, Brent."

"Cool it, Dan. That kind of talk can kill us. We won't achieve a damn thing with open hostility."

"Okay, okay."

"Exactly what did he say?"

"He said the plan contradicts his orders. SUBPAC said to sanitize Tango Four and that means all of it. When he says rendezvous with

Utah, that doesn't mean go someplace else. He asked me what would headquarters' reaction be if our patrol report states we disobeyed orders."

Brent suspected the captain had said more. "Is that all?"

Dan hesitated. "No."

"What else?"

"He said he'd expect that kind of advice from an officer like you but surprised to hear it from me."

Brent nodded, took a breath to speak, but remained silent.

Later he relieved Dan as conning officer before reaching *Denver's* rendezvous point three hours early. Bostwick, determined to be on time, ordered the high speeds needed to sanitize the entire area.

Exactly on time, the faint whir, whir, whir of *Utah's* propellers marked the mighty ship's passage overhead.

Denver initiated the rendezvous signal with three short pings on her secure depth sounder. *Utah* received the signals reflected off the ocean floor and replied with three of her own. *Denver* fell into trail five miles astern of the Trident submarine; an excellent peacetime tactic to detect an adversary lying in wait with intentions to trail *Utah* to her northern Pacific patrol area, but not a good one if an attack is in the cards.

Reluctantly Brent complied with the captain's orders. "Ahead one-third," he directed the helmsman and to the chief of the watch, "Chief, ease us down to three-fifty."

Chief Cunningham answered, "Ahead one-third, ease to three-fifty."

Brent said, "Left full rudder, steady two-eight-zero, belay the headings."

Helmsmen, while executing turns, usually announce the ship's heading every ten degrees unless ordered to belay them.

"Left full to two-eight-zero, belay headings, aye, Mr. Maddock."

"Sonar, Conn. Here we go, Hansen. Give me a report on anything that remotely sounds like a target."

"Good move, Brent." Captain Bostwick provided the young officer with a rare, but sincere vote of confidence, though to be short-lived.

"Conn, Sonar! Torpedo in the water bearing two-eight-five!"

Brent ordered, "Collision alarm!" A shrill signal made its piercing whoeee, whoeee throughout the ship. Henri, the quartermaster of the watch correctly anticipated the order and its follow-on. He initiated the gong, gong, gong of the general alarm and announced over the 21MC, "Man battle stations!"

Brent ordered, "Torpedo Room, Conn. Make tubes one and two ready in all respects."

Instantly, Brent knew he had made a mistake. The sound of water blown from WRT tank to the launchers deafened the sonar at the most critical moment. The background noise masked the torpedo's running sounds. For what seemed an eternity the torpedo tube blow subsided forty seconds later.

"Bearing to torpedo, Sonar!"

"Two-eight-four, drawing left."

Brent surmised correctly, *They're shooting at Utah.*

Wanting to acquire a bearing and range to the attacking Soviet with a pulse from the ship's sonar, Brent turned to Bostwick, and requested, "Permission to go active, Captain."

Silence ensued.

Brent demanded, "Captain!"

Bostwick made a stern and well calculated reply, "Not granted."

The sound of two distant explosions rattled *Denver's* hull.

Brent pleaded, "Captain … for chrissake. Permission to go active and get the sons of bitches."

"Not granted, Brent. It's too late. Let's not give 'em another aim point and another scalp for their belt."

"Let me shoot down the bearing line, then."

"No. They're out of range and they can outrun anything we throw at them. Secure the tubes and save the bullets. We're going to need them later."

Anger surged through Brent's chest but mostly at himself. He knew the captain had it right. They had blown their first mission, but better not to make matters worse by striking out in stupid anger.

Get above the layer, Brent thought then said, "Chief, five degrees up bubble, make your depth six-zero feet."

No response from Chief Cunningham as he sobbed uncontrollably. At that instant, sounds from a collapsing compartment in *Utah* rattled over the underwater telephone receiver speaker. The sinking Titan yielded to the sea and gave up the lives of Cunningham's former shipmates.

Calmly, Brent ordered, "Henri, relieve the chief of the watch."

The authoritative voice of the black quartermaster responded, "Aye, sir," and then ordered the helmsman, "Full rise on the fairwaters, five up on the angle, smartly to six-zero."

"Messenger of the watch, call the chief's relief," Brent said. Then he put his arm about Cunningham's shoulder and guided him to the ladder leading to the crew's quarters.

Doing what he could, Brent tried to comfort the COB. "Chief, I can't say I know how you feel. I've never been there. But I hurt for you, Chief, and for your buddies. I hurt goddamn bad."

Captain Bostwick hunched his shoulders and with no expression showing on his face, walked to his stateroom.

The 21MC crackled, "Conn, Sonar. Distant suppressed cavitation bearing two-eight-five, range opening."

The message described the distinct sound of an escaping submarine. Her work done the victorious Soviet sped off into the vastness of the Pacific Ocean.

Chapter 6

Eric Danis looked out his office window onto a magnificent view of the Mojave Desert. Though a seaman, the expanse and serenity of this intriguing land overwhelmed him. He made a mental note to find time to look into the many secrets that had attracted man to find an abode here over the past ten millenniums. He held a phone to his ear and heard the ring at the other end, twice, three times.

"Hello, Dave Zane speaking," came a distant voice.

"Hello, yourself. Eric Danis, here."

"I know that. I'd recognize that sandpaper voice anywhere. How are you, old buddy?"

The relief in Dave's voice said much. His friend had survived. A custom of their generation precluded emotional pronouncements.

"Figured I'd find you at the *Digs,* Dave."

"You figured right. If you believe the newsies, it'll be five years before we can go back to Bainbridge. The Soviets made a damn mess of it. Too hot for at least the time being."

Eric assured Dave. "Eve's here with me. The last we heard Sean got arrested for laying down in front of visitors at a Trident submarine commissioning ceremony. But he's still with us and I'll take having him alive any way I can get him. How about Bea? I trust she's well."

"Bloomin', Eric, just bloomin'. Since young Maddock showed up, things have gotten a lot better for her. She's a mite worried about him. I keep tellin' her a 688 at sea has a better chance of making it than us poor souls on terra firma. She's a woman, Eric, and needs assurances."

"Tell her I'm certain he's well and that's more than just a gut feel."

"Thanks, Eric. She'll be grateful for that, especially since it came from you."

"Least I can do for my favorite godchild."

"How we doin', Eric? Papers say we're gettin' our butts kicked."

Eric said with a grim voice, "We've lost just about all the hardware we needed to successfully carry out the Maritime Strategy. Add to that some serious casualties ashore, both military and civilian. Most of this is on the coasts. We don't know how they did it, but the areas attacked are dirty enough to keep us out for quite a while. Apart from facilities ashore, submarines seem to be holding their own ... just barely, but hanging in there."

"Guess the Maritime Strategy turned 'round and bit us submariners square on the ass. We went along 'cause it got us outta battle-group escort and freed us up for the forward areas where the good hunting is. Just didn't believe the Soviets would do what they did."

"Hindsight is 20/20, Dave."

"Well at least we saved something, Eric. The damn *I told you so* flakes from the candy-ass peace crowd piss me off. If we do get taken over, wait till they hear what the KGB has to say about their damn intellectual pontificating."

Dave regretted his words the instant they left his mouth since Eric's son was an avid peace activist.

If Eric Danis noticed, he didn't let it show. "Let's hope it doesn't come to that." *Hmm. What's the best way to hit Dave with this? A no brainer, just give it to him straight up.* "Dave, have I got a deal for you."

"Shoot. I got my hand over my butt."

"How would you like to be activated for temporary assignment?"

"A stupid-ass old diesel guy like me? What could I do for the war effort? Do I get paid? Better not let the newsies get hold of this. I can just see the headlines now. *Navy retiree, already getting paid too much for doing nothing, gets paid more for doing less.*"

Eric laughed. "This thing hasn't hurt your sense of humor one bit. Seriously, Dave, I need you to set up an emergency submarine base."

Not quite believing what he heard, Dave asked, "Set up a what?"

Although a patient man, Eric could get his back up on occasion. "Damn it! Hear me out."

Sensing his friend's stress, Dave said, "Okay."

Eric went on, "We've got boats at sea with no place to bring them home. All of our deep-water ports are unusable. We need something workable. Flimsy is good as long as it works. You're the best person up there to do this."

"Why do you say that, Eric?"

"Two reasons. You know the Washington coast like the back of your hand and what's needed to pull off a refit."

"Thanks for the vote of confidence, Eric. Got any specifics?"

"There are none. Find us a spot and then look around to see what you can lay your hands on to make it suitable for submarine refits."

"That's one hell of a job, buddy. It took eight years and three billion dollars for the base at Bangor."

"That's because you weren't running the job, Dave."

"I'd have cut it to four billion and twelve years." Dave paused then asked, "You're serious? You want to fire up an old fogy like me?"

"Look at it this way, Dave. We didn't pay you any attention when we owned your soul; so now we figure you owe us. That's one of the beauties of this country. We're the land of the second chance."

"Do I get a raise?"

"You'll be damn lucky to see another retirement check in the next ten years."

"In that case, I'll take the job."

Dave Zane realized the powerful vote of confidence he had just gotten from a man he held in great esteem. Old salts avoid maudlin so he said nothing. Dave gleaned as many details as he could from his old friend and after an exchange of pleasantries they hung up.

Eric drew a pair of black and bitters from the coffeepot behind his desk and summoned Dutch Meyer.

Dutch came into the office, took the coffee and seated himself in response to Danis's hand gesture. "Afternoon, Commodore."

Eric said, "Afternoon, Dutch. Thanks for coming by. Got a couple of things on my mind and need your help."

The stoic Dutch replied, "That's why they keep me on the payroll, Commodore."

"I'm worried about our aviators. We gotta find them something to get their teeth into. They've had their asses kicked and want to get even. Failure of the carrier battle group strategy does not reflect on these kids. From what I see, they're damn good. I get the feeling we give them nothing but make-work and I think they deserve better. I want you to dissolve the hard-ass attitude by some of our submarine staffers. You know who they are."

"No problem, sir. You're right. It's been bugging me too. I can fix that."

"Work fast. You only got a day to do it. There's something else I need you to do."

Dutch squirmed uneasily. "Something else, Commodore?"

"Yeah, Dutch. How's the old Chevy running?"

The old Chevy ... what the hell? Danis wants to buy my car? Dutch answered, "Not all that bad, I guess."

"Good. I want you to start driving north and gather up everything you can find to help set up a temporary submarine base."

Sitting back in his chair, Dutch thought, *Whew!* Then he said, "A temporary submarine base, Commodore? Where? When?"

"On the Washington coast as soon as Dave Zane gets off his sorry ass and finds us one."

"When did he get the assignment, sir?"

"About fifteen minutes ago."

"I see what you mean, Commodore. Those retired guys do take their own sweet time. When do you want me to start?"

Looking at his watch Danis replied, "Right now, Dutch. We gotta get a base for our boats because they can't stay out there forever." He passed the mustang a letter with a stack of duplicates. "This authorizes you to requisition anything we need, including the means to get it up there."

Dutch asked, "Where's *up there,* Commodore?"

"I don't know, Dutch. Here's Zane's phone number. Call him once a day and keep the pressure on. Dump whatever you find at the Coast Guard Station in Astoria, Oregon till Zane finds us a better place."

"This okay with the Coasties?"

"It will be by the time you get going."

"With all due respect, Commodore, how am I supposed to do this? Gather all the stuff, I mean."

"If I knew, I'd do it myself and wouldn't need you."

He glared at his boss for a second then Dutch said, "Aye, aye, sir," and turned to walk off, shaking his head in disbelief.

As Dutch left, the commodore said, "And, Dutch, don't forget to straighten out the staff problem before you go."

The two looked at each other and exchanged a grin.

"I won't forget, sir."

Vasiliy Baknov sat in the huge auditorium at the Vladivostok Naval Base among several hundred Soviet Pacific Submarine Flotilla officers. On a stage in the front, the briefer awed his audience with descriptions of overwhelming combat successes against the American Navy.

A large, backlighted world chart reached to both ends of the stage. Small red circles indicated locations of nuclear weapons strikes by both warring nations. The United States directed her nuclear strikes mainly against Soviet military air facilities.

The briefer stressed, "It is clear the main concern of the Americans is the defense of NATO; therefore, they hit our air bases harder than expected. This diminishes the speed of our thrust into Western Europe but will not stop it."

The speaker paused to let this settle in and then swept a light beam shaped like an arrow along and over the leading edge of the Soviet advance. "This line shows our current positions. The right flank is anchored in Belgium. To the south, our forces have entered France and Italy where widespread collapse of Allied forces is reported. Poland, Czechoslovakia, Austria, Finland and the two Germanys belong to us now. Only neutral Sweden impedes our drive through to the Atlantic."

Again, he paused then said while smiling, "Negotiations with the reluctant warrior proceed quickly and our tanks will soon roll over Swedish soil and into Norway."

Laughter erupted from the audience. Next, the pointer moved along the west coast of the United States. Red circles covered all the major ports. "Our strategy is to contain the enemy in his North American continent."

The white arrow pointed from south to north over the American east coast where red circles covered all the seaports. "We must prevent American supplies from reaching their NATO allies. Destruction of these ports has reduced the flow of war materials to a trickle and our Northern fleet submarines in the Atlantic are fast shutting that off."

The briefer turned to face his audience. "And now, for the vaunted American Maritime Strategy."

Again laughter, then an abrupt standing ovation as a periscope photo of the attack on *Savo Island* flashed on the screen, superimposed over the world charts.

"Sherensky ... Sherensky ... Sherensky." The chant grew louder and several fellow officers hustled the reluctant commanding officer up and onto the stage. *Zhukov's* Captain acknowledged his ovation in the traditional manner of applauding back to his audience. The din settled and the briefer continued.

"It appears our worthy enemy has prepared himself well but for the wrong war. He has bet all on the survival of fifteen attack carriers and has lost. Ten have fallen victim to our submarines and rest forever on the ocean floor."

Red triangles marked scenes of the related engagements.

"We destroyed two in Navy yards during the initial strike and three are bottled up in NATO ports." The pointer moved to Nova Scotia. "Two are here and one in the Mediterranean at Naples, Italy. The Americans expected us to fall back into a defensive line, but we came out on the attack. Our enemy believed we would strike with missiles, but we did our work with torpedoes. The balance of his six hundred ship navy, no longer with carriers to protect, is being destroyed as they flee to shelter."

Again, applause interrupted.

"Our work continues, comrades of the Pacific Flotilla. We learned from the Japanese Great Patriotic War experience. Do not permit an apparently beaten American foe to rise again and steal the victory. Show no compassion. We will shut off our enemy's supplies and render him impotent. We will destroy his morale by hitting him at every opportunity. We will not stop until the last capitalistic banner in the world has been hauled down and trampled into the dust."

The auditorium echoed with cheers as the briefer concluded his remarks and left the stage.

A circle of officers surrounded Sherensky, each to add his personal message of congratulations. Sherensky noticed Lieutenant Baknov standing nearby and beckoned to him. He raised the young officer's right hand.

"Comrade Baknov ... comrades. Behold ... this is the very hand that launched the torpedo strike against *Savo Island.*"

The young officer joined his captain and accepted the accolades.

Later Sherensky congratulated young Baknov again. "Vasiliy, you have done your work well. Fortunately, for *Zhukov* and me this word has not spread far. We need you for our next voyage and can't afford to have you promoted from under us. That will come soon enough."

A beaming Vasiliy responded, "Thank you, Captain. I'm honored and indebted to you."

Sherensky changed the subject. "It is good your mother can be with you these final days before our next mission. I once saw her dance at the Kirov ... long ago. I can remember very little but often heard my father and mother sing her praises. It is regrettable what happened. I hope the wounds you may have suffered are healed. You must give her my warmest regards."

Vasiliy nodded. "I will, Comrade Captain, and thank you again."

Take away stealth and a submarine's value is all but eliminated. It must remain undetected or forfeit its raison d'etre.

Reduction of radiated noise thus became paramount to mission success and resulted in new revisions to *Denver's* daily operations. A series of five clicks on the 1MC general announcing system would call the crew to battle stations and replace the noisy gong-gong-gong of the general alarm. The clicks plan, quite audible throughout the ship, provided for light sleepers to awaken the heavy ones as a backup measure. *Denver* transitioned from a peacetime to a wartime footing.

A stewardsman rousted Brent from a sound sleep and shook the dream matter from his head. He reckoned his dreams likely made no sense, so therefore impossible to recapture after awakening. No big loss, but for an unknown reason, he seemed to enjoy this one.

"Here we go again," groaned his roommate, Dan Patrick, "fifth time today." Both men, exhausted by lack of sleep, bore deeply traced lines in their faces.

They slept in blue patrol jumpsuits and needed only to slip on sandals, but with the compartment rigged for red, they had to grope for them.

Arriving at the Attack Center they encountered operational activity, plotting tables being set up, fire control systems activated and communications checked among the various combat stations. They used sound powered phones, as loss of ship's electrical power would render the MC systems inoperable.

Denver made her way westward across the widest part of northern Pacific toward the Sea of Okhotsk. Their orders read: *Breach the chain of Kuril Islands, proceed south to the Sea of Japan and conduct hostilities against Soviet naval units afloat and ashore.*

Brent took his Battle Station position as attack coordinator and wore a phone and headset to connect him to the torpedo room. He paralleled electrically transmitted weapons orders verbally to insure accuracy. In the Attack Center, he supervised operators of three MK 81 ACCs and a MK 92 WCC, responsible respectively for processing digitally formatted combat data and transmitting directions from the Attack Center to the torpedo room. He conducted transmission checks to insure the various equipments talked to each other accurately.

The executive officer asked, "What've we got, Brent?"

"Captain called us to battle stations, Jack. He's got something down there."

Jack hit the 21MC press-to-talk button. "Sonar, Conn, report the situation."

The captain's voice answered, "Possible contact, Jack. About three-ten, distant."

Trying to keep the edge off his voice, Jack asked, "Got a make on 'em, Captain?"

Bostwick replied, "Nothing. We're looking LOFAR and passive narrow band. We'll let you know."

Brent said softly, "Recommend come right to two-nine-five, Jack. That'll put the best part of our sonar array on 'em."

Jack nodded agreement. "Captain, Conn, coming right to two-nine-five for a better look. Recommend check the baffles."

The captain's voice had an edge, "That's well, Conn. We'll get the baffles. Don't want anyone sneaking up on us."

Silence hung over the compartment for nearly an hour while the crew waited at battle stations. They had secured from all other ship's activities, including the gaining of much needed rest, and their attentiveness diminished proportionately with time.

Brent considered the vastness of the ocean area where *Denver* patrolled. If the entire Soviet Pacific Fleet patrolled all routes available to *Denver*, one in a thousand represented the odds of an encounter. He reckoned distance to be covered and *Denver's* slow speed of advance. Provisions would not support a round trip at this rate. *Why in hell not race through this part and slow down as we approach the coast where encounters are more likely? Something's gotta give here.*

Captain Bostwick entered the Attack Center. "Secure from battle stations. Whoever he was, we couldn't find him."

Everyone thought, but dared not speak out, *another false contact.*

Dan responded to the captain, "Secure, Aye," and then passed the instruction to the Quartermaster of the Watch.

Continuing, Dan said, "Looks like you could use some shut-eye, Captain."

The captain wore the deep marks of his fatigue, circles under the eyes, drawn and sallow complexion and no visible expression on his face. Loss of *Utah* had hurt him emotionally and a sense of guilt drove him beyond endurance.

Bostwick responded to Dan's comment, "I'm a little tired, but right now Sonar's the right place for me to be."

Brent said, "Let me relieve you in sonar for a spell, Captain."

Looking surprised, the captain replied, "Uh … why thanks, Brent. I am pretty damn tired. Maybe I will hit the sack for just a bit. But I want to be called even if you suspect you have something."

"Of course, Captain."

Brent knew there was no need for anyone but the watch to be in the sonar shack. The men were more than competent to perform their jobs without officer supervision. But he volunteered for the job to take the edge off everyone's nerves.

With the captain out of earshot, Brent asked Jack Olsen to join him in Sonar where a heated discussion erupted.

Jack exclaimed, "No way, Brent. You been in the Navy long enough to know you shouldn't be talking like this."

"I'm not talking insubordination, XO. The captain's in trouble, and it's our job to help him. Did you read the Caine Mutiny?"

"We had to at the Naval Academy."

Brent went on, "Right. They vilified old Queeg, but the bastards in his wardroom should've born the guilt. They let him down. I think the Captain will do fine, but he needs propping up from us. You mind if I talk to him?"

Jack shook his head. "You piss him off every time he looks at you, Brent."

"Dan Patrick, then?"

The executive officer remained silent.

"Damn it, Jack. I want an answer. We owe the taxpayers a better return than what *Denver's* giving right now. Think on it, but if you don't have an answer by tomorrow, I'm gonna force the issue."

Lowering his voice, Jack said, "I'll get back to you, Brent. I hope you realize what you're laying on me."

Brent looked Jack directly in the eye and answered, "Yep." He did not add, *and you better do it.*

He didn't have to. Jack read Brent's mind perfectly.

Dutch Meyer sat in the well-appointed conference room of Pritchett Aerospace Los Angeles Office. He drummed his fingers upon an oak table to relieve apprehension over how he would procure vast amounts of material with only a blank promissory note signed by Eric Danis as compensation. A dainty cup and saucer sat before him. Dutch, happy Pritchett could still come up with good coffee, wrapped a massive hand about the cup, for its tiny handle could not accommodate his fingers.

A handsome, graying man in an impeccable three-piece suit entered the room, smiling warmly. "Good afternoon, Commander. I'm Todd Benson, Marketing Manager. Your visit is unexpected, but welcome. We always make way for the Navy. Is there something I can do for you?"

They shook hands.

Disguising his uneasiness, Dutch replied, "Yes, sir, matter of fact there is. I represent Commodore Eric Danis, Commander Submarine Squadron Three. We're assembling a temporary Submarine Base on the Washington Coast and I've been authorized to requisition equipment and weapons for the initial outfitting.

"How many Tomahawk land and ship attack missiles do you have ready for shipment? We need these immediately. Then, I'd like to see your production schedules for the rest of the year."

Todd Benson raised his hands in mock surrender. "Oops, you just moved out of my job code. Sounds like you need to talk to the *HawkProjOff* direct. Let me get somebody."

When Benson left, an attractive secretary arrived and asked, "More coffee, Commander?"

"No thanks." He watched her well-turned buttocks sway beneath a tight skirt as she walked away. He thought, *Maybe I'm not as old as I think.*

Dutch hated acronym buzzwords of the *in* set. *HawkProjOff* likely meant Tomahawk Project Office in Pritchett-talk. He felt buzzwords to be good only for covering gaps in real knowledge.

A stern looking man with rolled back shirtsleeves and a loosened tie entered the conference room. "I'm Al Mahler, Tomahawk Business Manager. Is there something we can do for you?"

Dutch liked the cut of this man, less handsomely appointed than Benson and spoke in whole words. He repeated the story given earlier to the marketer.

Mahler barely masked his astonishment. "You're quite serious?"

"Very serious. Those are my orders."

In steady tones, Mahler replied, "You understand, Commander, that none of these missiles are ready for delivery."

The business manager had drawn a line for the company's position.

"I'll take 'em in any shape you got 'em, Mr. Mahler."

Mahler said, "They're not signed off by the resident Defense Contract Administrator."

"That's okay. I'll sign for him."

Showing a hint of exasperation on his face, Mahler said, "But they have not completed acceptance testing yet."

Putting on his grimmest expression, Dutch said, "I promise you, sir, they're gonna get one hell of a test where I'm taking 'em."

Mahler shook his head then said, "This is absolutely out of the question, Commander. We can't do this. Why there's no—"

Dutch cut him off, "And, there's been absolutely no wars."

"You must understand—"

Dutch interrupted him again, "No, dammit, you're the one that's gotta understand. We got submarines coming in with empty launchers. We need those bullets to get 'em turned around and back out there into the fight."

The shaken but determined business manager replied, "I'm not authorized to release these missiles."

"Well you better find somebody who is, and tell him if action doesn't start in an hour—" then pointing to a wall clock, he continued, "one hour from now. I'm leaving here and I'm coming back with a detachment of Marines to take those goddamn missiles by force if I have to."

Dutch hadn't the slightest idea where he'd find any Marines much less how he'd get authorization to use them. He would do everything possible before he'd return to Eric Danis whimpering over failure to bring home the missiles.

"I'll get someone," Mahler said then left the room.

Dutch's heart skipped a beat when *HawkProgMgr* himself stood at the conference room door in a blocking stance. He looked sternly at the Navy commander. "I hear you need a few Tomahawks for some empty submarines."

"Yes, sir, I do."

"Helluva good idea. Let me buy you lunch and we can work out the details while we eat."

A wave of relief surged through Dutch as the two walked off to a plush executive dining room.

The manager apologized, "A hangover from prewar days. It takes us awhile sometimes for the message to sink in, but we're capable of making things happen pretty quick around here when we have to."

Over lunch, they formed a plan. Factory acceptance testing would be limited to the flight critical items and done immediately. The *birds* would be moved to Astoria as quickly as possible. In a few hours, the first truckload exited the plant gate and headed north on Interstate 5.

As Dutch stood up to leave, *HawkProgMgr* handed him a card. "Here, when this is all over come by and see me. We'll need a few bolts of your kind of cloth."

The two men shook hands and a relieved Dutch Meyer made his departure.

Chapter 7

Dave Zane scanned a cove cut into the rugged Washington coast by five million years of punishment from the sea. The harbor opened to pounding Pacific swells, but a sandbar reached northward from the southern end to the entrance. Shallow waters of the bar would permit the barges used to haul in equipment to be sunk to form a breakwater. Only the lack of a suitable overland access had prevented its previous use as a port.

The bay covered approximately two square miles and had ample deepwater. He took soundings earlier in the day with a fish finder Fathometer in a small boat he commandeered. The northern end of the bar dipped to a depth of seventy-five feet and formed a channel two hundred yards wide.

Dave figured two rows would do it, and the barges would not have to be stacked. "This will be it," he said then trudged five rugged miles back to the road and his car.

A short time later, he called Eric Danis from the *Digs*.

Eric kidded his friend, "Took you long enough."

"I know. Had the job all of two days now. Look, Eric, this place I found will do the job, but I'm gonna need some Navy clout. I got a plan, but I need help and equipment from the locals. Not sure how they'll take to jumping on an old retread's bandwagon though."

"You'll get the clout, Dave. Lay the plan on me."

"Okay. The whole deal will have to be afloat."

"Afloat? Hell, that's not new. We did it that way in Holy Loch."

"Right, Eric. But we had a submarine tender. Ours are gone now."

"You talk, Dave. I'll listen."

"I'm gonna anchor twenty-five to thirty barges in a cluster. They'll provide enough platform for our refit shops. I'll find the barges and tugs to haul them. There's enough stuff around somewhere, but I need a better fix on it. Our anchoring scheme oughta give us at least two alongside berths with two to three outboard. I can get cranes that'll reach out over the first two. We'll also need anchors and chain, but there ought to be plenty of that around."

Eric asked, "How about the reserve fleet?"

"How about ground zero? Can't be very far from there."

"Oops, I forgot."

Dave continued, "I'm going to need some muscle. I don't see us getting too much of this stuff on the strength of a handshake from old Dave Zane."

"You got it, Dave. Now, what else?"

"Heard from Meyer and he tells me there's some pretty good-looking bullets on the way. Where'd you find him? He's cutting his way north like a buzz saw."

"Grew him myself, Dave. You're right. Not a good idea to get in his way once he's turned onto a problem."

Dave gave Eric further details on his breakwater plan. "Two rows will keep out all but the worst and the most would happen then is we'd be shut down a day or two. Another thing. Don't lay any of that testing crap on me. What you're getting here is Zane eyeball certifications. We'll teach everybody to pay attention and keep out from under heavy things swinging overhead."

Eric asked, "What about power?"

"A segment of the northwest grid is only five miles east of the site. Doug firs will support the power lines and insulators for the stretch to the base. We can't build towers without clearing the wilderness and that might take weeks. I don't know about shore power for submarines, but I'll work on it. There's plenty of fuel for diesel generators so some of your prima donnas are just going to have to learn to live with them."

"Sounds like you might not have been wasting your time after all."

"Plenty to do to keep me off the streets and out of the bars. Just as well. Most of 'em are closed anyway."

"Think of how grateful your liver will be."

"Yeah, I suppose. When am I going to see some help, Eric?"

"When do you want them? I've got some pissed off aviators down here who are none too happy about having their carrier shot out from under them. They're convinced submarines are the best chance for getting even."

"Need 'em at Astoria right now. If there's not room enough for them at Clatsop County Airport, we'll move out some of the current tenants. I need some blue-suiters to take charge of the docks and staging area I got lined up down there. Can you get them moving in that direction?"

"They're aviators and we got plenty of airplanes."

"Good. Have them fly into Clatsop and I'll meet them there. Let me know when. And, Eric?"

"Yeah, Dave?"

"A lotta folks here are unhappy about what happened to Bremerton and the Port of Seattle. They're just about mad enough to build that submarine refit site for you."

"So no problems with the locals?"

"None at all."

"I figured that."

"Furthermore, Commodore, we're gonna whip their Red asses. Get an American's back up and somebody better watch his step. About now, I'd say we're bristlin'."

They exchanged good-byes and hung up.

Eric Danis wished he could find support for his friend's optimistic outlook among the dismal communiqués from SUBPAC on the war's progress. When operations turned conventional in Europe, Soviet movements ground to a halt and a version of Sitzkrieg in World War II developed. Soviet submariners replayed Hitler's early war triumphs in spades.

The U.S. Air Force provided troops and materials to hold the Soviets in check, but to turn things around more troops were needed.

The Pacific Theatre concerned Eric. Essential war supplies needed from Australia and South America could not be shipped by air in sufficient quantities to support America's war industries. Somehow, sea lines of communication must be reopened and protected from the Soviet Submarine Flotilla. U.S. submarines and their bases provided the best hope. Worst of all, the clock continued to run with no indication of things beginning to improve.

Eric wished to discuss all this with his old friend Dave, but security considerations prevented it over public phone lines.

Jack Olsen, Brent and Dan Patrick finalized a patrol plan for *Denver* and discussed it with Captain Bostwick in the wardroom. The skipper looked refreshed seated behind a steaming cup of coffee. After the last false contact, he'd fallen into a deep sleep that lasted twelve hours. During this period, the executive officer ordered the ship's routine relaxed and authorized all the sack time that could be squeezed in by the troops.

Dan said, "This plan exploits our acoustic advantage over anything they've got except possibly an *Akula*. Our chances of stumbling on one, or for that matter any other submarine here in mid ocean, is almost zero."

"I see," Bostwick said. "The old sprint and drift tactic," alluding to the technique of running along at high speeds for a given distance and then abruptly shutting down in order to catch a possible interceptor in the act of racing to reach an attack position.

Dan continued, "Right. And spacing runs at these speeds gives us a high enough speed of advance to reach Vlad with remaining endurance for nineteen days on station. It's a target-rich area with opportunity to even some scores."

The positive attitude expressed by his officers, coupled with a refreshing sleep, buoyed the captain's spirits. Bostwick had permitted the loss of the *Utah* to burden him beyond his capacity to perform properly, but sooner or later, he'd have to change that.

Napoleon once said, "There are no bad regiments, only bad colonels." Bostwick's Navy rank equated to an Army colonel. At the Naval Academy, he learned morale of the troops reflected confidence in him, their leader.

The captain's newly formed assertion that *Denver* would be successful grew into a fire that spread throughout his ship. A once demoralized crew, now aware of their potential to strike the enemy hard, knew these attacks would provide a needed lift for sagging spirits of their countrymen.

Bostwick declared, "On to the attack, gentlemen. You've worked up a hell of a plan and we're going with it."

Soviet naval policy required all ranks to be indoctrinated in ongoing military strategy. Most young officers found this boring, but Vasiliy Baknov thrived on it. His zeal grew from a natural hatred of all things American. He completely despised the capitalistic system, where dedication to one's own personal interests outweighed loyalty to the state. He believed this to be the Achilles' heel of the West and would bring about its ultimate downfall.

Fueled further by his father's defection to America, Vasiliy's anger left no room in his heart for forgiveness. The young officer often brooded over this moment and reaffirmed a long held determination to gain vengeance.

Vasiliy passed a fourth straight hour in the security vault, delving further into his favorite topic of strategic studies. Both elbows on the table, he considered the yet unread volumes stacked before him and rubbed his tired eyes. Fellow *Zhukov* officers had long since departed for the open mess hoping to avail themselves of vodkas which continued to be bought for the heroes of the *Savo Island* sinking.

He returned to his reading and reviewed several essays on current Soviet Navy planning. The Soviet approach offset an enemy goal to wrest control of the seas through their program, Maritime Strategy, where surface vessels carried the major load of combat operations. The Soviet Navy invested mainly in nuclear powered submarines of the attack class to counter this.

Soviet submarines enjoyed tactical advantage over allied surface warships and merchant ships, principally because they could remain undetected. They out-dove and outran everything in the U.S. anti-submarine warfare (ASW) arsenal except the ADCAP torpedo, carried only by U.S. submarines which the Soviets outnumbered five to one.

Aircraft carriers require twelve or more ships for logistic support, anti-aircraft warfare (AAW) and ASW protection. The collective radiated noise created by these ships made carrier battle groups easy to find and the Soviets quickly located them then maneuvered to point blank attack range.

The submarine is a lone wolf and holds exclusive advantage of surprise attack over all other warships. Best of all, they operate independently and need no support from other vessels.

A lone submarine and her crew of a hundred can disrupt the mission of twenty warships, manned by more than ten thousand seaman, a precedent established in the opening days of World War I. A German U-boat, manned by thirty-five seamen, attacked and destroyed an overwhelming superior force of three British battle cruisers manned by twenty-three hundred. Within an hour, three cruisers sank with the loss of more than fourteen hundred men.

From that day forward, submarines accounted for eighty percent of all combat related sinkings. If success in combat at sea accrues from sinking enemy ships, the smart money is invested in submarines.

Vasiliy wondered, *Are the Americans oblivious to these facts? Is this why they blundered into their Maritime Strategy? Or did inter-warfare group bickering result in the American Navy being fully prepared only to fight the last war?*

Between World Wars I and II, ignoring Germany's near victory through U-boat destruction of twenty million tons of allied shipping, American naval planners focused instead on the issue of whether traditional battleships or the newly conceived naval air weapon held the greatest advantage.

At the onset of the Second World War, the Japanese attack on Pearl Harbor showed naval aviation to be in the driver's seat. The fallacy in their theory revealed itself when Yamamoto's planes overlooked the submarine base while en route to battleship row to destroy ships that would have virtually no impact on the outcome of the war. Within a week the by-passed U.S. submariners deployed throughout the Pacific and began a campaign that would bring Japan to her knees by the end of the war.

U.S. submariners systematically deprived Japan of its desperately needed access to the sea. Subsequent actions reduced imports below levels needed to sustain the mainland, much less those required to support ground forces throughout the Southwest Pacific. At Iwo Jima, U.S. Marines captured a Japanese garrison that had undergone sixty-five days without replenishment due to the U.S. submarine campaign.

Vasiliy thought, *How good of the Americans to develop and battle test this strategy for us.*

The advent of nuclear propulsion in 1955 enhanced submarine warfare of a magnitude beyond what all other naval warfare acquired through postwar technology. Diesel-Electric powered submarines of World War II remained submerged less than fifteen percent of their total deployment time. Long transits could be made only on the surface where they remained defenseless against warships and air forces.

Nuclear powered submarines remain independent of the atmosphere indefinitely.

American turncoat John Anthony Walker's betrayal, with unwitting help from several allied nations, served much of this technology up to the Soviets on a silver platter.

Again, Vasiliy thought about the Americans. *Perhaps the greatest weapon we have against capitalism is their own greed.*

He recalled earlier *Zhukov* peacetime missions to monitor U.S. peacetime fleet exercises and observed repeated successful simulated attacks by 637 and 688 class submarines against carrier battle groups. He wondered whether the Americans knew of the Soviet surveillance and deliberately made themselves appear vulnerable. Now, Soviets subsequently confirmed these observations in real combat.

Soviet Intelligence also probed into the personal characteristics of prospective opposing warriors. Chinese General Sun-Tzu warned in 401 BC, *Keep your friends close but your enemies closer.*

American love of recognition supplied ample material to fill this Soviet need. Even officers of the *silent service* submarine arm shared an appetite for publicity. Character sketch brochures are handed out at Change of Command ceremonies, Submarine and Nuclear Power School graduations and Naval Academy yearbooks are compiled.

American newspapers openly published the detailed citations of officers being decorated. The Pacific Flotilla maintained an up-to-date directory on key officers serving in the U.S. Submarine Force.

Vasiliy believed this knowledge about his enemies would prove helpful in combat on the silent battleground and thought, *When we have prevailed and there are no more wars to fight and I am a full admiral, perhaps I shall write a book.*

Denver alternately raced then slowed and all but disappeared in the Pacific's murky depths. The crew liked their Captain's new look.

Gary Hansen quipped, "Sure is good to have my chair back."

He was sonar supervisor on Brent's watch and alluded to the captain's heretofore-continuous presence in the sonar shack. A new sign on the door proclaimed *Findin' Ivan* despite a standing order for posting nothing but official literature.

The glib Hansen reasoned, "We're at war now, a special situation not covered in the standing orders."

Not to be outdone the torpedo gang hung labels on each of the four-launcher breech doors: *Vodka Express, Moscow Mule, Bottom Line* and *Utah's Revenge.*

A standing submarine axiom goes, *clean ship, happy crew,* hence the forenoon watch of each Friday found the crew busy at field day. Every man not on watch rousted out and manned his cleaning station. All did their best to make their ship a comfortable and inspiring place in which to perform *Denver's* mission.

Initiated by the quick-witted Gary Hansen, the resumption of field day resulted in Ensign Woody Parnell becoming the butt of a prank by the crew. "Mr. Parnell, sir, we could clean these launcher doors much better if we had a bucket of steam."

The gullible Woody replied, "A bucket of steam? What good would that do?"

An almost too stern faced Hansen said, "Verdigris is what turns the breech doors green. A kind of plant, sir, and only steam kills it."

Hansen's explanation sounded plausible enough to Woody. "Why don't we get one then?"

"Can't sir. Only officers are allowed to draw steam on field day. Maybe you'd be willing?"

A bucket-laden ensign embarked upon endless treks throughout the ship, met at each destination by alerted sailors, each identified as a source of steam. The sailors would fabricate an excuse and send the confused Woody off to another source.

Eventually, the trail led to a sailor in the auxiliary machinery compartment who told Woody, "Only the exec can approve drawing steam on field days, Mr. Parnell. And it has to be in writing."

Woody found the executive officer in the wardroom at a meeting with the chief engineer.

Jack Olsen roared with laughter. "My God man, not the old bucket of steam gag. That one predates Nimitz's Midshipman days."

With a sheepish grin on his face, Woody Parnell departed for the torpedo room. *Number three,* he thought, considering the previous two times he had been tricked. *Three strikes and out. These bastards asked for it and now they're gonna get a page out of old Wooder's book of great ones.*

The Friday afternoon watch found the Captain in company with the COB and Exec, inspecting the ship. Bostwick surprised all with his adeptness for one-liners to individual crewmembers.

A young seaman exclaimed, "Wow!" after Bostwick finished with inspecting the Crew's Mess. "The captain knows my name."

Excitement mounted as *Denver* neared the Kurils and elevated the probability of contact with the enemy.

World War III had apparently stripped the seas clear of the many and varied shipping types that normally plied this ocean segment. *Denver* had nearly crossed the entire Pacific before making her first bona fide sonar contact. Made on Dan Patrick's watch, he won the conning officers' pool, all of fifteen bucks.

In keeping with the new look of no hasty calls to battle stations, the crew watch section performed target identification and ranging without officer supervision.

The lead sonar operator reported, "Conn, Sonar, this guy's on the surface. Lots of cavitation and screws too clunky for a warship."

Dan replied, "Conn, aye, Sonar," and then pressed the 21MC button. "Captain, Conn."

"Captain, aye, Dan. I heard all that. I'm halfway through a cribbage game with the XO. Work on the contact and I'll be up as soon as we're through."

A wave of good feeling surged through Dan. First contact in a possible combat situation and the Captain let him run with the ball.

Half an hour later, the captain entered the Attack Center. "What've we got, Dan?"

"Bearing three-two-five, drawing right and closing. Put him at about fifteen thousand yards, making eight knots on a northerly heading. Zero-one-two currently."

"Zigzagging?"

"No indication, Captain. From what I can tell, it's a fisherman with gear down. He's got some low frequency lines likely from vibrating net cables. We're looking hard to see if the noise isn't screening another unit lying nearby."

"Not likely, Dan. Any submarine out here would be guarding the Kuril approaches against guys like us. He couldn't hear us through that racket. Let's come to periscope depth and have a look. If your call is right, then we've got a ticket for some free distance. Take a thirty-degree lead and let's do it."

Dan replied, "Aye, Captain," and then to the helmsman, "Right full rudder, steady, new course three-five-five." Dan announced over the 21MC, "Sonar, Conn, unmasking to starboard. Check for contacts back there, we're coming to periscope depth."

Denver's sleek hull responded cleanly to Dan's direction as the captain took his place at number two periscope.

Bostwick ordered, "Up number two for a look around."

Immediately after attack scope's slender shaft broke the surface the captain swung it around in less than five seconds, too fast to see anything at long-range, but enabling him to spot a target close aboard that might have slipped by sonar. Larger ships pointing directly toward the listening hydrophones often masked propulsion sounds with their huge hulls. The quartermaster on watch assisted from the other side of the scope, his left hand locked over the captain's right to ensure optics rolled to low power to provide the widest field of view.

"Dip scope."

The quartermaster lowered the periscope enough to submerge the upper optics and left it suspended in the well.

Bostwick demanded, "Bearing to contact?"

Dan replied, "Three-two-eight from Sonar, sir. Still drawing right."

Nodding his response, Bostwick said, "Observation. Up scope."

Again, the huge shaft lunged from the periscope well.

"Quartermaster, put me on the bearing."

The ACC Operator reported, "Three-three-three relative, sir."

After the scope aligned, Bostwick studied the contact for three seconds.

"Bearing, mark!" The captain signaled for the scope lowered by lifting handles to the stowed position. It dropped completely into the well this time.

The quartermaster responded as he read the numbers from the bearing and range repeater, "Three-two-nine, Captain."

"Angle on the bow, starboard forty. Estimate range at twenty thousand plus. All I can see are her sticks."

The ship was hull-down, meaning only her masts could be seen above the horizon.

Bostwick asked Dan, "Distance to the track with a forty degree lead?"

Dan ran some quick calculations. Using target range and angle on the bow, he determined distance to the target's projected track ahead. "Fourteen thousand, sir."

"Good. Give me the forty lead. We'll close at twelve knots. Plan to pass ahead by two thousand yards and adjust speed to stay a few decibels below him. With all the noise he's making, we oughta be able to go pretty fast without alerting anyone. Be sure you're well clear ahead, Dan. We didn't come all the way out here to get tangled in some damn fishnet."

"Aye, sir," then Dan ordered *Denver* to a depth that eliminated propeller cavitation from higher speeds. "Play our cards right and this gambit will buy us sixty or so free miles, Captain."

"That's how we'll play 'em," said the captain then changed the subject, "the nerve of that guy. Fishing away like he doesn't know there's a full-blown war on. Guess he's still gotta make a living."

The captain left the Attack Center.

Wonder of wonders, thought Dan, *... can this be the same man who a few short weeks ago drove us all to exhaustion?*

Brent appeared in the control room to relieve the watch.

Acknowledging Brent's presence, Dan said, "Good to see you."

"Can't say I'm glad to be here."

"C'mon, Brent. You love this. What better watch to breach the Kurils than Mad Maddock's?"

Dan referred to the chain of islands that separated the Sea of Okhotsk from the Pacific Ocean, a natural focal point for Soviet defense, but thus far, none encountered.

Brent thought, *They probably don't think we're capable of offensive missions.* He asked, "What've we got, Dan?"

"Among other things, the first real contact of the whole damn patrol," then went on to tell him of the captain's plan to use high-radiated noise from the contact to mask *Denver's* high-speed transit.

Listening intently, Brent had conditioned himself to be suspicious because disaster had a habit of showing up along with peak optimism. He learned playing football at Annapolis to not sit on a big lead with a full quarter left to play. Brent caught a side-glance of Quartermaster Henri who badgered his predecessor for every crumb of detail, a reassuring sight for any watch officer.

Later, Brent reckoned the range to the fisherman had opened sufficiently and its noise reduced to the point that *Denver* could no longer hide in its shadow so he reported this to the captain. "We've resumed stealth tactics, Captain," then continued, "I'll shorten the legs. This breach track is too restrictive for north-south run options if we encounter trouble. Costs us time, but if somebody's out there, this'll improve chances of detecting him before he reaches attack range."

"Do it, Brent," replied Bostwick over the 21MC.

As Brent and Henri huddled over the plotting table to layout new projected tracks, an ear-shattering explosion rocked the ship. The force of the blast knocked both men to the deck and the compartment plunged first into darkness and then silence.

Chapter 8

Captain Igor Sherensky congratulated the young communications officer on the thoroughness of his pre-sail briefing. *Zhukov* officers had been bombarded with volumes of intelligence information and the time had now come to put it into action.

Following the *Zhukov* commander, the navigation officer began his presentation. He taped a large chart of the Western Pacific onto a bulkhead in *Zhukov's* wardroom. A tracking line began at Vladivostok winding its way seaward through the Kurils and then via the southwest Pacific to the approaches at Fremantle, Australia.

The navigation officer began his briefing with, "Visual aids to shipping navigation end at Vladivostok. Thereafter, shallow water presents a problem only at the Kurils."

Lieutenant Vasiliy Baknov asked, "Why not proceed via the South China Sea? The shorter run will give us more time on station."

Captain Sherensky answered the question. "We have lost track of three American SSNs in the Western Pacific. Best guess by our intelligence people places them in the South China Sea area. Better we go around them."

Vasiliy added, "If they are 688 class, Comrades, we'll not find them. We go deeper and faster, but they are much quieter. To find them, we must be able to hear them and that is unlikely."

Zampolit Poplavich, leapt upon every occasion to remind *Zhukov's* officers and crew that he would tolerate no faultfinding with any segment of the Communist System. "We must have confidence in our Comrades of the intelligence division. Their information thus far has led us to victory."

Sherensky replied, "And we have confidence, Comrade Zampolit."

Problems enough with day-to-day management of a warship left the Captain with no desire to agitate Poplavich. Sherensky considered the zampolit system a detriment at any time, but particularly in time of war. Placating the zampolit was the best hope of silencing him.

Sherensky said to the navigation officer, "Please continue."

Directing his comments mainly at Vasiliy, the navigation officer proceeded, "For most of the track, we're free to operate at maximum speed, but not while we're in the South China Sea. It's too shallow to accommodate the depths we need to suppress propeller cavitation at high speed."

Being a step ahead of the dynamic Baknov pleased the navigation officer as he continued with, "Once on station, runs between merchant ship attacks will lengthen as we systematically destroy them and shut down the flow of materials to the Americans. This obviously changes if the allies cooperate and put their ships in convoys. In this case, we'll finish them off quickly and get home early."

Laughter erupted among the *Zhukov* officers, confident after their victory over *Savo Island*.

The navigation officer asked, "Questions? None then? If you please, I yield the floor to our distinguished weapons officer," he said, making a mock bow and removing his chart.

Vasiliy gave his mates a rare smile. "It is good to see *Zhukov* louts give the respect due to the best among them," he quipped.

Others laughed and hissed their protest.

Normally deadpan, the junior Russian's bright mood surprised all, but the levity dissolved as he refocused attention on business at hand. "Our principal weapon against merchantmen is the missile. America made a major investment in missile defense for aircraft carriers so we used torpedoes. Merchant ships will be spread out and difficult to defend. The long range of our SS-N 21s shortens the distance we must run between targets."

Next, he explained *Zhukov's* defense against U.S. submarines. "An escorting 688 comprises our greatest obstacle in attacking a widely dispersed convoy. They have sonar sensitivity and stealth needed to breach our track as we preoccupy ourselves with targets. An ADCAP Torpedo could bring our mission to an abrupt end."

Again, the zampolit interrupted, "Comrade Baknov, apparently you attach no significance to the findings of our comrades in intelligence."

"I do, Comrade Zampolit. I want only to be certain we have a plan if—"

The zampolit became irate and interrupted. "There are no ifs. The probability we will encounter a 688 is inconsequential and unworthy of our attention. I would thank you to not waste our time preparing for action that will not occur."

Vasiliy felt deflated. He wished to explain his planned evasion tactics devised by him and implemented throughout the Pacific flotilla.

Captain Sherensky gave the young officer an understanding wink and Vasiliy sat down.

The captain concluded the briefing. "Comrades, we come to the end of our refit and prepare to sail again. The days ashore have been good ones and the honors given to us for past successes taken with gratitude and humility. Past victories have meaning only in history books. Let us be mindful of Japan's failure in the Great Patriotic War.

"We must prevent the wounded warriors from rising again and taking victory from us. You have done your work well and our ship has been expertly serviced. We are ready for combat, Comrades, so I now enjoin you to pass these final days in happiness with family and friends."

Sherensky thought, *I must defuse this growing hostility between Vasiliy and our learned zampolit. But how? Both are so obstinate.*

Quartermaster Henri looked at Brent, his hand already on the collision alarm switch. Brent's nod gave the needed order and the alarm wailed its warning throughout the ship.

Taking the 1MC mike Brent ordered, "All compartments report your condition, forward-aft. Flooding reports immediately on the nearest intercom."

Henri picked up the sound-powered handset to receive reports.

Brent ordered, "Ahead standard, make your depth one-three-zero feet," then demanded over the 21MC, "Sonar, Conn, what've you got?"

Gary Hansen replied, "Nothing, sir ... nothing before the bang. Reverberations from the explosion blocking out everything."

Turning to the quartermaster, Brent asked, "How we doing, Henri?"

"Good so far. All compartments reporting normal. No flooding." At that instant lights flickered throughout the ship. "Only Maneuvering to go and the noise definitely came from forward."

Brent said, "We hit a mine. We'd have heard the inbound noise of a torpedo. Sonar, Conn, reversing course to starboard. Conduct active, repeat, active search of sector east of north south, max range five thousand. Report all contacts immediately."

The captain shouted over the 21MC, "Belay that order! Sonar, do not ... repeat ... do not go active. Brent, I'm on the way to the Attack Center."

"Aye, sir," replied Brent.

Captain Bostwick arrived and demanded, "Report the situation."

Brent's gut flipped over. "Everything inside the hull is normal, sir. I think we hit a mine. A small one. Maybe an MZ-26. They're ship laid with a case depth near thirty-four meters, just about where we are. Likely activated by our electric field."

He did not want Bostwick to read this as a smart-ass *I told you so* but feared it came across that way. The current that created this field was by design. Hull mounted sacrificial zincs disintegrate to insure good electrical connectivity between them and the propeller they protect.

Brent had urged the captain to install a shaft grounding wire, a copper braid that rode over the top of the shaft just forward of the seal to prevent the electric field. He reckoned protecting *Denver* took precedence over the propeller shaft. In the same conversation, Brent also suggested eliminating the weekly steam generator blow-downs as a noise reduction measure. Bostwick rejected both recommendations.

Continuing, Brent said, "They're only one point three kilograms of explosive, Captain, but enough to puncture the outer hull and make us noisy."

Bostwick demanded, "Sonar contacts?"

"None, sir."

"Why did you order us to go active? Do you want to alert the whole damn Red Navy?"

"No sir. But if someone's in the area, they heard the explosion and know we're here. Active doesn't show 'em anything they don't already know. If we find somebody, it gives us a leg up. We got a bearing and a range while he only has a bearing."

The captain snapped back, "Stuff the goddamn tactics bullshit, Brent. I have the Conn. All ahead full, right full rudder, steady course east. We're getting the hell out of here."

The helmsman replied, "Ahead full, right full, steady east, aye, Captain."

Brent advised, "Sir, I recommend increasing depth ahead of the cavitation curve."

Bostwick snarled, "Damn it Brent, I have the Conn," then followed the recommendation with an order to the proper depth and rate of descent.

Denver picked up speed and a loud howl grew from the region of the ship's starboard side. By then, Jack Olsen had reached the Attack Center.

Brent looked first at Jack through a pleading expression then said in the calmest voice he could muster, "Captain, we've got to slow down. If this mine field's patrolled, we're playing right into their hands."

The captain glared at Brent with a look of fury beyond rationality. The howl became deafening as *Denver* approached full speed.

Moments passed. Finally, the captain ordered, "Ahead one third. Mr. Olsen, you have the Conn. Mr. Maddock, report to my stateroom immediately."

Half a minute later, the showdown began. The captain took his place behind a small table but did not invite Brent to sit.

Agitated, Bostwick opened with, "Mr. Maddock, I've put up with all the bullshit I'm going to take from you. Do you understand?"

"No, sir, I don't understand. I'm not fighting you, sir, I'm—"

"You've been second-guessing me in front of the crew with your goddamn cutesy tactics show. You bitch at me for wanting to run back where we know it's safe because you think it'll make too much noise. Yet, you want to bang away with active sonar. Now what the hell?"

"I needed a quick look, Captain. Something might have been lying in wait and close aboard. A few pings would have spotted him. Now noise from the damaged hull sends a beacon to anyone who wants to take us. The enemy will know we're running east at full speed when they hear the noise. That knowledge gives him tremendous tactical advantage."

"Enemy, you say. What enemy? No one's out there or he'd have gotten us on the way in."

"Our tactics, sir. Not much chance he could find us before we found him. Your own plan of using the fisherman to screen us likely prevented our being detected."

"Like I said, Maddock, I'm tired of your half-assed theories. There's nothing where we came from except that damn fishing boat. Consider yourself off the watch bill until further notice. I'm not putting you in *hack* because it's unfair to the others to pick up your workload."

An officer in *hack* is confined to his quarters.

Brent saw the futility of attempting to reason with the Captain. *Denver's* new look abruptly became a memory. Crisis had plunged the captain back into his black mood.

"If that's all, Captain?"

"That's all. Now get the hell out of here."

An urgent call from the Attack Center on the 21MC interrupted Brent's departure. "Captain to the Conn! Sonar holds contact on a probable submarine bearing zero-eight-zero, closing rapidly!"

Dave Zane surveyed the activity that accompanied establishing his new submarine base. Scarcely three weeks into the project, Dave had already assembled a cluster of barges for living and working areas and had them moored in place. Makeshift shelters, in some cases tents, housed the base facilities.

"This sure does beat all," Dave said to Dutch Meyer. "Takes a war to get us off our asses and out from under the bureaucracy. The damn environmental impact study for this alone would take two years."

Dutch had joined Dave Zane at the makeshift refit site. He added, "Every time I bust a rule to get something done on schedule … makes me feel good all over."

"Know what you mean, Dutch."

They ate lunch prepared in the open eating area under a canvas fly covered field kitchen procured from nearby Fort Lewis Army Base. They looked out to sea via the harbor entrance where sunken barges formed the first line of an improvised breakwater and savored a long, bright day in May that signaled the approach of summer.

"Make damn sure you don't tell your California buddies about this, Dutch. We don't want them coming up and crowding out us natives."

Grinning, Dutch said, "Nothing but rain, rain, rain. Can't see how we stand it up here. That's my message."

"You got it, Dutch." Then Dave continued with, "Gotta give Danis's aviators credit. They sure know how to get things moving."

"The commodore can get blood from a stone," Dutch added. "But these guys are good. Did you see how fast they converted that empty field in Astoria to a full-fledged Navy supply depot?"

"Yeah ... and they did a helluva job getting stuff staged so it could be here when we need it. That Carter guy moves well. I heard he flew off *Savo Island* when she got it and had to eject and dump his F-14 in the drink near a destroyer to get picked up. Lucky for us he made it. Likely he figures he's got some payback to do."

"You're right, Dave." Then turning his attention to the shoreline east of the base, Dutch continued, "that break in the woods must be the power coming in. How do you figure to get it out here from shore?"

Dave's face brightened in one of his trademark squinty grins. "Lay the cables on the bottom. Don't believe I'll call the county electrical inspector. Chalk that project up as another success by the flyboys. I don't know where they got the people and power lines to do that job."

"You probably don't wanna know."

Dave asked, "What's happening with the Torpedo Range stuff?" referring to a torpedo proofing facility based to the north of them on the Washington Coast normally used to test anti-submarine torpedoes.

Dutch reasoned the sudden abundance of Soviet targets provided a much better *test bed* so he converted the network of range hydrophones to serve as a submarine warning system for the new base. "Going real well ... already using the stuff from the range seabed. This, plus all their spares makes a pretty good network out to about a hundred miles."

"That oughta give us plenty of warning."

"Yeah, but that's only part of the problem. Once we spot 'em, there's nothing we can do. We don't have the resources to keep an airplane on station full time and the flyboys say we're talking at least forty minutes from a cold start ashore. That's too long."

Dave asked, "No way of getting a weapon on the target?"

"You got it, but at least it'll give us early warning. As soon as the breakwater goes in, we've got some Vulcan-Phalanx anti-missile guns to sit atop of it."

"You figure the Soviets will attack with sub-launched land attack missiles?"

"Wouldn't we? We've learned the hard way they're not as dumb as we figured. They took great pains to knock out our sub-bases in the first strike. It's logical they'll come after any temporaries we set up. Cable will be our biggest problem."

"Turn Eric's flyboys loose. If there's any cable available, they'll find it and get it here."

"Good idea, Dave. But we've dumped on 'em so much, I hesitate to add to the burden."

"It appears to me like they thrive on it. Put it to 'em this way. Right now they're agonizing over how they're gonna run electric lines on the bottom between the shore and here. And you need a hundred miles of cable for that damn array of yours. Tell 'em if they get your cable, you'll lay their power lines."

Dutch smiled. He had already begun to convert an aging tugboat into a cable layer.

Changing the subject, Dave continued. "Ya know, Dutch, we're really putting together a helluva base for that half-assed boss of yours. When do you figure his nibs will put in an appearance?"

"As soon as you make him a place to sleep and install a telephone."

Dave's grin broadened. He nodded toward the breakwater. "Here it is. Would you look at what's poking its nose around the point?"

"Where the hell did you come up with that ... and I don't want to know how much it cost."

One hundred and thirty-two feet of the most palatial yacht either of them had ever seen slipped easily into the harbor and proceeded to the barge cluster. COMSUBRON 3 floating headquarters had arrived.

Quartermaster Henri calmly activated five clicks on the 1MC and called the crew to battle stations. He had practiced this enough so the real thing went off smoothly.

Brent followed his captain to the Attack Center.

Bostwick demanded, "What've we got, Jack?"

"Diesel boat making high speed on the battery. No bearing change, getting louder."

Brent considered his predicament for only an instant then jumped in anyway. "Sonar, Conn, we need an ident."

The captain glared at Brent and Jack Olsen glared back at the captain. The young officer had proven Bostwick wrong, but the situation appeared perilous so he yielded to Brent's actions.

Gary Hansen's voice crackled over the 21MC, "Got a make, Conn. *Tango*." Hansen used the NATO designation for the Soviet Navy's top diesel-electric submarine.

Brent exclaimed, "He's close then! Damn close! No time for a range, Captain, recommend an ADCAP right down the bearing line."

Bostwick ordered, "Get it ready!"

Taking his station behind the ACC, Brent ordered over the sound powered phones "Make ready tubes one and two in all respects. Quickly!"

The ACC operator repeated the order, followed by "Aye, sir," and then fumbled with a switch.

"Steady, just like we always practiced."

Brent figured a junior officer commanded the *Tango* on minefield patrol. He showed inexperience by racing in for the kill. Destruction of an American submarine would likely net him an Order of Lenin and command of a newer ship, a *Victor III*, an *Alfa* or if lucky, an *Akula*.

Calling for computer-generated torpedo presets on the MK 81 console, Brent read the display, made two adjustments and ordered them entered.

After what seemed an eternity, though only a minute had passed, the torpedo room watch reported, "One and two ready with the doors open."

"Recommend shoot, Captain," said Brent, fresh from a dressing down for doing just that.

The captain found his voice. "Gyro angle and range."

"No time, sir. It's now or never. He might be inside minimum enable range already."

Bostwick hesitated.

Brent ordered, "Fire one!"

Denver gave her customary shudder as the torpedo left the launcher. The wailing, high-pitched sound of an accelerating ADCAP could be heard clearly through the ship's pressure hull.

The captain ordered, "Fire two, Brent."

"Aye, sir. Fire two in a minute-thirty seconds."

Brent gritted his teeth at having to correct the Captain, but construed lack of a reply from Bostwick to be his assent.

Bostwick asked, "This course good for the wire?"

Brent thought, *Wire's not a factor with the target this close.* He let it pass. "Good heading, Captain," he responded.

Apprehension shown in Hansen's voice as he announced, "Conn, Sonar. Torpedo running down the bearing line."

"Want to check fire on two, Captain. If this guy's close and we get him with one, number two might not see him and start looking for us. I've got Doppler Enable out," a feature that accommodated attack against a motionless target.

The captain ordered, "Check fire tube two."

Brent said, "Henri, give me a mark at one-plus-sixty seconds."

The steady Henri repeated, "Mark at one-plus-sixty in fifteen—"

An ear-splitting explosion obscured the rest of Henri's sentence.

So much for the eager bastard's Order of Lenin, Brent thought.

Silence for a second after the explosion then a chorus of cheers resonated throughout *Denver*. They had finally drawn Soviet blood.

Capitalizing on the moment, Brent turned to the captain and extended his hand. "Congratulations, sir. You got the son of a bitch."

Bostwick hesitated an instant then with some uncertainty, he took Brent's hand, shook it and smiled. "Why thank you, Brent."

The others joined in expressions of congratulations with flurries of handshakes and back pats.

Brent ordered the torpedo room over the 21MC, "Close the outer door on two, drain down and secure." But being the eternal skeptic, he directed sonar to monitor the target. "He might still be dangerous, Sonar. Report everything. Listen for launcher sounds or running torpedoes."

Hansen responded, "Aye, sir. There's too much reverberation from the explosion but not enough to blank a torpedo. We don't hear any."

"Let's hope we don't."

Hansen reported, "New noises from the target sir. It's a groaning sound. Like—" He stopped in mid-sentence deciding not to make the analogy to *Utah's* demise. "I think she's gone, sir."

An air of sobriety replaced the excitement in the Attack Center. The enemy submarine yielded to the common foe of all submariners, the relentless ocean depths. The ocean crashed in and drove the hapless *Tango* ever downward. Tremendous pressure crushed the hull like an eggshell and snuffed out the lives of her crew.

The tactical margin between the victor and vanquished is extremely narrow.

Dave Zane relayed the message from Eric Danis that *Denver* had survived.

Bea threw her arms about her father and began to sob.

He comforted his daughter. "Why ole Brent's likely conducting patrols in the Pacific and having a fine time."

"Oh, Daddy, I'm so ... so grateful. God, I'm so grateful. I thought the worst."

"Hell, Bea," he said, releasing her and smiling into her eyes as he had done throughout her life, "nothing them damn *Sovies* got measures up to a 688. Brent will be back before you know it and likely with a couple of Red scalps in his belt."

Bea recomposed herself. "Thanks, Dad, but I'm still worried. Be sure to tell Eric how much I appreciate the message."

Dave took the opportunity to probe for what future she saw for Brent. He knew of her bruising from the disastrous affair and couched his words in terms easy for her to evade.

Looking away and scratching behind his left ear, a gesture that signaled meaning beyond his spoken words, he asked, "What's in store for Brent after *Denver*? His tour must be just about up by now."

Her father's giveaway quirk betrayed his intention to exploit her good mood and she responded, "Brent and me ... where do we go from here, you mean?"

Crinkling his face into a squint-eyed grin, he said, "Well, seeing as you brought it up, the thought did enter my mind."

"I'm very fond of him, Dad. And I believe he feels the same way about me. He's a sensitive man and a good catch. We've made no plans, but he discusses the future often. It's always in terms of us. He wants children."

Dave exclaimed, "Damn it, you know my dream is to bring a grandson up here! How long do I have wait?"

"Till you stop being so cantankerous. From my seat, that could take awhile."

"Okay, okay. I get the message. What else is coming down with Brent?"

"Before the war started, we planned for me to join him for a month in San Diego. Brent expects orders and would take some leave before the next duty station. He wants to know if it's okay by me for him to request the east coast."

"Asked? That's the kind of question a naval officer asks his wife, not his girlfriend. Likely that's another damn thing that's changed since my day. How do you feel about this?"

"Would I marry him? I'm not ready to say that. We've got some distance to run. You know he has an ex-wife and a son."

"Didn't his wife remarry? You've got no competition there, Bea."

Dave's hopes for Brent and his daughter showed clearly.

"Can't you see there is, Dad? I can't compete with a ghost, and sometimes, that's how his ex comes across to me."

Chapter 9

Captain Bostwick entered the *Denver* wardroom, where his officers had assembled for a war conference. The ship meandered along at one-third speed, all unnecessary machinery secured to reduce radiated noise. This all but eliminated the probability *Denver* would be detected and improved her own ability to detect enemy ships.

The captain smiled a greeting. "First, let me say how proud I am about the way you've handled things."

Brent tried unsuccessfully to capture Bostwick's eye. The young officer sought reassurance that his conduct during the *Tango* kill vindicated him in the eyes of his commanding officer. He also felt that the captain's apparent surge of self-confidence might evaporate in the next crisis.

The captain said, "We've given our countrymen something to cheer about … God knows, they need it."

Brent liked what he heard, but not the implied message. He felt the captain had unusual ideas on what comprised success. They had failed in their mission to screen *Utah* and crossed the entire Pacific Ocean with little to show for their efforts, only a diesel-electric submarine.

Bostwick went on, "We've been hit, but not hard and have a fair understanding of the damage. Fortunately, we had no personnel casualties. Now, I want to review the facts and identify available options."

Jack Olsen spoke. "The engineer thinks we can fix it."

Raising his eyebrows Bostwick asked, "Fix it? We're banged up outside the hull. We can't make that repair submerged."

Nodding toward the operations officer, Jack said, "Dan."

"We can do it on the surface, Captain."

An astounded Bostwick questioned, "On the surface? In the middle of the Pacific with enemy control of the air?"

His tone hung like a pail of ice water about to be doused on the plan.

Dan spread out one of the charts obtained by Quartermaster Henri on the eve of their departure from Bremerton. "Not in the open sea, sir." He pointed to their present position. "We're a hundred twenty-five miles southeast of this small cluster of islands in the Kuril chain. We can approach submerged, then anchor on the leeward side of one of them."

His impatience blatantly apparent, Bostwick demanded, "And then what?"

Dan made his voice steadier than his conviction. "Surface after dark, anchor, and conduct the repair."

The captain countered, "Are you out of your mind? The soundings on this chart alone are not reliable. How good are they?"

"My guess is not very good at all. But we have a Fathometer."

"What about the mine field?"

The captain clearly wanted no part of the idea.

Brent jumped in. "They're probably MZ 26s, sir, moored at thirty-six meters. We can avoid that depth by running shallow. We have to anyway in order to make landfall at periscope depth."

"We've run checks, Captain. The noise threshold from the damage is acceptable at six knots. At five, we can be there in little more than twenty-four hours."

The captain's arguments quickly diminished and he grasped for straws. "What about Magnetic Airborne Detection equipped aircraft?"

"MAD range is a thousand feet, okay for localizing, but not for search. It's even worse in shallow water. You would not believe how much junk sits on the bottom that will distract it."

Bostwick had to hear the plan out, though he searched his mind for reasons to disapprove.

Next, the engineer spoke, "If we keep the hole above the waterline, the job should be fairly simple. We'll burn off the jagged edges and then weld a piece of plating over the hole. Grinders will smooth it up. We'll rig blankets around and over the worksite to keep the bad guys from spotting weld flashes."

Bostwick's hostility to the idea became more open. "What about airborne radar?"

Several officers showed understanding expressions for the captain's point of view.

Dan replied, "It's useless once we're close in. There's so many other land targets, we'd never be picked out of the clutter."

The captain quizzed the chief engineer for more details on the repair plan and then retired to his stateroom for a private conference with Jack Olsen.

Bostwick closed the door and gestured menacingly at his executive officer. "For chrissake, Jack, why the hell didn't you nip this stupid idea in the bud before it came to me?"

Jack hesitated, recognizing the Captain's tone and knew the going would be rough. "I'm not sure it's such a bad idea, sir."

"You're right. It's not a bad idea. It's a shitty idea, and we're not going through with it. Now dammit, Jack, we got our ticket home. A war wound, and in spite of it, we went on to kill an enemy. Nobody expects any more from us."

An overpowering personality had earned Bostwick a perfect track record for getting Olsen to knuckle under.

Out of character, Olsen responded, "Captain, I disagree."

"Disagree?"

Bostwick had never heard these words from his executive officer.

"Yes, sir, the plan is sound. Risky, but sound. The way I see it, we collect a salary all our lives not for what we do in peace but for what's expected of us in war. We're capable of doing much more than we have so far. We've got to do it, or we live a lie."

Olsen astounded even himself with the passion of his response.

Denver's captain bristled. "Dammit! Jack. Now I see it—first Maddock and now you. Well let me tell you, Buster, I'm in command of this ship and if you care about your future in this man's Navy, get back in that wardroom and work up a plan for getting us back to the States."

"Are those your orders, Captain?"

"You goddamn betcha."

"I'll carry them out, sir." Then Jack astounded himself again by saying, "But I will insist on including transcripts of this meeting and the wardroom meeting in our patrol report. It will describe in detail recommendations from the officers and your decision."

"That includes you?"

"It does, Captain."

"You son of a bitch. You'd really do that?"

Jack's threat struck the captain at his most vulnerable spot. "I will, Captain. And, if I may, the remotest possibility of cowardice in the face of the enemy all but rules out your flag chances."

Bostwick snarled, "Get the hell out of here."

Jack Olsen knew he'd won one. *About time,* he thought.

Eric and Eve Danis sat in the tiny backyard of their rented house in Ridgecrest, California. The town grew up in the Mojave Desert with the Naval Weapons Facility and housed the people and businesses that supported the activities there. A spectacular sunset concluded a clear day and now they conversed beneath a brilliant canopy of stars.

"Eve," Eric said, breaking the silence, "it's downright embarrassing how I'm letting this desert grow on me."

Twenty-two years of marriage had brought them to near perfect harmony. They could sit for hours without talking and still derive great pleasure from just being with each other.

"It would be embarrassing if it didn't," Eve replied. "I've always wondered how people who live out here could stand it. Now I know why they never want to leave."

"I always thought we'd only settle near the ocean in retirement. Now I'm not so sure," he said.

Retirement? Eve had not heard the word mentioned before now. "Is this an announcement?"

He replied, "Announcement? Oh, no, but then maybe so. Every now and then, my brain pops out things that I'm not sure I'm ready to say. This job is up in three months and there are plenty of young bucks who'd like to push me off this springboard."

Eve felt a surge of pity for her husband. The road to this point in his career had been a long and hard one with seventeen years at sea, running the gauntlet of junior officer assignments, executive officer and then command. He had served six years in the latter capacity, four as captain of a 688 class SSN and two in a Trident. Sixty percent of his years found Eric at sea and away from his family.

She asked, "Why don't we talk about it?"

"Ya know, Eve, it'll be the hardest decision of my life. No one knows better than you how hard I worked to make flag, but if it's not meant to be, it won't happen."

"You've got plenty of good company. A lot of good men don't make it, simply because there're not enough promotions for all who deserve one."

"You're right, Eve. And a lot of guys deserve it more than I do. It won't be easy to quit, especially in the middle of a war. This gives me another option. Maybe obligation is a more appropriate term."

"Obligation, Eric?"

"Step down and take a lesser assignment. One that's really not a challenge but in need of being done. It'll take some crow eating for an anointed squadron commander to fall back into the trenches, but I can do that."

Eve asked sympathetically, "Is that what you believe you should do?"

"Yes, I really do. After thirty years at the trough, I owe the Navy. In peacetime, the best favor I could pay them would be to get out and make way for the next guy. Go home and write articles for the Naval Institute on how things should really be done. Go to Submarine League Symposiums and make small talk with the good old boys. God, I'd love it, Eve, but can I really do that? Guess I'm scared that if I stay, everyone will think I'm a die-hard and want to hang around just to see if lightning strikes later."

Reaching over, Eve took her husband's hand. "Eric, you've got no worries. Everyone who knows you is in your corner, and that includes all the best submariners. They will know what you're doing, and the rest can damn well go to hell," Eve said with an uncharacteristic show of candor.

Eric smiled. "You sure have a way of cutting to the issue, Eve. I'll think on it of course, but I'll likely take the reassignment. Couldn't live with myself if I didn't." Then changing the subject, he asked, "How do you feel about packing up and driving off to Washington State?"

"Actually, not too good," she replied. "I know why I like the desert so much. I see you every evening at five o'clock sharp. Think about it. We've not had that throughout your entire career. I'm used to it now and I know what happens when you get submarines to play with."

Eric dodged her with a subject change. "These flyboys are very good, Eve. They stay on top of things and keep me informed. Hate to admit it, but Gerry Carter's the best Chief Staff Officer I've ever had. He's got me calibrated and starts jobs before I even assign them. He's already in Washington State and will likely get me home early up there just as he does here. You know Carter's the real thing if he can impress Dave Zane, and Dave can't say enough good things about him."

Eve said, "Seeing Dave would be compensation for heading up that way. And Bea, too. I haven't seen them since Dale's funeral. Do you know how Bea's doing?"

"That dumpy little girl has grown into a beautiful young woman. Dave says she's interested in young Maddock on *Denver*."

She teased her husband. "I thought she'd be smart enough not to go after a submariner."

"Well now, you didn't do too bad. Lucky for you they built Conn College across the river from the submarine base," he said referring to Eve's Alma Mater in New London, Connecticut where he met her while in Officers' Basic Submarine school.

"Just the other way around, dear man. Lucky for you they built the Sub Base across the river from Conn College. We were there first."

He thought for a moment. "Maybe we're both lucky."

They exchanged a smile and Eric continued, "Do you have any regrets, Eve? I know it's been a tough road for you … nursing a bunch of young wives while I played at sea. And maybe seeing even less of me during my shore duty while in Washington. The damn Pentagon's a treadmill. Where else can a man spend so much time on the job and get so little done?"

"No harder for me than for you, though I didn't like sea duty a bit," Eve confessed. "There seemed to be such a finality about it when the ships deployed. We had no contact. At the Pentagon, you were done in when you came home, but at least we got to say hi to each other. Not so with sea duty. And Sean liked having you around."

"Well he sure kept it a secret from me … our son the poet. If only he could write poetry."

"Don't be so cynical, Eric. He's so much like you it's frightening. Maybe that's why I hated sea duty the most. I could do many things for him, but I couldn't be you."

"I'm proud of Sean. He stands his ground. He's likely matured beyond the points of view that got him into his current situation. But he's burned too many bridges and doesn't know how to get out."

"I wish you and Sean would resume talking to each other."

"He has that option and I don't want to push it. He's only nineteen. I remember how I could get my back up at that age. Maybe he'll come to Mark Twain's conclusion. At fourteen, he considered his father so ignorant he could hardly stand to be near him, but when Twain reached twenty-one, his dad astonished him with how much he had learned in seven years. Maybe I'll be that lucky."

"Still, I'd be happy if you'd try harder."

"I will, Eve. I promise." Eric bent over and kissed his wife. He found her lips softer than their usual peck. He kissed her again, this time harder. "What do you say we turn in early and make it an unprecedented two times in the same week?"

"With that kind of romantic talk, how can a girl resist," she replied. Holding hands, they walked into the house.

Captain Bostwick yanked his head from beneath the periscope yoke and snapped the handles to the stowed position, the signal for his assistant to lower the scope.

Quartermaster Henri announced, "Number one coming down." He rotated the control actuator, and the huge shaft hissed into its well.

Brent said, "Too dark to get much on the peri-viz monitor, Captain. What's it like up there?"

The captain had not followed through with the threatened action to remove him from the watch bill and Brent continued to stand his watch.

Bostwick replied, "Bleak, but good. No evidence of anyone on the island, but to make sure we're not spotted, we'll wait till after dark before surfacing. Take a single ping sounding, Henri."

Henri said, "Single ping, aye, Captain," and then operated the Fathometer. "Hundred and twenty feet under the keel, Captain. That's a charted sounding of 188, sir."

Adding the recorded sounding to the submarine's keel depth, Henri compared it to what the navigation chart showed for their position. The young black took every opportunity to insure everyone knew nothing slipped by him.

Bostwick, resenting Henri's unneeded detailed explanation, took a breath to respond but let it pass. "Okay, Brent, do race tracks here for thirty minutes. Mix up the sounding intervals, but average three per minute. If they fall below a hundred, head east immediately and call me."

The captain turned to Henri, "That's *below* the keel, Petty Officer Henri," making his point after all.

Brent believed he would never understand the captain's attitudes. He had a habit of disapproving plans and recommendations, but once having bought in, he would reverse his attitude completely. Brent considered the captain performed a masterful job of directing his ship to an anchorage in uncertain waters.

He reckoned Bostwick's self-confidence grew as a function of time. *The more we're successful, the more effective he is. Unfortunately, reversal makes his self confidence crash.*

Effective commanding officers innovate in the face of disaster. Bostwick possessed the fundamentals but lacked the ability to pull it all together on his own.

Brent ordered, "Up number two for a look around, Henri."

The young black responded, "Two coming up."

Placing his face against the eyepiece when the upper window broke the water, Brent led Henri in a wild circular dance as they swung the scope around completely within five seconds.

"Dip scope," and the shaft lowered about six feet and stopped.

Henri said, "Mark your depth, Chief." He double-checked to be sure the scope upper optics remained beneath the surface.

Cunningham replied, "Six-eight feet and steady."

Three pay-grades senior to Henri, COB carried out the order without hesitation. Submariners do not stand on ceremony.

"Getting pretty dark up there," Brent noted. "I need a final look at the tangents," referring to the bearings of both extremities of the island. "Up scope." Again, the hissing as the scope rose and the metallic clack of the yoke butting against the upper stops. "Put me on Henri, left tangent first."

With his hands over Brent's on the periscope handles, Henri rotated counterclockwise. "Should be right about here, sir."

Brent cried out, "See it!" He then shifted to high power and trained the scope one degree to the right. "Bearing, mark."

Henri recorded the bearing and did so again when Brent marked the right tangent. The sounding checked with *Denver*'s plotted position. "Everything perfect here, Mr. Maddock."

"Pretty good set of charts you swiped for us, Henri," then ordered, "Have the engineer assemble his repair party in the Attack Center."

The six-man patch party included the auxiliary officer and five enlisted men, all warmly dressed. Each man carried a piece of the equipment needed to make the repair. They had gas cutting torches, an arc welding kit, several tool bags and a deck plate from the machinery compartment to make the patch.

Brent reported over the 21 MC, "Repair party assembled in the Attack Center, Captain. All preparations completed for surfacing."

Bostwick replied, "Okay, Brent, I'm on the way."

Reaching the Attack Center the captain raised number one scope for a final look. A dark moonless night, coupled with a low heavy overcast that obscured the stars, made *Denver* difficult to spot with the human eye.

With a calm voice, Bostwick said, "Soon as we're up, we'll proceed directly to the anchorage. Get as close to the island as we can but no less than ten feet below the keel. We'll drop at ten feet. Too dark for tangents so we'll wing it. Henri, you been keeping a tight DR?"

The captain referred to a dead reckoning track, which employed times, course and speed changes, computed to the ship's position and recorded on the chart.

Henri responded, "The tightest, Captain."

The two exchanged a grin.

Bostwick addressed the auxiliary officer, "Bill, when the bridge reports hatch clear, I want you to go out on deck with the Chief and get back with a quick report of the damage, got that?"

"Got it, Captain."

"Raise the ESM mast and do a complete electronic countermeasure search."

An ECM antenna sat atop the ESM mast. A short time later the operator reported, "No contacts except for distant aircraft radars."

The captain said, "We'll have those continuously," then ordered, "Leave the mast up and search for anything significant. Keep me informed."

Brent replied, "Aye, sir, we'll do it."

Bostwick took a deep breath then turned to his conning officer and said, "Okay, Brent, let's go."

Inwardly, it infuriated him to converse with young Maddock, but Bostwick put his money on the best officer he had for the operation.

Henri announced throughout the ship on the 1MC, "Surface, surface, surface."

The sound of high-pressure air rushing into the ballast tanks briefly masked *Denver's* sonar. The submarine shuddered to the surface and held.

After initiating a low-pressure blow to remove remaining ballast, Brent climbed onto the bridge and at once inhaled the smell of marine growth that had accumulated in *Denver*'s superstructure over the past four weeks beneath the Pacific. It reminded him of the prophecy in the opening chapter of Herman Melville's *Moby Dick*, "One day you will smell land where there is no land." The prophet alluded to the scent of marine growth that had accumulated on the great white whale—the same odor as from a landfall.

Looking around, Brent saw nothing. A shaft of light burst from the deck hatch as the two engineers came up to assess the damage. *Damn*, he thought, *shouldn't have done that.* Flashlight beams moved ahead of the two men and he could hear metallic sounds from their belt guides as they dragged along the safety track.

Brent shouted into the 21MC Box, "Bridge testing."

Henri's voice called back, "Loud and clear, Bridge."

"Heading and distance to the anchorage?"

Very much on top of the situation, Henri reported, "Two-eight-two and we're steady on it. Estimate four thousand yards to drop, sir."

"Good, have the anchor party stand by in the torpedo room."

Ahead of the game again, Henri said, "They're standing by with phones manned."

"Very well. All ahead one third, give a mark every five hundred yards till a thousand and then every hundred."

"Five till a grand, then hundreds. We'll monitor for ten below the keel," he repeated.

Brent felt as though he should commend Henri on the spot. *Why waste my time telling that smart-ass what he already knows?*

"Captain up!" Bostwick announced as he climbed onto the bridge. He focused his binoculars and looked on the damage. "Doesn't seem to be too bad, Brent. The hole's about three feet in diameter with all the edges turned in so we won't have to cut them off. The engineers are cutting and bending enough plating to cover the damage. They estimated they'd need about three hours."

"Plenty of night left for that, Captain."

"I'd feel a lot better about the night in a World War II scenario. Too damn much technology around now to help the Reds find us."

Hesitating Brent said, "It's the hand that's dealt us, Captain. We'll play it best way we can."

Bostwick didn't acknowledge Brent's remark. "Going below," he said and left the bridge.

Brent warned the bridge watch to keep a sharp look out as *Denver* proceeded toward her anchorage. Henri had started on the hundreds when the captain's voice interrupted him on the 21MC. "I'm going in to ten below the keel, Brent. Keep a sharp look out ahead. I don't want to hit anything."

Denver stopped engines at fifteen feet and began backing. She had just a bit of sternway when the anchor let go. The current and a little bit of wind kept them off shore; a perfect situation. To get the hole fully above the waterline the ship had to be rolled slightly to port by partially counter-flooding the ballast tanks. The engineers already began welding the preformed plating to the upper side of the hole. Their makeshift blanket tent did an excellent job of screening light from the arc torches.

An hour passed, two hours and then three.

Brent thought, *So much for the optimistic engineers.*

Quartermaster Henri broke the silence with his 21MC transmission. "Thirty minutes on the outside is the latest estimate on repairs, Bridge."

"Bridge, aye, conn," Brent replied then asked, "Tracks laid out for getting back to deepwater?"

Henri gave the expected reply. "That's affirmative, sir."

"Aye, pass the word on to the cap—"

The topside port lookout interrupted, "Contact, sir! One-nine-five and closing."

Turning around, Brent spotted the running lights of a small ship. A simultaneous view of both sidelights meant the ship headed directly toward *Denver*.

He ordered through a megaphone to the repair party, "Secure the work topside, all hands lay below on the double!" Then on the 21MC, "Captain to the bridge. Closing visual contact true bearing one-eight-zero, six thousand."

Henri replied, "Captain has the word, Bridge. We're securing the deck hatch when the work party is below."

Bostwick called out, "Captain up," the edge on his voice apparent. "What've we got, Brent?"

Brent pointed aft. "Whatever he is, he just came around the point, sir. This close to the field, my guess is a mine layer."

The captain asked, "Can we get him with a torpedo?"

"Too high risk of missing, Captain, and it would alert him to our presence. Shallow water and tight gyro angles. Even if we did hit him, he'd radio the whole damn Soviet Air Force and they'd be on our backs before we reached deepwater."

His voice betraying both anger and fear the captain snapped, "What do you recommend?"

Brent calmly replied, "Sit tight, sir. He's not looking for anything and doesn't expect us to be here."

The captain said, "Why the hell did I ever let you jackasses talk me into this?"

Once again, Bostwick proved not equal to the pressure.

"Port sidelight beginning to mask, Captain. He'll pass astern, but not very far."

The captain exclaimed, "Listen! The son of a bitch is so damn close we can hear him."

The *rum, rum, rum* of the ship's single diesel engine could be heard clearly and the bearings abruptly drifted quickly left.

"Shsssh," Bostwick hissed.

Tension levels mounted. Although no one aboard the unidentified ship could possibly hear voices from *Denver's* bridge, its closeness made silence a psychological factor. The ship passed a scant half-mile astern then its propulsion sounds stopped. The vessel began to drift slowly away with the current. Next, the red glow of her port sidelight reappeared, followed quickly by the green starboard sidelight. She pointed directly toward them again.

Bostwick said, "Oh shit, they've found us."

"No, sir," Brent replied, "I think we're just too good at selecting an anchorage. We must be in her favorite spot."

At that instant, the sound of the ship's anchor splash and the running of chain through her hawse pipe rang through the still night. Brent estimated the range to be a thousand yards astern and blocking *Denver's* escape to sea. She'd likely run out fifty yards of chain and give *Denver* a little more breathing room. But daylight would come in a few hours and illuminate the trapped *Denver*.

An irate Bostwick said, "Okay, Mr. Smart-ass tactician, what the hell do we do now?"

Chapter 10

Dave Zane demanded of Dutch Meyer, "Now what the hell does that commodore of yours think we can do with that mess?"

They watched a 688 being towed around the breakwater, one of the partially overhauled ships Eric Danis had turned out of Bremerton on the eve of the attack.

He continued, "I told him yesterday it would be at least a month before we're ready for work and already he loads us up. That thing is in such pitiful shape, you have to be an expert to tell it's a submarine."

Dutch replied, "You really want to hear what he expects? He wants it fixed and sent to sea. That's what."

"Damn it, there's nothing we can do to fix it now. It's only gonna be in the way and delay us from doing more important jobs so let's anchor it outside."

The old mustang indulged himself a grin, "You tell the skipper that, Dave. He's been sitting on the bottom of Puget Sound for the past month, bailing out water from a leaky patch; his crew has no idea of what's happened to their families, and the only thing keeping them going is a desire to get their ship into action. If you're gonna tell him he has to anchor out, give me half an hour to draw a crowd, 'cause I can collect fifty bucks a ticket for this show."

"All right then, what do you suggest?"

"We both go down to the berth, welcome him to the facility and ask what we can do for him."

Grinning, Dave asked, "Am I really getting that old, Dutch?"

"Yeah, and twice as ornery. Let's go."

Mooring USS *Newport* showed the crew's lack of practice since arriving at Bremerton more than six months ago. The ragtag gang assembled by Dave had no experience at all. Both ship's crew and Dave's men sensed the other's problems and therefore performed the operation devoid of bickering and catcalling as the gap closed between the ship and dock.

The *Newport* officer-of-the-deck ordered the brow set in place and Dave went aboard.

What Dave considered an extremely young officer gave the order, "Attention on deck."

A crisp salute from the younger man showed Dave at least some facets of his day had survived. Dave, caught off guard by the courtesy, removed his hands from his pockets and assumed a semblance of the military position, which had evaded him since completing active service. He returned the salute in the prescribed manner of a retired officer by standing at attention.

The submarine's skipper said, "Good afternoon, Captain Zane. I'm Phil Reynolds, commanding officer. Welcome aboard *Newport*."

Dave thought, c*ommanding officer? He looks younger than my paperboy.* "Well," Dave hesitated, but for only an instant. "Welcome to our base, Captain. We don't have much here yet, but seeing you're our first customer, it's all yours."

Dave extended his hand and the submarine skipper took it with a firm grip and shook it.

Commander Reynolds said, "Please come below, sir."

Both men proceeded to *Newport's* wardroom where Dave accepted the customary offer of a cup of coffee.

Dave began, "Well how did you enjoy the bottom of our Sound?"

"Frankly, sir, I've only been in a few places I liked less."

"Perfectly understandable. How did things go back there? You're the first guys out. What can you tell us?"

Shaking his head, Reynolds said, "Not a nifty place to be. We heard the racket and just sat tight. That place is now as hot as a firecracker. Once in a while after the attack, we'd pop up at night and send monitors out to take background readings. The Reds used some pretty dirty stuff. Are you familiar with the term salted weapon?"

"Isn't that when they capture neutrons in the material to be blown up? Spreads around a lot of contamination."

"That's right, sir."

Dave felt uncomfortable with the respectful form of address. He'd rather be called by his first name but had to come to terms with being back in the Navy.

Reynolds continued, "From what we found, they used a cobalt sixty isotope. Its half-life is five years. It's spread all over the southern part of Puget Sound. Even with leaching from heavy rainfall, we can't get back into Bremerton for at least a year."

"How'd they do that? The technique you described requires a pretty good-sized device. It couldn't have been delivered by a ballistic missile."

"That's right, sir. I think we now know what the Soviets did off the Swedish coast a few years ago. A Foxtrot submarine ran aground there; and nearby, the Swedes found marks of a remotely piloted tracked vehicle on the seabed. Somehow, they got similar vehicles into Puget Sound undetected. They loaded them with the dirty stuff, drove them to desired burst points and programmed them to detonate concurrently with the missile attacks."

It struck Dave that young Reynolds had gotten it all pretty well together. His tone level steady and he took no delight in using his observations to focus attention on himself. He didn't need to. Dave liked the notion that his country still produced officers of this quality.

"What made you think they used RPVs?"

Reynolds smiled. "We bottomed near Hat Island. One evening after we surfaced an irate local approached us in his boat and raised hell. He wanted to know if we were responsible for destroying the clam beds. Actually, Captain Zane, we found this refreshing. Here we were, recovering from a nuclear attack, up to our buns in a full-fledged war, and this guy could still worry about clams. The small space occupied by *Newport* could not have wiped out his bed, so I asked if he would show us where they were. He did, and my divers uncovered the tracks. Ivan had been there.

"We figured the rest by deduction. But here's the really funny part. The guy came back and let us have it again. He claimed he argued against bringing the carrier battle group into Everett, Washington in the first place. Had they listened to him, the Soviets wouldn't have run their tracked vehicles in there and this reinforced his position. After the war, he'd go to Washington, DC and say as much. What a feisty guy.

"He'd been there two weeks when we saw him and he's already a goner. It would've done no good to tell him that. We thought it best to let him live out what little time he had in a place he obviously loved."

"You did the right thing."

"From what we could tell, sir, Bremerton and Everett got hit hardest. Lucky the battle group left port a few days earlier. The Soviets likely intended to deny access to any port facility that we needed to conduct the war. I suspect there's a bunch of other places in the Sound with wiped out clam beds too. Whoever directed the RPV movements reached station early with plenty of time to practice."

"As far as your ship went, how did things go?"

"On the plus side, we performed our mission. We survived the attack and brought you a hull to repair. But in the yard before the attack, we lifted the reduction gear casings and found wiped bearings on the port low speed pinion and high-speed gear. We ordered replacement bearings but had to deploy before they arrived. Unless you got a line on some, I'm afraid we're nothing but a spare parts bin."

"How long have you been in command, Phil?"

"I relieved my predecessor two months ago in the yard."

Dave paused for a moment. If he found the bearings, he had no one at the *Pitstop* capable of making repairs of this magnitude and did not wish to offer any false hope. During their short acquaintance, Dave developed a fondness for young Reynolds.

"Look, son ... er, Captain. We've performed a kind of miracle here just getting this place set up. We just might have another one up our sleeve."

Jack Olsen said, "An armed boarding party is our only option. We can't hide by bottoming with only ten feet beneath the keel. Slipping past them undetected is out of the question, unless they're deaf and blind."

Captain Bostwick addressed his hastily assembled council of war, "What do we know about the target?"

A long-term submariner contention is: *There are only two types of ships, submarines and targets.*

Nodding, Jack addressed the weapons officer seated at the end of the wardroom table. "Brent?"

Brent continued to function well despite the captain's now open hostility toward him. "Yevgenya class, sir. No more than ten aboard. Sonar got a make on her. A one-lunger diesel propulsion system. A couple of sweeps with a Don II Radar just before she anchored is consistent, although common, with a number of warships that size."

Bostwick asked, "Brent, any chance she detected us?"

"None sir. We're well inside the width of a Don II transmission pulse and no suspicious radio intercepts. Real problem is the damn radio. We intercepted her anchoring message and the power of the response signal indicated a transmitter's fairly close. Maybe even on the island itself. We've got more reason than just the minesweeper for being out of here and submerged before daylight."

Dan Patrick added, "If we get caught, we've had it. The Soviets have the hardware they need to keep us from reaching deepwater."

Captain Bostwick agreed to let the boarding party go. "Okay. It's our only chance. Who'll lead this? Brent?"

Jack replied, "He wants to, Captain, but he's too important to the success for the rest of our mission."

The captain gritted his teeth as he asked, "Who then?"

"Woody, sir," Dan replied. "He's right out of the Academy and he's the most recently trained in infantry tactics. He's also in the best physical shape."

Considering Dan's choice, Bostwick thought for a moment. *True. Green, but tough and smart.* "Okay, Woody, you got it. Some of my classmates led platoons in Vietnam as second lieutenants and gave good accounts of themselves. We're banking on you."

Grinning, Woody said, "I won't let you down, sir."

Moments later, Brent assembled Woody Parnell and twenty enlisted candidates in the crew's mess. Quartermaster Henri, not a nominee, suspected a mission planning session in the works and slipped into the meeting uninvited.

Brent outlined the situation and a plan. "Our major goal, prevent the Soviets from reporting *Denver*'s presence. Eight men, under command of Ensign Parnell, will take a rubber life raft and approach the minesweeper. Silence is paramount," Brent cautioned. "If they hear us before we get to the radio transmitter, it's over. Blowing it up is the first order of business. Next, the crew must be terminated. We can't take the chance of someone reporting our presence."

The crew winced upon hearing these sobering words. Submariners are trained to sink ships and other submarines. People died but from less personal actions. *Denver* troops found the concept of one on one, kill or be killed to be a new and unnerving one.

"Our best point of entry is from astern." Brent pointed to a large, hastily drawn representation of the minesweeper.

"Ensign Parnell and one troop will board. Parnell will move up the starboard side and the other up the port, each with a satchel charge. I don't know which side the radio shack is on, but the one who finds it, open the door and neutralize the occupants, silently if you can. Then set the charge alongside the transmitter and activate the timer. You'll have ten seconds to put some distance between your buns and the charge."

Low remarks and repositioning of feet by the candidates reflected mounting concern and excitement.

Brent continued, "The sound of either gunfire or the explosion will bring the enemy out on deck. Hopefully, it will be the latter. The radio shack could be unoccupied. The explosion alone could bring the enemy out unarmed, but the sound of gunfire … well, you know what to expect then.

"Either sound will cue the rest of the attack party to move out, three port and three starboard. Cover the exits. Let as many get out as you can before opening fire. There's supposed to be ten aboard but maybe a few more or less. Questions? Make them brief. We don't have a lot of time."

Hesitating for answers and when none came, Brent asked, "Okay then, volunteers?"

Twenty-one hands shot into the air.

"Thanks, men," Brent said then chose a first class petty officer and six others.

The stern voice of Jacques Henri demanded, "Mr. Maddock, I don't see how you can pull this off without the benefit of my experience. What you just described is like a normal Saturday night in East St. Louis."

"We need you for the rest of our mission, Henri. We can't afford to lose our leading quartermaster."

An irritated Henri went on, "Are you saying I'm indispensable, sir? Look, you're sending Barnes because he's heavy on explosives. He's the logical choice to accompany Mr. Parnell to the radio shack. You need a petty officer to control the rest of the troops while they wait for the noise to start. And, in the event of casualties to the bomb squad, someone has to pull off the rest of the job. Like I said, you need me on this one, sir. Besides, I won't need to darken my face."

A nervous laugh came from the assembled submariners.

Someone asked, "What about your teeth and eyeballs?"

The crew laughed louder this time.

After considering Henri's request for a moment, Brent said, "Okay, Pruitt, Henri gets your seat. The rest of you guys get out of here so we can get ready."

After a flurry of handshakes and wishes for good luck Brent, the captain and Chief Cunningham stood topside to see the raiders off.

Taking Henri's hand, Brent stumbled to find a suitable expression.

Henri said, "Trouble with you white guys is you don't know how to handle emotion."

The two men embraced without embarrassment.

"Just get your sorry ass back here, Henri. I need you to beat up on during my watch."

"Treat me right and I'll bring you a Red scalp."

The small raiding party boarded the raft and disappeared into the darkness.

Brent admired the manner by which leadership fell so naturally to the young black petty officer and wondered from which band of fierce warriors had Henri descended.

On board the raft, Woody ordered the four paddlers, "Quietly, quietly," as much to quell his own butterflies than to reduce noise made by the crew.

Either a weaker than estimated current or lesser distance between *Denver* and the minesweeper shortened the raiders' transit from what they anticipated. Before they realized it, the raft had reached the minesweeper and moved along its starboard side. Blisters of rust flaked the paint and red streaks ran down to the water line. The sound of a running auxiliary engine, probably a diesel powered generator, masked what little noise the sailors made as they fended their craft off the sweeper's side by hand.

Woody saw no one moving about above deck so he ordered the raft repositioned at the stern according to plan. He and his men, dressed completely in black, including gloves and stocking caps, moored their tiny craft with quarter inch nylon line to the enemy ship. They sat quietly for a moment and listened. No sounds other than the generator pierced the quiet night, and the raiders' heartbeats made a deafening sound in each man's ears.

Heretofore unseen steel shown in Woody's baby blue eyes when he ordered Petty Officer Barnes, "Okay, let's go."

Being the first American warrior to occupy Soviet territory thrilled Woody as he leapt onto the deck. He hoped time would soon find many followers. Being careful, Woody looked into the glass of each deckhouse porthole while moving up the starboard side of the sweeper and detected no movement.

No surprise, he thought. *It's 0300.* At anchor with a crew of ten, all except perhaps an anchor or engineering watch slept soundly in their bunks.

He scaled a ladder to the bridge. Still no Soviet crew encountered. He quickly located the radio shack just aft of the bridge. An artistic radioman had painted a tier of lightning flashes on the door, the traditional symbol for radio transmitting equipment.

The radio shack had a porthole. Woody looked in and detected no apparent movement. He attempted to open the door. *Oh shit! It's locked and we didn't bring anything to bust it open.*

Someone made a sudden movement on the bridge. A click sounded as Woody cocked his pistol.

A hoarse whisper sounded from Petty Officer Barnes, "*Denver.*"

No password had been established, but when Barnes heard Ensign Parnell's weapon being cocked, necessity gave birth to invention.

Woody explained the situation about the locked door.

Barnes exclaimed, "Dammit! What'll we do, sir?"

"These bulkheads can't be more than quarter inch plate. The transmitters are against the bulkhead on the portside beneath the antennas. If we put both satchels against the outboard bulkhead and set them off together, it ought to do the job. What do you think?"

"Yes, sir. These charges are big enough to knock out anything."

Woody snapped back, "Okay, let's do it."

At the raft, Henri heard the approach of stepping feet as the Soviet sailor on anchor watch made a routine walk about the weather decks of the sweeper. Henri thought, *That asshole's gotta be blind not to see our mooring line.*

Clunk … clunk … clunk. The man walked past the raiders then stopped.

Henri drew the only knife that someone had the foresight to bring on the mission.

The enemy sailor turned around and walked back then put his hand on the mooring line.

Henri grasped the man's wrist and dragged the surprised sailor into the raft. Henri's right arm, coiled like a cornered rattlesnake, delivered the blade to the man's rib cage.

"Aaagh." The young man expired and was the first Soviet to fall in hand-to-hand combat in World War III.

Relief at Henri's victory and apparent solution quickly ended.

A nearby voice cried out, "Tovarich! Tovarich!"

None in the raft spoke the language, but all recognized the tone. More than just one enemy prowled about and the survivor had to be suspicious. A light flashed, blinding the Americans, quickly followed by a burst from the Soviet's AK-47 blasting its rounds into the raft.

Henri's M-16 silenced the attacker, but not before two men of the *Denver* raiding party fell dead into the sea. Air hissed through bullet holes in the raft.

Henri ordered, "Okay, Honkies, up and out. Shit's hit the fan!"

The four surviving *Denver* crewmen leapt onto the sweeper deck and moved forward according to plan with two on the port side and two starboard, instead of three as originally planned. A sudden earsplitting explosion ripped through the darkness as the charges set by Woody and Barnes destroyed the radio shack and its transmitter. No one emerged from the deck access door and hatches.

Woody and Barnes shouted in unison, "*Denver, Denver,*" as they raced aft, not wanting to be mistaken for Soviets.

When Woody met Henri, he yelled out, "We got the transmitter. Hang the rest of the charges over the side and we'll blow up the rest of this tub. Then get our asses outta here."

Henri responded, "Feel like swimming back? Ivan made some serious holes in our raft before he bought the farm. No, sir, Mr. Parnell. It's two down and eight to go, that is unless you got some of them in the radio shack."

"Only eight left … let's go get 'em."

A deckhouse door burst open. Two Soviets emerged firing wildly but American M-16s dispatched them before they could inflict damage.

Woody yelled, "Henri! Have the troops each stand by a door. On my whistle, open it and toss in a grenade."

"That's a bummer, sir. The only doors unlocked will be the ones they want us to open. I got a better idea."

"Let's hear it."

Henri quickly explained, "There's a gas-engine pump on the fantail. There's gotta be gasoline too. Let's dump it down a ventilation intake, and then toss in a match. Keep those doors and hatches covered till I get back."

Leaving the others, Henri disappeared, but quickly returned with a gas can.

Woody ordered, "Take a couple of men and get the pump. We don't know what they have stowed below decks, but you can bet there's plenty of mines. Starting a fire might blow us all sky high. We'll run the engine exhaust into the fresh air intake and gas them with carbon monoxide. They won't know what happened."

They found a ventilation intake aft of the bridge not far from the destroyed radio shack then fitted the pump hose over the engine exhaust pipe, while two of the raiding party removed hand lugs that held the grating in place. Henri inserted the hose and gave several pulls on the start rope. The engine sputtered to life and he set it to full throttle.

Woody shouted, "Okay, Henri, find me something to break the padlock on the radio shack door. Let's see if there're any goodies in there."

"Yes, sir. But first, I'll report our situation back to the ship. They must have heard the noise and will want to know what's happening."

"Good idea. Do it."

Henri directed his Aldis lamp toward *Denver*.

On board *Denver* the port lookout exclaimed, "Signal! Captain."

Bostwick ordered, "Quartermaster," and the petty officer began to record the message.

> *Transmitter, destroyed. Two casualties. Life raft gone.*
> *Four Soviet dead. Remaining crew trapped below decks.*
> *Pumping gas engine exhaust into ventilation intake.*

Brent thought, *Somebody over there's really thinking.* He correctly assumed it to be Henri. *Good thing he went along on the raid.*

The captain asked, "How do we get them back without a life raft?"

"We'll have to go to them. Pick up the anchor, then drive over with the outboard," said Brent, referring to the electric powered secondary propulsion motor that rigged out from beneath the engine compartment and able to be trained through three hundred sixty degrees for direction control.

The captain agreed. "Get the repair party back up and finish the ballast tank patch."

"Aye, sir."

Back on board the enemy vessel, Henri said to Ensign Parnell, "We don't have to break the door down. The hole from the explosion is plenty big enough to get in."

Before the young black could stop him, Woody leapt through the hole and entered the radio shack. Instantly, two pistol shots shattered the stillness.

Woody spun, fell to the deck and lay motionless.

Henri held his M-16 around the edge of the hole and sprayed a full magazine into the radio shack. He removed the empty magazine and snapped another one into place. His flashlight probed the smoke-filled compartment and fell upon a youngish sailor, slumped against a bulkhead, barely alive. Blood flowed from both nostrils and multiple wounds in his upper body. He appeared to be no older than Ensign Parnell.

The young Soviet had no idea of their meaning, but the last words he heard came from Henri. "Sovie bastard!"

Henri emptied the entire magazine into the twitching corpse.

Tears streamed down Henri's face. In his mind, he had failed the important charge he'd given himself; bring Ensign Parnell back alive. He knelt and lifted the officer's head into his lap. "Damn it, why in hell did you have to run in there?"

Henri's grief came to an abrupt end as Woody sighed, "Beats the hell out of me, Henri. You're not gonna tell Mr. Maddock about this are you?"

Woody became conscious and raised a bloody hand. Two bullets had struck him, one in his arm and the other in his thigh.

Anchor lights on the minesweeper continued to burn although the balance of her crew had succumbed peacefully to the carbon monoxide gas pumped into the ventilation system.

Denver made up alongside the first enemy warship to be seized since Rear Admiral Dan Gallery captured the Nazi U-505 in June 1944. The raiding party, welcomed home, embarked upon a new fame that would follow each for the remainder of his time in *Denver*. But the pain of losing two crewmen put a damper on this.

A submariner's belief goes: either all the ship's company is lost in combat or none is. There would be no grief experienced among the crew in either case.

Woody Parnell, cherubic warrior, acknowledged his shortfall for racing into the radio shack to the extent he felt no gratification over his spectacular achievement. The *Denver* crew boarded the sweeper and seized anything and everything that might be useable on their own ship. These included two cases of vodka and several tins of suspicious looking and smelling caviar.

Dan Patrick made the most important find, a crypto machine and key lists. If the sweeper could be disposed of in deepwater, the Soviets would consider these items lost and not compromised. They could prove valuable in the months ahead.

Daylight would soon be upon them and they'd have to get moving.

Brent tried another of his *Mad Maddock* schemes on the Executive Officer Jack Olsen and Lieutenant Dan Patrick, beginning with, "Okay, XO, this is gonna sound wild, but I think it'll work."

Jack Olsen wore a cynical expression. "What've you got for us this time, Brent? Paint us like a sailboat and do the rest of the trip to Vladivostok on the surface?"

Grinning, Brent said, "If Tom Edison worked for you, we'd still be reading by candlelight."

"Never mind the analogies; just give me your latest."

Continuing with some enthusiasm, Brent said. "I think we can get a few miles courtesy of the sweeper."

"Okay, give me the punch line." Then Olsen asked, "How will we do this?"

"Henri says the sweeper has an autopilot. We'll fire up his diesel, give it turns for ten knots and set the AP for the heading we want to make good. This'll double the advance speed we can make safely through this area. It'll give us a noise blanket for as long as the Soviets let us get away with it."

Shaking his head Jack asked, "Won't Ivan get suspicious when he doesn't hear from this guy?"

"Let's hope they figure he has radio problems and is heading home to get it fixed. Conveniently, that's the same direction we need to go."

Jack frowned, "What if they don't and they send somebody out to check on him?"

"We'll run submerged and use the floating wire as a detonation cable. We can run it through a cooling water intake or something on the sweeper. Our engineers can figure it out. We'll use the cable to detonate an explosive charge set in the middle of the sweeper's mine load. We want to sink him in deepwater so Ivan can't find out what we took.

"If a helicopter comes, let it get close enough and maybe we'll make history. The first submerged submarine to down an aircraft."

Jack looked to Dan Patrick. "What do you think?"

Dan replied, "What I always think, XO. Maddock is mad as a hatter, but then this whole damn war is madness so why not? I say let's do it."

Jack replied, "Let me get the captain. If we're going to do this, we gotta move out."

"Give me a break, Jack. I gotta low-key my advice to the old man. Can't you and Dan pass this off as one of your children?"

Mulling it over for a moment, Jack actually enjoyed the new hold he had gained on Bostwick so he said, "Okay, Brent."

Brent rose to leave, but Jack stopped him. "Look, Brent. You're a bit short of pats on the back lately. For whatever it's worth, we'd be damn well hurting without you."

Pausing, Brent's face began to flush as he said, "Thanks, Jack. I really appreciate that."

Jack said with sincerity, "Not half as much as you deserve."

Chapter 11

Naval Aviator Commander Gerry Carter performed well as a front man for the submarine squadron. Given an assignment, he regarded success to be routine. He looked beyond specific instructions and carried out intent, as well as the letter of each order.

A qualified and motivated cadre had been assembled to establish Eric Danis's submarine repair facility. It included the Bremerton yard personnel squirreled away by the resourceful Dutch Meyer on the eve of the Soviet attack. The men now needed expressions of reassurance and resolve from a strong leader to guide them through a dilemma that exceeded any other in the history of their country. Their morale hinged on this and Commander Carter ensured the need would be filled.

Thus, Carter conducted the commodore's arrival in the manner of military shows during World War II that did much to restore the morale of the country after a stream of successes by the Japanese. A tough talking military leader was just the ticket and Carter made the pomp of Commodore Danis's arrival at the repair facility second only to General Douglas MacArthur returning to the Philippines.

The day typified a Pacific Northwest prelude to summer, sun shining brightly while a gentle northwest breeze swept over the cluster of unkempt barges. Carter arranged the officers, twenty including the hapless *Newport* wardroom, into a single rank. Behind them stood the civilians mustered to man the base along with *Newport*'s enlisted crew on either side.

The small tug that carried Eric Danis northward from Grays Harbor now made its way alongside.

Carter commanded, "Attention on deck!"

Military personnel snapped to the traditional position.

Danis stepped onto the new base, his military bearing impeccable and wearing an expression that both reassured and warned the men assembled.

Rendering a smart textbook salute, Commander Carter said, "Good afternoon, Commodore. Welcome to SUBRON 3 Repair Facility."

Commodore Danis returned the courtesy with equal precision and said, "Thank you, Commander Carter. My first perceptions are equal to the excellent reports that precede my visit," then he turned and approached his old friend Dave Zane, took his offered right hand and held it for a moment as he continued, "Let me set the record straight. From this date forward, the correct nomenclature for this operation is Zane's *Pitstop*."

Dave replied, "Hi, Eric. I hope that title doesn't scare away any customers."

The two exchanged warm expressions that grow only from many years of mutual respect and admiration.

Commander Carter led the commodore among the ranks of officers and introduced each one then the designated leaders among the civilian workforce. Next, the commodore gave the shortest and most important speech of his life. The words would be crucial to the success of his operation so he chose them well. He often thought of what he would say then went with his instinct, which always worked best for him. He directed Carter to have everyone stand at ease and when the order was executed, he assumed an uncharacteristic pose; cap pushed to the back of his head, hands on hips, he straddled to a comfortable position.

Danis began, "I'm damn tired of having my ass kicked by the Reds. And I'm even more tired of doing too little about it. From the looks of this operation, I stand among determined and competent people who share this point of view. I won't waste time with platitudes. Instead, I'm going into those fancy quarters Captain Zane commandeered for me then get out of this sailor suit and into some working togs. I'll be around for the rest of the day for head-to-heads with each of you. I want your views on the way things go so I can understand the problems as you see them. As far as the war goes, we may be down but we're not out. Operations like Zane's *Pitstop* will do much to get us into a winning position. And we're going to win."

He paused a full thirty seconds and appeared to scan each man's face individually to make sure his message sunk in—then continued with, "I'm touched by your warm welcome and I thank you. I'll close with instructions that we'll all hear often in the weeks to come. Back to work. We've got to get this place ready to fix submarines."

Lieutenant Vasiliy Baknov attended a morning operations briefing and listened to the local summary in order to keep abreast of things because *Zhukov* would deploy within the week. The briefing officer directed his pointer to the northern edge of Proliv Yekateriny pass near the southern end of the Kuril chain.

"We have detected several explosions in this area, however, the area hydrophones detect no signs of the enemy's presence."

Vasiliy was immediately skeptical. *The only American warships able to reach that area are submarines and likely undetectable by our ancient hydrophones.*

The briefer continued, "The area is heavily seeded with small mines … perhaps too heavily. An occasional porpoise or sea lion sets one off and that," he said with a smile, "in turn sets off our ASW forces. These mines are tiny and cannot destroy a submarine, but they make enough noise to alert us and provide warning if one tries to pass. Damage to a submarine is minor, but its stealth is compromised, especially at higher speeds. This neutralizes the 688 class acoustic advantage and makes it inadvisable for him to continue his mission. With no capability to repair such damage at sea, they must make the long return trip across the Pacific to the shambles of their submarine bases."

I wouldn't be too sure of that, Vasiliy thought. *Submariners must be resourceful to survive, including those of our enemy.* He wasn't quite certain how it could be done, but if *Zhukov* sustained damage off the American coast, much scheming and trying to make repairs would precede giving up before making the forty-five hundred mile voyage home.

The briefer droned on, "Actually, our dense field of small mines does not work as expected. There are many false alarms. Explosions are investigated by patrolling *Tango*s, but zeal to make a kill has already resulted in two of them striking mines themselves. We suspect this is the case now."

Again, the briefer smiled and said, "Our young *Tango* commanders are reluctant to report self-sustained damage."

Quiet laughter ensued.

Next, he presented the current weather and the seventy-two hour forecast then asked, "Questions, comrades?"

Vasiliy spoke up, "Yes, sir. What is the contact approaching La Perouse Strait?"

"It is a reydny traishchik." (Russian for roadstead minesweeper.) "He has apparent radio problems and is returning for repairs. Other questions? No? Very well then, this concludes the morning briefing."

More than two days had passed with no Soviet warship in the area making a report and Vasiliy felt uncomfortable over lack of concern shown for the explosions. He thought, *Very unusual.*

Recognizing Sherensky among the departing officers, Vasiliy, said, "Good morning, Captain."

Sherensky replied, "Ah Vasiliy. Good morning to you. And what brings you here? I believed you would be with the others enjoying shore leave this last week in port."

"I thought the same of you, sir."

"Perhaps we two are the only worriers. This must be so. I don't even see our learned zampolit among this morning's assembly."

"Comrade Captain, do you believe our waters are clear of American submarines as Intelligence seems to think?"

"Frankly, no. But if they're present, it is in extremely low numbers. Insufficient to impact our current plan. It means simply we must be alert when we leave Vladivostok. It will be good training for us and peak our readiness before we reach station."

"Might it not be wise for *Victor* IIIs, or perhaps an *Akula,* to conduct a search of our home waters? Those wild men with their mine fields are ineffective and our *Tangos* no match for a 688."

Zhukov's captain changed the subject. "Vasiliy, your enquiring mind pleases me. I know this will accrue much benefit to us before this war is over. But caution ... our zampolit, shall we say, is no giant when it comes to wisdom, and you give him much cause to be alarmed. He considers ... well, he believes your father's defection counts against you. He looks for reasons to report you to the party, not because you are disloyal, but because it gives the impression that nothing escapes his scrutiny. These observations and subsequent reports strengthen his reputation ... if you follow my meaning."

The captain's comment about his father made Vasiliy furious, but he masked his feelings. No one hated his father more than he, but the Zampolit Poplavich held this over his head.

"I understand, Comrade Captain, and I thank you. I will exercise greater care."

Vasiliy sought revenge against those ultimately responsible for his continuous anger, the Americans. *Find and kill a 688.* He knew only those fortunate enough to find them before being found would harvest these fine ripe plums. The 688 peacetime exercises had shown this many times over.

Killing the first 688 delivers a crushing blow to fading American hopes. This attack submarine is vaunted as the finest warship in the world. *When it too falls to the Soviet juggernaut, all will be lost and the paper walls that protect my father will collapse.*

Vasiliy planned to play a major role in this Soviet victory.

Aboard *Denver*, the quartermaster reported to the conning officer, Dan Patrick, "Sounding two thousand fathoms."

This depth matched the charted one and verified their position sixty miles east of La Perouse Strait, the last narrow passage before reaching their target area. Once clear of the Strait and in the Sea of Japan, they again become the needle in a haystack. Noise from the minesweeper masked their passage through the waters where implanted Soviet listening systems searched for them.

Dan reported via the 21MC, "Wardroom, Conn, pass to the captain we've crossed the two thousand fathom curve, three hundred fifty miles to the hunting ground. Add to that, I don't think we need Ivan any longer."

Bostwick replied over the 21MC, "Captain, aye, Conn."

Brent, seated with the captain and the others in the wardroom for the evening meal, smiled. *Another Mad Maddock scheme has paid off.*

The captain instructed, "Dan, we'll wait till after dark and torch her. This'll give us the option of surfacing and doing the job manually if our remote doesn't work."

"Conn, aye, Captain," Dan replied. "For Mr. Maddock, it's warm and cozy in the Attack Center."

Brent's signal he had the next watch.

Bostwick's response, "He's right here and has the word."

The seas rolled gently under a solid overcast, hence spotting *Denver* from the air would be highly improbable, and she held at periscope depth. Noise from the chugging diesel powered minesweeper masked all sounds from *Denver* but did the same for other contacts in the area. Periodic periscope sweeps ensured their path clear of surface contacts.

Dan filled the high power optics with the hapless minesweeper. He thought of her grisly cargo of deceased Soviet crewmen. They had fought bravely, but the advantage of surprise permitted the *Denver* raiders to prevail. The Soviet crewmen had been laid to dignified rest in their bunks. Jack Olsen then read a short memorial service for the dead of both sides over the 1MC before *Denver* submerged.

How sad, Dan thought. *Hours before, alive and the hated enemy, but now harmless corpses. They deserved and got reverence from fellow human beings.*

"Down scope," Dan ordered.

The 21MC blurted a message, "Conn, Sonar, contact two-eight-zero, drawing right, closing, no ident."

"Surface or submerged, Sonar?"

"Can't tell. Never heard anything like this. Maybe a helo?"

"I'll check it. Up number two for a look around."

The quartermaster reported, "Two coming up," as the shaft hissed from the well.

"Put me on zero-nine-zero," Dan said. This bearing relative to the ships head coincided with the target's reported position. "Bearing, mark," then Dan yanked his head from beneath the yoke as the scope lowered. "Captain, Conn, helo inbound. Two-eight-zero true. Sonar, contact confirmed with visual."

Jack Olsen responded, "Captain's on the way, Conn."

Dan gave the order to the ordnance crew standing by in the radio shack. "Radio, Conn, prepare the charge for firing."

On his arrival, the captain demanded, "Chopper got us, Dan?"

"No, sir. He's heading straight for the minesweeper."

"Charge ready?"

"Checking, sir. No grounds as of thirty minutes ago."

"Fire the charge as soon as it's ready."

"Aye, sir, but if we wait till the chopper crew boards the sweep, we'll kill two birds with one stone."

Bostwick snapped, "Can the tactics shit, Dan. Just do as I say."

Jack Olsen had arrived and exerted his newly discovered leverage. "Dunno, Captain. Sounds like a good idea to me. We'll know if the copter goes into the ASW mode 'cause he'll have to dunk an active sonar and we'll hear that."

Bostwick hesitated. "Think so, Jack? Okay, let's give it a shot. I have the Conn. Give me a hand here, Dan. Up scope for a look at the helo," the captain ordered.

Dan demanded via the 21MC, "Bearing, Sonar."

A voice from the Sonar shack responded, "Three-zero-zero true, drawing right, Conn."

With the scope out of the well, Bostwick pressed his eye into the optic. "Put me on the bearing," he ordered.

Swinging the scope around, Dan called out the numbers when it reached the bearing. "One-one-zero relative!"

"Bearing, mark," Bostwick said then signaled to lower the scope. "Not doing any ASW. He's high-tailing it directly to the sweeper. Charges ready?"

Dan acknowledged they were ready for firing from the ordnance crew. "Checked and ready. No grounds, Captain. It ought to go."

"It better. We only get one chance."

"Another look, Captain?"

"Nothing to see. Have Sonar advise us when the helo bearings merge with the sweeper's."

By that time, Brent reached the Attack Center, he was elated to find Bostwick's on again, off again self-confidence restored. The captain was in control and performing superbly.

The sonarman reported, "Conn, Sonar, helo in the baffles, lost in the minesweeper noise."

"Conn, aye, Sonar," Dan said then asked, "Another look, Captain?"

Bostwick ordered, "Up two." He knelt at the well and pushed his eye against the lower optics as soon as they cleared. Dan snapped the handles into position and horsed the shaft to the Captain's ordered bearing.

An instant later, the captain signaled, "Dip scope."

The shaft stopped hissing when the upper optics submerged a few feet below the waves.

The captain briefed the Attack Center crew, "Chopper's circling the sweeper. Sea state is a low three but solid overcast with enough whitecaps to make us too hard to spot. I'll take look around a minute from now. Give me a mark, quartermaster."

The quartermaster replied, "Mark in a minute, Captain."

Brent noted how quickly the crew rallied to self-confidence shown by their leader. Bostwick again demonstrated when once committed, he performed well. The scope had been in the air less than a second, yet the captain had gleaned all he needed to generate a plan.

If only the captain could set aside his blind ambition to make flag rank, Brent thought, believing this to impede planning and most likely accounted for the rift between Bostwick and him.

Bostwick said, "I figure the helo will put a man aboard when they don't see anyone on deck. That's when we'll let 'em have it."

The quartermaster exclaimed, "Your sixty mark, Captain!"

The captain acknowledged the mark and said, "Okay, Dan. A three sixty in low power. We'll dip then do sixty-degree increments in high. Stagger the intervals and drop the scope in three seconds whether I'm done or not. Got all that?"

Dan replied, "Got it, Captain."

"Look around, up number two."

The scope hissed from the well, the captain at the eyepiece and rotating before the upper stops engaged. Snap went the handle signal and the scope quickly lowered.

With a steady voice the captain said, "Okay, Dan, up scope for the sixties. On the bow first, high power."

Dan stood on the opposite side of the scope, placed his left hand over the captain's right and rolled the optics to high power. "You're in high, Captain," he said.

Bostwick blurted the words most feared in the Attack Center. "Oh shit!" followed quickly by, "Dip scope!" He went on, "More company. Top hamper of several warships. Mark this bearing, quartermaster."

"How many?" Dan asked.

"At least three, Dan. Maybe more. Between ten and fifteen degrees off the bow moving northeast, I'd say. Fifteen thousand and beyond. Bad part is they're probably talking to the helo and he's gotta be pretty dumb not to suspect and report something. Okay, let's go back to the sweep. Up scope."

The huge shaft snapped again up into the stops, with the captain's eye in place. "Hot damn!" he exclaimed. "Fire the charge!" He left the scope up and waited.

Dan quickly ordered, "Radio, Conn, fire the charge!"

One, two, three passing seconds seemed like an eternity, then the rumble of an explosion shook *Denver's* hull.

Bostwick cried out, "Got 'em both, now let's go deep and get the hell out of here."

Dan offered, "Maybe we got 'em before the chopper contacted anybody, Captain."

The captain replied grimly, "And maybe we didn't."

Eric Danis had changed to his work khakis, ready to leave his plush quarters on the yacht, when a knock on the stateroom door interrupted his departure. "Come in," he said.

Dave Zane thrust in his head, a squint-eyed grin spread over his round face. "Best we could do on such short notice, Commodore."

"I need to know two things, Dave. One, am I going to have to put up with that commodore bullshit from you? And two, how much did it cost and how much trouble did you get me in with this damn yacht?"

No one could hold a grin as long as Dave Zane. "Commodore, I'll take 'em one at a time. One, just as long as I have to put up with this captain bullshit; and two, nothing. The owner's scared to death to take this thing to sea with a full-fledged war going on and nobody wants to buy it for the same reason. He's so damn happy to get out from under moorage payments. We got it for nothing."

Danis indulged himself a laugh. "You mean we're mooring it here and not charging him anything?"

"You can't expect me to think of everything. I'm an engineer, not a bean counter."

"Seriously, she's a beauty, Dave, and I thank you for it. But on the matter of titles, I'm afraid we got another one of our famous Mexican standoffs."

"Half a victory's not all that bad," Dave replied then changing the subject, "I'm sure you've got Eve in tow. How is she and where are you staying?"

"Thanks for asking, Dave. Eve's great. We moved into the thirty-second place since we got married. A small house in Grays Harbor. How she does it and maintains that steady attitude, I'll never know."

"Face it, Eric. You chose well. At least there's some good in all this. Maybe now I'll get you out to the *Digs*. And having Eve along is a bonus. Bea'll be glad to see her. They got a lot of catching up to do. I'd say at least eight years worth. This weekend, or whenever you can."

"I'll check with her. This weekend's likely a good time to give her a break from setting up."

"Good. That place of ours cries out for company."

"How do things go here, Dave? Gerry Carter tells me you're a magician. I hear you want to start fixing propulsion reduction gears. That'd be a helluva coup if you could pull it off."

"Need to bend a few rules."

Danis asked, "When did that ever stop you?"

"Glad to hear you say that. I've got a fix on some parts. Took the bull by the horns this morning and got them moving in this direction. We got no one who's ever done that before. But Carter's found a guy and I'm gonna talk to him this afternoon."

"Fine, Dave. Keep moving on this one. I won't second guess you, but keep me informed. I need to know what lies to tell when the higher ups start asking questions."

"You bet, Eric. But now tell me, what's happening to us? The whole damn country, I mean. Are we gonna win?"

He invited his old friend to be seated. "Dave, we got the age-old problem. Politicos got elected in peacetime. War changes everything and they don't know how to handle it. They can't grasp the notion that winning the war is more important than getting re-elected."

"Lucky we had Roosevelt. He could handle both sides of the coin. Coming into office at the onset of the Great Depression made him tough and inventive, tools he needed for dealing with the war. But are you saying there's a chance we'll put our tail between our legs?"

"Frankly, yes. It's not at all like the last one. Back then wide oceans kept the bad guys far enough away for us to train men and crank out equipment. We had no complex manufacturing or training issues. Not so today. Ocean widths are no longer a factor. Everything's harder and takes more time. And we can't replace losses in a few months like we did after Pearl Harbor.

"Our biggest job right now is to signal the government that we can come back. We need a big victory, like Midway. Submarines are all we got left so it'll be with them or nothing. Otherwise, a growing faction in Washington sees merit in knuckling under … and there are a lot of influential writers pushing this."

"You know, Eric, I figured that might be the case. Damn it, the issue's no different than what we had during the American Revolution. A lot of people saw the easier road of giving up, but thank God, enough troops with spine forced the issue. Sure, it'd be easier to fold to the Reds, like the candy-ass peace crowd touts with their intellectual bullshit. The same group that bitched so much about the Gulag Archipelago detentions will end up there if they win and Soviet history repeats itself."

"Simply put, Dave, we need a hell of a victory. The Soviets know this and will avoid a showdown."

"Maybe they'll do something dumb."

"So far, we have the monopoly on that. The Soviets are not fools. They know what makes pabulum for our special interest groups and play the *Simon-pure* logic of their intentions through our own media. And it's damn effective."

"Hopefully, we got enough hard-asses left that won't sit still for that."

"I hope you're right, Dave. President Dempsey's no FDR, but he appears to be his own man. He got the job as a compromise candidate in the last election, but the war snapped some backbone into him. He's trying to rid himself of bureaucratic deadwood. We gotta give him something to cheer about before the next election or he'll get dumped."

"In that case, you better put this on and get your commodore butt out there and find out what goes on in this here submarine fixing operation," said Dave as he handed his friend a freshly painted white hard hat with a naval officer's device on the front over the letters, COMSUBRON 3. "This'll give 'em plenty of warning you're comin'."

"Thanks, Dave," said Danis setting the hat on his head at a jaunty angle. "Now let's go have a look at Zane's *Pitstop*."

Brent completed his post watch check of the ship and stopped in the wardroom to play a tape and have a cup of coffee. He found Dan Patrick there listening to the sound track of *Dirty Dancing*, a Brent favorite. It surprised Brent because Dan had the reputation of being *Denver's* number one sack rat. He planned to hear a classic, a part of his continuing effort to cultivate a taste for it, one of Bea's passions. So far, he'd warmed up only to Rachmaninoff's Symphony Number Two because part of it sounded like Barry Manilow's, *All By Myself.*

Smiling at his friend, Brent said, "Wonder of wonders. The Patrick machine's alive, well, functioning after midnight and before breakfast. I'll call the quartermaster and have him log this historic event."

Dan grinned as the tape rendered *Hungry Eyes.* "Shush, no talking in church. Damn that tune turns me on. Did you watch Patrick Swayze and Jennifer Grey do this scene in the movie? Or had you fallen asleep by then?"

"Missed the flick. We're divided up into *doers* and *watchers*. I fall into the former category."

"Maybe so, Brent, but in my book, just watching them is enough doing for me. Anything new on the watch?"

"No. We're barreling ass toward the op-area. The engineers did a great job on the patch. No indication on the noise level monitor all the way to full speed. It sure is a relief to be back in deepwater. We need it for acoustic advantage if we expect to find anybody and I sure as hell hope that's why we came out here."

"Ah, mad … mad is the warrior. Pardon me if I reject this opportunity and continue to indulge in prewar decadence."

Brent wondered, *Is Dan right? Am I really so wrapped around the tactics axle I can't do anything else?* Brent tried to make conversation by asking, "What do you plan to do when it's over, Dan? The war, I mean."

"Guess that depends on who wins."

"Us, of course. If we don't, what the hell does it matter anyway?"

"See how easy it is to fish you in, Brent. Why don't you back off a fathom or two? Maybe some problems would go away if you opened up a bit. But first, let me answer your question. I really don't know. I've given the Navy a fair shot but really don't think it's my bag. The law has appeal and maybe politics. How about you?"

"Looks like it will be something other than the Navy. The pasting I'll get from Bostwick will put those lights out."

Dan used a comforting tone knowing how much Brent loved the Navy. "Might not be all that bad. Maybe Bostwick's all bark and no bite. The patrol's been successful enough for the Captain to blow his horn. To complete the picture, he's gotta drag us along with him. I hear Woody's nominated for a Navy Cross."

Brent asked, "What about the others?"

"Silver Stars for Henri and Barnes and Bronze Stars for the others, including posthumous awards for the casualties. Can't believe anything short of a Silver for you with all you've done." Dan did not believe this but felt it would sit well with his friend. "The Navy means a great deal to you, doesn't it, Brent?"

"I owe it just about everything."

Dan responded with a question. "No big family shoes in need of filling?"

"Not really. My father died ten years ago."

"What did he do?"

"Worked."

Dan had long noticed Brent's reluctance to talk about himself. "I don't mean to pry, but it's sure hard to get anything out of you. We've known each other for two and half years and I don't even know where you grew up. You oughta let me in on what matters to you. Example. You come down here every night to learn about classical music, but never ask any of us about it. Woody's damn near an authority on the subject. He'd be happy if you'd ask him."

"I don't know about all that." Brent remained silent a moment then finding the situation awkward; he groped for the right words. "But your friendship is very important to me, Dan, especially right now."

"I won't push it, Brent. You're a big boy. Maybe a little softening up might help your case with the Old Man."

Brent looked at his friend and spoke sincerely, "Thanks, buddy."

Dave Zane looked up from his desk and out the window of his shack-turned-office. He caught the forms of Gerry Carter and another man climbing aboard the barge that supported the repair facility offices.

Must be the new man to lead the Newport reduction gear repair effort.

Carter and the newcomer entered the office.

Gerry said, "Dave Zane, meet Darby Cameron."

Chapter 12

Eric Danis thought, *He sure is a teacher,* during his interview with Commander Jim Buchanan, USN, the new prospective commander of *Denver*. He had initially discovered Buchanan's knack for building student confidence by reading records of his past assignments at the United States Navy Submarine School. Danis hoped the command change would restore the morale of *Denver's* officers, who he believed to chafe under Captain Bostwick's bit.

Danis asked, "I'm trying to recall. Did our paths ever cross?"

The new man spoke with a trace of New England twang. "They did, Commodore, though I'd be surprised if you remembered me. You were exec on board the tender in Holy Loch in seventy-nine when I was on a Boomer. My first assignment out of sub school."

"Well, I'm sure if I thought about it, I'd fit you into some of the great memories I have of that wonderful place."

Jim Buchanan's face brightened as he remembered. "It is nice there. My wife met me after a patrol in the summer of eighty. We spent two weeks together and had a wonderful time."

"Eve and I loved it there too. We managed to get a few beautiful weekends in the West Highlands. It's easy to see why the Scots have such passion for their land."

"Sir, this is my first visit to the Pacific Northwest and it reminds me very much of Scotland. It's rustic and untamed by comparison to the rest of the country. Don't you think so, sir?"

"Now that you mention it, Jim, I do see the resemblance. But we have a ways to go to fully measure up."

Jim agreed, "Quite a way if we're to match the Scottish cost of living. But we do have a start, don't we, sir?"

"That we do, Jim, that we do." Then getting down to business, Eric continued, "You're getting a helluva fine ship with *Denver*. As you probably know, they're just out of overhaul and in pretty good shape. Only problem is they're in WestPac and not due back for a month."

"Well let's hope it's with a few scalps in her belt. We need some good news for a change. In the meantime, sir, I have no illusions about the future commanding officer bit. Please put me to work wherever there's a hole I can fill. I've been sitting on my duff at submarine school the past three years and I'm ready to put my hands back on some hardware, even if it's a knuckle-buster. You've worked a miracle out here and I want to be part of it. Just give me a steer and I'm off."

"I appreciate your attitude, Jim. I understand you taught in the Tactics Department at sub school. I'd like you to review our weapons overhaul setup and then give some thought to an ASW defense scheme we've worked up. Lieutenant Commander Dutch Meyer runs both operations and can use the help."

Jim laughed then said, "Not the same Dutch Meyer from Holy Loch. That turkey was a lieutenant when I first showed up as a JG. He ran my ass all over the tender. I probably needed it, but don't tell him that now that I rank him."

Danis said with mock caution, "Well don't be too hard on him."

"Nobody in the whole Navy could be tough on Dutch. It'll be a pleasure working with him again."

"Now, about quarters. I'm spending my evenings at home ashore and you're welcome to these."

Jim smiled, showing his appreciation for the offer. Quite tempting, but an established custom of the service is that generous offers by high-ranking officers are expected, but always politely declined.

"I'm afraid I might get too used to this. Thank you, sir, but I'll find a place to stash the bones."

"Well then," Danis replied, "Welcome to the *Pitstop*. It's good to have you here."

"It's damn good to be here, sir."

At battle stations aboard USS *Denver*, Captain Bostwick ordered, "Give me the course for a thirty degree lead," as they closed upon the first big game of the patrol, an *Alfa* class submarine.

Brent thought, *Damn it. The typical attack trainer solution. When the hell will Bostwick realize this is not a drill to be graded by the*

Squadron Commander and cited in his next fitness report? This is war and for all the marbles. "Recommend point the target with no lead, Captain. He's too close to worry about torpedo run. This'll reduce his chance of hearing us and we can shoot into his baffles."

Captain Bostwick did not respond immediately, but after a moment, he ordered, "Rudder amidships, steady."

The helmsman responded with, "Amidships, steady two-three-five, Captain."

Bostwick gave progressive rudder orders which kept *Denver*'s bow in a tight point on the target as it rumbled by to the West, not more than a mile away.

Brent thought, *Those arrogant bastards. They're making fifteen knots and more noise than a sea bag full of broken dishes.* He learned during earlier surveillance operations they could be much quieter at those speeds. *Maybe it exceeds the Alfa Soviet comprehension that a U.S. submarine could reach this position undetected.*

"Tubes one and two fully ready, Captain," reported Brent. "Presets entered and matched," having already advised the skipper but believed he needed a subtle reminder.

"Want to be sure he's beyond enable range before we shoot."

The executive officer said, "Target speed fifteen, Captain. That's 500 yards every sixty seconds."

Even the XO wants to shoot now, Brent thought. *This guy can accelerate and go fast, maybe more than fifty knots. Wait too long and an ADCAP will have a helluva time catching up.*

A minute went by. Two minutes. Brent could stand it no more. "Recommend shoot, Captain."

The captain continued with Attack Teacher doctrine. "Match bearings and shoot."

Brent reasoned, *With the target twenty-five hundred yards away, matching bearings takes valuable time and adds nothing to success probability.* He disregarded Bostwick's command and quickly ordered, "Fire one!"

The ACC operator activated the launch key.

Sonar reported, "ADCAP running on the bearing and masking target, Conn."

The captain asked, "Doppler enable in?"

Brent replied, "In sir. We have wire continuity."

Denver continued to communicate with the weapon as it sped toward the target. The display on the MK 81 console presented a chart of the attack area in miniature. It included *Denver*'s, the target's and the torpedo's positions, continuously upgraded. All eyes, except the ever-wary Brent's, focused on the console. He scanned other visual indicators in the Attack Center, particularly those transmitted from sonar.

First, it appeared as a flicker, a transient in submarine jargon on the Acoustic Intercept Receiver display. The second flicker damn sure wasn't a transient and the third one confirmed it.

The calm sound of Brent's voice did not reflect the churning in the pit of his stomach as he announced, "Inbound torpedo in the water, not ours."

Fear on Bostwick's face and in his voice, he asked, "Where?"

"No bearing, Captain," then Brent ordered, "Ahead flank, left full rudder. Torpedo's gotta be coming from the target. There it is on the AIR, sir. I'm launching a countermeasure. Torpedo Room, flood and release ETC (Electronic Torpedo Countermeasure)."

A minute after Brent's assessment Sonar's report came. "Inbound torpedo, Conn, bearing three-five-five."

Brent advised, "Captain, we've gotta go deep enough to suppress cavitation at evasion speed. About a hundred above test will do it."

Bostwick repeated the order to Chief Cunningham who quickly executed it. *Denver*'s hull nudged downward and rolled slightly away from the turn as the ship accelerated to maximum speed.

The Torpedo Room watch reported, "ETC away."

Brent had taken charge even though not on watch and ordered the helmsman, "Steady two-seven-zero."

This angered Bostwick, but fear kept him from overruling his young nemesis.

The helmsman's voice cracked slightly, showing an edge of fear as he repeated, "Two-seven-zero, aye," and not alone among the crew, grateful knowing that Mr. Maddock had taken the reins.

Brent demanded, "Bearing to the inbound."

Sonar responded, "Zero-zero-five."

Forcing a relief sound into his voice, Brent said, "We're gaining bearing on it. It hears the ETC and is heading that way."

Bostwick finally spoke. "Classification on the unit, Sonar."

"We're working it, sir."

Brent wanted to know the target's maneuver and how it avoided the ADCAP. Noise from the inbound torpedo masked the *Alfa* and made it impossible to assess the tactical situation. The Soviet weapon grew closer and the *ping-ping-ping* of its active search could now be heard. Stern faces stared at the AIR display. Abruptly, the interval between pings shortened.

Dan Patrick exclaimed, "Oh shit! It's acquired us!"

With an emphatic tone, Brent declared, "No! Too far away. It acquired the ETC and attacking there."

Bostwick demanded, "You sure?"

Brent thought, *What the hell difference does it make if I'm wrong? We're dead if it gets us and there's nothing we can do about it anyway.* Brent considered this a good time to let Bostwick resume charge and save some face. *Get him involved.* "Captain, recommend ride the cavitation curve to one fifty feet, sir. We've got a strong thermal layer at two hundred. Suggest we put it between us and the weapon."

The captain ordered, "Make your depth at one-five-zero, chief. Ahead two thirds."

"Need a bearing to the target and our ADCAP when we can get it, Captain. Should be around zero-one-five."

This time, Bostwick did not respond.

The Sonar operator announced, "Best make on the unit is an ET-80 A. Getting fainter."

All in the Attack Center breathed a sigh of relief. Perspiration soaked the backs of patrol shirts and glistened on each brow.

The captain came back with, "Conn, aye, Sonar. Do you still hold the *Alfa* and our weapon? Should be somewhere to the northwest."

Sonar replied, "Standby, Conn." Twenty seconds passed. "I hear the unit, but no target."

The captain acknowledged Sonar's report.

Chief Cunningham reported, "One fifty and holding, Captain."

"Good," said Bostwick. "We'll stay at battle stations while we sneak the hell out of here."

He did not intend to look further for the *Alfa*.

Later, Dan and Brent discussed the incident privately.

Dan asked, "What do you figure happened, Brent? I thought we had the bastard cold. How do you think he found us?"

"He heard our torpedo. He certainly didn't hear us when he went by his closest point of approach and we were in his baffles when we heard his fish. He used the inbound torpedo as an aim point 'cause he knew it came from us."

"But how did he get so quiet? The exec and captain figure we've been led down a primrose path here. The Soviets knew we conducted peacetime surveillance and likely used noise augmenters to cover up how quiet they really can be. Now the war's started, they turn 'em off."

"I don't believe that. Low frequency lines from Soviet boats have always been strongest and augmenters can't reach down that far. It defies the laws of physics."

"Then how do you account for their disappearing like they did? To outrun the ADCAP they should have made enough noise to hear them all the way back in San Diego."

"I don't know what they did, Dan. Somehow, they dodged our Sunday punch. It's gonna be a long war if we can't figure out how they did it."

Dave Zane greeted his new prospective employee. "Have a seat, Mr. Cameron."

"I'm more used to Darby … if that's okay."

Dave sensed the newcomer's apprehension and set about relieving it. "That'll be fine, Darby. I'm told you know something about main propulsion reduction gears."

While sitting down, Darby nodded and said, "I've replaced a few in my time, but I'll need to do some reading up. Do you have anyone else with experience or do you want me to train the workforce and run the operation?"

"You've keyed onto a major piece of the problem. We lost the documentation at Bremerton. Can you take a stab at it?"

Darby whistled softly. "I can, but it'll be reaching way back. Do you have the parts?"

"They're on the way. We're breaking a few rules, but then I guess the Soviets are too."

Darby said, "Damn nukes didn't invent bearings or the Babbitt metal they're made of. Hell, I've replaced a lot of bearings on Jimmy and Fairbanks Morse engines. We can get Babbitt to melt down from diesel locomotives that aren't running now because they're the same engines used on our diesel boats. We'll disconnect *Newport's* reduction gears from the main engines so they can be jacked while steaming and then I'll build and install the bearings. We'll cull out enough guys from the ones you got here to help work on it. You know we'll be breaking some rules for doing this without certified people, but what other choice have we got?"

Dave noted Darby's memory remained sharp and felt the working details would be equally so. "We know that. Our boss, Commodore Danis, says he'll bend everything short of risking major damage to the refit facility."

"That's a pretty broad latitude," Darby said.

"Danis has a pretty broad charter."

Darby would have liked it better if he had the reference manuals so he asked, "Did you try to get documentation from someplace else?"

Knowing the importance of Darby having some sort of check on his memory, Dave answered, "We're trying, but all our leads end up in situations similar to Bremerton's. Maybe some troops in *Newport* are experienced enough to help you out."

"Good idea, Captain Zane. I'll take anything I can get."

Dave winced at the title but hadn't made peace with Eric, so he let it pass.

Continuing, Darby added, "Submariners are known to squirrel away a lot of stuff so I'm sure we'll find some goodies in *Newport*."

"When did you last work on reduction gears?"

"About five years ago. An opportunity for promotion came up in the weapons inspection area and I've been there ever since."

"Well, Darby. You're the only game in town so the job is yours if you want it."

"Thanks," Darby said then his tone grew somber, "but there's more and I don't want to start off by blindsiding you."

"What's that?"

Darby related the problem with *Denver*'s eject pump and the action by the Civil Service Board dismissing him. He remained quiet after his story and looked at Dave through a grave expression.

Dave reflected a moment then said, "Darby, there's no question you did wrong and that won't be tolerated here. However, you impress me as one who appreciates the importance of this work and will perform it in a conscientious manner. All of us have had our letdowns. Probably the difference between you and the rest of us is that you got caught. I suspect the experience will work to my advantage because it'll make you more cautious. I'm willing to take the chance. The job's yours if you want it."

"What about Commodore Danis and the submariners? I'm told they won't let me back aboard their ships again."

"Manning this outfit is my responsibility and I'm sure Danis won't second-guess me. Now for openers, let's you and me walk down to *Newport* and get our arms around that repair plan. It's going to be a bitch."

The two men stood. Darby Cameron smiled for the first time since the near sinking of *Denver*. They shook hands and walked out into the makeshift facility.

Dutch Meyer explained the plan to build an ASW defense system with bottom-mounted hydrophones to Jim Buchanan. Gerry Carter sat in on the meeting in the Weapons Repair Office.

Beginning the meeting, Dutch said, "We have already planted a hydrophone and the test results look pretty good. Using a calibrated noise source, we start at the hydrophone then move away from it till we lose the signal. This set of curves shows we covered all approaches against the best they've got down to four knots. Below that speed we generate a few gaps, but our overall detect, localize and classify probabilities are above eighty percent for all targets."

Jim liked the mustang's concept and voiced his enthusiasm and support.

Dutch continued, "Weapon placement is the big problem. We don't have enough resources to keep a plane on station twenty-four seven. We'd need too many ships to cover the entire area and they'd make enough noise to mask the targets. They'd actually provide a beacon for anyone trying to locate the *Pitstop*."

Jim said, "You've solved half the classic problem, Dutch. Quieter they get, the more hydrophones we need. Spreading them over the defending areas is doable. Trouble is we only get a peek at the target and he's gone before we can get a weapon on him. What's realistic in terms of aircraft support, Gerry?"

Gerry answered, "I've checked out the runways and facilities at Hoquiam. The footprint's okay for S3A Vikings and we can support three of them there."

"How soon can we be up and running?"

"A month, give or take. I've got a fix on some reserve troops in the area that are in pretty good shape. We have the birds. Fortunately, somebody stashed some surplus 3A's at Phoenix, Arizona and they're ours for the taking. Couple of rubs though."

Jim asked, "What's that?"

"Fuel is the biggest one. We're damn short of it and Air Force requirements for the European Theater sucks it down like it's going out of style. We've got no petroleum coming in from the sea and mainland American resources are not up to it."

Dutch asked, "What's the other?"

Gerry explained, "We'd need seven hundred and twenty hours a month to give you full coverage. With three planes, we can provide about half that. If we had the fuel, of course, which is simply not the case."

Jim inquired, "What's your Viking's top speed with a pair of MK-50 torpedoes aboard?"

"A little better than mach point eight five."

Jim asked, "How long after alert at the field can you hit that?"

"Five minutes, give or take, depending on the weather."

The three bent over an area chart that Dutch had prepared showing the hydrophone locations, along with Hoquiam airport.

Making some fast calculations, Jim stepped off the critical distances with a pair of dividers then said, "No way. We've got to think of something else. Back at the sub school, we'd brainstorm a problem like this as a Prospective Commanding Officer class project. A lot of good ideas came up and occasionally a solution. Maybe we can try that?"

Dutch answered, "Sure. We'll take a shot at anything."

Looking up from the chart, Gerry said, "This might be a stupid question, but a check of Jane's shows this guy can lob an SS-N-21 to sixteen hundred nautical miles. Isn't that outside the hydrophones?"

Jim knew weapons systems and responded to Gerry. "That's true, but those long-ranges are for nukes. He'll need conventional weapons against the *Pitstop*. His only chance is to come in close to launch them. Shooting conventional 21s outside the hydrophones will diminish his accuracy and improve our chances to detect and destroy the inbounds. He's gotta launch from inside our phone array if he expects to do any good and he knows that."

Dutch asked, "What do you know about Sealance, Commander?"

Jim wanted to invite the mustang to drop the title, but on the verge of command, he couldn't afford to damage that certain mystique so essential to the job. "I've got a fairly good idea. It's designed as a submarine launched weapon and can boost an MK-50 torpedo out a far piece."

"That's right, sir."

Jim added, "But you have to know target location, course and speed if you expect to do any good with it."

"My array does all that," said Dutch. "I got to wondering whether we could anchor a barge within range of the hydrophones with a couple of ready Sealances on it. That would cut the time from initial contact to weapon on target down to almost zero."

Jim liked the idea and said, "You'll have an alignment problem. It can't be maintained with the barge swinging back and forth in a seaway. I like part of your idea, though. But why not cluster the missiles on a platform and set them on the bottom?"

Dutch shook his head skeptical of the question's validity. "On the bottom?"

"Why not?" Jim asked. "They're designed to fly from a watertight composite capsule launched by an SSN. The materials don't interact with seawater so you could leave 'em there indefinitely. Make the platform good and heavy so it'll sit still then index guidance systems to north with gyro monitoring of earth rate. That'll solve the alignment problem."

Dutch exclaimed, "Damn! Sounds wild as hell, but right off the top, I can't see anything wrong with it."

Jim went on, "No wilder than putting them on barges. They'll be invisible to satellite surveillance and improve the chances of surprising the hell out of any Soviet submarine that pokes his nose in here."

Gerry asked, "Reds still operate their satellites?"

"We never touched them. And we still got ours too."

Dutch cautioned, "It's later than we think then. They must know about this place by now and we can expect them to come after it."

Gerry asked, "You want me to put a hold on the Viking operation?"

Jim replied, "No. Our little deal might not work and even if it does, we'll need S3A's for follow-on attacks. One MK-50 is not likely to damage an *Akula* enough to stop him from launching his 21s. We can vector your birds on top and rub a hell of a lot of salt in his wounds. The initial damage will make him noisy and easier to track."

"Could you vector us on top of the target?"

"No," Jim replied, "but if you drop an explosive charge, we'd hear it and vector you from there. Will that work?"

"Like a charm," said Gerry.

"Good," replied Jim, nodding. Then he said to Dutch, "It sounds to me like we better get moving."

Gerry added, "Yeah, we better do that before some government analyst gets wind of it and proves it can't be done."

The captain's attitude toward Brent deteriorated at an accelerated rate. He considered the young officer as the genesis for all *Denver's* problems, Bostwick's problems, actually. With a short time to go as CO of *Denver,* he would likely emerge in excellent shape for flag rank, particularly if the patrol had any kind of success at all. Timing meant everything and with an American public hungering for good news, it would be perfect for Bostwick. But he regarded Maddock a liability to this goal, rather than the asset he truly was.

He admonished Brent by listening to his comments then didn't acknowledge him. He did this when convened in the wardroom to determine how the *Alfa* got away and nearly killed *Denver* in the process.

Bostwick opened the meeting. "I don't need to say how important it is for us to learn from what happened today. If the Soviets have developed a method to counter a 688 then the war could well be lost." He studied the face of each officer in turn to ensure the gravity of his message had set in then continued, "Dan has assembled all the tactical data recorded during the event. Dan?"

Dan Patrick discussed each data point in painstaking detail. He invited interruptions for clarifications and got many.

When Dan finished, the captain spoke again. "I suspect one or a combination of three things could have happened. One, the *Alfa* had an escort that detected and attacked us. Two, *Alfa* used a noise augmenter that he secured when he heard our torpedo. Concurrently, he fired back at us and then began to evade. The third would be a bona fide fluke. We just picked a bad time to shoot, maybe just as he slowed down to clear baffles. Thoughts, anyone?"

Brent considered his predicament but knew nothing he could say or do would damage his career any more than it already was. *So what the hell?* "I have problems with all three, Captain."

Tension filled the wardroom. Emotionally drained from the *Alfa* close call, none wanted another knockdown drag-out session between the Captain and Brent.

Continuing, Brent said, "Most of us have heard *Alfas* on surveillance missions. He's much quieter than this guy showed us today. An escort would have to go ahead in order to do the *Alfa* any good, and he would have to pass right by us. If he didn't hear us then, he sure wouldn't have with the *Alfa* in between.

The trouble with two is securing a noise augmenter does not affect an active acoustic torpedo at close range. With his target strength, our ADCAP should've seen him right after enable and that's the same problem with number three. He did something planned and it worked. We've got to think this through more carefully."

Brent did not raise his eyes to the captain, whose face had become flushed. Bostwick took a deep breath then spoke softly and with self-control, "Take charge of this meeting, Jack. Report to me what you conclude our plan should be," then he left the wardroom.

No one spoke for several moments.

Brent broke the silence. His stomach churned, but he knew the train had to be set back on the tracks. His voice cracked slightly as he said, "I think they know a lot more about our tactics than we give them credit for. For openers, how would we defend ourselves against a 688 if we knew her attack style? I think that's the direction we should take."

Dan added, "We need more data. We can't throw up our hands based on this tiny sample. We gotta figure out what to do next time."

"Shoot," Jack Olsen said. "Start the ball rolling."

"Attack with a bow aspect. It'll be completely different and give us more advantage. We're obviously quieter, 'cause he passed right by and never heard us."

Brent responded, "Think about what happened today. That tactic would have shortened his torpedo run, reduced the gyro angle, and because he wouldn't have to reach back into his baffles to find us, would've counter fired against our ADCAP much sooner. I don't think we'd be alive for this meeting had we used that tactic.

"Damn it ... guys, listen! This guy is not the submarine school attack trainer out here. If we screw up we're not just going to hear the voice of our friendly instructor saying 'Bang, gotcha,' over the 21MC."

He turned to Dan who ground his jaws and bowed his head in embarrassment. "Dan, I'm sorry. Maybe we let the pucker factor have too much control. I poke at your idea but have nothing better to offer. And I don't defend the tactics of this afternoon. They damn near got us killed but did permit us to escape. Let's not throw the baby out with the bath water."

Jack Olsen asked, "What's your suggestion, Brent?"

"I say we stay with the game plan for now, but pay more attention. Next time, have Sonar tape the whole thing and we'll analyze it from here to kingdom come. In the meantime, let's study the stuff Dan assembled for us. If anybody sees anything or even thinks he does, speak out."

Jack asked, "Further comments? Okay everybody, let's get some rest."

All rose to leave.

Jack stopped Brent. "Stick around. I'd like to talk a little."

Brent forced a smile. "Gee. I wonder whatever about?"

After the others left, Olsen said, "The hostility between you and the captain has reached the point where it can no longer be ignored. Letting it get out of control is dangerous for all of us. Because he is the captain, we owe him loyalty. I think you understand that and probably even practice it better than the rest."

Surprised to hear this, Brent did not interrupt.

"You understand tactics head and shoulders above anyone else in *Denver*. I think you also recognize the captain's ego has a tough time handling this. You don't rub his nose in it, but on the other hand, you don't let him make any mistakes. This patrol, whether he realizes it or not, assures fulfillment of his lifelong dream of making flag. The nation needs heroes and *Denver* will provide the first news worth cheering about. Your hand in the success of this mission has been pivotal. The captain might even recognize this, but I doubt he'll admit it. Keep doing more of the same, however, I want you to do one thing."

"What's that, Jack?"

"Be sure there are always some officers around when you give him advice. Me preferably, but anybody will do."

Brent scoffed, "The captain never talks to me directly so it'll have to be in a group."

"I've noticed, but just in case."

"You got it, boss."

"Brent, I know how much the Navy means to you and how all this must make you feel."

Brent thought, *Damn it! It's the last time I tell Dan anything.*

Jack went on, "Nothing in this life is certain, but I've gained a sort of stranglehold on the old man that puts me in a good position to ensure he doesn't hurt you. I give you my word, Brent, I'll pull that string as hard as I can and I have reason to believe I'll be successful."

A great load had been lifted from Brent's shoulders; he smiled and said, "Thanks a lot, Jack. Ya know, it's too damn bad the skipper chose the political route and not the tactical one. Once he settles in, he's damn good. His problem is he hasn't given it enough thought so he doesn't have the self-confidence. And he's too proud to take advice from us."

"Well, he took the political path and that's what we have to live with. At least until we get back and he's relieved. The situation is survivable for you, at least in my view. Just keep up the good work."

"I'll give it my best shot, Jack."

The executive officer left and Brent indulged himself a few quiet moments to enjoy his rejuvenated spirits. He searched through the box of cassettes and selected a Cleveland Symphony rendition of the Nutcracker. He did not understand the music, but it helped him to recall his first and penance date with Den Mother to thank her for rescuing him and his drunken cohorts.

The overture had barely finished when Woody Parnell hobbled into the wardroom for the first time since being wounded. "Hi, Brent."

"Hi, yourself, hero."

Recognizing the music, Woody exclaimed, "Ah ha! Peter Ilyich Tchaikovsky. Did you know he only wrote the ballet? The actual story is by E. T. A. Hoffman. Wanna hear all about it?"

Brent replied, "You bet your ass," and thought, *Dan absolutely gets no more from me.*

Chapter 13

Jim Buchanan thought, *It's sure good to be at sea again, even on a tugboat.* He stood on the tiny bridge of a yard craft converted to a cable layer by the resourceful Dutch Meyer. Slight of build, his face in its apparent perpetual pleasant expression, Jim's pale blue eyes squinted through the black rims of his navy issue glasses. Under normal circumstances, failing eyesight would have precluded his command tour but war changed that. Three years ago, he believed his career as a seagoing officer had ended.

A superb teacher, his value to the Navy continued in a different vein and the best and brightest among submariners benefited from Buchanan's able tutelage. His knowledge and passion for tactics combined did much to prepare embryo warriors for the grim days no one realized lay ahead. Although unplanned, Jim's path choice proved to be the exact medicine needed to mend his career. War generated a vital and immediate need for his expertise in the conflicts that now raged in the silent battleground.

Evening neared and golden sunrays brightened the final hours of a beautiful spring day off the Washington coast. Underway for nearly twenty-four hours, the snowcapped ridges of the Olympic Mountains had fallen below the eastern horizon.

Jim said, "Looking really good, Dutch. As long as we use the same Loran-C rates you planted the hydrophones with, we've got no worry about geographical position error. All we need is the location of the missiles relative to the phones."

Both men nursed hot cups of coffee. War shortages be damned, black coffee is the lifeblood of seaman; and sailors always find ways to get it.

Even the inscrutable Dutch Meyer found it difficult to contain his excitement over the impending test.

Jim said, "This oughta give you some empathy for women, Dutch. Now you know how they feel when they're about to give birth."

Dutch chuckled at the analogy. "That's new ground for me, Commander," he said then got back to the business at hand. "There's a crew ashore listening on the phones. They're marking our position hourly. I'll check for deltas when we get back and that should be the frosting on our cake."

A small barge astern on a bridled towrope yawed from side to side in the moderate seaway. Behind it, a cable paid out connecting it to the shore-based test equipment. A canvas tarpaulin covered its deadly cargo of four encapsulated Sealance missiles.

Jim asked, "How long to station?"

"About an hour and a half. It'll be totally dark. I'm glad as hell you thought about satellite surveillance. I'd never have covered the missiles. Think they saw me plant the hydrophones?"

"Maybe they did, but figured you were a fishing boat. From all appearances, both would look like the same thing and there are plenty of them out here."

Two hours later, Dutch and his small crew made final equipment adjustments on the barge. They communicated with flashing lights because radio transmissions were almost certain to be intercepted.

The quartermaster signalman reported, "Message from the barge, Commander, READY FOR TRANSMISSION CHECKS."

Jim replied, "Aye, send it."

Dutch Meyer ordered the shore-based test team over the trailed wire, "Spin 'em up and enter test coordinates."

The system reacted perfectly and Dutch reported to Jim, again via flashing light.

Jim exclaimed, "Damn! Absolutely no reason they won't do the same thing sitting on the bottom."

Returning to the bridge, Jim directed the quartermaster, "Send the following message, EXCELLENT. COMMENCE SINKING OPS, then said, "and add to it, AND GET YOUR FAT ASS BACK HERE."

The astounded youngster asked, "Really, sir?"

"Really, sailor." *Denver*'s prospective commanding officer had a good chuckle then went below for another well-deserved cup of coffee.

An hour later, the barge rested on the bottom armed with four tactical Sealance missiles at the ready. With target data provided by hydrophones on the seabed, they could place a deadly MK 50 Torpedo quickly upon an unsuspecting target. The tug and its elated occupants made its way back to the *Pitstop*.

Captain Sherensky squinted as the briefing officer pointed to a spot on the Washington coast. His aging eyes were troublesome, but he would not reveal this to the medical division until his tour as *Zhukov* commanding officer ended.

"Satellite surveillance shows naval activity here. Based on the amount of equipment being moved in, it is likely a refit facility. We shall permit the Americans some time to make substantial investment then knock it out with an SS-N-21 land attack missile. We will permit their hopes to build then dash them again. Several days ago, the Americans towed a disabled 688 class SSN, likely dragged from Bremerton yard on the eve of the war and hidden until our attack abated."

Immediately, thoughts came to Sherensky's mind. *Does not sound good. The Americans must have expected the attack and competent submariners took action. They are a force to be reckoned with. Better such thoughts not be spoken aloud in the presence of so many zampolit.*

The briefer's pointer indicated the position of Bremerton then he continued. "There may have been others as our satellite is unable to discern submarines among the rubble here. Perhaps they evacuated all of them. The one we have found appears without propulsion and it is not likely the cautious Americans will permit such extensive repairs at a temporary base."

More thoughts by the Soviet captain, *American writers make much of Soviet problems with submarine nuclear propulsion systems and conclude this an indication of poor combat readiness.* He did not consider the flawless American peacetime reactor safety record an intimidating factor in the current fight.

Vasiliy Baknov also sat in the audience, equally unnerved over the briefer continually finding no significance to new findings on the Americans. The Briefer apparently ignored the lessons of World War II. Admiral Yamamoto's prophecy given the day after Pearl Harbor,

'We have succeeded only in awakening a sleeping giant and filling him with a terrible resolve.' He thought, *Surely we will not let that happen again.*

Many questions ran through Vasiliy's mind. *Where were the surviving submarines? How did they know to leave? Had they cracked the most closely held secret in Soviet history and knew of the planned attacks? Also, why wait to hit the replacement bases? Surely, the Americans recognized the Soviet submarine land attack capability and prepared accordingly. Why not dispatch Zhukov to hit these bases before suitable defenses can be installed instead of diverting her attacks on dispersed merchant ships in the Southwest Pacific? How many days have passed since the Tango went missing? How do we explain her fate?*

Warned by his captain, Vasiliy would withhold his concerns lest the shortsighted zampolit interpret them as more evidence of his disloyalty to the Party.

The briefer continued, "Our submarines of the Northern Fleet have denied allies use of the Atlantic. Materials and personnel must be flown, thus draining resources of the United States Air Force. And the shipments fall well below the allies' needs. Our fighter-bombers further impede this effort and our superior numbers take their toll. The Americans are unable to replace losses without replenishing strategic materials by sea and they are not likely to recover this capability. Time is a comrade for our cause, but to exploit it, we must maintain control of the sea. Our submarines are pivotal in this endeavor.

"Put up the chart of the waters adjacent to Vladivostok.

"We have a visitor in the Sea of Japan. Intelligence concludes with high probability it is the USS *Denver*, a 688-class attack submarine, recently completed overhaul at Bremerton. Her tactical priorities are questionable. She torpedoed and sank a tiny *reydny traishchik* that cost much less than the ADCAP torpedo that took her to the bottom with ten of our brave comrades. Our *Alfa* class *Legeroff* reported an attack by a 688 near this position."

A spot-point flashed three hundred miles northeast of Vladivostok.

"The attack failed, thanks to a newly developed defensive tactic, the *Zhukov* Maneuver, named for the ship that originated it. A description is included in all your operational packets and is now tactical policy.

Familiarity with this maneuver is a required pre-condition to all future deployments."

Vasiliy's heart throbbed with excitement. His child, the *Zhukov* Maneuver had saved a Soviet submarine. *But what went wrong? It should also have resulted in the death of the 688.*

Later Sherensky discussed the briefing with his junior officer. On hearing of Vasiliy's concerns, the captain comforted his weapons officer. "Ah, Vasiliy. You wish to have everything at once. Be happy for enabling us to fend off the enemy. You have silenced a major impediment to our war plan. If we continue to nullify the cream of the American battle fleet, we're sure to win. Let's not draw hasty conclusions based on a single engagement. We'll continue to perfect the *ZM* and I shall ensure our learned zampolit knows of your hand in this important achievement."

Saving his comrades in *Legeroff* pleased Vasiliy, especially because two of her officers were personal friends, but he still felt deprived. He hungered for vengeance against an enemy he believed responsible for his and his mother's grief.

Later Vasiliy visited the security vault and paged through the intelligence brochure on *Denver*. *Zhukov* would sail in a few days and with luck would encounter this hapless 688. He found foreign names difficult to pronounce, Bostwick, Olsen, Patrick. *Ah, there he is, my counterpart. Lieutenant Brent Maddock, weapons systems officer. U.S. Naval Academy, 1982, submarine school, nuclear power school, previous service in a 637 class, married, one child,* Vasiliy read. The intelligence community had not yet recorded the divorce. *So here is my foe*, thought Vasiliy and said aloud, "I look forward to our meeting and providing you a peaceful sleep beneath the waves."

That evening, Vasiliy and his mother dined at a Vladivostok restaurant on the eve of *Zhukov's* deployment. Ekaterina looked well for a woman in her sixties. Years at the dance preserved for her the figure of a most attractive woman.

"I have an announcement, Vasiliy. I'll stay here at Vladivostok until your return. There is little for me in Kiev and summer will soon be upon us. Spring is lovely here and I plan to enjoy every second."

"This pleases me. You will stay in my apartment, of course."

"No, Vasiliy. I have taken a flat in the new building. You must permit an old woman her independence."

"If you say so, Mother. But if you change your mind, I'll leave a key."

At that moment, the waiter brought their drinks. They touched glasses and toasted with excellent vodka. In the Motherland, there is no other kind.

"To your success and good fortune, my son."

"And to yours, Mother."

"I've already had more than my share of success. And what need has an old woman for good fortune?"

He revisited his all consuming vendetta. "To repay you for the cruelty life has shown you because of my father's cowardly act."

"Vasiliy, you must learn to forget. Put the pain and anger behind us and make the best of our remaining days together. You smile so infrequently. Why is this? A mother's favorite gift is a smile from her handsome son."

"My life's a constant reminder of father's disdainful act. It follows me constantly, most lately in the attitude of comrade Commander Poplavich, our zampolit. He regards my father's defection as cause to question my loyalty to the Party."

"Pay him no mind. You do well in the Navy and I am proud. Now make me happy. Put this anger aside and enjoy your life. Find a good woman and give me a grandchild to dote over."

"War is not a proper time to bring children into the world. Perhaps when Capitalism is destroyed, the world will again be such a place."

"Ah, Vasiliy, you turn even pleasant thoughts into grist for your vendetta. Learn to forgive Yuri. He loved us but he is an artist. Art can be a cruel master."

He had never heard his mother speak her husband's name. Before, it had always been your father or my husband.

She continued, "He could not find artistic freedom here. You see some of this yourself, Vasiliy, in the actions of the zampolit. You have ideas about your profession but they are thwarted. Try to understand. If we continue to find cause to put off the important things in our life, we'll never get to them."

She reached across the table and pressed her son's hand.

Vasiliy did not agree but could not bring himself to deny his mother her tender moment. He blamed America for the misery she tried to hide, as well as for the plight of the downtrodden throughout the world. He intended to play a major role in hastening the defeat of his hated enemies.

"You have given me much to think on, Mother, and I shall," Vasiliy lied.

Eve Danis exclaimed, "Bea Zane! Ooh, your mother. You have so much of Dale it's like seeing her again."

Bea had driven to Hoquiam to gather up Eric's wife for a weekend at the *Digs*. They had not seen each other for over ten years so the women embraced warmly. Eve and the Zanes had been close friends when their husbands shared junior officer days.

"Mrs. Danis, it's great to see you again and looking so well."

"Please, Bea, call me Eve. Mrs. makes me feel so ancient, which I am, of course."

"If you're ancient," Bea hesitated then used the offered invitation, "Eve, I hope time flies by quickly, because I can't wait to look that good."

"A way with words … from your dad, no doubt. He was full of them. Never believed him but loved hearing what he had to say. When will I see him?"

"This evening. He's really excited about the weekend. Whenever Captain Danis comes to town, Dad tries to get him out to the *Digs* but it never works out. It took you to come along to make it happen."

"I'm pleased to be the culprit."

Bea changed the subject, "So, how do you like Hoquiam?"

"I really can't tell the difference between here and the other places I've lived. Just put our things around and from the inside, all houses look the same. So far I've only been out enough to hit a few grocery stores."

"You'll love Washington, especially in the spring. We get great weather and best of all, no food shortages at the *Digs*. We live on clams, fresh salmon, Dungeness crab and fresh veggies from the garden. Old Dad, the squirrel, has laid in a lifetime supply of vino.

There are enough empty cardboard wine boxes under the house to be a fire hazard."

Eve replied, "I'm so excited."

"Then let's be off. It's not all that far but the roads there are not the best."

They drove west out of town on state highway 109 that bent north along the coast ending at Ocean City State Park. The park, originally intended as a year-round 170-acre campsite, featured ocean beach, dunes and dense thickets of shore pine. Campers came to watch migratory birds and to comb the beaches. War changed it to a refugee camp. Makeshift shelters built by nuclear attack survivors marred a once idyllic site.

Refugee agencies provided food, medicine and other essentials. Early arrivals fabricated domiciles from many of the existing structures but tents and other shelters made from plastic sheets abounded throughout the makeshift camp.

Obvious burns and loss of hair by many of the survivors signaled they'd not likely survive. Their spirits, despite all that had happened, seemed high. The world's highest standard of living does not soften Americans to the point of being unable to adjust to disaster. For the third time in this century, they exhibited no intention of knuckling under to hostile attempts to control their world. Not a distant war in a strange land, but an offense to their own treasured quality of life and they would not tolerate it.

Continuing their conversation, Eve said, "It's dreadful to think of what these poor people have lost, but at least they have their lives. Material possessions can be replaced."

"Most of the workers who man the base live here. It's good that it's spring, especially for the children. Winters here can be cruel." Pointing off to the west, Bea continued, "The base is about five miles over that way."

They left the paved highway and drove onto a gravel road leading to the *Digs*.

"Well Bea, let's hope the boys get done with what they have to do so we see them at a decent time for dinner tonight. I'm so happy to be rescued. I can't stand to look at another packing box."

Bea replied, "The fate of a Navy wife. You become a moving specialist."

"On that subject, I hear there's a thing between you and Lieutenant Maddock on the *Denver*. Is that talkable?"

"It is. Brent's very nice and we see a lot of each other. That is when he's here. The *Denver* is out, you know."

"Oh there has to be more than that. You wouldn't deprive a snoopy old lady of grist for her mill?"

"Not a bit, Eve. It's more than just a passing thing. We do discuss the future. Nothing definite, mind you. No proposals or rings yet."

"Are you in love with him?"

"In love? Yes, I think so, but neither of us has mentioned it. Brent makes it obvious he cares for me. He's a good listener and very considerate. He took me to the Nutcracker on our first date ... his first ballet. A real chore for him but he toughed it out with not a single complaint."

"When I was a girl we called that sort keepers."

Bea said, "Maybe that's the problem. Brent's too good to be true."

"That's a problem?" Eve smiled.

"He was married but now divorced."

"Oh?"

"Brent wants stability. I get a sense he's ready for another marriage but needs to be certain it will succeed. Frankly, Eve, Brent is not an easy person to get to know. He sends signals but doesn't volunteer anything. It's easy to tell when you're into a sensitive area with him because that's when the simple yes and no answers start. There are problems too."

"Aren't there always? How dull life would be without them."

"I'm not sure Brent is totally out of love with his first wife. They have a son he adores. He didn't want the divorce."

"Has she remarried?"

"Yes, and here's the funny part. He likes her husband. It's as if he still feels responsible and wants to be sure she's well provided for. I don't know if I can really handle that."

"She's no threat, Bea. Apparently, she doesn't want him and has made another commitment. I suspect his ex-wife is only a perceived obligation. But show me a man who honors obligation and I'll show you a winner."

Bea seemed relieved to change the subject. "Well, here it is."

They turned off the gravel road and into *Digs'* rustic driveway. Mid-afternoon found the sun high in the western sky. The Pacific opened in a vast panorama of esthetic beauty, revealing nothing of the lethal and hostile devices concealed within her depths. The women were pleased with the prospect of what the weekend would bring and delighted they'd be together with Eric and Dave for the first time in many years. Both wondered how many more remained in the offing but neither confided this feeling to the other.

Lt. Vasiliy Baknov had the watch when the attack came. Sounds of an ADCAP torpedo racing toward *Zhukov* could be heard through the hull, striking terror into hearts of the crew but the men went about their business like the professionals they were.

Keeping his voice steady, Vasiliy ordered, "Open the muzzle door and fire," as he sounded the collision alarm, which quickly brought Captain Sherensky to the Attack Center and *Zhukov* to her highest state of watertight integrity.

Zhukov shuddered as the ET 80A ejected from its launcher and turned to the bearing of the inbound ADCAP.

Vasiliy had planned everything down to predicting time of the attack to within three hours of when it occurred. He had pre-positioned a torpedo in a flooded and pressurized launcher so he could counter-fire almost at the instant the michman detected an inbound torpedo. A rough pre-positioned gyro angle setting in the torpedo would direct the weapon toward the baffles, the general direction of attack correctly expected by Vasiliy.

The *Akula* had entered Vasiliy's Zhukov Maneuver by the time Sherensky arrived.

Vasily reported, "Inbound bearing changing rapidly, Captain, running up the starboard side. The maneuver is working. I'm certain it can't find us."

"Let us hope not. How long has our unit been running?"

"One minute, Captain. If the Americans play their usual game, we'll hear an explosion in two minutes, fifteen seconds."

Sherensky marveled at Vasiliy's composure. While the others held their breath, Vasiliy concerned himself only with the prospect of a kill. If successful, Vasiliy's quick shot would give *Zhukov* the margin they needed to evade the inbound. At minimum, it would put the attacker on the defensive and cause his evasive actions to sever the torpedo guide wire.

The michman reported, "Enemy weapon opening ahead."

Vasiliy gloated, "Ah, good. Now all that remains is to await the explosion of our torpedo." Certain *Denver* was the attacker; he tried to recall names of officers he'd read about in the intelligence directory. *So, Lieutenant Maddock, it appears we will not be adversaries much longer.* Vasiliy counted down the seconds, "Five, four, three, two, one—"

No explosion.

His frustration mounting, Vasiliy said, "Comrade Michman, search the target area and report."

The michman replied, relief clear in his voice, "A high noise level, steady bearing, growing fainter."

Vasiliy exclaimed, "Damn all! He's running for it. If he goes to maximum depth, our weapon won't catch him. He must have fired from a greater range than estimated. Comrade Captain, we need weapons with greater catch up margin if we expect to sink 688 class submarines. Let us go after him, Comrade Captain."

The captain held a decidedly different point of view. He grew up in a submarine force, a distant second to the Americans. Deployment of the 688 class in 1974 appeared an insurmountable gain by the west. But with help from the Walker spy ring and new propeller technology sold to them by allied countries, they produced equipment that brought them closer to the Americans.

A Voltaire quote hung on the wall of Admiral of the Fleet Sergey Georgyevich Gorshkov's office, "Better is the enemy of good enough."

The admiral lived by this. Therefore, Sherensky considered having made good his escape from a 688 to be good enough. "There is no need to sink him if he cannot hurt us. We evaded him easily."

Zampolit Poplavich berated Vasiliy, "Our mission, Lieutenant Baknov, is to forge into the Pacific and destroy the enemy's ability to replenish and rearm himself, not sink harmless submarines in the Sea of

Japan. Do you suggest we disobey our orders and risk this ship in combat against a unit that shows itself to be of no value to the enemy?"

Sherensky took a breath to answer but thought better of it. He had warned young Vasiliy about the seriousness of his situation with the vindictive zampolit. Vasiliy had either forgotten the warning or believed his advice would be taken in the context presented and not as lack of confidence in the Soviet system.

Vasiliy replied, "We cannot expect the Americans will remain baffled by our new tactic. It is only a question of time before they discern it. This 688 has been frustrated twice and gains new experience with each escape. We must prevent this tactic from returning to America for pass off to its other submariners."

The zampolit folded his arms stoically. "Do not bore me with your self-fancied wiser view of our mission than the one given us by our leaders. Simply answer my question."

Immediately, Vasiliy realized what he had done and attempted to make amends. "Forgive me, Comrade Zampolit. I fear I permitted the power of the moment to blind my better judgment."

"You would do wise to think well on those words."

The zampolit departed the Attack Center, walked directly to his tiny office, closed the door and unlocked his file cabinet. Withdrawing a folder marked Lieutenant Vasiliy Baknov, he opened it and made some handwritten entries.

Eric Danis said to his friend as they turned into the driveway of the *Digs,* "This place is gorgeous. Damn it, Dave, how come you've never had me out here before?"

Dave replied in a somber tone, "One more comment like that, sir, and it'll be no vino for you for the rest of the weekend."

The balmy weather of the spring afternoon yielded to a stiffening breeze from the southwest and skies became leaden in color. A mild surf showed the coast's wild beauty.

Eric greeted his wife Eve with a kiss. "Hi, Sweetheart. Hope you got everything done before you left."

Dave shook a finger at Danis. "Eric is really asking for it today, Eve. Don't know what we're going to do with him." He hugged her warmly. "Sure is great to see you again." Holding her at arm's length for a better look, he continued, "Glad somebody in the family managed to keep their good looks. You know, Eve, there's a lot of handsome and available guys around. Take me for example. Maybe you should give some thought to throwing the old man over."

Eve replied, "And lose all that good Navy retirement? Same old Dave Zane."

"Maybe you could find a rich one. From the looks of you, you could do a lot better than the old sea dog here."

Laughing, Eve said, "I'll think real hard on it, Dave. First, line up all the available candidates and have them wear net worth labels instead of nametags then I'll let you know."

After Bea and Eric exchanged greetings, he asked, "What about all that lovely weather you keep promising me, Bea? You lure me up here then damn near blow me away."

"That's because you blew all the other invitations, Captain Danis. The *Digs* has its own personality and maybe thinks you don't like it."

With a serious tone, Eric said, "Bea, now that I'm finally here, I sure regret the missed opportunities. It's truly gorgeous. I envy you and your dad. And about this captain nonsense ... only old codgers get called that by beautiful women."

Losing herself in an engulfing smile, Bea regained her composure. "Comments like that'll only get you the best dinner you ever had," she bragged.

Eric asked, "Bea, how about a glass of wine? Your dad says I'm cut off."

"From a bottle of our very best, saved specifically for this occasion. If Dad doesn't clean up his act, he gets one from the box. Cook's the only one who does the cutting off around here."

Dave wailed, "See, Eve. I'm always the one that gets picked on. Eric here puts up all the flak and I have to pay the dues. Now I ask you. Is that fair?"

Eve shook her head. "Tsk-tsk. Scapegoat's written all over you, Dave. But you look none the worse for the wear."

"Well if I at least look good, I can live with that."

Dave opened a bottle of vintage Chardonnay and the old friends toasted their reunion before a roaring fireplace.

Raising his glass, Dave said, "To friendship. May it remain endless and the walls of these *Digs* provide it an equally endless retreat."

Voices joined in the coziness of the rustic family room, "Hear! Hear!"

Outside the weather increased to a full-fledged Sou'wester.

The women excused themselves to attend the finishing details of dinner while the men settled in before the fire for another of their chats.

With the ladies gone, Dave said, "Eric, I know us old EDOs," referring to his Engineering Duty Only designator, "got no business knowing how the big war is going, but what can you tell me? A lot can be concluded from the lack of anything encouraging coming out of Washington."

"A pregnant observation, Dave. Lack of even a little fabricated good news is unnerving."

"Anyone back there think surrender's a viable option?"

"There are folks who'd answer yes to Patrick Henry's question, 'Is peace so dear and life so sweet it is to be purchased at the price of chains?' And you know the damn special interest groups control the country."

Dave added, "And the irony is politicians need the majority to get elected. What's wrong with this picture? Is anybody doing well for us? Besides the Armed Forces, I mean."

"Right now, it's an Army-Air Force show. Apparently, they got things checked in Europe. Not sure how long they can hold out. Everything has to be flown in and the Soviets don't have that problem. Wasn't it Sherman who said 'More beats better every time'?"

"You got me, Eric … you're the history buff. So what about tactical nuclear weapons? They in the picture?"

"Not really. The Soviets want to be sure there's something left if they prevail. They don't want to win an empty bag. If TacNucs do come into use, it won't be limited to Europe. Their land attack cruise missiles would make things damn tough. The SS-N-21 has long legs and can be submarine-launched off our coasts. We'd shoot down some of them but not enough to make a difference. Both sides are holding their breath 'cause TacNucs run up the chance of escalation. Neither wants that, particularly the Soviets."

Dave said, "Well it's not very damn likely we'd be first to use them. How about our new buddies, the Chinese? They like the Soviets about as much as we do."

"Not much help there either, Dave. Look for China to ride the fence and jump in on the winning side when that becomes apparent."

"Looks grim, doesn't it?"

Eric thought for a second. "If we don't regain control of the sea, we've had it. Despite the great job we're getting from the Army and Air Force, we need the ocean to cart in and deliver the stuff required to win the land war."

"So Eric, you think our submarines are doing any good?"

"We won't know that till they start rolling back from patrol. And the jury's still out on whether we can support them adequately with *Pitstop* operations."

"Submarines are our only real hope for regaining sea control. Can they do it?"

"If we can knock off enough Soviet front-line nuke submarines, I think maybe we can. But it's got to be their new stuff, not the old dogs and cats you and I used to chase around. If we can pin them back to first and second-generation equipment the job's doable. With 637s, 688s, and patrol aircraft, we ought to be able to secure enough water to move the stuff we need. If we could get the bastards to meet us in a big showdown, we might pull it off. But they're too smart for that. They're winning; they know it, so why should they change anything?"

"They'll have to invade to get us to knuckle under completely."

"Yeah, Dave. They can take their own sweet time about it and consolidate the rest of their holdings worldwide while they cut us off from what we need to mount opposition. Then they can strike at their leisure."

"You might be right, Eric. Damn it, you're probably right. We'll just keep doing what we're doing and count on you warrior types to figure something out."

"President Dempsey comes across stronger than he did during the election. But he's got a lot of influential defeatists to fend off in addition to the lack of any good news we're unable to provide."

Dave exclaimed, "Damn! Now that makes me mad. When I think of those people we saw along the road on the way up here. They're not quitting and they've got a helluva lot less to cheer about than Dempsey's wimps. These people deserve better than that."

"Don't prejudge Dempsey. He might surprise us if we can give him some indication we can win. If we can't, then his decision boils down simply to how many lives we lose before he cries 'Uncle'."

The phone rang as a gust of wind rattled the windows so hard they seemed on the verge of shattering. Bea picked it up and after a short exchange with the caller, summoned Eric. "It's the base. Commander Carter."

"Evening, Gerry. What's up?"

"Bad news, Commodore. Waves are coming over the breakwater and breaking the base anchor chains. Not sure how much longer we can keep it off the rocks."

Chapter 14

Brent and Dan Patrick met with Jack Olsen in the Wardroom to determine how the Soviets evaded the *Denver* attacks. Convening such meetings is a command responsibility, but Bostwick avoided it. Olsen then had to initiate the session, though it made him uncomfortable to do so. Additionally, Bostwick had confided to Olsen his concern over their inability to unscramble the mystery and that it justified aborting the land attack against Vladivostok. The captain argued the attack failures signaled a fatal vulnerability leaving *Denver* with no capability against threat submarines. Sharing this with Brent and Dan would have the effect of dumping fuel on the captain's fire so Olsen remained silent on the subject.

Their brainstorm session carried well into its second hour and nerves had grown ragged when Brent used a tone that annoyed Dan. "Whatever they're doing is simple. Plain as the nose on our faces but we're not seeing it."

"You and your thoughts, Brent. I've got a bellyful of both. Damn it! We've been turned back six times. Let's face it. These guys know far more than we give 'em credit for."

Jack Olsen spoke with a tone that signaled the two lieutenants to contain their emotions. "That's exactly why we gotta figure it out. So let's use our energy for that instead of bickering."

Shrugging off Dan's put-down, Brent said, "Not only figure it out but bring the answer home with us to spread it around. You're right, XO. We need to get cracking and time is running out."

Brent broached the Bostwick-Olsen issue over the land attack in his next comment. "We're now down to two ADCAPs. We oughta hoard these for self-defense on the trip home. I suggest we move the land attack up and get out of here a few days early."

Both pair of eyes turned toward the executive officer as he said, "A good thought, Brent, have you worked up the target package?"

They didn't need a target package. SUBPAC's directions required none. Brent knew Olsen wished to exclude the land attack from the meeting agenda and correctly sensed the reason: the captain's reluctance to pull *Denver's* trigger against Vladivostok.

"A few more items on strike timing should do it, XO. I'll have it for you in two hours."

"Good, Brent. Now back to the subject at hand."

Both Olsen and Patrick knew Brent had the best grasp on tactics so they yielded the lead to him. "I believe we have plenty of data from our busted pick operations. Each time a target was well within range it has evaded our torpedoes. I've arranged all the shots into this matrix." He unrolled a large piece of plotting paper onto the table. "The most significant is Doppler but we eliminated that with our one-two combination, first Doppler in and then out. And we've worked both sides of the layer."

Dan asked, "What about countermeasures?"

"Can't eliminate them so they remain a possibility. Sonar recorder data for all shots showed nothing. They shoot back immediately, likely to make us evade. Bottom line, nothing definitive. Maybe they've got a countermeasure we don't know about."

"Why do you think that?"

"Not a lot to go on but what little we have shows our torpedoes continue beyond where we think the target is but don't attack anything."

Jack asked, "Something wrong with our torpedoes, maybe?"

"Possible, but contradicted by the *Tango* success."

Dan suggested, "He was coming toward us. The rest were going away. Could that be it?"

"I don't think so, Dan," said Brent. "The only difference is the Doppler. The weapon shouldn't care whether it's up or down just as long as it's there. But right now, we gotta consider everything. That answer leaves us trouble. Shooting only bowshots oversimplifies his counterattack problems. Our second attack, you remember, the *Akula* came closer to cooking our bacon than I like to think. If we were on his bow when he shot, there's no doubt we'd be history. We do know he makes initial detection on the noise from our torpedo."

Olsen exclaimed, "Damn it! We make the quietest submarine and the noisiest torpedoes."

"Next time we're in town, mention that to Den Mother's dad, Dave Zane. He oughta be good for two hours on the subject."

"Okay, wizards," said Olsen. "Keep the big think on it. We'll meet again in the morning."

The two left and Jack braced himself for the next meeting with Bostwick. Subject: Move up the Vladivostok strike.

Eric Danis and Dave Zane covered the final mile of their abruptly initiated journey on foot through a newly carved trail built to facilitate bringing power lines to the *Pitstop*.

Dave berated himself. "How could I be so dumb? Worst storms are out of the southwest and I missed the anchor points completely."

Strong southwest wind pressured the chains one at a time, depriving them of collective holding power. However, sufficiently stout all together, one alone couldn't carry the entire load, therefore the anchor chains broke one by one like pulling open a zipper.

Eric took everything in his customary matter-of-fact stride. He knew Dave had done a great job just getting the project moving. He also knew omissions would reveal themselves and be corrected as they emerged. Irony here, the first storm threatened to destroy the entire operation. This would seriously, if not fatally, delay turning around submarines desperately needed for the war effort. Eric had learned over the years that frustration did not help, hence wasted no time on it. But this obstacle challenged his emotional control to a new high.

Upon reaching the beach, they discovered the pounding surf had severed telephone lines and communications with the *Pitstop*. The heavy seas also prevented reaching the facility by small boat.

"Damn!" Eric cursed and for the first time seeming to vent wrath upon his old friend, "Didn't anyone consider a simple walkie-talkie backup radio?"

Dave made no reply.

Eric continued, "I've got a wounded birdman in charge out there who's never commanded anything bigger than a ten-foot rowboat ... and I can't even talk to him."

"He's got seamen out there with him, Eric. Gerry knows how to get the right advice. Count on him."

"What other choice do I have?"

Despite the breakwater, waves broke over the barges and soaked Navy men and civilians working side by side, in what appeared a losing fight to save the *Pitstop*. Both reserve anchors had been dropped at the anticipated pressure points. But they'd see no strain until the next anchor chain parted so the domino effect continued. The problem could be delayed but not resolved.

One of the two available tugboats had a towrope wrapped about its propeller and couldn't move. Even both tugs working in tandem would not provide sufficient power to hold the barges in place.

Gerry Carter asked of Jim Buchanan, Phil Reynolds and Dutch Meyer, "Okay experts, what the hell do we do now?"

The inventive Jim Buchanan had no suggestions. "We shoulda used the tug to drag the anchors out till the chains strained before we dropped them."

With growing impatience in his voice, Gerry said, "Shouldas don't help. Where does this leave us?"

Nothing came forth from the three submariners.

Time was running out so Gerry scrambled for a solution. "Phil," he asked, "that ... what did you call that thing on *Newport* ... the outboard?"

"Secondary propulsion system."

Gerry's irritation began to show. "Yeah. Well whatever the hell it is, can it move your ship against this wind?"

Phil answered, "Yes, sir, it can. But it can't hold something the size of this base against the storm."

The confidence in Gerry's voice did not reflect his true feelings. "It won't have to. That sewer pipe of yours is gonna perform its most important job since they built it. It's about to become a thirty-six hundred ton anchor."

Puzzled, Phil asked, "What are you talking about?"

"This. Make up all the bitter ends of the broken anchor chains to the *Newport*. Fire up your outboard and haul them into the wind till they're as taut as you can get them. Then submerge and sit on the bottom."

The idea struck Reynolds like a kick in the solar plexus. Less than two weeks ago, he had ended a miserable six-week stint on the bottom of Puget Sound and had no wish to enact another similar demand upon his crew.

Phil snapped back, "I want to discuss this with the commodore first."

"You just did," Gerry said. "Captain Danis is not here and that makes me the commodore. Get moving or in another thirty minutes this base and that goddamn derelict of yours is gonna be scrap iron on those rocks over there."

Grateful that darkness hid the grin on his face, Jim thought, *Damn! These aviators are made of the right stuff.* He placed a hand on the shoulder of the stammering submarine commander. "Come on, Phil. Let's get moving."

Making up the anchor chains to *Newport* sapped the remaining stamina of the men struggling to save the *Pitstop*. The job finished, Commander Reynolds ordered the mooring lines slipped to save time when normally, they would have been taken in and stowed. *Newport* moved slowly into the teeth of the storm. The nest of barges, a scant hundred and fifty yards from the rocks and bearing down on them, the final anchor chain snapped, quickly finishing the job of tightening the anchor chains to *Newport*. Buchanan and Reynolds stood on *Newport's* bridge and immediately recognized the situation.

Buchanan shouted above the storm, "Okay, Phil, let's do it!"

Reynolds pulled the diving alarm and the two dropped below decks and secured the bridge access hatch. Popping ballast tank vents roared above the wind and *Newport* settled to the bottom. Momentary banging and grinding rumbled through the hull as the monstrous submarine rolled ten degrees in the direction of the storm then held.

Ordering the number one periscope raised, Reynolds scanned the *Pitstop* then yelled out, "Yahoo! She's holding."

Back on the *Pitstop*, Dutch Meyer took Gerry Carter's hand and gave it a hearty shake. "Congratulations, Gerry. We got an even strain on all the chains. We're home free."

The fatigued aviator turned submarine squadron Chief Staff Officer gasped, "Damn! You guys really do earn your submarine pay. But seriously, Dutch, what the hell will I tell Danis when he gets back and finds *Newport* on the bottom?"

Dutch had a witty comeback for everything. "All you need to say is 'Good morning, sir. How do you like having the most expensive anchor ever built?' Danis will like that. Being first is important to him."

Dutch Meyer and Jim Buchanan had earlier discussed a test plan to demonstrate their new concept: detect an intruder with the sonar array, attack it with a Sealance missile launched from the seabed and finish the job by vectoring S3A aircraft over the damaged target to drop MK 46 Torpedoes. They would move quickly, but carefully, one step at a time and today focused on getting a missile onto a simulated target noise source.

Meyer would take one of his improvised cable layers to sea and suspend a noise source in the vicinity of the hydrophones planted to monitor the sea approaches to the *Pitstop*. He'd then record his position using the Loran-C.

Jim Buchanan remained ashore to monitor hydrophones from the blockhouse, a hastily constructed cover for the acoustic recorders and weapon control panels.

He exclaimed to the hydrophone operator, a sonarman borrowed from *Newport*. "There it is!"

The operator said, "Got it, sir." The youngster read off target coordinates and Jim recorded them.

As the numbers appeared at the precise position where Dutch had been dispatched, Jim thought, *Good.* He then had the operator double-check the reading. "Doesn't look right, sailor," he fibbed, "Try it again. Reset the display."

The second reading identical to the first one assured Jim the array could pinpoint a noise source. Now they had to demonstrate a Sealance payload could be dropped on the target vicinity.

Jim activated one of the four missiles atop the sunken barge many miles at sea. The guidance system responded. He then set in the target coordinates and had a fire control technician; also commandeered from *Newport*, verify them.

After validating the numbers, both on a scratch pad where he had written them and on the array display itself, Jim said, "Checks." He then ordered the fire control technician, "Verify presets."

The youngster replied, "Read-backs correct, sir."

"Give me the numbers. I want to be sure."

The operator re-verified them.

Jim ordered, "Fire one!"

The operator depressed the firing key. A *Missile Away* light came on in response to the preset wire being broken when the missile floated free from the barge and began its buoyant ascent toward the ocean surface.

Radio silence had been imposed, again for security reasons; hence, Jim would wait for Dutch to return with the full results. The monitor would show the running torpedo sounds blended with the sound source if all went well.

Buchanan and Dutch had joked about the peacetime amenities for safety, once ironclad but now dispensed because of wartime urgency. The Federal Aviation Administration would not be notified and the missile had no provisions for command destruction in the event it miscued and headed in the wrong direction.

Dutch complained, "Now, what will I do if it hits us, Jim?"

"Cheer," said the ever-flippant Buchanan. "If it does, we'll have succeeded beyond our wildest dreams."

"Look closely," Dutch warned. "It should be coming in any time now."

He would know within a few seconds when the Sealance MK-50 Torpedo payload impacted in his area. He had six pairs of eyes in binoculars, each scanning sixty-degree segments of the horizon.

The men searched diligently then heard the most terrifying words to be spoken during a naval operation. "Oh shit!"

Someone yelled from the flying bridge. The entire crew hit the deck, each making his own separate thud but combining into a single loud one. An explosive *CUSH* preceded the crew being doused with seawater as the Sealance payload knifed into the water a scant twenty-five yards astern.

Dutch thought, *Missed us but think I'll cheer anyway.*

He raced to the passive monitoring equipment, turned up the speaker and monitored the display. The MK-50 ran into its search pattern. Abruptly the pitch increased as the torpedo made passive detection on the noise source and shifted to high speed to attack the target.

The weapon continued re-attacking until its endurance expended and then sank. Later came the sound of an explosion as the weapon struck bottom and detonated.

Dutch quipped, "Even the warhead works."

Ashore, cheers erupted in the blockhouse where positions of the exploding warhead blended perfectly with the noise source.

Next day, data sets collected afloat and ashore melded to show the 'Meyer-Buchanan one-two punch' would provide a lethal welcome to any submarine approaching the *Pitstop* with hostile intentions.

The time had come. Jack Olsen took a deep breath and knocked on the captain's stateroom door.

Bostwick grumbled, "C'min."

Stepping inside, Olsen replied, "Afternoon, Captain."

"Yeah, Jack. What's up?"

"Got the plan for the land strike, sir. We need to move it up a few days. We're down to two ADCAPs and ought to get out of here before they're used up. There's no reason for us to hang around."

Bostwick spoke as though he'd give the matter some thought and already discussed it with his executive officer, but in reality, he hadn't. "Damn it! Jack, I already told you we're not doing this."

A fragment of the captain's ability to intimidate him remained so Jack set his jaw and stood firm. "We have to, sir."

"We have to die and pay taxes. And frankly, I'm not sure about the latter."

"Here's the plan, sir."

The captain snapped, "How much longer do you expect me to put up with this mutinous bullshit?"

"It's not mutinous, Captain. It's our orders. We have no cause for failing to carry them out. And our country needs the good news."

Bostwick resisted, "We won't make it out of here to give it to 'em if we conduct that strike."

"I disagree, Captain. We've been shot at six times and always evaded. Only thing that can reach us quick enough after the launch is an aircraft. Their air dropped CP-45s are useless against a 688."

"You've been talking to Maddock. That son of a bitch thinks he knows everything. He's got it in for me and he uses you to pull my chain."

Jack's voice remained steady and firm. "He doesn't, Captain. He feels you're a very capable officer. He considers his recommendations to be the best expression of his loyalty. He's sorry you misconstrue—"

"Damn it, Jack! Knock off the bullshit? You know Maddock hates my guts and nothing would make him happier than to see me go under."

"I know nothing of the kind, Captain, but that's not the issue here. We've got to decide about the land attack."

"What the hell option do I have? If I don't go along, I'm stuck with the threats you've laid on me about what happens when we get back."

"Put it in any terms you like, sir. Anything I'd say back home is invalid if you've got sound logic behind your position. I'm the one at risk if you do."

"Okay, you bastard let me see the damn attack plan. But remember and you pass this along to that arrogant running mate of yours. The Navy lasts a long time and if we survive this, I'll be well positioned enough to make you both damn sorry."

The last of the new anchors hit the sandy bottom, this time arranged to hold things in place against the next Sou'wester. Eric Danis had assembled Dave Zane, Phil Reynolds, Dutch Meyer, Darby Cameron and several *Newport* engineer officers for a final run through of the *Newport's* reduction gear repair plan. Gerry Carter and Jim Buchanan, Danis's advisors-at-large, rounded out the group.

Commodore Danis began, "Gentlemen, your time is too valuable to be wasted in meetings just to keep me informed so we'll make this brief. However, I want to take the opportunity to express how pleased and impressed I am with Gerry's inventive and decisive action during the big blow. It saved our bacon or at least prevented a disastrous set back of six months or more.

"Congratulations, Gerry. I want you to hold school on these guys to see if you can load them up with that kind of initiative."

All laughed.

Jim Buchanan said, "You've got your work cut out for you, Gerry. Submariners fit into the spectrum somewhere between Louis XIV and Attila the Hun. Some pretty hard heads to crack."

The men laughed again.

Danis added, "And while we're giving out kudos, the 'Meyer-Buchanan one-two punch' is a show stopper. I want a tight report to pass off to the other refit sites. Make it crisp, hard and no windows for some damn vested agency to poke a stick through."

Jim smiled at his boss and said, "Yes, sir."

Turning to his weapons officer, Danis asked, "Dutch. How are the Sealance reloads coming?"

"Four more rounds on station and eight ready as soon as the crew gets back with them."

"I don't want to know how he did it but Dave Zane got *Newport's* new reduction gear."

Dave replied, "Commodore, are you saying I'm devious?"

Not fully recovered from the bad feeling brought on by his error on the initial anchoring plan Dave had self-medicated with humor.

Danis asked, "How else could we have gotten this place set up?" signaling no intention to wallow in what might have happened. He went on, "Mr. Cameron has the experience needed to fix *Newport's* main bearings. You've all met him so let's drop formalities and get on with it. Darby?"

Standing before the very men that Brent Maddock once declared would not permit him ever again to work on submarines, Darby Cameron set up a homemade easel with briefing sheets attached. War has a way of neutralizing such pronouncements. He opened with a plan view of the *Pitstop* with marked locations for positioning *Newport*, the crane and the bearings.

A little nervous at first, Darby quickly settled down. "Here's the materials flow. The locations are spotted within the crane's reach, *Newport* and the repair parts."

He covered a myriad of details including moving parts from the dock to the ship, installing them, the procedures for meeting stringent precision requirements, testing the work and the closing up process then finished with, "Our watchword when in doubt will be STOP. It's gotta be right the first time through because we won't get a second chance." He added the customary, "Questions, gentlemen?"

Danis asked, "None? Very well then, let's get on with it. Dave, stick around will you?"

All the others rose and left.

After pouring each a cup of coffee Danis said, "With all the hustle and bustle of getting this thing up and going, Dave, it occurs to me I–" Eric grasped for the right expression, "I just don't show you enough appreciation. I depend on you for everything. This whole damn operation couldn't be pulled off without you. Two other facilities on this coast are at least two months behind us and started before we did. None of these would even dream of attempting this repair.

"You came up with the materials and know-how to put *Newport* back together. How you did it will always be a mystery to me. You've got her within two weeks of being able to deploy. Maybe I expect you to just sense my appreciation. That's wrong and I want to set the record straight."

Dave turned and looked out to sea through a porthole in Eric's palatial accommodations. He blinked hard and absorbed a tear that threatened to fill his eye.

"Eric," he said, "between you and me, I think we're going to win this damn war."

Captain Bostwick, back in his Jekyll role, took absolute charge of the situation. It amazed Jack Olsen how the morale of his troops rose and fell with the skipper's moods. If he lived to be a hundred, Olsen believed he'd never fully comprehend the psychology of leadership.

He stood before a 1MC microphone and addressed his crew, "This is the Captain speaking. I'm proud of how you've prepared *Denver* to deliver this first American strike against the enemy. We'll hit the

Vladivostok Naval Facility, home of the submarines that have hurt our cause the most. We attack and then return home to rearm for more and greater strikes. I expect all to give their usual outstanding performance. God bless, good luck and man your battle stations."

A cheer erupted from the troops as they proceeded to their posts.

Brent took his position behind the Attack Control Console. He had reprogrammed the combat system to load target coordinates into the twelve land attack Tomahawk missiles in the vertical launchers.

Captain Bostwick said with confidence, "Okay, we'll shoot above the layer then duck below to evade counterattack."

This wasn't Brent's choice of tactic. He thought, *It's exactly what the opposition expects.* He'd have remained above the layer believing aircraft dropped torpedoes would be likely set to run below it. Brent deduced in any case, the best Soviet air dropped device fell well below the 688-performance envelope. He wisely chose not to reveal this and detract from the captain's moment.

The captain ordered, "Make your depth six-two feet, smartly," and then, "Make ready twelve TLAMs. Flood and open the muzzle doors."

"Six-two smartly," Chief Cunningham responded followed by Brent's acknowledgement of the TLAM orders.

After raising the number two periscope the captain took a look around. The closeness of the landmass unnerved him. He observed darkened ridges on the horizon and discerned a clear light pattern that outlined the port. At 0300 Vladivostok time human activity would be at its lowest, a big factor in both hammering the enemy and making good an escape.

He commanded, "Report when TLAMs fully ready."

Brent responded, "Aye, sir. Eight preset and matched. Expect the rest in four minutes, Captain."

Bostwick ordered number one periscope raised to conduct an electronics countermeasure search.

The ECM console operator reported, "Many shore-based and surface ship radars, Captain. No ASW aircraft."

What jackasses, Bostwick thought. *With all our recent local exchanges, you'd think someone on the staff would know we're in the area. They must know we've got land attack missiles. Are they truly that arrogant or just plain stupid?*

With a crisp tone, Brent replied, "Twelve birds ready, Captain," showing a lack of any emotion, accumulated from the long and arduous training sessions he had conducted.

Captain Bostwick's voice also betrayed no emotion. "Fire missiles in sequence, one through twelve."

Denver rumbled and shuddered as missiles departed her vertical launchers. In short order, the last bird had departed and the launchers secured.

Brent reported, "Twelve away, Captain. Recommend we haul buns, sir."

Bostwick wasted no time. "Right full rudder, all ahead full."

The helmsman acknowledged.

"COB, take us all the way down."

Cunningham replied, "All the way, aye, Captain," and then to the helmsman, "Fifteen down on the angle."

Denver responded eagerly to her first directions to embark on the initial leg of the homeward bound trek. The crew sensed this and their spirits soared.

How anti-climatic, Brent thought. The attack began and ended quickly and left no sense of having engaged the enemy. *Denver* crewmen saw or heard nothing. Weeks would pass before they'd know how well the attack succeeded, if at all. Maybe a satellite scan would provide a quick look.

Brent knew twelve conventional warheads would do only minor damage to Vladivostok's extensive Naval facility. However, its effect on Soviet national morale could be substantial. During WWII, the Doolittle raid inflicted only minor damage to Tokyo but seriously impacted morale of the Japanese populace.

Above the surface, twelve missiles roared into the sky with a great show of smoke and flame. This fireworks-like display ended abruptly. Rocket boosters burned out as air breathing missile sustainers took over and drove the weapons below the radar horizon to cruise altitude. Here they spread out and raced toward various landfalls where radar altimeters would plot ground contours and match it to profiles stored in the missiles' Tercom computers. Most went in the direction of the submarine refit facility, two sped toward ammunition bunkers, one to the suspected location of the Flotilla Headquarters and the last missile headed toward a Navy antenna farm on the far side of the city.

A Soviet radar operator detected the initial launch but quickly lost contact when the missiles dropped to cruise altitude for short and quick deliveries of their payloads onto their designated targets. *Denver* had been well positioned for the attack. Close to shore, the shortened runs deprived Soviets of reaction time needed to mount adequate defenses.

Ironically, the first warhead struck Flotilla Headquarters, taking the life of the intelligence briefer who had failed to properly identify and assess the threat posed by *Denver*. He misread the intelligence data and numbered her among the 688s not equipped with vertical launchers. Consequently, he did not anticipate a land attack. One hundred fifty officers and men died in the Flotilla Headquarters.

The surprise attack raised havoc on the waterfront where personnel comprised the major casualties. An *Alfa* and three *Tango* submarines fell victim to the assault. Two Tomahawk warheads detonated among the ammunition bunkers. They failed to penetrate any walls; thus, no sympathetic explosions among the stored explosives.

Damage inflicted upon the facilities would be quickly repaired.

Ekaterina Baknov slept in her modest condominium. Since the conversation with her son on the eve of *Zhukov's* departure, she thought often of the joyous days with her husband in the months following Vasiliy's birth. She recalled the last time they danced Adam Adolphe's *Giselle* at the Kirov. *How high he had lifted her and how much love they felt.* These happy thoughts accompanied her as she drifted off to sleep three hours before the attack.

The high-rise apartment, erected just weeks after the missile tracks had been laid out from landfall to the antenna farm, had not been taken into account. If the building had been five feet shorter, the Tomahawk missile would have over flown it. It wasn't. The hastily constructed structure collapsed when the missile struck it dead on and snuffed out the life of Ekaterina Baknov and the other occupants.

Chapter 15

Eric Danis had been there and done that enough times to make it harder to explain to Captain Tim Hopper, the *Pitstop* wasn't prepared yet to fill his requests, repairs beyond the means of ship's force, clothing, mail, and most importantly, salad, the first commodity to expire after leaving port. Last salad served to Hopper's crew had been sixty days ago.

Danis said, "I wish I had better news, Captain."

Captain Hopper, the Commanding Officer of the Trident submarine USS *Idaho*, The latest arrival at the *Pitstop* after eighty days submerged in the emptiness of the Pacific Ocean, said, "Thank you, Commodore. We've had time to accept the probability that most of our families did not survive the attack on Bangor. But still, it's overwhelming. Getting back brings it all up again but we'll deal with it, sir."

Almost at a loss for words, Danis forced a smile, nodded and said, "Captain, I don't envy you your job right now."

Hopper attempted to put Danis at ease. "I guess it's not the best time to ask for groceries but we are a little low. Right now, anything but dry stores would be like Thanksgiving for us."

"That we can handle. The food supply around here is great. I'll have Commander Carter get right on it."

"What are chances of getting my troops ashore, sir? I know this operation is anchored out and your hands are full. But my guys have been a long time at sea."

"Of course we can. Forgive me for not thinking of that." For an instant, Eric's many happy homecomings flashed through his mind and he knew the *Idaho* crew could not find what they hoped for, however, Danis thought even a little change of atmosphere might help. "We've got eight to ten boats a day running between here and Hoquiam. I wouldn't exactly call it the big apple of the West Coast but I think your troops will find it lively enough."

Hopper asked with reservation, "I guess there's no chance of replacements?"

"No, Tim. My orders are to turn you around and get you out of here in a week. Hopefully, we'll scrape up a relief crew and call you back later. But for now, tea and sympathy is the best we can do."

"I understand, Commodore," said Captain Hopper as he rose to leave then extended his hand.

Danis took it warmly and said, "Congratulations to you and your crew on an outstanding patrol, Captain."

"Thank you, sir. I'll pass it along to them."

After Captain Hopper left, Danis summoned Gerry Carter. "What can we do for these guys, Gerry? They're really down. Eighty days sealed up in that overgrown sewer pipe and then going out for eighty more after a week ashore. That's damn near inhuman. Hopper's the first officer I ever spoke to that I couldn't look in the eye."

"Commodore, you can't do anything for them."

For the first time the laid-back Eric Danis raised his voice to the chief staff officer. "What the hell do you mean, Gerry?"

Gerry responded quietly. "I mean exactly that, sir. We're in a war now and it makes a personal hell for everyone. There are no more carriers so I won't get to do what I trained for all my adult life. Young Reynolds is damn lucky to get a command back and wouldn't have if it weren't for you and Zane.

"Commodore, at the risk of sounding like the script from a grade-B war flick, you can't take on the personal problems of everyone that comes in here. You'll be overwhelmed. You got too damn many problems of your own. Trust me, sir. These guys are big boys and can take care of themselves. War makes 'em grow up fast."

Eric Danis smiled and doing his best impression of James Cagney playing Captain Flag in the World War I film, *What Price Glory* said, "Why am I so hard on 'em? Because I love 'em, that's why."

Both men laughed.

"You got it, Commodore."

Finally up and about, Woody Parnell spent a lot of time in the Attack Center learning the duties of a conning officer. A strong youngster, his wounds healed quickly and he took on light duty, mostly learning details of running a conning watch. He enjoyed the new hero status resulting from his minesweeper action and basked in the awe of younger crewmen.

Life aboard an attack submarine in the forward areas has only moments of excitement; the rest is passed waiting for something to happen. Consequently, many of the off watch crew hung out in the Attack Center. If anything happened, it broke there.

Gary Hansen also spent much of his off watch time there to gain a better understanding of how the boat drivers used the information he sent them from Sonar. This helped improve his personal efficiency at his end of the 21MC.

Sounding a bit like a complaint the young petty officer said, "Here it is mid-May and the baseball season's six weeks old. And we don't know a thing. Wonder how the Twins are making out?"

The helmsman asked, "Are they even having a baseball season with war 'n everything?"

Woody muscled his way into the conversation. "Sure they are. Didn't stop 'em during the last one."

Another troop volunteered, "But that wasn't a nuclear war, Mr. Parnell."

"Well neither is this one," Woody said. "At least not anymore."

Hansen expressed his wish for a bit of major league baseball news. "I, for one, would sure like to get the ball scores once in a while. Twins made some good trades over the winter and oughta be doing pretty good. And I got a high school buddy supposed to move up from the farms this spring."

Woody offered, "Hansen, I can get the scores."

"You can, sir? How do we do that halfway on the other side of the world?"

With a matter-of-fact voice Woody said, "SATACBAK BRAVO, that's how."

Hansen shook his head. "Never heard of that, Mr. Parnell."

"It's a radio term, Hansen, Satellite Tactical Backup, Bravo. Never gets used because it's a backup circuit. They have to test it, though, so they'll send almost anything. Sports scores mostly, 'cause it helps morale."

"Why don't we get 'em, sir?"

The rest of the watch troops in the Attack Center also expressed interest with enthusiastic anticipation.

Woody shook his head. "Can't. SATACBAK B is a surface ship system. But maybe with the right parts, I could modify one of our receivers to copy it."

Hansen exclaimed, "You could, Mr. Parnell? What do you need? They might be in our spare parts bin."

"Yeah, Hansen. Actually, it wouldn't take much, resistors and capacitors mostly. I'll make you a list."

Within a day, Woody had the list. The enterprising Hansen found everything except one component among the sonar spares. Hansen made his way from stem to stern, trying to trace down a resistor with unusual power tolerances and finally found it in the communications' electricians bin. It cost him two Penthouse Magazine back editions, fair exchange in his view for getting the ball scores.

With great pride and anticipation Hansen delivered the resistor to Woody.

"Hey, that's all right, Hansen," Woody said as he received the part. "Shows how green I am to think we didn't have this kind of stuff aboard, otherwise, I would have set this up a long time ago. Now understand, nobody else can be in the radio shack while I work on this. Crypto stuff in there, you know, only officers and radiomen allowed."

The delighted Hansen replied, "Yes, sir, understand perfectly. When do you think we'll get some scores?"

Woody furrowed his brow and muttered, "Mmm," then said, "today is Thursday. By Monday, I should be able to summarize the weekend in the majors. With a little luck, might even have the standings."

"That's great, Mr. Parnell. This is the absolute most."

"Like to do what I can, Hansen. Make sure all the guys know that."

"I'll tell 'em, sir. I surely will."

Word spread throughout *Denver* like wildfire. On Monday, they would have a summary of the weekend ball scores and maybe standings and records of all major league teams. Spreadsheets developed and pools initiated among the *Denver* gambling set. During the morning watch on Monday, a grim-faced radioman walked from the shack and posted a sign.

A summary of the weekend baseball scores will be posted on the radio shack door at 1500, compliments of Ensign Parnell.

Ignoring a myriad of questions, the radioman re-entered the cipher-lock door. At 1500, a group of some thirty enlisted crowded into the area immediately adjacent to the radio shack. The same radioman emerged and again, without saying a word, posted a replacement sign.

Scores announcement delayed until 1800. Reason: Failure to take Daylight Savings Time into account and movement into a new time zone to the east.

This elated Gary Hansen, as he'd be off-watch at that time. At 1800, he and fifty sailors struggled for the limited space available. A few of the more serious gamblers stood to win enough to buy a new car when they returned to port.

Again, the stern-faced radioman emerged. He removed the old sign and with dramatic flair, he unfurled and posted a new one.

Weekend ball scores: four to three, one to nothing after fourteen innings, eight to seven, and here's a real blowout, seventeen to four. The rest are fairly average: four to three, three to two and seven to five and so forth. All that's needed to get team names and current standings is to douse this sign with a bucket of steam. –Ensign Parnell.

The crowd quickly diminished as each read the bottom line. Among the last, Lieutenant Commander Jack Olsen turned away only to be confronted by the grinning Parnell.

With a laugh in his voice, Woody said, "C'mon, Exec, not the old baseball score gag? Old hat even before Farragut joined the Navy."

A series of five 1MC clicks interrupted the ball score gaggle, the new signal established to quietly call all personnel to Battle Stations and the crew scurried off to assigned posts.

Captain Bostwick made the customary demand when he reached the Attack Center. "What've we got?"

With Brent on the watch, Bostwick omitted the usual first name address to his conning officer. This had become so routine the young officer scarcely noticed.

"*Oscar*, Captain. Bearing zero-four-five, closing fast. Sounds like he's coming home and anxious to get there."

"Aye, what do you figure the range?"

"Quite a way out, Captain. Can't believe the racket he's making. Either no one's warned him we're here, or he doesn't give a damn."

Despite his adverse feelings toward Brent, the Captain knew no one understood how to fight a 688 better than this young warrior so he asked, "What do you think about letting him have it head on?"

"Terrifies me, Captain. Shortens the range too much and the last few guys damn near ate our lunch at close range. Let's shoot at his stern. This'll give us more time to collect data on the evasive maneuver if he uses it. I'm convinced that whatever they're doing is simple and we gotta figure it out."

"Okay. Let him go by and we'll shoot two. One above and one below the layer."

Brent thought, *Damn it! It didn't work last time so why do we think it will now. But go along. Life's too short.*

The attack party sweated out the final moments. Six of the last seven engagements with the enemy found them running for their lives. All expected a torpedo from the target back down the bearing line. Nonetheless, they did what had to be done.

Brent thought, *Damn these kids are tough.*

The *Oscar* passed closer than any previous target, which assured a good estimate of target range and speed. Brent correctly anticipated Bostwick's cautious nature would result in shooting at long-range. *Denver* could fire at minimum enable range and make it tough for the *Oscar* to avoid the ADCAP; but Brent conceded firing at short range also increased danger of a successful counterattack.

Bostwick read Brent's mind and beat him to the punch.

"We'll let this turkey open out to six thousand yards before we let him have it."

Denver launched an ADCAP, ending with the same results identical to all the previous engagements. Sonar detected a torpedo from the target immediately after the attack was initiated and Bostwick ordered the same tactics that had previously saved his ship. Unfortunately, noise from *Denver*'s ETC jammed the acoustic recorders and precluded gathering further data on the enemy evasive maneuver.

Having reached evasion attitude and assured the Soviet torpedo now expended its remaining energy against the ETC countermeasure, everyone aboard knew *Denver* once again had successfully evaded an enemy counterattack. A collective sigh of relief went through the ship.

Brent suddenly shattered the Attack Center discipline of silence. "I've got it, Captain. I know where the son of a bitch is. The only place he can be. On the surface."

Bostwick demanded, "How do you know that?"

"He knows we're attacking him as a submarine so he's become a surface ship. Why not? The Reds own the surface and air. He's got nothing to worry about up there. Recommend come to periscope depth for a look."

"Damn it! Brent."

"He's up there, Captain. Trust me."

The captain made no response.

Jack Olsen said, "Let's try it, Captain. What've we got to lose?"

Captain Bostwick's face slightly flushed in anger, but he ordered the ship to periscope depth and there wallowing in the seaway, he saw a huge *Oscar* class submarine, apparently having planed to the surface so his attacker would not hear the ballast tank blow. He had performed a classic airless surface.

Bostwick ordered, "Make ready two TSAMs," using the acronym for Tomahawk Ship Attack Missile. "We'll blow the son of a bitch out of the water."

Brent grabbed Jack by the arm and dragged him to a corner of the Attack Center. "Don't let him do it, Jack. We're onto 'em. Knowledge of the tactic is way more important than the kill. This guy can't hurt us from where he is. He's going home to get patched up. If we've got this thing figured out right, a lot of Soviets will buy the farm."

Jack said with an exasperated tone, "Damn it, Brent, stop talking in parables. What're you trying to say?"

"What we've just found out is more important than killing a dilapidated *Oscar*. Shut the old man down. I don't envy you the job."

Grinning wide, Jack blurted out, "Think so, Brent? Watch this."

Returning to the open Attack Center area Jack Olsen announced in a loud voice, "Let the turkey go, Skipper. Bring the straight scoop back on what these bastards are up to and we'll bust a lot more than an

Oscar junkyard. Letting this guy go will make us look a hell of a lot better than we do already."

Bostwick, concerned an ASW aircraft would fly down the TSAM contrails and put a weapon on *Denver,* flooded with relief at Olsen's recommendation. "Good thinking, XO," he announced in a loud voice. "Now, let's concentrate on getting this crew back to the States for some well-deserved rest."

Bea called out as she returned to the *Digs* early from shopping, "Dad, are you home?"

Dave replied, "Uh ... out on the deck."

He appeared to be gasping and out of breath. He wore sweats and looked as if he had been exercising.

Curious, Bea asked. "What's this all about, Dad? When did you stop conserving energy for filling and lifting vino glasses?"

"Oh," Dave said, looking a bit startled then explained, "lotta work at the *Pitstop* and I gotta stay fit."

An implausible answer, she thought, but she did not push it and only murmured, "*Mmmm.*"

Eager to change the subject, Dave said, "Got some good news. Brent should be back in about a week. Keep that under your hat though. No one's supposed to know."

Bea's expression revealed her elated feelings. "Oh, Dad, that's great. When did you hear?"

Putting on a serious expression, Dave said, "Gotta be careful about that. Let's just say I know and Eric cleared me to tell you."

"Tell Eric I said he's a sweetheart. Is there room for *Denver*? How many are in already? Three at least and the *Idaho* makes four."

"When your old Dad makes a refit base, he includes room for everything. Actually, we can handle up to eight but only reach four with the crane."

Bea had no interest in details but her dad loved to go over them so she listened.

"We got transformers and can provide shore power for all of 'em. Hell of a lot better than sitting alongside with reactors critical. Or worse, those noisy damn diesel generators."

Bea asked, "Aren't *Idaho* and *Newport* due to leave?"

Dave shook his head. "No secrets 'round here. Where'd you hear 'bout this?"

"Common knowledge, Dad, *Pitstop*'s the biggest business in Grays Harbor County. Local prices rise and fall on that kind of news. Don't think any of it's shared with the Soviets."

"This is what we get for living in a free society."

"A lot better than the alternative. Am I mistaken or is this what the war and the shooting are all about? Yet you get plenty of security when you need it."

"I suppose you're right, little girl. Now let me see what you got in those paper sacks."

"Feast your eyes, Dad. Then go fire up the grill and we'll feast the bodies." She held up a pair of Spencer rib-eye steaks for her dad's approval; after Dungeness crab, his favorite food.

Patting his stomach, Dave said, "Be sure to trim the fat off mine. Gotta get this middle under control so start watching what I put into it."

Bea thought, *What's going on here? First the exercise, now the diet. And a 'lotta work at the Pitstop' doesn't hold up.* She made a mental note to coax the truth from her father but not now.

Dave fired up the grill then disappeared into the bathroom. He emerged a short time later, changed from the grimy sweats into jeans and a plaid shirt, his face scrubbed and shaven.

"I'm honored, Dad. What's the occasion?"

"Oh, nothin'. Just felt grubby and thought I'd buff up some. How long till dinner?"

"About half an hour," Bea said, believing her father would use this to gage whether he had enough time for one or two glasses of wine.

"Good. Gives me time to walk up and get the mail."

"Dad, the mail hasn't been delivered since the war started."

Dave said with a deliberate nonchalant tone in his voice, "Person up the road agreed to pick it up and drop it by."

Bea went on with dinner preparations but wondered about her dad. Twenty minutes passed and he had not returned so she walked to the door for a look toward the mailbox. A woman who looked to be in her forties stood beside her bicycle and chatted with her father.

Bea thought, *So much for the Pitstop story.*

Captain Bostwick announced, "The last place they'll expect us to exit is over the same track we entered by."

Brent knew the captain to be capable of sound thinking. *He can be good when he has to. If only he'd be consistent.* They knew the type and depth setting of the minefield and avoided it, another sound decision initiated by Bostwick.

The executive officer conducted religious services for the two *Denver* seamen as they passed the site where they had died in battle during the minesweeper fight.

Denver pushed out into the expanse of the Pacific and headed for home. The probability of a chance encounter with the enemy almost nonexistent, the men relaxed. The crew took time for reading, studying for advancement in rate examinations and reflection on the impact war would have on individual life game plans. They experienced emotions not felt by American submariners for nearly forty-two years: the constant pressure of being in a combat zone where at almost any moment, an enemy device could fracture their fragile cocoon and admit the deadly ocean. With all this behind them, it felt as though a great mantle had been lifted from their shoulders

A man of his word, Jack Olsen could be counted on to defend Brent's interests as he had promised so Brent gave a lot of thought to what the future held. But Bostwick, a clever man, would not be easily fended off. Destruction of Brent's career had become a vendetta for Bostwick. Brent hoped Olsen would be successful.

What of Brent's relationship with Bea? The thought of seeing her again excited him. She had shared love with him like none before. Thoughts of having her by his side for the long pull pleased him. He had stored details of their time together in his mind for easy recapture.

Beautiful Bea put up a halfhearted struggle against his efforts to fondle her breasts while riding back from Seattle on the dark fo'c'sle of a late ferry. It had been a great evening on the town together. They'd spent the night in an available room at Bangor BOQ. Before dawn they'd arose and hastened to the Zane home, before Dave awoke, to preserve appearances. Then, throughout the day, both paid the price for their sleep-robbed night. Brent's daylong fatigue kept him mindful of the beautiful feeling growing between them and their need to acquiesce to it. These thoughts and others filled extra time afforded by the combat-free long transit.

His second passion, undersea warfare tactics needed to get the war turned around. He frequently dueled with his favorite competitor, Dan Patrick and often engaged him for long discussions.

Sitting in a tiny stateroom they shared with two other officers, Brent opened with, "Dan, how do you figure we oughta deploy the new Sealance? We gotta think it through ourselves. The war won't let it get to the range so we can screw around with it there. Instead of practice rounds on fleet exercises, it'll be the real thing, where we gotta get it right the first time."

"I haven't thought that much about it, Brent. Captain says the DCNO, Submarine Warfare, OP-02, all but killed it. It's a long-range weapon and the threat got too quiet to be tracked at those distances. He says a high-speed, short-range, quiet torpedo is needed. I think he's right. We'd have a lot more scalps in our belt than the one *Tango* with a weapon like that."

"You're right, Dan, and so is the captain, but we've painted ourselves into a corner where that can't be done."

"How'd we do that?"

"Look at our hull designs. We bought higher speed and lower radiated noise levels at the cost of greater volume. In thirty years we doubled the size of our submarine."

"I don't see the point."

Brent assumed his lecturing voice. "Obvious. Submarine launchers haven't changed in more than seventy years. While hull designers solved problems with greater size, the weapons crowd had to make do with the nominal twenty-one by two hundred forty-six inch launchers. It's grown only three inches in diameter and added a mere twelve inches in length from one we started out with eighty-seven years ago. Great for anti-surface ship weapons where radiated noise doesn't matter but definitely a factor when the target's another submarine. After we assumed the ASW mission, the launcher size got a lot of lip service but no action."

"Great history lesson, Brent, but isn't this discussion about Sealance?"

"Just a little background on what created the situation."

Dan enjoyed his friend's theories but he always thought it took Brent so damn long to make his point. "You got some ideas or you wouldn't corner me on the subject."

"The OP-02 hypothesis is wrong. We do have a long-range track capability."

"You can't revoke the laws of physics, Brent. The quieter they get, the closer they have to be for us to hear them."

Brent exclaimed, "Right! But we're quieter. Suppose we make contact, like we have been. First hearing transients and next enough broadband noise to positively identify and track. We've shown we can get around to his baffles without being detected, right?"

"Yeah but so far we're still dealing with him at the same range. Detection range won't change with a Sealance missile aboard."

"No, Dan, we get a new option. We get a good range and speed when the target passes so we can compute where he is even beyond effective sonar range. We'll also know transients are from him and can use them for bearing spots. We let the range open till he can no longer hear our launcher noise and then let him have it. An MK-50 Torpedo drops in on him and he has no idea where it came from. And look what this does. To evade, he's gotta increase speed, gets noisy and we start tracking him again. We refine the range for a follow-on shot. If the MK-50 is dropped on the far side of him, he comes racing back toward us and we nail him with an ADCAP. Make sense?"

"Yeah, Brent, but the current submarine mindset is don't let a target get by."

"Right, but letting a target get by means we don't let it get beyond effective weapon range. The Sealance extends that. We got a sales job in getting submariners to see it that way."

Dan grinned at his friend, "As Tonto said to the Lone Ranger, 'Why you say we, white man?'"

Zhukov ploughed into the southwest Pacific, principal mission, shut down the flow of enemy war materials. Ships of many non-belligerent nations also used the sea-lanes; hence, this made problems. Would-be world conquerors shared a common problem throughout history. Success depended solely upon how well peoples of the world accepted the emergent regime. Now, with a favorable outcome approaching greater reality, the Soviets sought to mollify non-belligerents while concurrently snuffing out the ally's ability to continue the war. Unrestricted submarine warfare against all merchant shipping in the Pacific would not achieve this end.

Commander Poplavich addressed the *Zhukov* officers, his frequent speeches always long but never meaningful. Each pair of eyes rolled as the zampolit began, "Comrades, we must make the peoples of the world see the value of being freed from suppression of capitalism's mantle. This cannot be achieved through inadvertent destruction of non-belligerent merchant ships. We have been given direction to attack only those belonging to, or known to be carrying contraband to the allies."

Captain Sherensky asked, "Will this prove to be difficult, Comrade Zampolit? Many allied ships fly foreign flags."

"You are right, Comrade Captain. The capitalist system strangles ship owners to where ships must be registered out of country in order to turn a profit. Identifying flags alone will not solve our problem. We have a list of American ships and the foreign flags they fly. With the help of this directory, conveniently provided by one of the Allied Nations, we can identify those ships."

Sherensky did not like the idea at all. It restricted operations to daylight hours, thus cutting valuable operation time in half. Their long-range missiles permit simultaneous attacks against widely dispersed targets and now this crucial advantage will be nullified for political considerations.

Zhukov's commanding officer thought, *War and politics do indeed make strange bedfellows.*

The zampolit said, "Questionable ships will be stopped and boarded."

Astonished gasps spread among the officers. Vasiliy restrained from asking the obvious question, not wanting to further damage the view of him held by Poplavich.

Another officer asked the question as though he had read Vasiliy's mind. "But Comrade Zampolit, won't this show the enemy exactly where we are? Under satellite surveillance, our position will be broadcast to the allies who will use this information to avoid us. This is to say nothing of sending his own submarines to the area to attack us."

The zampolit understood nothing about tactical problems and considerations that affected *Zhukov's* ability to carry out her mission. His job, enforce political direction from the party and leave Sherensky to clean up the mess. Poplavich often muddied those waters by presenting his own tactical solutions then challenging party loyalties of those who questioned them.

Poplavich rattled on, "We've already shown American 688s pose no real problem. As a safety measure, however, *Zhukov* will re-submerge after the boarding party is dispatched and then standby at a predetermined position and await a light signal to return and recover our men."

A knock at the wardroom door interrupted the meeting. A radioman entered and handed a message to Sherensky. While the zampolit continued his lecture, the Captain read the message, his face folded into a grave expression. He pocketed the paper and refocused his attention on the meeting.

Vasiliy thought, *This ridiculous scheme not only restricts us to daylight hours but also to sea conditions that permit operation of Zhukov's flimsy life raft for the boarding party. Why are we concerned about sinking a few neutral ships? No country in the world is capable of resisting, so why not exploit it?*

Half an hour later, the zampolit closed with his usual party pep talk.

The captain said, "Vasiliy, come to my stateroom, please."

Here it comes, Vasiliy thought, *the zampolit has finally done me in.* The fat now apparently in the fire, he regretted not having attacked this most recent party stupidity with full vigor. What did he have to lose?

When they reached his stateroom, Sherensky said, "Please sit down, Vasiliy. I have grave news."

Sherensky read the message, which reported the death of Ekaterina Baknov during the American raid against Vladivostok. Also in the message the flotilla commander had added his personal condolences and stated all in the Motherland mourned the passing of this great artist.

Setting his jaw tight, Vasiliy held back the tears. As Sherensky rose, the younger man stood with him.

The captain placed a restraining hand on Vasiliy's shoulder. "No, stay here a while," then Sherensky left.

Despite his best efforts, Vasiliy's eyes flooded with tears and he wept. The tragic event fueled his hatred for Americans and helped him to regain composure. He remembered his last visit to the security vault and the likely name of the submarine that had launched the strike against Vladivostok, the USS *Denver*. He had forgotten the officers' names save one. He'd seek out the man who launched the weapon against his mother and personally take the life of Lieutenant Brent Maddock.

Chapter 16

Positions of each hydrophone in Dutch Meyer's array along with the location of the Sealance missiles showed on an old IBM PC screen. A computer wizard from USS *Newport* worked up a systems program and now enjoyed his achievement by tracking *Newport* through the approaches to Zane's *Pitstop*. Radio transmitters and receivers added by Meyer converted the austere Blockhouse into a top-notch command center.

A radioman transmitted to Birdman Four, the radio voice call sign for an S3A Viking pilot en route to a coded position designated as Springboard with serpent assigned as the code name for the submarine *Newport*. "Estimate time on top of Springboard in two minutes. Have serpent for you, over."

The airman responded, "Springboard in two, Bottom."

Bottom identified the command center Blockhouse.

Dutch Meyer wanted the plane to drop a small explosive charge to fix its position in order to vector it on top of *Newport*.

"Roger, Four, request boomer on top, over," said the Blockhouse radioman, referring to the explosive charge.

Birdman Four responded, "You got it, Bottom."

Two minutes passed then the message came from Birdman Four, "Boomer away at Springboard, one-five-one-three-three-zero Zulu. Let us know how we did."

The transmission relayed a worldwide date-time-group used by the United States Navy with numbers 1 and 5 meaning the date, 1330 the twenty-four hour clock and Zulu meaning Greenwich Mean Time. All U. S. military units use this time code system as a standard to avoid confusion when combat and training operations are conducted within various time zones throughout the world.

A short time later, the PC screen displayed an explosion close in to Springboard and the computer immediately generated intercept data for transmission to the aircraft. A series of coded numbers, giving the time, distance, course and speed of *Newport*, accompanied the message.

"Now give us a boomer on the serpent, Birdman Four."

"Roger, Bottom, tell 'em to watch their ears."

Forty seconds later, the boomer signal merged with *Newport's* position, winning a cheer from all in the Blockhouse.

The watch officer, a submariner, exclaimed, "This beats all! Never believed I'd help zoomies drop trash on one of our pipes." He radioed the S3A, "Great job, Four. Put a scalp in your training log."

"Roger, Bottom. Now find me the real thing."

"Soon as we do, you got 'em. Four released to dry feet."

Bottom then cleared Birdman Four to return to base.

The watch officer thought, *Wow! Somebody sneaks in here and we bang 'em with a Sealance. Then Birdman comes out and drops the kitchen sink on 'em.*

Days later and with the first *Pitstop* refit completed; *Newport* had patrol orders in hand.

> CLEAR SEAWAY FOR IDAHO DEPARTURE. UPON COMPLETION, PROCEED TO SOUTHWEST PACIFIC AND ATTACK/DESTROY ENEMY ASSETS.

Everyone turned out to see *Newport* off. Commander Phil Reynolds, looking more like he should be leading his company onto the parade ground at the Annapolis Naval Academy rather than taking a warship to sea, personally thanked each person with a hand in getting his ship ready for war. This involved a good number but he didn't miss anyone.

The *Pitstop*'s informality did not include provisions for a band but a temporary public address system played recordings of Sousa marches in the background.

Phil Reynolds' sense of humor revealed itself in the form of a large pasteboard box near the gangway. It bore a sign,

> ALL WHO'D GIVE THEIR LEFT ARM TO BE GOING WITH US — PLEASE DROP THEM HERE.

At their pre-sail meeting, the commodore commented to *Newport's* skipper on his youthful appearance. Then Reynolds reminded the commodore that as a Lieutenant, Danis was two years younger than Reynolds at the time he took command of his first submarine.

Danis then congratulated the *Newport* skipper. "You did a superb job, Phil. You know Captain Zane wrote *Newport* off as a box of spare parts when you showed up here, but you sure turned that around. Your ship is the first distinguished graduate of what we hope will be a long list from *Pitstop*."

"Captain Zane says a lot of things, sir, but his bark is much worse than his bite. He can resist anything but a challenge. We're very lucky to have him, sir."

Next, Phil sought out the ever-busy Gerry Carter. "Thanks for everything, Commander."

Carter took the young skipper's hand and shook it firmly. "Even for turning your ship into an overpriced anchor?"

"Especially for that, sir. You taught us we're all in the same Navy despite the badges on our shirts."

"If you find the bastard that sank *Savo Island*, make a big hole in him for me."

"That's a promise, sir."

The public address system, at maximum gain, blared *Anchors Aweigh* as a pair of tugs rotated *Newport* and pointed her bow toward the harbor entrance. The submarine's air horn sounded a long resonant blast, in compliance with Rules of the Road, but actually signaled a final expression of gratitude to all at the *Pitstop*.

Dave continued to watch after the crowd dispersed to the next job. *Newport* glided along slowly till she cleared the breakwater. Then her propeller dug into the sea and thrust her ahead at full speed. White foam contrasted with her sleek black hull as she slipped majestically out to sea.

With well-deserved satisfaction Dave Zane thought, *This is what it's all about.*

Later, Blockhouse notified squadron operations that *Newport* had crossed the hydrophone array and performed the identifying maneuver.

Dutch Meyer took the phone call.

The watch officer said, "She sure is quiet, Commander. Held her less than three minutes."

Dutch added, "And *Newport's* at high speed. If someone tries to sneak in, we're only gonna get a peek so our trigger finger better be quick."

A furious Vasiliy Baknov believed sea conditions to be marginal for transfer of personnel from the rubber raft to ladder of a Peruvian tanker. The zampolit had lectured on a Communist Party mandate that South American countries, a key factor in winning hearts and minds of conquered peoples in the Western Hemisphere, must be handled with care. They had been exploited far too long by capitalist American greed and the Soviet Union would show them a better way.

These platitudes did little to aid Vasiliy and his boarding party as they struggled to leap from raft to ladder. Soaked through, Vasiliy's group appeared more as a pack of drowned rats than warriors from the most powerful Navy in the world.

He thought, *Too bad Poplavich didn't have to drag his fat-ass up this ladder. Maybe the Party policy would become less important to him.*

Vasiliy gave the elderly tanker captain before him a crisp salute. Unfamiliar with such protocol, the captain made a sincere, if ungainly effort to return the gesture.

In Spanish, the ship's captain said, "Welcome aboard the Peruvian merchant vessel, *Bolivar.*"

Through his interpreter, Vasiliy announced, "We will examine your ship's papers and inspect cargo for contraband. You will be delayed as little as possible."

The Russian interpreter translated Russian to English then in turn English to Spanish by the tanker's interpreter. Vasiliy did not like the looks of the ship's young translator ... *The cut of his clothing, perhaps.* To Vasiliy, the man's accent and demeanor appeared very much American. Additionally, he appeared more annoyed over the search than the ship's captain. He grew suspicious when the *Bolivar* translator read the papers in English.

"Do not be too concerned, Comrade Lieutenant," said the Soviet interpreter. "The important words are the same in Spanish as English. I am certain we are being told the truth."

Bolivar's papers showed her to be a tanker loaded with Malaysian crude oil, bound from Sarawak to Lima. The papers also showed deck loads of teakwood and hemp.

Vasiliy believed the *Bolivar* interpreter grew more pugnacious with each completed inspection; the sort of smug look expected from an American who succeeded in hiding something from the boarding party. He thought, *That bastard's an American, I know it. Perhaps we should take him prisoner then conveniently lose him overboard on the way back to Zhukov.*

All tanks proved to be filled with crude as shown in the manifest. The deck loading correlated correctly also, except for several tons of copra, not considered contraband.

When the *Bolivar* interpreter accidentally struck Vasiliy's chest with his elbow while retying a deck load strap, Vasiliy lost control.

Quickly drawing his pistol, Vasiliy pointed it at the interpreter and snapped in Russian, "American bastard!"

With terror in his eyes, the young man looked first to the *Zhukov* interpreter and then back at the Russian officer's angry stare. Vasiliy stepped forward and struck the man's face with his pistol, knocking him to the deck unconscious.

The Soviet interpreter exclaimed, "Comrade Lieutenant! This must stop immediately."

Vasiliy growled back, "What do you know? He is an American, I say."

Several tanker crewmen attempted to scurry the young man off but Vasiliy stopped them by gesturing with his pistol. "I want to see this man's papers."

Panic showed on the crewmen's faces as they wondered what else might be in store.

Bolivar's first mate located the injured man's papers and presented them for inspection. They identified him as a Peruvian national. This did not placate Vasiliy. His mother's death at the hands of Americans had driven him beyond being rational.

The Soviet interpreter demanded, "You must apologize, Comrade Lieutenant."

Vasiliy snapped back, "Never!"

Then he ordered a light signal to the submerged *Zhukov* where he knew a periscope monitored the tanker. He led his party down the ship's ladder where they again performed the acrobatics of re-boarding their raft.

Zhukov resurfaced in the tanker's wake after *Bolivar* had been released and directed to proceed on course. On *Bolivar's* bridge, the injured interpreter, head bandaged, reported to his captain that aside from a headache, he felt well.

The captain said, "I am sorry, Manuel. If the son of a bitch had put that pig boat anywhere near my bow, I'd have cut him in half."

Neither Vasiliy nor his interpreter picked up on the slight English-accented Spanish by *Bolivar's* captain, the only American on the tanker.

The *Pitstop* PA system blared *Anchors Aweigh* to welcome home rust-streaked *Denver* as she rounded the breakwater and pushed her way into a beautiful June morning. She moored outboard of three 688s, two having deployed from Bremerton by order of Commodore Danis on the eve of the war. The third, like *Denver,* a WestPac returnee, had deployed from Pearl Harbor before the war started.

With the *Denver's* brow set in place, Commodore Danis strode briskly across and greeted Captain Bostwick. "Welcome home, Hal. And congratulations. There's some great satellite before and after photos of your Vlad attack."

The captain said, "Commodore, it's great to be back. Hey, looks like you've been pretty busy," as he gestured about the facility.

"A few things going down here. Enough to get your good ship turned around and back out there to do us some more good."

Bostwick did not want to hear these words. He thought, *Surely my relief must be aboard.*

Danis continued, "But there's some bad news. You're going to have to give up *Denver.* Jim Buchanan's onboard with orders as your relief."

"Oh, no." Bostwick feigned disappointment, "Don't I get at least one more shot at kicking Soviet butt?"

"It'll be a long-range kick, all the way from the other Washington. You're reporting to a flag maker job on 02's staff."

Bostwick thought with great relief, *Right on.* "I'll go wherever I'm sent, Commodore, but I sure hate to give this up. Would you like to come below?"

"Lead the way, Skipper."

Brent did not see her at first. Bea stood behind a group of workers congregated to form a welcome home contingent. The crowd parted for an instant and he caught his first glimpse of her. Back lighted by the bright sun, she looked quite feminine in a light blue dress. *How wonderful to see you*, ran through Brent's mind as he raced across the brow, threaded his way through the welcome-home crowd and took her in his arms.

As they embraced, applause arose from *Denver's* main deck, led by Dan and Woody.

The pair yelled in unison, "Hi-ya, Den Mother."

Bea and Brent waved their response.

When he caught his breath, Brent said, "Can't tell whether my mind or body is happiest to see you."

Smiling at him, Bea asked, "How 'bout we run a contest?"

"I'm game," and then his tone grew serious. "Bea, I didn't know if you survived the attack. It had me worried sick. You told me you were going to the *Digs*. I figured you reached there before the attack came but I didn't know. Commodore Danis knows how things are with us and I banked on hearing from him if anything bad had happened. That kept me going, Bea. He did a great job of letting the crew know about families when he could. Each time he learned something, he'd squeeze it into the limited radio broadcasts we received."

"He is a dear, that man. Stuck his neck out a foot but let me know *Denver* survived. And he sent me a heads-up on your homecoming." She could not help but smile each time she looked at Brent. "And that's how I knew to look so beautiful today, even though you didn't say so. First time I've worn a dress since you left."

"Oh damn, Bea, you are gorgeous. Guess you're gonna make me eat crow for not saying that right away?"

She shrugged her shoulders and said, "For a while."

They boarded *Denver,* went below and joined an impromptu gathering in the wardroom. The captain had ordered up two bottles of Vodka and some cans of caviar recently liberated from the hapless Soviet minesweeper. A similarly supplied party, under auspices of the COB, had broken out in the crew's mess.

Commodore Danis quipped, "It's against Navy regulations to partake of alcoholic beverages aboard a United States warship except for medicinal purposes. Don't know about you, Captain, but I feel sick as hell."

Bostwick replied, "Me too, Commodore. I've had a headache ever since I woke up this morning. I'll have the corpsman write us a prescription."

"Mark of a good commanding officer. Action first, paperwork later."

Of the caviar, Woody Parnell said, "This stuff's not half bad once you get it past your nose."

After Bostwick poured each glass full, Danis announced, "May I propose two toasts? The first, to victory."

"Hear! Hear!" All replied and savored their first sip of the vodka.

Danis raised his glass again, "Goddamn Josephus Daniels," the traditional Navy toast to the World War I Secretary of the Navy, who decreed no alcoholic beverages permitted aboard U.S. warships.

"Goddamn Josephus Daniels," chorused fifteen voices.

Upon realizing Bea had no security clearance, Danis drew her and Brent aside. Danis wanted to be sure no word of *Denver's* contact with the Soviet minesweeper went beyond the room. "You know, Bea, Captain Bostwick got this Vodka in Seattle before he left."

Bea replied, "Where else, Eric? I'm a Navy junior, remember?"

Eric nodded. "Good. While I've got your ear, I hear some good things about this fine young man of yours. But this is not the time to embarrass Brent."

They responded with a smile.

Maintaining a transparent air of aloofness, Danis continued, "Look, I'm sorry Bea, but your dad will be tied up here the rest of the day so would the two of you mind running out to the *Digs* to see if Dave drank that bottle of champagne I left cooling in the fridge?"

Brent replied, "You heard what the commodore said, Bea. It's a lousy assignment, but somebody's gotta do it," and the two departed.

Initially unnoticed, Jim Buchanan entered the wardroom and poured himself a glass of vodka. Suddenly Captain Bostwick's voice boomed above the din. "Jim Buchanan. You rascal. You've come to take my ship from me and I refuse to give her up."

The two shook hands. Jim served with Bostwick at two previous duty stations and knew him well. He easily saw through Bostwick's statement and knew that nothing could please Bostwick more than his springboard assignment at OpNav.

Jim said, "I trust you had a great patrol, Hal, but not too great. You're a big pair of shoes to fill just for openers. War hero status on top of that makes the job near impossible."

Bostwick beamed. He took the compliment well.

Continuing Jim said, "Seriously, Hal, can't tell you how happy I am for the opportunity to command *Denver*. I look forward to seeing the patrol data. A lot of good lessons there, I'm sure."

"I'll have Jack Olsen work up a schedule. Relief in a week sound okay?"

Danis interjected, "How about two days, Skipper? This time next week, you'll be head down and butt up in the Pentagon. War has a way of making things happen quicker."

A tone of mock surrender in his voice, Bostwick replied, "Guess we heard what the boss said."

Later, after the festivities on *Denver*, Eric Danis and Dave Zane sat in the commodore's office. Eric and Dave had grown up together in a different time and the thought of arranging for young Maddock to go off and make love to his friend's daughter gnawed at Eric's conscience a little.

Dave reminisced, "These homecomings are great, Eric. I remember how Dale and Bea would drive to the boat to greet us. Soon as we got home, I threw a handful of dimes onto the lawn and told Bea she could keep all she found. Said I tossed out ten but it was actually nine. After that, the second thing I did was to take off my shoes."

In his own inimitable way, Dave let Eric off the hook.

The interpreter immediately contacted the zampolit upon his return from the *Bolivar* boarding. Poplavich then went to Sherensky and demanded, "Comrade Baknov must be relieved of all duties. This is necessary to deter others who might be similarly disposed."

Sherensky thought, *Winning a war is challenge enough for field commanders without the second-guessing of political twits.*

Zhukov needed the talents of Vasiliy to perform her mission so the captain attempted to reason with the obstinate zampolit saying, "Ah yes, Comrade Zampolit. Lieutenant Baknov is clearly out of line. I shall require him to support the sound Party guidance. I shall discipline him immediately but must prevent the loss of his valuable role in the success of our mission."

Poplavich did not like Sherensky's tone but neither did he wish to be identified as one who deprived *Zhukov* of needed services. "Go on, Comrade," he said.

"First, we make it known to him he will no longer serve as a boarding officer. Then his indiscretion will be made known to all in *Zhukov*."

The captain figured the crew would probably applaud the news of Lieutenant Baknov's action but did not share this with Poplavich.

The zampolit asked, "And then?"

"We let Vasiliy know the Party is not without compassion then permit him to make amends through demonstration of his loyalty. Require him to assist you in preparation and delivery of political lectures to the crew. And fine him twenty percent of pay for twelve months." Sherensky looked for expression on the zampolit's poker face but found none. "We'll set the time as one year before amnesty. In the meantime, we keep the advantage of his weapons and combat training. Believe me, Comrade, this could be very important to us before the mission is over." *Make the zampolit realize Vasiliy may be key to getting Poplavich's abundant ass safely home.*

Poplavich considered the proposal a moment. Though not making it known, the zampolit had no true wish to die for the Communist Party despite the fact it would earn a plaque in his memory to hang in the Kremlin. Having the arrogant Baknov under his thumb had a certain appeal and he saw logic in the balance of Sherensky's plan.

"Yes, Comrade, Captain, we shall do as you wish but I insist on confinement after his next indiscretion. Is that understood?"

"Clearly, Comrade Zampolit."

A knock on the captain's stateroom door interrupted their meeting. A messenger reported that a zampolit and commanding officer eyes-only message had been received and they personally must complete the decryption.

While Sherensky typed in the plain language text, the decrypted message rolled out on a tape from the crypto machine and read:

ZAMPOLIT/COMMANDING OFFICER EYES ONLY. TO ALL UNITS. MOVEMENT OF NORTHERN FLEET SUBMARINES TO PACIFIC VIA BERING STRAIT TO SUPPORT ANTI-MERCHANTSHIP CAMPAIGN WILL COMMENCE LATE JUNE. PACIFIC FLOTILLA REACTOR POWERED SUBMARINE UNITS CURRENTLY DEPLOYED PROCEED TO STATION DESIGNATED IN WAR PLAN. THERE, SCREEN BERING SEA TO INSURE SAFE PASSAGE OF NORTHERN FLEET UNITS. DEPART IMMEDIATELY TO VICINITY LATITUDE FORTY-FIVE NORTH, LONGITUDE ONE SIX FIVE EAST AT BEST SPEED. FURTHER INSTRUCTIONS TO FOLLOW.

So, thought Sherensky, s*omeone near the top is finally convinced the Pacific Ocean is far too large for the plan we have been embarked upon.*

Bea's dress, a puddle of blue, blended with the bright afternoon sun on her bedroom floor. Brent watched her as she slept. Her rich brown hair lovely even in disarray, she lay on her back uncovered from the waist up. The late spring afternoon warmed them and he savored this view of his ladylove. They'd yet to seek out Eric Danis's bottle of champagne; but after Brent lighted Dave Zane's inventive wood fired hot tub would be a good time for that. Their initial physical reunion completed they settled down to the mental one.

Marriage had never been broached but this did not preclude Brent from thinking of *Bea decorating their apartment, shopping together, long motor trips into the mountains for skiing in winter, entertaining friends at home and raising a family.* They'd have children and fill the void left by his estranged but beloved son. War cannot defer such things. Life goes on, for there are always wars and those who survive them.

Brent fully intended to be involved in raising his children, even if it caused him to leave the service. This reality put his problems with Bostwick into a different perspective. Should he be fortunate enough to secure her promise, Brent would not let this marriage fail like his last one. Bearing such pain once in a lifetime is quite enough and he would not let it happen again.

At Annapolis, the student prince-like backdrops for Brent's courtship of his first wife kept them from discerning the true substance of lasting relationships. The robust Pacific Northwest setting of his time with Bea bristled with reality and gave him confidence his deep feeling for her did not impair his judgment. His mental reunion with Bea proved more voracious than their physical one.

Bea stirred then awakened. They embraced warmly.

He whispered, "Hi lover. You're so beautiful."

She recovered from her sleep and said, "Can this be really happening? The world turned upside down and here we are, like nothing else matters."

He regarded her tenderly. "It doesn't."

Again, they held each other tightly.

Brent said, "At risk of shattering the mood, I haven't had a thing to eat for twelve hours."

"So that's how it is. Ravage my body, raid my refrigerator and then away for new worlds to conquer."

"No. I'm not done ravaging your body just yet. Just a little hungry, that's all."

They shared a laugh then arose to replenish their inner persons. Seated on the deck and looking out onto the Pacific, they watched the blue sky yield slowly to gold as the sun approached the horizon. Bea prepared a supper of cheese, French bread and smoked salmon. Eric's champagne, a Piper-Heidsieck Brut, vintage 1979, proved the pièce de résistance.

Brent asked, "How much better does life get?"

"If I've ever been happier, it's completely escaped my memory."

He looked at her with affection and said, "Good. That's how I want it for you."

"Well tell me lover boy. What happened out there?"

"You know Bea, if I told ya, I'd have to kill ya afterwards."

"I'm a Navy brat, remember? Who are you trying to kid?"

"Actually, my big problem is the captain." Brent summarized the main events of the patrol as they related to the deteriorating relationship between Bostwick and him. "Jack Olsen gave me some assurances but I wouldn't give a fig for my Navy future if the captain has a final say."

Bea said in a comforting voice, "Dad always says nothing happens in a vacuum. I know Eric Danis thinks highly of you."

"Let's hope everything goes well. Look, Bea, can we talk about something else?"

She responded with, "Did you find the actual fighting very scary? I mean, if you feel like talking about that."

Brent set his jaw. "Damn scary. Anyone who says he's not scared in combat is either an idiot or a liar. It's hard to summarize. When the bell rings, you go at it and the only thing on your mind is get the son of a bitch before he gets you. But when it's over, like after we got the *Tango*, it gets rough. We sent a bunch of guys to the bottom of the ocean, who were probably a lot like us. Only difference is our ancestors caught the boat and theirs didn't. I had to force myself not to think about it. But the bell would ring again and we're right back at it. Man is the only truly mad species on this earth."

Indicating she understood, Bea took Brent's hand and smiled. She had known Brent for eight months and she learned more of his private feelings in this talk than in all the others combined. Brent arose and walked to the hot tub on the edge of the deck. He thrust in his hand and tested the water. He removed the robe he had borrowed from Dave Zane and climbed in. The warm water instantly relaxed him.

"Ever make it in a hot tub?" he asked.

Brent feasted his eyes an instant on Bea's nakedness before her body slipped beneath the water and she came to him.

Gerry Carter recognized the importance of the Soviet intelligence find immediately. Not a submariner of the old guard, he excused himself from *Denver's* welcome home party and returned to his office.

He wanted to get the minesweeper crypto machine quickly into the hands of those who could best exploit it. With lives at stake, the war revised and elevated priorities accordingly.

Carter arranged for an immediate flight to deliver the machine to the Naval Security Group Detachment at the National Security Agency, Fort Meade, Maryland. It being Friday, he called ahead via a secure phone to ensure suitable personnel would be on hand to make the assessment. Gerry located an old aviator friend, Captain Marty Baker turned intelligence specialist because of deteriorating eyesight.

Captain Baker answered his phone with the usual military greeting then said, "Hey, Gerry, great to hear from you. The word floating around here is you defected to the submarine force."

Gerry said, "Must not be a lot of worthwhile news if that's all you hear."

"Just wanna keep ya on the step. Now what's on your mind?"

"I'm flying a package to you, Marty. Can't discuss it on the phone but I think it needs your immediate attention. It should be at Andrews between three and four this afternoon. Think you could have it heloed out to Fort Meade? In case it's late, somebody should hang around. Do you read, old buddy?"

By virtue of Gerry declining to mention it on the secure phone, Marty sensed the importance.

"You think the war ain't going on back here too. We're an around the clock operation. Even the civil servants hustle," replied Marty, "but just to make you feel good, I'll stick around myself."

"Thanks, pal. I knew I could count on you."

"Okay. That means you buy next time you're out this way."

Gerry kidded, "Do they allow seeing-eye dogs in DC bars?"

A day earlier, on the other side of the world, another segment of the drama played out. At 0400, a message addressed to all Pacific Flotilla submarines had been transmitted over the VLF fleet broadcast for the fifth and final time. This task complete, the watch officer at the Vladivostok Communication Center reviewed a backlog of messages received from units operating in the Seas of Japan and Okhotsk. A message from the *Tango* submarine *Tolstoy* reported problems with her crypto equipment and requested re-encryption and retransmission of important radio traffic on the back up system. The procedure called for a decision in these matters to be made by a designated communications officer but it seemed routine enough for the watch officer to handle the matter himself.

Shortly, a shore to ship HF (High Frequency) transmitter relayed the message directly to *Tolstoy* from the same antenna field spared when Ekaterina Baknov's apartment building intercepted *Denver's* TLAM. A U.S. surveillance satellite recorded the message and relayed it to the National Security Agency for entry into a massive database.

The Soviet watch officer filed his report of the routine action and went on with his duties.

In late afternoon the next day, Captain Marty Baker's phone rang.

Crypto analyst Pete Ryan said, "Hi, Marty, that's a neat piece of junk your buddy sent us. Giving us all kinds of good dope, like this one, REYDNY TRAISHCHIK ZERO ONE SIX REQUESTS NEW STOCK OF VODKA ON NEXT REPROVISIONING. How can we lose with this kind of inside dope?"

"All of it like that?"

"Worse. Wanna hear some more?"

"Spare me, Pete. I'm heading out. I'll be home for most of the weekend if you need me."

Marty had already left and locked his office when the phone rang again. He hesitated a moment, unlocked the door, stepped inside and took the call. "Captain Baker here."

Pete Ryan answered in an uncharacteristic staccato voice, "Get your ass down here, Marty, on the double! Your aviator submarine buddy found the second Rosetta Stone. I've activated the emergency recall. I want every cleared and qualified analyst in here immediately ... government, consultants, beltway bandits ... the whole damn lot."

Marty whistled. "That big?"

"You bet your ass it's that big. And get somebody from the White House over here, right now!"

Chapter 17

Commodore Danis despised Bostwick's condescending manner as the two conducted a private conference in the commodore's office. They discussed turning over command of *Denver* to Jim Buchanan.

Bostwick opened, "Jack Olsen's on top of administrative matters so no problem there. We're a little out of date on registered publications and code lists, but I'm sure we can fix that over the next few days."

Smiling, Danis said, "That's good, Hal. What about personnel?"

"Pretty good shape there too, I'd say."

On a more serious note, Danis said. "I notice everyone except Lieutenant Maddock has been nominated for a decoration. Is there any particular reason for that?"

"Lieutenant Maddock has just not measured up, sir. We discussed his case after the overhaul, and with your advice, I gave him a second chance. He blew it, pure and simple."

"I'm sorry to hear that, Hal. When your crew was debriefed about unscrambling the Soviet's new evasion maneuver, I heard his name mentioned frequently and favorably."

Not budging off his original assessment, Bostwick said, "Maddock is good at some things, but fails to round out in other important areas."

"Specifically?"

"Specifically by not adhering to priorities set by the commanding officer. Maddock marches to his own drum and is not a team player. He's a master at opening arguments that end up undermining the crew's morale."

"How do you plan to deal with this, Hal?"

"I won't drop that sack on Jim Buchanan, Commodore. I'll get Maddock replaced and surface him before I'm relieved."

"Have you written Maddock's fitness report yet?"

"I have, sir. It's adverse. I'll give it to him for comment as soon as he gets back. I'm told he's on a social mission and not expected back until tomorrow."

"Hmm? Too bad you have to take that measure, Hal."

"Why? If you'll pardon my language, sir, it's exactly what the wise bastard deserves."

"I didn't mean too bad for him. I meant you."

Bostwick's startled expression revealed where his true priorities lay as he asked, "Me?"

This'll be a piece of cake, Danis thought. "Yes. Two items. First, we have an appointment with the President to hang a Congressional Medal of Honor on you at the White House on Tuesday morning. Now we'll just have to send somebody else. SUBPAC regs require a full investigation into adverse fitness reports prior to the reporting senior's transfer. As you know, insubordination in the face of the enemy is a serious charge and we'll need you around to substantiate that.

"Fortunately, *Butte's* back at a *Pitstop* near San Francisco. They had a good patrol so maybe her skipper can keep the White House appointment.

"Second reason, the investigation puts you under tight scrutiny. We'll need all the details. I'm sure you're clean as a whistle, Hal, or you wouldn't be doing this so I don't see a problem. You're aware flag infighting gets awfully tough and the number of good people always exceeds available promotions. You gotta consider possible effects of perceptions generated, even if they're erroneous ones. The weight of a feather could tip the balance."

Bostwick thought, *This Goddam lame duck is fitting me on again.*

The war had eliminated Bostwick's end-run routes. Additionally, getting the *Pitstop* up and running so quickly may well have tossed Danis's hat back in the ring for promotion to flag rank. In any case, Bostwick felt a tilt with Danis at this time could be the kiss of death. He paused for a moment.

The commodore correctly construed Bostwick's silence to mean he had no good response. "We're at war, Hal. This changes things." Then Danis gave Bostwick a graceful out. "You're badly needed back in Washington, and quite frankly, the country requires a hero. Success of your patrol, particularly the strike against Vlad, puts you in great shape to take an essential bow for the country. Your decision must be driven by what's in the best interest of the service."

"You shed a light I hadn't considered, Commodore. I wasn't taking the global view. For the good of the service then, I'll withdraw the adverse."

"Good, Hal. In order for this to look right, toss in a nomination for a Silver Star for Maddock. Just sign the letter and a blank fitness report. I'll have Olsen take care of the citation and fitness report details. I'll be sure he does right by you."

"Thank you, Commodore."

Danis again showed Bostwick how easily he could be pushed over, but took no delight in this. It would likely be a long war, and Bostwick could contribute much before it ended.

Wanting to part on the best note possible, Danis said, "Hal, you've done a marvelous job with your command. Bottom line, with the country at low ebb, *Denver* pulled off a spectacular military feat and restored national self-confidence. You're the officer who prepared the ship and crew for this and I'm proud to have had you in my squadron.

"My fitness report will reflect this, along with my strongest recommendation for promotion to rear admiral. I wish you every success in your next assignment and the increased responsibilities that are sure to follow. I leave you with this thought, Hal. Combat brings out the best and worst in military officers. Those who recognized the need for transition when the country moved from peace to war and adapted went far. Grant, Pershing and Eisenhower to name a few."

"Thanks, again, sir. I appreciate the advice."

As he left the office, Bostwick's smile did not reflect the anger that burned in his chest.

On the other side of the country, Captain Marty Baker waited in the anteroom outside the Oval Office in the White House. He did not fret over the delay, for he had already set machinery in motion to provide military commands with the material his staff had uncovered so no valuable time was lost. He'd never been in the White House and had yet to meet face to face with a sitting President, an overwhelming concept for Marty.

Gerry Carter, he thought, *gets me into more damn trouble.*

The naval aide emerged and ushered Marty into the office. "Mr. President, Captain Baker of Naval Intelligence, sir."

"Good evening, Captain. I hear you have some news for us." Andrew Dempsey recognized the usual signs of stage fright and lightened the atmosphere." What you've turned up couldn't come at a better time." President Dempsey nodded toward the Chairman of the Joint Chiefs of Staff and the Chief of Naval Operations seated at a conference table. "As you can see, I've assembled all the king's men, but we don't have horses anymore."

Everyone chuckled at the President's joke. Ten others, all civilian officials, except for the President's Naval Aide, sat about the table.

The President continued, "May I present General Schultz, Joint Chiefs Chairman and one of your own, Admiral Baines, CNO."

Both officers said in unison, "Captain," and extended their hands.

Next came a flurry of introductions to the civilian officials, too quick for Marty to remember them. He did recognize Senator Darrel Manning who the President had narrowly defeated in the last election.

Introductions over, Marty got down to business. Shaky at first, but quickly getting into a rhythm, he provided a short overview of the *Denver*-Soviet minesweeper incident. President Dempsey preferred the adventurous details but permitted him to be pushed along toward the real meat of the briefing.

Marty cautioned, "It's essential this be held in strictest confidence. The Soviets give no indication they know what we have."

The President said with obvious delight, "Very good, Captain. Please go on."

Continuing his briefing, Marty said, "This is an exceptional stroke of luck, sir. The equipment recovered from the minesweeper is low security and used only for local operations. For some unknown reason, the Soviets used it to retransmit a message sent earlier on their high security fleet-wide broadcast system. Having both messages enabled us to crack the higher code. We're now able to decode previous and present Soviet naval radio traffic."

This statement brought both senior military officers to the edge of their chairs.

General Schultz exclaimed, "What a break! You're telling me we know what they're going to do before they do it. Does the Army have this yet? We need this in the European Theater, and we need it now."

Marty said, "Your Army people are hard at it, General, but so far, no joy. This is a naval code not used by the Soviet Army. Frankly, we're amazed this happened. A simple bust by the Soviets, and we hope nobody catches it."

Senator Manning asked, "Are you certain we're not being fished in, Captain?"

"That cannot be ruled out, sir. But everything points to this as the real thing."

Admiral Baines declared, "This is hot, Mr. President. It could turn the whole Pacific war around. What do you have on their current ops Captain?"

Marty read the message to all units of the Pacific Flotilla directing them to proceed north to screen units of the Northern fleet in the Bering Strait. "We've analyzed traffic leading up to this. The logic for their plan is clear. Soviets have problems of separating potential friends from known enemies in their submarine campaign. Treading so carefully severely limits the area a single unit can cover. The only solution is more submarines. They need the Northern Fleet units. I think we got 'em where it hurts. Unless they can shut down the Pacific to Allied shipping, we're going to get back on our feet."

President Dempsey asked, "How do we exploit this?"

The CNO, a submariner, replied, "Mr. President, if we deploy our units quickly, it'll be like shooting fish in a barrel. These guys are so precise. They've told us not only where they'll be, but when they'll be there. And these Northern Fleet submarines are mostly old dogs and cats our guys can hear for a country mile."

Even though he sensed optimism by his military chiefs, President Dempsey chose to use caution. They had known of the Soviet's preparations for war, yet couldn't stop them. Could history be about to repeat itself?

The President's staff got their jobs through owed favors for help given during his campaign for the White House; none experienced warriors but they carried tremendous political clout. Several sat in Darrel Manning's camp and believed the President should consider sending out peace feelers. Only a major triumph of Allied arms would turn them around.

The President wanted details on how this intelligence find might be converted into a meaningful victory. "Admiral Baines, give us your views on what should be done."

"If the Soviets continue to carry out this plan, we get unbelievable tactical leverage. We could sink enough assets to make them pull in their horns. This will give us sea room to bring in supplies needed to take the offensive. That's what saved their bacon in the second war. The Soviets know first hand of our vast manufacturing capabilities and they realize the only way to nullify this advantage is to isolate us from our needed raw materials."

The President asked, "Can we expect the Soviets to maintain their schedule? Seems to make their movements awfully predictable."

Marty responded, "Mr. President, experience shows Soviet naval units to be more regimented than ours. It's likely a Communist Party mandate. Anything but total compliance is construed as disloyal. If they change anything we'll know because we've broken their code."

Pausing for a moment to absorb what Marty said, the President then asked, "What forces do we have to pull this off, Admiral?"

Admiral Baines answered the question. "Twenty to twenty-five attack submarines in the Pacific, 688s and 637s, both superior to the Northern Fleet units. And we'll bring some Atlantic Fleet boats to the party by sending them under the polar ice cap."

"Do we have someone good enough to run the operation out there?

Smiling, Admiral Baines said, "We have the best, Mr. President. Captain Eric Danis, Commander of Submarine Squadron Three. USS *Denver* of his command recovered the crypto machine."

He had twice unsuccessfully argued the case for Eric Danis at flag selection boards but retained his unshakeable faith in Danis's ability as a solid combat commander.

Addressing his aide the President said, "Yes, the USS *Denver*," then asked, "Aren't they scheduled for something here at the White House soon?"

The aide responded, "Yes, sir. A Medal of Honor presentation for her commanding officer, Captain Hal Bostwick."

Marty winced. "If I may suggest, Mr. President, the Soviets don't suspect anything. *Denver* is the source of this find. It might not be a good idea to focus attention on her just now."

Baines said, "Good point, Mr. President, let's hang that Medal of Honor on someone else this time around. I know Captain Bostwick, and I'll make it up to him."

The President concluded, "Very well then, gentlemen. It appears our work is cut out for us, so let's get to it."

Eric Danis entered the communications center housed in a small building erected nearby his yacht-headquarters. He responded to a summons from Gerry Carter who maintained his usual placid demeanor only with great difficulty. "I think we've got a live one, Commodore. Read this, sir, it's an action message to COMSUBPAC and information to all Pacific Submarine Squadrons."

> TOP-SECRET (NOFORN) INTELLIGENCE REVEALS DETAILS OF MASSIVE SOVIET PACIFIC FLOTILLA SUBMARINE MOVEMENT TO SCREEN ENTRY OF NORTHERN FLEET UNITS SOUTHWARD THROUGH BERING STRAIT. DETAILS OF MOVEMENT COVERED IN SEPARATE MESSAGE. FOR COMSUBPAC, DISPATCH ALL AVAILABLE UNITS IMMEDIATELY. INTERCEPT AND DESTROY ENEMY UNITS ENCOUNTERED. COMMANDER SUBMARINE SQUADRON THREE DESIGNATED OFFICER IN TACTICAL COMMAND. MORE TO FOLLOW.

Looking well satisfied, Danis said, "Guess we're finally gonna mix it up a little. Gerry, initiate a general recall. I want Dave Zane in here pronto. He's gotta do what he has to do to get everyone out of here. That's four 688s. We'll need every damn one of 'em, regardless of condition. Tell no one anything other than what they need to get their jobs done. A leak can blow the whole operation."

"The recall's already out, Commodore. I figured you'd want to talk to your skippers. They're on the way over here."

"Good, Gerry. Get young Maddock of *Denver* here too. He's our guru on Soviet tactics and we need a dump on what he knows."

Carter replied, "Yes, sir, and there's a special item for you from the CNO."

Eric opened the message and read:

> PERSONAL ADM BAINES TO CAPTAIN DANIS. CAN THINK OF NO ONE BETTER TO CARRY THIS BALL. EVERYTHING DEPENDS ON YOUR SUCCESS. GOOD HUNTING AND GOD SPEED.

Eric knew being closest to the combat area drove his selection as OTC but the expression of confidence from his old mentor pleased him.

Midnight oil burned throughout the *Pitstop* as his staff formulated plans and hastily buttoned up submarines for sea. Jim Buchanan delegated Jack Olsen to complete details of the change of command. They'd forego the customary ceremony and replace it with a simple handshake in the presence of the assembled crew.

At dawn, four 688s stood ready for sea with fundamentals of their operation plans in hand. They'd proceed toward the Aleutian chain and enter the Bering Sea between Unimak and Unalaska. Next, they'd move off shore from Attu Island and form a line between there and the Soviet Komandorskiye Island. From there, they would pick off any screening units of the Pacific Flotilla as they made their way into the Bering Sea. Details would follow based on subsequent information received on Soviet movements.

One of Dave Zane's crews spent the entire night installing an experimental laser communications device. It would provide *Denver,* designated flagship from which Eric Danis would coordinate the attack, with a high security system for transmitting instructions to his task force. Gerry Carter argued unsuccessfully that the operation could be best directed from ashore.

Danis replied, "Gerry, as a young submariner about to deploy on a special operation, our skipper fended off an abundance of useless advice by referring would be advisors to a speech given by Roman Consul, Lucius Aemilius Paulus in 164 BC. Commissioned to fight the wars in Macedonia, inundated with many and conflicting directions, he addressed the Senate. Bottom line, Paulus said he'd take advice only from those willing to go with him to Macedonia.

"I'm a warrior, Gerry, not a senator. My direction will have more meaning if I'm out there sharing the dangers. I'm going with my troops to Macedonia."

From this came the operation plan title, MACEDONIAN.

The time for good-byes came. Eric Danis had two big hurdles, his first one, Dave Zane.

Dave cautioned, "Now damn it, Eric, you be careful out there. Take it from somebody who knows. It's sure nice to sit around and do nothing but walk to the mailbox once a month for a retirement check."

"You don't think I'd be dumb enough to do something stupid, do you, Dave?"

"No. I just figured I'd like to lower you down the hatch on the end of a mooring line at least one more time."

Eric recalled the incident in Holy Loch and laughed. "So, do you think we're not too old to get that smashed, anymore?"

"Problem with us is neither of us are too old for anything. And I don't want to see that change. God bless and go get 'em, Eric."

They shook hands and Dave turned to walk away.

"Dave," called Eric.

Dave stopped and turned; the two shared a serious expression.

"See ya, old buddy."

After a silent nod to his old friend, Dave turned and walked off.

"Well, Babe," Eric said to Eve, who had made her way to the *Pitstop*, "this has to be good-bye number three hundred and forty-two."

"Three hundred forty-three and I like even numbers."

He wanted to say more but couldn't. Fortunately the expression on his face told how much this dear wife and companion meant to him. "I love you, Eve, sweetheart."

"I love you, Eric. Please come back to me."

"I will, Eve. Believe me, I will."

They kissed and Eric boarded *Denver*

Meanwhile on the dock, Brent held Bea tightly.

"I'm worried, Brent. The feelings you told me about after sinking the enemy submarine … they're hard to get out of my mind. When I think of our afternoon, the *Russian Brent Maddock* fills my mind. He'll never return to his love. Such simple things decide who comes home and who stays out there."

"Don't worry, Bea. It doesn't help anything. Trust, hope and pray. You know I'll do everything I can to be sure *Denver* comes back and me with her. I've never told you this, Bea. I love you."

"I feel the same way, Brent. But I need assurance there's a future with some guaranteed time in it for us, before I can say it."

"I understand," then he kissed her and walked the brow to *Denver*.

Back at Fort Meade, Maryland, The Crypto Analysis Center bulged with personnel. They quickly worked out a computer program that produced plain text from Soviet encrypted traffic upon receipt of each intercepted message. American naval officers read messages ahead of the intended Soviet recipients.

Pete Ryan said, "I can't believe how much these guys talk about what they're going to do. New traffic identifies every Red Pacific Flotilla Unit, where they are, the points they'll pass through and when.

"Marty, look at this. They're forming a picket line a hundred miles seaward off the lower end of the Kamchatka Peninsula all the way to the Strait. That's right where they should be. If they reach station before us, we've got a helluva tough row to hoe."

"Right," said Marty. "They control the air around there too. We can't operate anyplace but underwater so I guess it's the submariners."

Pete asked, "Your buddy Carter out there with 'em?"

"No. They had to leave somebody behind smart enough to keep the submariners' repair facility from being blown away in the next storm."

"How do you think we'll do out there, Marty?"

Furrowing his brow, Marty replied, "Tough call. The more dope we send, the better so let's stay on top."

"Well, we'll pump it out as fast as the Reds pump it in. Just hope our guys are swift enough to move through all that paper."

President Andrew Dempsey looked at his watch. Senator Darrel Manning had left the President waiting at least twenty minutes for their appointment. Normally the President's secretary cancelled late shows after five minutes, but this time the senator had him over a barrel. Public sentiment grew steadily against the war and Congress realigned itself accordingly. Manning led the war issue charge and now had enough votes to override a veto and force the President's hand.

The President adamantly opposed surrender despite popular opinion to the contrary. He believed it the wrong decision and needed time to turn the public around to his view. He hung everything on success of the impending undersea battle in the Bering Sea. *All the American people need is a single bit of evidence that we can fight back,* Dempsey reasoned. *Damn, I hope our submariners give them that.* He believed of Manning, *The arrogant bastard's ego is big as a house but if I stroke it right, he'll give me the time I need,* so Dempsey restricted his irritation to merely grinding his teeth.

Andrew Dempsey had defeated Manning by a mere thread in the last election. A major plank of the Dempsey campaign asserted the job of President had grown too big for one man. The voting public needed a greater voice in selecting those who would exercise much of the power so the President's nominating committee identified prospective Cabinet appointees prior to the election. Dempsey did not like the idea because it diminished his authority over Cabinet members.

These concerns had come home to roost, for much of his Cabinet's advice reflected Manning's position. The Secretary of State ran his Department autonomously and regarded the President as a figurehead to preside at formal state functions and ceremonies, the real business of the Executive Branch carried out by the Cabinet. Senator Manning in his capacity as Chairman of the Senate Foreign Relations Committee wielded tremendous influence over the Secretary of State.

At twenty-three past ten, Senator Manning entered the Oval Office and made no apologies for being tardy. Tall, slender and in his late fifties, the senator cut a handsome figure. Despite his hectic schedule, he reserved an hour each day for his squash game. Reputed to be brutal on the court, he eliminated all opposition with ease.

As the two shook hands the senator opened with, "Good morning, Mr. President. I trust you're having a good day?"

"Good morning, Darrel," replied the President then gestured for the senator to be seated. "The term is your nickel, I believe."

"Ah, yes, sir. I did schedule the meeting as I recall."

The President thought, *Damn, I wish I had Manning's diction. It's magnificent. He can make small talk in the men's room sound like a major political address.*

"Did I get your agenda, Darrel?"

Ignoring the barb, Manning said, "Mr. President, I'm anxious over the progress of this war. All the signals are dismal as you well know."

"We don't have a lot of good news, Darrel, but we've been at this thing for less than three months. Five months passed in World War II before the first win at the Midway. Up until then, the Japanese kicked our asses all over the Pacific."

Not approving the use of coarse language, Darrel Manning ignored the analogy. "I see no comparison at all, sir. Today the problem is simply one of supply and demand. Our demand for resources continues to rise and by far exceeds our supply, much worse our ability to re-supply. Further, we have no capability to change that. We live with the results of building our forces upon fifty years of bickering among our service chiefs, rather than filling the needs of a major power."

"What do you see as my alternatives, Senator?"

"Stop this madness. We're losing far too many American lives for no purpose. Unless a clear path to victory is identified, continuing the war is an emotional, not an intelligent alternative."

The President sighed, "What do you recommend then?"

Manning considered out-dueling the ineffectual Andrew Dempsey as hardly a triumph and felt no elation at this sign of the President weakening. "I recommend you contact the Soviet Premier and inquire of his terms for ending this war. I know how difficult this is but you have nothing to offer the American public except defeat at the hands of the Soviets. You have no other choice."

"Such an inquiry to Premier Rostov is tantamount to surrender. It signals we're helpless and have nothing left to bargain with. We need more time to at least show the Premier there might be something important he must lose in order to defeat us."

The senator asked, "And what might that be?"

"Success in the coming Battle of the Bering Sea."

Responding to the President's answer, Manning shook his head and asked. "You'd hang your hat on that flimsy peg? I demand you perform your duty, sir. I shall return in a week's time to hear your answer. I will not sit idly by and permit the issue to remain unanswered after that time."

Chapter 18

Commander Buchanan quickly adapted *Denver* to her assignment as flagship for Operation MACEDONIAN. With no staff aboard, Eric Danis looked upon the new skipper as his Chief of Staff officer, with *Denver* Operations Department doubling up to perform both staff and ship functions. Brent Maddock devoted a lot of his efforts to tactical planning.

With the little time he could spare, Buchanan walked about the ship, meeting his crew and familiarizing himself with the general material status. He found both men and equipment to be in good shape. His efforts also elevated the crew's confidence in him. Buchanan led by precept and example, not by fear as did his predecessor.

In the Attack Center on Brent's and Henri's watch, the new skipper greeted the two men with a cheerful, "Good morning, Petty Officer Henri. Are you keeping Mr. Maddock on the straight and narrow?"

Henri answered, "Good morning, Captain. Matter of fact I am, sir, but he's a slow learner."

The captain asked his conning officer, "Going okay, Brent?"

Brent answered, "Just fine, sir. We're right where we're supposed to be and so far haven't missed a radio broadcast."

Buchanan said, "I almost wish we *would* miss a few. Maybe the Soviets plan to win by giving us more information than we can possibly read before the war is over."

Ever apprehensive, Brent asked, "Should this make us suspicious, Captain? Seems like we're getting an awful lot of detail. Luring us into a trap, maybe?"

"So far, their actions confirm what we've learned about Soviet Naval operations. They use their new technology to tighten control from ashore. We watched this during their fleet exercises. They don't leave engagement details to their commanders at the scene."

Buchanan thought, *Lucius Aemilius Paulus didn't know how lucky he was not to have all this technology back in his day.*

Brent replied, "Guess that was a dumb question, sir."

"There are no dumb questions in this business, Brent. And none of us have all the answers. Everybody tosses what he knows into the pot. Most of this is being tried for the first time and needs all the devil's advocating it can get."

Henri spoke after the captain left. "Different kind of wind than the one that used to blow through here, sir."

Brent did a poor job of masking his pleased expression. "Don't have the slightest idea what you're talking about, Henri."

Later, Dan Patrick, MACEDONIAN Operations Officer, briefed the attack plan to the *Denver* officers at a wardroom meeting. Commodore Danis wanted a final review before transmitting it via the new laser system to a communications satellite for rebroadcast to all other MACEDONIAN units.

Dan opened with, "Twenty-three SUBPAC units are proceeding to the area. Fifteen Atlantic Fleet units from SUBLANT are heading this way under the polar ice cap but won't be here in time to make the rendezvous. No plans for them yet."

He moved a pointer over a collage of charts covering the planned engagement area then continued. "MACEDONIAN will be carried out in this big triangle. To orient you, here's Severo Kuril'sk atop of the Kuril chain and the southwest corner of the area. The southeastern corner is at Kiska here in the Aleutian chain. Then we go north to Saint Lawrence Island just below the Bering Strait. This landmass running from Saint Lawrence back to Severo K is Koryakski and the Kamchatka peninsula. And here is the port city of Petropavlovsk."

Hesitating for a moment, Dan let the geography lesson set in. "First, the Soviet's plan. A hundred sixteen submarines from their Northern Fleet will attempt to transit the Strait en masse then fan out to establish control of merchant shipping in the Pacific. These are old *Hotel*, *Echo* and *November* classes, along with *Yankee* and *Delta I* ballistic missile submarines converted to attack class in compliance with SALT II. They're noisy. If we get to them before they reach the open ocean, we'll clean up big time."

Woody Parnell asked, "Why do they need so many submarines?" The young officer had fully mended and stood watch as Brent's assistant conning officer. "Long-range anti-ship missiles oughta do the job for them with what they got right now."

"Too hard to separate the good guys from the bad," Dan replied. "The Soviets believe the war's in the bag and they want to capture some hearts and minds. Additional submarines are needed to do proper target discrimination. Okay?"

Woody nodded.

Dan glanced at the commodore and Buchanan, but neither provided anything in the way of expression. The new skipper's ever-pleasant expression gave Dan more encouragement than he had heretofore been accustomed to. "Their screen consists of top Pacific assets: *Akulas*, *Victor IIIs*, *Mikes* and *Sierras*, all pretty hot ships. They equal or exceed our 637s. But we know where they are and where they'll be deployed. I can't tell you how we know this; just that it's the straight dope. Most of us have been on SPEC-OPS and know how that goes. The Soviets have a three-stage plan. First, form a screen between Komandorskiye and Attu north of and parallel to the southern MACEDONIAN boundary. A column of submarines will move along here."

He ran his pointer along the Soviet landmass. "Larry, a nickname for Saint Lawrence Island, is at the pack ice boundary. They'll be hard to detect until they're ten miles from there. Background noise can be almost deafening and we can't pick targets out of it."

An officer asked, "Why do they send their screen under the ice, then?"

"We really don't know," Dan answered. "Probably think we're a lot better than we really are. With an offshore screen in place, the mass exodus from the Arctic begins with the units moving close to shore as they dare. When they reach this point," said Dan, indicating a spot marked on the chart fifty miles above Komandorskiye, "the screen guarding the southern approach pivots east and opens the end of a funnel to protect the transits as they move into the Pacific. Everyone understand?"

All nodded.

"Good," said Dan. "Now here's the plan."

The chief engineer asked, "Who in hell opened this cookie jar? This stuff is so hot, it's smoking."

Dan replied, "Like I said earlier, need to know, but if you like that, we got tracks, intended positions and estimated times of arrival of the southern screen. It's like the Kremlin is directing a parade. A 688 is assigned to each screen unit with a 637 backup. Intercepts are scheduled concurrently as we can make them. This prevents a missed attack from creating an alarm for the others. We scheduled intercepts to occur here," he said, sweeping his pointer along a line thirty nautical miles south of the screen intended position. "It'll be during daylight hours. Our erstwhile Cannon Cocker will explain. Brent?"

Brent took the pointer from Dan. "Cannon Cocker? Remember, the only purpose for the rest of this junkyard is to get my bullets into firing position. So look upon yourselves as my chauffeur."

Laughter filled the wardroom while Brent stole a glance at the new skipper. *Damn*, he thought, that unreadable expression. He made a mental note not to get in a wardroom poker game with the captain.

He went on, "We'll use what we learned on the last patrol. One, we know he'll shoot back if we fire a torpedo at him; and two, we know he'll surface to evade. He has no reason not to 'cause he owns the surface and air here." Brent spread out a chart depicting the plan for individual attacks and used the pointer to aid explanation of each planned tactic. "We solve problem one with a Sealance. After initial contact, we'll track him out until he can't hear our launcher and then let him have it. A 637 stationed ten miles up range from the target will listen for the Sealance payload, an MK-50 torpedo. When they hear it, they'll come to periscope depth with a pair of Encapsulated Harpoon Anti-ship Missiles at the ready. That's how we solve problem two."

An officer asked, "What happens if the target doesn't surface?"

"The MK-50 should get him, Brent replied. "If it doesn't sink him, it'll make him noisy and the 637 will move in and finish him with an ADCAP."

Another officer asked, "What if he doesn't surface and the MK-50 misses?"

"Then we find out why we collect submarine pay. We'll have to sneak in and go one on one. I don't have to tell anyone who made the last patrol how hairy that can be. Questions? None? Okay, back to you, Dan."

Dan resumed, "A sub-task group of one 688 and three backup 637s will provide a similar welcome for the offshore screen. They're spaced far enough apart so they can be taken one at a time. The intended tracks we have on them are tight also. Maybe Ivan believes this whole war is nothing but a fleet exercise but we'll take what he gives us. The rest of MACEDONIAN forms a gauntlet for the Northern Fleet submarines to run. We should really clean house if this thing goes as planned. Questions, comments?"

"Yes, Dan," Brent replied. "What about our brother submariners from the Atlantic? If we're successful in turning the Reds back, SUBLANT units will be well positioned to attack the retreat."

Looking over to the commodore, Dan said, "Nothing like this is planned." Then asked, "Is there, Commodore?"

Commodore Danis replied, "No, but it should be. Good thinking, Lieutenant Maddock. We'll work something up and pass it along with our next transmission."

Lieutenant Vasiliy Baknov said to his commanding officer, Captain 1st Rank Igor Sherensky, "Finally we take the American submariners seriously."

He fully agreed with new orders re-directing *Zhukov* from screening the Northern Fleet transit to land strikes against the new American submarine bases. *Zhukov* proceeded east toward America.

Vasiliy discussed such matters with Sherensky only with the zampolit out of hearing. "It is well we do this, Comrade Captain. Otherwise, the lessons of World War II are ignored. The attack on Pearl Harbor achieved nothing for the Japanese but unite the Americans in a common cause. Their planes over-flew the submarine base to attack a row of overage battleships that would have little effect on the war's outcome. American submarines went on to strip Japan of the sea power she needed to succeed. Despite outward appearances, history shows the Americans to have won at Pearl Harbor."

The captain chided, "Ah, the ever-serious Vasiliy. What shall you do when there are no more Americans to fight?"

"I worry over permitting the enemy to recover his ability to refit submarines. The World War II analogy fits well."

"I am more in the mood to hear you confirm rumors of you and the delightful young nurse at Vladivostok Naval hospital."

Vasiliy smiled but a sounding alarm spared him from providing Sherensky his tidbits.

An excited voice over the general announcing system ordered, "Man action stations!"

Both men raced to the Attack Center and heard the michman report a contact to the northeast, closing rapidly.

Sherensky ordered, "Stop engines." The target would pass close aboard and he had no wish to be counter-detected before attacking. As the crew readied the ship for combat, the target roared toward *Zhukov's* starboard side at a range of five hundred meters.

The michman reported, "A submarine of the 688 class."

Sounding extremely eager, Vasiliy said, "Here is the target we must kill, Comrade Captain."

With a steady voice the captain said, "Make ready two launchers."

Then Sherensky recalled the counsel of his own captain when he served at the grade of junior lieutenant in his first submarine, *Beware of the first impulse.* Sherensky's mind raced. *Think this through. What are the odds?*

He estimated one in a million that one of these ships would pass by so close within the vast size of the Pacific Ocean. Yet, this near impossible probability occurred during the 688's most vulnerable period; the sprint leg of her sprint-drift transit tactic employed so successfully by U.S. submarines. *Zhukov* found the target through pure luck.

Later, he would dwell on this. *This is too good to be true.* Then it came to him. *A great prize, the 688, but what of counterattack? Worth the risk? Zhukov stalks much bigger game, the submarine refit bases. Destroying one of those meant neutralizing all the units that subsisted there. Risk of getting killed by this lone 688 must not be taken.*

The eager Vasiliy announced, his hand upon the firing key, "Ready to fire, Captain."

The captain ordered in his firmest voice, "Check fire! We'll let this one slip away. We've far more important fish to fry."

Vasiliy could not believe the words he had just heard. His hand tightened on the firing lever and actually moved it half an inch. Then his oath of obedience outweighed his hatred of Americans and he removed his hand from the lever.

The captain ordered, "Secure the launchers."

Repeating the order, Vasiliy said, "Secure the launchers."

He wondered if the target could have been USS *Denver*. Had he missed a golden opportunity to settle accounts with Lieutenant Brent Maddock?

Phil Reynolds and all in *Newport* would never know how close they came to an eternal rest in the depths of the Pacific Ocean, within half an inch of motion by the hand of a man, whose hatred for Americans defied belief.

Captain Marty Baker completed his briefing to the President on the latest MACEDONIAN developments. His third visit to the White House found him much more at ease.

President Dempsey asked the CNO, "What's your learned opinion, Admiral Baines?"

"Guarded optimism, sir. Everything we have points to the Soviets moving to plan and unaware of what we know. Mr. President, if this continues like it has, we should eat their lunch."

The President asked, "A decisive battle?"

The CNO said, "Decisive in terms of winning the war? No, sir, but it'll crack one of our biggest nuts; open up the Pacific Sea lanes. And from my seat, only a security breach can stop us. Unfortunately, those are easier to come by than we like to believe."

Turning to Marty the President said, "And your thoughts, Captain. Do you think we have them fooled?"

"I do, sir," Marty replied. "As the Admiral points out, all the data shows their plan to be authentic and they carry it out on schedule. If they are as precise as their plan, we'll strike a major blow."

The President went on, "Would either of you hazard a guess as to how many submarines both they and we might lose in this scrape?"

Baines responded, "With the element of surprise on our side, I'd say we should knock out up to fifty of them, sir."

The President asked, "And what should we expect?"

"We hold the element of surprise so I expect light casualties, sir, especially against the northern fleet. Our ships have substantial acoustical advantage over them."

"When will it start?"

Marty answered, "Twelve hours from now, Mr. President."

At that instant, the President's intercom buzzed.

Pushing the talk button the President said, "Yes, Mrs. Bonner."

"Senator Manning, Mr. President."

"I'll take it."

The President put Darrel Manning on the speakerphone because he knew it irritated the senator. The President could be very ornery when he wanted to.

"How are you this fine morning, Darrel? I've got the Navy in tow, Admiral Baines, and Captain Baker from NSA. You might recall them from our meeting the other day."

It did upset Senator Manning when the President put him on the speakerphone with other people within earshot, but he pretended it didn't and said, "Aha, the best audience I could have hoped for. I just received a call from my Associated Press source. I'm told a story is coming over the wire stating we've broken the top Soviet Naval code."

Marty looked at the Admiral, each with a stunned expression on their faces then Marty quickly scrawled a note.

President Dempsey replied, "Well, Darrel, you really come up with some good ones. I'll check the Navy out on that," as he read the hastily written note.

> GET OFF THE SPEAKERPHONE AND SAY YOU'LL CALL HIM BACK ON A DIFFERENT LINE. THEN TELL HIM WE PLANTED THE STORY BECAUSE WE WANT TO DISRUPT THEIR COMMUNICATIONS. THEY'RE A LOT LIKE US, SKEPTICAL ABOUT WHAT THEY GET FROM THE PRESS.

The President went off the speaker and told Manning he would call him back on his private line then dialed the senator's number. "I got rid of my company," he lied. "Now keep this under your hat, Darrel," then delivered Marty's message, paraphrased to his manner of speech.

Manning asked, "Do you think it wise to fool around like this? Maybe the Soviets are about to pull off something big. Perhaps we should move our meeting up. Timely action on your part could save a lot of American lives and property."

"Good point, Darrel. I'll think on that. Call if you have anything else for me."

The two hung up.

The President asked Marty. "How bad is this?"

Marty said, "Let's hope you just bought us the twelve hours we need. After that it'll be too late for the news to do the Soviets any good."

President Dempsey asked, "How did I do this?"

"By undermining the validity of the news release. It's your private line, sir, but it's on a public telephone system, almost certainly tapped at a dozen or more places. Transcripts of your comments are most likely at the Kremlin already and it'll make them vacillate. Changing the primary code in the middle of a big operation is more risk than they'll want to take."

The President's face brightened. "Next time those jackasses from CIA tell me military and intelligence are mutually exclusive terms, I'll know what to say. Nice job, Captain."

Brent's final lingering doubt dissolved when an *Akula* passed overhead at the precise depth and speed as ordered in her sailing directions, within a mile of the designated track and off schedule by only twenty minutes. "This is unbelievable," he said, "unique in the annals of military history. Never has a warring nation lost so much advantage through a single screw up."

Jim Buchanan compared it with the loss of Robert E. Lee's special order number 191. Wrapped around three cigars, two union soldiers found a copy and turned it over to their commander, General George B. McClellan. The find revealed Lee's entire battle plan, in particular, the intended movements of his troops, a major contribution to Lee's defeat at the Battle of Antietam.

Dan Patrick added, "But the rigid compliance with orders," then asked, "do you suppose the zampolits keep a close check on their positions to ensure orders are being carried out?"

Buchanan replied, "If they run true to form, yes."

Neither Brent nor Dan could resist being in the sonar shack for the initial contact with the enemy. Shortly, the call to battle stations came and the Denver crew commenced their initial MACEDONIAN attack.

The conning officer briefed Captain Buchanan on the tactical situation when he arrived at the Attack Center. The ship transitioned from normal cruise to full combat readiness.

Once in the *Akula's* baffles and assured *Denver* would not be detected, Buchanan took the 1MC mike for the general announcements system and addressed the crew, "This is the Captain speaking," he said in a firm voice and chose words to enhance the crew's confidence. "We are in contact with the enemy, an *Akula* class submarine. She is opening to the north and gives no indication of having detected us. We'll let the target open to beyond his effective counterattack range and fire two Sealance missiles at him. I expect all hands to give their best. I'll keep you informed."

The crew liked this, one of many changes since the tenure of Buchanan's predecessor. This new skipper made each crewman feel the importance of his role in the ship's mission. They liked that.

Captain Buchanan released the 1MC press-to-talk switch, turned his attention to the Attack Center Battle Station crew and calmly said in a soft, controlled tone, "Well gentlemen, let's find out how good we are at a submarine *first*, letting a target get by and open to long-range. Dan, when will the target be there?"

"Computed target will reach firing range in twenty-three minutes, Captain."

Buchanan nodded. "Thank you, Dan. Jack, that gives us enough time for two streets of cribbage ... you ready for another lesson?"

Astonished, Jack Olsen quickly read Buchanan's strategy. He'd just expressed confidence in the attack party. "You're on, Skipper." The two disappeared, heading for the wardroom.

Broad grins spread across each face in the Attack Center. Even the stoic Jacques Henri could not resist initiating an exchange of wit. "Now what's different about this picture?"

Brent replied, "Don't know, Henri. For some reason I find it hard to remember."

Twenty minutes later, Dan announced on the 21MC, "Captain, Conn. Three minutes till shoot, sir. Brent recommends spin up the birds, flood and open the outers."

"Do it," came Buchanan's casual reply.

Dan demanded over the 21MC, "Sonar, Conn, hear anything?"

Gary Hansen's voice replied, "Nothing hard, Conn. Occasional transients on the generated bearing line."

"Conn aye, sonar. Give us a mark on the next one for fire control. Pay attention all the way 'round. Don't let Ivan sneak up and get us napping. We'll give it one more baffle clear and we're ready to shoot."

Hansen replied, "Sonar, aye."

With the baffle clear maneuver completed, Hansen reported, "No contacts, Conn. Here's a mark for fire control. A good one."

Dan ordered, "Conn aye, sonar. Match bearings, Brent."

"Matched," replied Brent.

Next, Dan notified Buchanan over the 21MC, "Captain, Conn ready to fire, sir."

With his trademark soft monotone, Buchanan asked, "What are we waiting for?"

Initially taken aback by the captain's casual approach, Dan quickly recovered. "Final bearing and shoot!" he ordered.

Brent called out, "Bearing matched, fire one!"

The launcher gave its customary shudder as it expelled the new missile into the seaway.

Sonar reported unnecessarily, "Rocket motor start."

The booster ignited at the surface and the noise could be heard in the Attack Center on the underwater telephone speaker. The long-range combined with *Denver* being in the target's baffles prevented the event from being detected by the hapless *Akula*.

Buchanan called on the 21MC, "Conn, Captain. I'll be in sonar. Check fire on two but be ready. We'll use the bearing to the MK-50 explosion as a spot when we hear it."

Dan replied, "Conn aye, Captain."

Grinning, Brent asked, "Why didn't you ask who won the cribbage game, Dan?"

Hansen reported, "Torpedo running on the target bearing line."

Brent exclaimed, "Damn! Now if we only got the range right!"

Seconds later the rumble of a warhead explosion sounded over the underwater telephone. Cheers erupted throughout the Attack Center.

Hansen reported, "Conn, Sonar, explosion. Can no longer hear the MK-50."

"Conn, aye, Sonar. Listen closely and see if you can find out what the target's doing."

Five miles north of the wounded *Akula*, SSN 637 Class USS *Clamagore* heard the same commotion and scanned the area with short periscope looks. Suddenly a huge black hull pushed its way above the waves and *Clamagore* released a previously readied salvo of two Encapsulated Harpoon Cruise Missiles. At mach point eight five, it didn't take long for them to reach the target. In less than a minute, each bird made its terminal maneuver and cracked into the hull of the unsuspecting submarine. Just minutes later the foundering *Akula* disappeared beneath the waves forever.

Identical scenes played out six more times across the lower boundary of MACEDONIAN, destroying the entire Soviet screen. Satellites received reports from the laser equipped 688s and rebroadcast them to the MACEDONIAN Flagship.

Commodore Eric Danis said to *Denver*'s new commanding officer, "Ya know, Skipper, I'm sure glad the Soviets obey the rules. Do you think they even close cover before striking?"

Denver joined other SUBPAC 688s and 637s making their way into what history would record as The Bering Sea Fish Barrel Shoot. MACEDONIAN units charged with disrupting the Soviet offshore screen succeeded beyond their wildest dreams, again because the Soviets followed instructions to the letter. The Soviets sacrificed stealth, the most important submarine asset and paid for it dearly.

U.S. forces dispatched twelve Soviet offshore screen units before the Soviets caught on and sent desperate messages to the Northern Fleet units ordering them to withdraw and advising the *Zhukov* maneuver had been compromised. Most of the soviet submarines well south in the Bering Sea en route to the Pacific Ocean received the warning too late. By then, SUBLANT units had completed their transits and blocked the Soviet escape routes.

Commodore Danis ordered transmission of instructions to attack.

FLASH PRECEDENCE TO ALL MACEDONIAN
UNITS. INITIATE ATTACK ON NORTHERN FLEET
130130Z. PICK ONE OUT OF THE FLOCK AND
SHOOT. GOOD HUNTING AND GOD BLESS. ERIC
DANIS SENDS.

High radiated noise levels from the older Soviet ships masked the approaching attackers who fired at point-blank range. Some units, having received the withdraw message and hearing distant explosions, retired toward shallow water and surfaced, hoping to take cover among the many inlets in the Kamchatka Peninsula. American submarines followed as close as they dared and attacked with anti-ship missiles. MACEDONIAN units performed like a school of hungry sharks in a feeding frenzy.

Finally, Commodore Danis said to Captain Jim Buchanan, "I think we've done as much good as we can. I'm concerned our guys might get too cocky and take unnecessary risks."

Jim nodded. "I agree, Commodore. The fight actually ended when we took out their high priced hardware. But additional kills boost the morale factor. The country needs this."

Danis replied, "Good, Jim. Draft a withdraw message. I'd like score reports as units cross a line two hundred miles southeast of Kamchatka. It's risky, but folks at home are long overdue for some good news."

Jim grinned at his boss. "I'll do that, Commodore. And may I extend my congratulations, sir, to the first victorious commander in a major naval engagement in more than forty-seven years?"

The commodore's eyebrows arched. "Thank you, Jim. By God, you're right. The thought never occurred to me."

"Didn't it, sir? Welcome to Macedonia."

Darrel Manning frowned. The importance of this meeting caused him to be on time, not his norm for visits to the White House. With irritation building, he waited in the anteroom. He glanced at his watch and looked up to see the President dismissing the CNO and other high-ranking officers from the Oval Office.

President Andrew Dempsey said his good-byes then invited the senator to come in. "Please forgive me, Darrel. The situation briefing went long this morning. I apologize for making you wait."

Manning managed a half smile. "They look like a casting call for a Gilbert and Sullivan Opera, Mr. President. I didn't know you were auditioning this morning. No more secret code games with the Soviets, I trust?"

Another man waited in the anteroom but Manning made no move to invite him into the Oval Office. The President gave a wink to Mrs. Bonner and closed the door behind them.

The senator talked down to the President. "Sir, I trust you've given our last discussion some serious thought. The situation deteriorates hourly and you have no solution. I urge you to accept the futility of our circumstances. For God's sake, find the courage and do the right thing. It's the only alternative you have."

"And what is that, Darrel?"

Shrugging off the President's glib attitude, Manning believed the President attempted to buy more time. *Damn it! This time I'll hold the jackass's feet to the fire.* "Contact the Soviet Premier and ask what are his conditions for ending this madness."

"And if I'm not quite ready to do that?"

"Then you leave me no alternative, Mr. President. I have the means to force your hand and will do so if you don't have the good sense to do it yourself. A growing congressional majority stands behind me. And other national factions in the private sector—very powerful ones, I might add—share my views."

"Your brain trusts, Darrel? Your circle of so called intellectuals who never dirty their hands making a living in the real world but earn their keep by telling the rest of us how we should?"

President Dempsey finally got his back up with the senator. How good it felt.

"Mr. President, I didn't come here to discuss the credentials of my advisors and supporters. They're firmly established and well respected in their fields, enlightened people who know how to separate emotion from substance. Now, may I have an answer, sir? Will you give me your position in this matter?"

The President recalled the man sitting in the anteroom and suspected the connection. "Do you know how I might contact Premier Rostov?"

Manning's face spread into a half smirk, half smile and sensing he'd won, he fell back into his respectful mode. "I took the liberty, sir, of inviting Senor Miguel Pinta, Cuban Ambassador to the UN. He's agreed to carry a message to the Soviet Premier for you. And he'll do this verbally if you like. I urge you, sir, at least establish contact. This act alone will result in the saving of countless lives."

President Dempsey furrowed his brow. "Very well, show Mr. Pinta in please."

"You have a message for Premier Rostov then, sir?"

"Yes, I do."

Miguel Pinta entered the Oval Office and introductions exchanged. Following introductions, Senator Manning stood to his full six feet three inches, his gray pinstriped three-piece suit hanging perfectly over his handsome frame, the picture of a man in control of the situation.

"Senor Pinta, I believe the President has a message he wishes you to deliver to the Soviet Premier."

While smiling the Cuban nodded in anticipation.

The President calmly said, "Please advise Premier Rostov that if he hasn't already done so, he should count his submarines. I suspect he'll come up about sixty-three short. Tell him also we will run up that number a lot higher if he doesn't withdraw them from the world's oceans and damn quick. Now, if you gentlemen will excuse me, I've got a war to win."

Not a vindictive man, however, President Dempsey did enjoy inflicting an occasional barb. "Darrel," he said as the senator began to walk out.

Senator Manning turned back and replied, "Yes, Mr. President?"

"If your party is stupid enough to nominate you again next year, I'm gonna whip your ass big time."

Chapter 19

Dave Zane, Bea, Gerry Carter and Eve Danis raised their glasses to the American success in the Bering Sea. Sketchy but conclusive news of the events at sea dominated the media. Izvestia, principal Soviet newspaper, did not address American claims of submarines destroyed but alleged great numbers of unsubstantiated kills by their own forces.

A beaming Dave Zane added, "And to Eric Danis, hero of the Bering."

All chorused, "Hear! Hear!"

Eve acknowledged the toast to her husband then quickly changed the subject. "Well, Dave, when do we meet her?"

Forcing a puzzled expression, Dave asked, "Who?"

"Cat's out of the bag, Dad. Eve knows about Carolyn joining us this evening."

Dave wore a baffled expression, followed quickly by one that signaled he understood. "Oh, Carolyn Ladd. Almost anytime now."

Gerry Carter gave an exaggerated imitation of Dave twisting his head to look up the path toward the mailbox. "And all along I thought you had a stiff neck, Dave."

Bea attempted to bring her father back to reality. "C'mon, Dad, you don't have to be so cool. She's lovely and I hope to see a lot of her." Bea had already told Dave her mom would be pleased he had found someone to brighten his life.

With a whining tone in his voice, Dave said, "Well now, there you guys go. Invite someone over who's been good enough to pick up the mail for me and everybody starts drawing conclusions."

Eve smiled at her old friend. "Dave Zane ... I don't believe this. You're actually blushing. I thought we finished with that years ago."

Dave threw up his arms. "See, Gerry? Don't try to understand what these females get in their bonnets. Only the two of us here got any sense. Let's go out on the deck and enjoy what's left of the sunshine."

Gerry took his shot at Dave. "Gonna fire up the hot tub for Carolyn?"

Dave complained, "Three against one. It's a damn conspiracy!"

The two seated themselves on the deck.

"What'll happen to you, Gerry? I mean, where'll you go after this?"

"Too busy to give it much thought, Dave. I guess as long as Danis is happy with me, this is a pretty good spot."

"Old Eric likes you alright but he's due to move on, you know. Next Squad Dog might want his own boy."

"You're right, Dave. I shouldn't get too comfortable. Unless the surface Navy makes major breakthroughs in antisubmarine warfare, carriers of the future will have a pretty small role. And that's what I do. Fly off carriers."

"Don't write the bird farms off just yet, Gerry. There's gonna be wars after this one. You can bet on it. Nuclear weapons make big fights too dangerous for both sides, so we'll likely shift to small ones. And we're gonna need some way to get your planes to the action. Actually, in little wars, it'll be the submariners who'll shop for new missions."

Changing the subject, Gerry asked, "How come you never got into the Nuclear Power Program? The commodore tells me you're likely the hottest submariner he ever knew."

Dave chose his words carefully, "First, don't believe everything Eric says. Second, you keyed on a sore subject. I applied for the program as a Lieutenant, qualified submariner and qualified for command. Thought I was on the fast track, till my application bounced."

"Bounced? With all you had going for you? How come?"

"I didn't stand high enough in my class at Annapolis."

Gerry shook his head in disbelief. "What's that got to do with anything? Some of our hottest pilots graduated by the skin of their teeth. Performance on the job has nothing to do with class standing. Our certification processes are rigorous as you'll find anywhere and it's based solely on how well you fly the plane. How do the Nukes justify this academic thing?"

Dave replied, "They don't have to. However, word floated around that low class standing is tantamount to lack of ambition."

"That's unrealistic. If we applied that policy, we'd never have enough pilots to fly our planes. Why did the top submariners put up with this?"

"Good question."

Gerry believed Dave's explanations but could not understand them. "Edmund Burke was right. The only thing needed for an operation to fall flat on its face is for 'enough good men to do nothing.' If anyone tried to inflict this on the Naval Aviation community, all hell would break loose. Remember the admiral's revolt of '49? Most of the guys who fell on their swords were Naval Aviators."

"We're the silent service, Gerry. We take our lumps and don't whine. Somebody might look on it as sour grapes."

"So you're not pissed over this?"

"I didn't say that. But the rejection dead-ended my submarine career. Turned out I liked it but becoming an EDO was initially a salvage job."

From inside the house, Bea interrupted their conversation, "Dad, Carolyn's here."

Dave's face brightened and he hurried into the living room.

"Hi Carolyn, meet my friends Eve Danis and Gerry Carter. We just toasted our boss's big win in the Bering Sea."

Dave filled a wine glass for Carolyn as Bea, Eve and Gerry greeted her. Slight of build, mid-fifties with wavy light-brown hair that showed a trace of gray, Carolyn vindicated Dave's enthusiasm. Faded blue eyes twinkled from a face that retained much of its earlier beauty.

Carolyn said, "Thank you, Dave," taking the glass from him, "and congratulations to all of you. Such wonderful news just when we really needed it. My fourth graders were so excited when they heard I'd be seeing people from the Sub Base this evening."

"Well that's good," said Gerry, and then gesturing toward Dave, "Are they as excited as *our* fourth grader?"

Dave complained, "See, there you go again. Been a hard afternoon around here, Carolyn. Maybe you can establish some good order and class discipline."

Zhukov prepared for its strike against the new submarine base on the Washington Coast. They slipped quietly toward the *Pitstop* to enhance stealth and increase success probability.

Vasiliy said, "Comrade Captain, there is no good reason for why we should not approach to within visual distance. It ensures better accuracy for our missiles and could permit us to see and verify explosions in the target area."

Sherensky replied, "We must not be too eager, Vasiliy. If we venture too close, we fall within range of ASW aircraft. Our missile contrails point directly to our position, an excellent aim point for aircraft torpedo drops."

"The ancient MK-46 torpedoes, Comrade Captain. Even the Americans have no confidence in them. They made twenty thousand for use against the four hundred submarines we had at the time."

"We can't afford to be cocky, Vasiliy. There are disturbing messages in the recent radio traffic. We've changed our code for some unknown reason. By now our submarine numbers in the Pacific should be increased by more than a hundred, yet radio traffic is lighter."

Vasiliy rationalized, "Perhaps we've become more skilled and less guidance is needed from ashore. But, yes, Comrade Captain, what you say is cause for concern. But caution must not deter us from our hard won initiative against the Americans."

Commander Gerry Carter picked up the phone in his office aboard the commodore's yacht.

"Got a live one, Commander," cried the excited voice of the watch officer at the Blockhouse.

"What've we got, Todd?"

"This guy's an *Akula*. Wrong kind of lines for one of ours and didn't perform the ID maneuver. Permission to let him have one."

Gerry thought, *Damn it! Where in hell are the submariners when you need them?*

The Blockhouse watch officer pressured Gerry for an immediate decision. Gerry pondered, *Was this an Akula closing to attack the Pitstop or an errant home comer, who either forgot the identification maneuver or never received it?* And Gerry's advice came from a hotshot fighter pilot with only fifteen hours training.

Considering the facts, Gerry reasoned, *Can't be one of ours. They're all coming back from the Bering and at least a week out.*

"Shoot!" he said, grinding his teeth in a futile effort to release stress then added, "And scramble the birds."

The watch officer replied, "Will do." He unlatched and closed the firing key. The missile had been spun up and initialized with target coordinates. He picked up the phone and called Navy Air Hoquiam.

"This is Bottom. Scramble two! Coordinates to follow for live serpent when airborne."

The array operator checked flashing numbers on the digital timer. "Should see the fish about now, sir ... yep, there it is."

With no speakers, the running torpedo showed up on a computer driven cathode ray display.

Lieutenant Vasiliy Baknov had the Attack Center watch when an excited michman, reported, "Torpedo astern, closing fast!" terror clear in the man's voice.

Vasiliy ordered, "Ahead full!"

Zhukov's huge seven bladed propeller bit into the sea and accelerated the giant hull toward its maximum speed of more than forty-two knots.

"Which quarter?"

The michman exclaimed, "Starboard!"

Calmly, Vasiliy ordered, "Left full rudder to course zero-seven-zero, fifteen degrees up, to depth—"

A sharp explosion at the rear of the ship interrupted the order and threw everyone to the deck. The ship's lighting lost, the crew groped about in darkness. A deafening squeal shattered the customary soft hum of the rotating propeller shaft, telling Vasiliy they had been hit close to the main seal.

He ordered, "Stop engines," and the noise dissipated as the main propulsion shaft slowed to a halt.

The Blockhouse watch officer reported to the S3A pilot, "Birdman Leader your coordinates grid, zero-four-two-zero for the boomer."

The sonar operator reported, "Losing contact but he's not going anywhere. I think we hit him in the screw and he's shutting down."

"Boomer away," crackled the voice of Birdman Leader.

"Okay, get us a good mark, sonar."

The sonar operator's excitement mounted as the chase heated. "There it is, sir, mark it!"

The watch officer called, "Leader, boomer two one-one-six Zulu and fourteen. Vector two-one-five, six miles to serpent. Target has stopped. Set Doppler out on the fish." Removing Doppler from the torpedo acoustic homing equipment enabled it to attack a submarine sitting motionless.

Leader reported, "Roger all, Bottom. Starting the run," quickly followed by, "Fish on the serpent at two-one-one-eight and thirty-five, Bottom."

The watch officer ordered, "Watch for the fish, Sonar."

"Got it, sir, and right on the last serpent position."

"Another torpedo, Comrade Lieutenant!" screamed the terrified michman, "closing from dead ahead!"

Vasiliy knew they could do nothing. Their best speed would be less than seven knots and to do this would provide a perfect noise source for the weapon to home on. Perhaps the Americans' lack of confidence in the MK-46 torpedo would be justified. Vasiliy departed the Attack Center for the Sonar compartment in order to gain a better perspective of the tactical situation. He'd nearly pulled his body through the operations compartment watertight door when the second torpedo struck. The concussion slammed the heavy door on Vasiliy's arm, nearly severing it above the elbow. He fell to the deck and lay motionless.

Sonar reported the MK-46 Torpedo warhead explosion, "Got 'em again! Hey, this is some kind of alright."

Gerry Carter had reached the Blockhouse; confident they had an enemy submarine under attack. A friendly would have surfaced immediately and be screaming his head off.

The watch officer contacted the second S3A to reach the scene, "Birdman Two, a boomer at the mark."

Two answered, "You got it, Bottom."

A second MK-46 made its way toward the champion Soviet *Akula*, its lucky streak ended by the Meyer-Buchanan one-two punch.

Shock from the third explosion silenced *Zhukov's* steam turbine driven generators, leaving only limited capacity storage batteries to supply ship's power.

"Flood auxiliaries," ordered Sherensky. He knew his ship could no longer function. He bet all on a desperate gamble to perhaps save a few of the crew. "We will sit on the bottom, where maybe the torpedoes cannot find us. When things grow quiet, we will float up to the surface and abandon ship."

The zampolit screamed at Sherensky, "You will surrender this brave ship? Disobey orders and abort our mission? Get hold of yourself, Comrade Captain. Don't make it necessary for me to take command and finish the mission myself. This will be reported."

Sherensky looked at Poplavich through a disgusted expression. "Comrade Zampolit. You are an idiot."

Bottoming *Zhukov* spared her further torpedo hits. As Sherensky had predicted, things quieted and the victorious American aviators withdrew. Hours passed and soon loss of the submarine's atmosphere control equipment left all hands struggling for breath.

The captain gathered the crew in the messing area and explained his plan. "You will assemble beneath the hatches. When you are there, I shall order all the main ballast tanks blown. Be prepared for violent angles. We continue to ship water and have no power to pump it back into the sea. When we reach the surface, open the hatches and leave. Get clear of the ship quickly as you can for she will not remain up there for long. The strong among you must help the injured."

Scanning the drained faces of the sailors who had served him and *Zhukov* so well, the captain said, "I am proud to stand among so brave a crew. I wish you all the best of luck. Go to your posts now."

With the main ballast tanks blown, the bottom released its hold on the stricken submarine. Mercifully, she steadied at a moderate angle as the ship slowly moved toward the surface. When there, as the captain ordered, crewmen opened the deck hatches. Heavy from so much flooding, *Zhukov*'s hatches failed to clear the surface and a deluge of seawater poured back through them and into the ship. Only a few escaped but had nothing to keep them afloat other than their ability to swim. This small number did not include Sherensky and the zampolit.

Commander Carter would never know his order for Blockhouse to fire against an unknown submarine, resulted in the destruction of the ship responsible for shooting the mighty carrier *Savo Island* from beneath his F-14 fighter jet.

The MACEDONIAN Flagship, basking in her recent victory, made a triumphant way homeward beneath the summer calmed waves of the northern Pacific. Spirits soared and the crew anticipated a well-deserved respite ashore. Their victory removed the pall of gloom, which hung over their country since the opening of hostilities. Now, in addition to refurbishing *Denver*, they would take the first small steps toward restoring lives set awry by the war.

Jim Buchanan addressed the commodore and several others in the *Denver* Wardroom. "Well Commodore, looks like our country might be off the endangered species list. I wonder how the Soviet Naval Staff will explain this one to the Politburo."

"We did well, Jim. No question about it. But we're a long way from taking the offensive. We've checked them for a time and now the balance of this war will involve only conventional weapons. The Soviets have more forces than us if it goes to a war of attrition and they showed during World War II they're willing to expend them."

All officers not on watch sat about the wardroom enjoying a cup of coffee and a break from generating mountains of paper that would comprise a consolidated action report. Reports of success by other MACEDONIAN units continued to flow in via fleet broadcasts, some including short congratulatory messages inserted by the crypto clerks, who bent the rules to do so.

Brent added, "I think no country ever won a war only by defending itself."

Buchanan replied, "That's right, Brent. We've got to seize the initiative if we expect to win this one."

"It can be done, sir. We just have to stick to our game plan."

Captain Buchanan said, "Our game plan depended on the survival of fifteen carrier battle groups, Brent. It'll be pretty hard to enact it without carriers."

"I don't mean that one, Captain. Major wars start with an opening strategy that gives way to the real world when the shooting starts. Always happens that way. Our original plan conceded force levels to the Bloc and rested the Allied case on superior equipment. That part worked. Granted, we had a little luck with the Soviet code bust but we did well in the Bering because our stuff's better and we used it right."

The commodore's face brightened into a warm smile. His long-term hunch about this young officer vindicated protecting him from the barbs of Hal Bostwick. "Our success is due in no small part to your efforts, Brent. Key to the big win was taking out the southern screen first. Otherwise, we'd have engaged the Northern Fleet while being harassed by their best equipment. Your Sealance tactic gave us the upper hand and nullified the enemy's ability to strike back."

Buchanan added, "We owe Brent another one, Commodore. I understand he unscrambled the surfacing tactic the Soviets used to evade. He also advised against making an attack, which would have put them onto what we knew. It cost *Denver* a scalp for her belt but paid great dividends in the Bering."

Danis said, "Well you made up for it this time. Four scalps, I believe."

"Something like that, sir. And just so all this doesn't go to Lieutenant Maddock's head, let me bring him back down to deck level. Brent, you've got your refit work list and justifications ready for when we hit port? That's only a week from now."

Brent took the remark in stride. "Getting on it soon as you and the commodore let me off this paper chase, Captain."

Buchanan joked, "Let me see. That should take just about, uh—seven days."

They all laughed.

Determined to have the last word, Brent, said, "Not to worry, Captain. Woody Parnell, ably assisted by straight man Petty Officer Hansen have it just about done. Cribbage, anyone?"

A knock sounded at the wardroom door. Chief Cunningham then entered uninvited followed by a group of enlisted crewmen, an event unprecedented even in the informal atmosphere of a submarine.

The group pushed forward as a radioman handed a clipboard to the commodore. "Message for you, sir."

Eric Danis took it and read:

> TO ALL MACEDONIAN FORCES, FROM THE PRESIDENT OF THE UNITED STATES. YOUR COUNTRYMEN ARE INDEBTED FOR THE VALIANT AND SELFLESS EFFORTS GIVEN IN VICTORIOUS BATTLE DURING THIS CRUCIAL CHAPTER IN OUR REPUBLIC'S HISTORY. FOR REAR ADMIRAL ERIC DANIS, CONGRATULATIONS ON YOUR WELL DESERVED PROMOTION. ANDREW J. DEMPSEY.

Chief Cunningham stepped forward and said, "The captain told us something like this might happen, sir, so we took the liberty of making these up for you. They should do till you get ashore and find a proper pair."

The COB presented Eric with two rear admiral silver-star collar devices fashioned by a gifted auxiliaryman.

Eric Danis took the gift. With just a trace of emotion in his voice, he said, "Thank you, Chief. Thank you very much indeed. I can think of no greater honor than to wear devices of this rank fashioned by a combat submarine crewman. I could find no better pair ashore."

Although Eric Danis believed his storm had long passed, a vindicating bolt of lightning reached back and struck home.

End